SC MacAlpine presents -

From the Diaries of
Becka Skaggs, PhD.

Introducing *The COSMIC TWINS*

Today's adventure:

What Little Girls
ARE MADE OF

© SC MacAlpine.

All rights reserved. This book or any portion thereof may not be reproduced or used in any manner whatsoever without the express written permission of the publisher except for the use of brief quotations in a book review.

ISBN: 978-1-66782-456-7 (printed)

ISBN: 978-1-66782-457-4 (eBook)

TABLE OF CONTENTS

CHAPTER - LIFE	1
CHAPTER - MY LIFE	27
CHAPTER – HOLDING ONTO LIFE	42
CHAPTER – A GREEN LIFE	47
CHAPTER – LIFE GIVER	68
CHAPTER – ZESTY LIFE	73
CHAPTER - ICU LIFE GIVERS	82
CHAPTER – THE TWINS SHARE LIFE	100
CHAPTER – LIFE QUESTIONS	114
CHAPTER – ENERGY IN LIFE	135
CHAPTER – LIFE TAKER	141
CHAPTER – LIFE TAKER DOWN UNDER	153
CHAPTER – LIFE ON THE RUN	175
CHAPTER – CAT AND FOWL LIFE	192
CHAPTER – TALL DRINK OF LIFE	210
CHAPTER – LAW-GIVER OF LIFE	234
CHAPTER – LIFE ANEW	242
CHAPTER – MY CYBORG LIFE	249
CHAPTER – METAMORPHOSIS: LIFE AS THE PERIWINKLE PRINCESS	272
CHAPTER – SUPERHERO LIFE: THE EARLY YEARS	311
CHAPTER – LIFE WITH A LOVE BUG	331
CHAPTER – ISLAND LIFE LOST	356
CHAPTER - CLIMAX FOR LIFE DOWN UNDER	361
EPILOGUE – WHAT LIFE??	388

CHAPTER - LIFE

August 19, 2004, my fourth birthday.

Mom picked me up from daycare and we stopped at a convenience store before my birthday party. I had no siblings, but many cousins. A family-sized birthday would include 15 people, easily. So, Mom bought beer and wine, but she had already been drinking. I knew it when she picked me up. I tried to ask her to take me to the dairy queen for ice cream, just so we wouldn't drive for a little bit. It was only an extra block out of the way. But nobody listens to me!

I was "aware" at my birth. I can't say I remember everything since. I can say I am aware of things. Much more than adults are used to kids being aware of, anyway. At least they never saw a kid like me. The problem with me is I remember their stuff and throw it back at them when they get mean. "Yeah, Marjorie! You don't like me mean? Don't you be mean first!"

Oh, excuse me. Sorry. That was a flashback. My brain is wired that way. Weird. That's what those doctors tell me, anyway. Who am I to argue with the doctors? I'm just a kid. No, I hadn't started arguing with the doctors, yet.

Sorry, I got sidetracked. Just after starting my story, too.

As I was about to say,

Before I could finish getting all the "ice cream" words out of my mouth, Mom said "We Don't have time, I am running late already. We can't stop for one more thing."

Then she added, "Buckle up. We're going!"

Those were basically the last sane words I ever heard her speak.

Mom took off out of the parking lot, turned right (thank gawd!!) and zoomed toward home. I was still trying to get my belt in the buckle. There was no car seat, but I felt safer in the back. Thankfully, I was in the backseat holding the seat belt when she blew through that intersection with the red light against us. I remember barely seeing the flash of something entering my vision way over to the right. Then, all sound stopped. I think my holding the seat belt kept me in the backseat, I think.

There must've been noise, as I think about it after the fact. It was just not making sense.

It's a car wreck, Mom!

Did I say that out loud?

I'm not sure. I can't hear.

Did time stop? What's happening?

A flash!

Roaring waterfalls covering all my senses.

Sudden jolts of energy, shocks.

Bumps.

'Ouch that hurt!!' from my internal voice.

Many bumps.

Strange sounds

Unhg!

More Bumps.

Owf! 'Can't breathe. No air in my lungs?'

What Little Girls Are Made Of- From the Diaries of Becka Skaggs, PhD

Another bump.

'Too many to track now.'

Legs over my head. Aagh!!

More shocks to my body.

Uncontrolled screaming heard. No, it's not me. Is it mom?

Arms over my head.

Ceiling. Numph! Ooch!

On the floor.

Bump! Back on seat.

Going around. 'What the….?'

Screams of terror!

Bumping. Mumphf!! Now what?

'Look out Head!' Oomph!!

I bounced to the seat, but not quite on the seat.

More breaking glass.

Shoulder.

Waawmf!

Bouncing.

Arm. "Yeoww!!"

'THAT was me out loud!'

Not quite on the floor. Wait?

A moment of nothing.

No screams.

'We stopped bouncing?'

'Moving? No.'

Everything has stopped. No more sounds. No more bouncing, no movement at all.

I can't hardly think of anything for about 30 seconds. Just listening and getting my bearings. Then,

I let out this "Whaaaa!" and a wailing crying thing. My body made me stop the crying and squirming.

'Ouch! Jeez. Quit yelling girl!' I scolded myself.

'I'm alive.'

'What's that? Something sticking me? I don't know.'

Am I ok? I'm not sure yet. Mother is my first concern.

"Mom? You, ok?"

I am feeling something wet on my back.

"Did we stop? For good? We were rolling, right??"

Then my mind starts trying to find answers.

Did we land in water?

Where was there any water?

I don't remember…NO!

There is no water anywhere on the way home.

No stream. No lake.

Not even sprinklers or a roadside ditch.

What Little Girls Are Made Of- From the Diaries of Becka Skaggs, PhD

So, why am I getting wet? It's in my back. Something is…

I can't reach it….my arms aren't moving.

"Mom! I can't hear you! I'm right here, Mom. I think I'm ok. Mom!! Can you hear me?"

Something wet. Sticky.

"Mommy! You okay?" I'm really struggling to breathe.

Something smells, Mom. Do you smell that?

I don't feel my legs.

OK. I think I am hurt, Mom

I don't know what that means, really. If I was hurt, wouldn't I be really crying my eyes out? I'm not crying. Not crying at all, Carol.

Mommy, talk to me!! I can't do this by myself.

Oh, crap! I'm not talking out loud anymore. When did that happen?

Mommy where… are you……. (I release my breath, and I fade to black)

* * * **FIRST BREAK** * * *

"OW!"

I heard that.

"Mom? You, ok?" I said it as loudly as I could. I'm not sure how loud I can talk.

"Yes, honey. I think so. My head though. I have the biggest splitting headache! I am so happy to hear you, and that you are okay, baby girl." Mom suddenly stopped talking, like just the sound of her voice made the headache worse. Then a "uh…nooohh" …...

5

Then she began to whisper more in a broken way. It was a way of speaking I was not used to hearing from her. It was broken into small bits of sentences. A few sounds at a time, then just a sighing sound. Maybe she was voicing frustration from not being able to think clearly from the pain of her headache? I couldn't be sure. I couldn't see her. I was stuck behind the driver's seat, and it really hurt, but I was definitely stuck. Maybe if Mom could move and ease the pressure on the seat, then maybe I could move.

Just a little. All I need is just a little.

"Mom? Can you hear me?"

I could hear only the same sighing, whispering (breathing?) sound.

Mom? See if you can move your seat up a little for me, please? I can't move. I'm really stuck, Mom."

No response.

"Mom. Come on, Mom! You gotta move the seat for me, Mom. I'm just stuck, that's all. If you could just move the latch for me, I might be able to get enough room...."

Minutes must have passed. How many? I really don't know. Maybe a lot.

Then came a sound from the front seat.

"Oh, my baby girl, I love you so much."

Then Carol continued.

"Everything is just fine."

Her breathing was very labored, heavy at times. I swear she stopped breathing at least once, for like a whole minute, then she gasped for air.

She was not fine.

"No, Mom! It's not! Everything is NOT fine!"

What Little Girls Are Made Of- From the Diaries of Becka Skaggs, PhD

I'm talking out loud again. Good, because I need to say some things to my mother!

"I am trying to be adult about this, Carol, but you are NOT fine. Everything's NOT fine!"

Then I began to sob uncontrollably, again, until the pain forced the tears to stop.

"I'm stuck, Mom! You must move. Mom, you have to move!"

When the tears let loose, I suddenly realized how much pain I was in.

"Mom. I'm really hurt, Mom." Now even the pain couldn't stop the tears from blinding me.

"Can you hear me, Mom? I really need you to move, Mom. Please?" Errrgh, I, can't… move…trying, mom… nothing."

With each word I tried another angle, another bit of energy to move myself so I could finally get my left shoulder and, therefore, left arm that was getting crushed, off the floor. I feel like I'm partly upside down. That must be a reason my arm is feeling crushed.

Maybe my butt, if I tighten my stomach muscles and then my butt muscles. I must try.

"Ok. Stomach" I say to myself. "Yes. You can do this, baby abs."

Yes. Tightened.

"Ok, easy", barely whispering to myself now. "C'mon little butt easy, tighten. Ok. Yes! Good. Hold!"

Now, Can I turn my waist a little to my….AH!

"Dammm, that hurt!! Ok, Ok, I won't do THAT again!"

I must catch my breath.

"I really need to move, Mom."

"Mommy?"

"I don't know, Carol….my mind isn't straight…...please help us."

All between bouts of sobbing now. But if my crying got too heavy, the pain in my back reminded me not to move. So, I could only try to keep mom awake with my words.

I couldn't reach mom. I couldn't see her. My head was closest to the driver's-side rear door but was closer to the floor than the door, if that makes any sense. My legs felt like they were still up on the seat, but I could only see one. I can't feel my left leg. Which leg is that I see? My foot I see has a right shoe on it. I hope that means that is my right leg.

I am lying here dying, trying to keep my mother awake so we both don't die, and I am keeping myself entertained with sarcasm. OK, Let's have another hope. I hope we both survive, and each still have a sense of humor when it's all over. Then, when I'm sarcastic, Mom will still laugh. I really miss that.

Ohhhh, don't start thinking about things you miss, you big baby. You are just gonna start sobbing again and you already know how much that can hurt!

Note to Self

Then a new, but very familiar voice, appeared from the darkness.

"Carol! Honey?"

Who the heck was that?? Grandma? Grandma Fran? Are you here?

Grandma, HELP!! HELP US!! Grandma, I'm stuck back here!

Wait. I'm not talking out loud. I have to talk out loud so she can hear me. Or grandma won't know I'm hurt. How could she know? She's looking for Mom. I'm Becka.

Geeez! She knows who I am, you goof!

She's not looking for me though. I have to yell.

What Little Girls Are Made Of- From the Diaries of Becka Skaggs, PhD

I can't yell. Grandma. Can you hear me?

I can't even hear me. How do I expect Grandma Fran to hear me? Sheeesh!

Ok. Relax. Easy, long inhale, and now....

"Grandma, I'm here! Grandma, I am SO glad to hear you! I'm in the back seat. I'm stuck! Mom got us in an accident."

Oh gawd, so out of breath. Owwwiee!! That hurt like hell!!

Crying begins again, and then the pain stopped me!

I actually talked out loud. I'm so proud of myself. I'm pretty sure I was yelling. So, where is everybody? Why is no one here? Grandma? You're not here??

I am not thinking very clearly. I'm pretty sure that's not good. Smells and sounds....I'm not sure what is a hallucination and what is real.

I don't know why I'm wet. Something in my back really hurts. My left shoulder is touching the floor but its my arm that feels crushed. And definitely asleep, poor little guy.

My back is stuck against the seat bench portion and my chest is against the back of Carol's seat. Pretty sure my neck will be sore for a while after this. That's just what I need, a crink in my neck!

NO, I don't!! I didn't mean it, Mr. Universe, if you're listening. Please don't give me a crink in my neck. I really don't need one of those. *sniffle*

It's my birthday. The Birthday that shall never be forgotten in the History of the Entire Known Universe! Rebecca Dall Skaggs 4th Birthday, August 19, 2004. Whoopee! Sadness strikes again.

OUCH!!! Dammit! Becky, quit hurting yourself. And get used to your name. YOU picked it out 16 years from now.

Wait. What?

16 years from now? I also remember something about 95 years. Things are definitely not right with Rebecca here. What is happening to my mind?

* * * WRECK Break * * *

Where are we again? Besides this stupid car wreck???

Oh! Grandma? Oh yeah!!

"Grandma? You still here? I need you to help me. I can't…get…. free."

Where did grandma go?

"Fran? Carol? I…."

Many minutes go by, again

"Grandma? You still here? I'm sorry I fell asleep."

"Grandma Fran. Listen to me."

I tried to keep my voice as calm and steady as I could. "I need you to call 9-1-1."

* Time slips by. Nobody is here to keep track. So, there is no way I can know how much time slipped by *

I keep falling asleep. I must stay awake. If I fall asleep, I may never wake up again.

NO!! That's NOT happening! We are NOT giving up!! NOOO!!!

I must try to stay awake. I have too much life ahead. I was born with so much love. I need to feed children!

I'm overtaken by the sadness of these thoughts.

What Little Girls Are Made Of- From the Diaries of Becka Skaggs, PhD

I am only 4 years-old today. I must love before I die. I must love people. I need to love children. I need to love animals. I must find my soulmate. I cannot give up now. I have to stay awake!

more minutes go by

I fell asleep again. Ok. I'm a little bored sitting here waiting a rescue.

NO, that's not right. That's not the reason I fell asleep, you big goof.

I'm hurt. I must stay awake for Carol. I must rescue Carol.

I'm not thinking clearly. Something strange is happening to my head.

My mind decides to go into its own narrative. I could not stop the thoughts.

'I am born a human girl. Generations are depending on me so they can be born. I cannot stop my life now. Who would I be to deny all those future people their lives? I was MADE to put people on this planet. Why would I be made that way just to have it all taken away before it could even start? That makes no sense. No! I am not going to believe that nonsense!'

And it has more for me to hear, if that is indeed what I am doing. Hearing.

'All we are discussing here is the fate of people. If The Universe created me to bear children, why would she take all that away just 2 winks into my life? No! That is cruel!! I do not believe a deity must be cruel. No, I refuse to believe that nonsense.'

'9-1-1'

'9-1-1'

'Grandma?

'NOW! Please. Grandma?'

'Carol??'

Then my hearing returned.

"OH-H-H no. I am not really talking, am I?"

"Again."

"Shoooooot. I haven't been. But now I am. So why am I now? I am definitely confused."

'Did you hear that Becka? We know we are confused.'

"We?"

"Who's here?"

"Oh, crap!"

'How do I keep my mind from wandering off and speaking with its own voice? Isn't that what I just did? I can't seem to find any ways so we can stay awake ....'

Black

More minutes go by

An electronic voice begins a narration, as if a training application had just been opened and is now playing automatically on a distant device. No, not a device. It seems to be telepathically implanted within my young and injured mind.

The narration continues in a series of lessons that seem linked by chains of thought rather than particular topics.

Narrator: *The cold of space is only cold because there is no heat source nearby. But what does that really mean? Our sun radiates its heat out into space, and we get warmed by it here on earth. People then ask,' How does that really happen? What is the science behind it all?'*

Uhhh, what is this? Who is doing this? Am I awake? Am I really hearing something? A radio somewhere? Owww, my back really is hurting. Ohhh...who?? Uhhnn......can't think. So groggy...

What Little Girls Are Made Of- From the Diaries of Becka Skaggs, PhD

Narrator continues: *I mean honestly?? There must be something in space that is a conductor of heat, otherwise it could go nowhere. It would have to throw hot particles at you to get you warmed up. You don't say? The sun DOES throw hot particles at us? Yes. They are called "Solar Wind" and they are charged particles that come from the sun.*

Ohhh, so there ARE particles of matter in "empty" space. Now things are starting to make sense. I'm dying, yet I'm still learning. What is going on? I'm learning science while dying??

And I fade to black, again.

* * * Narrator Needs a Break * * *

Young Narrator: *So, all that emptiness of space is not empty at all. But it is not all made of particles from solar winds. That is a very small percentage of the matter in space, actually. Whatever the rest of space is made of, it is made of a material that propagates light. And it allows light to travel at a constant acceleration of 186,000 miles per second per second. Acceleration is velocity that keeps getting faster every second. Acceleration is a mathematical construct that allows humans to better understand our universe and how it is made. The entire universe is made of one thing: not matter, but energy. Energy is matter, and energy is NOT matter.*

Wait. This is a girl's voice. Who's talking to me? Somebody is talking to me. I am getting information here. HELLOOOOO! I am right here talking to you!!

Young Female Narrator: *I am. That is all you need to know at this time, Rebecca. Now, shoosh! Rest. Listen. Conserve our energy.*

I guess I faded to dark gray because I can still hear, I think.

The young electronic narration continues: *That is the perfect paradox! The perfect paradox can only be so because it is factual. It is true! Es Verdad! [a little girl says "teehee"]*

The entire universe is made of paradoxes. One paradox after another. Over 80% of Earth's species must propagate by enjoining opposites within their population. The genders tend to be the way we differentiate opposites, but that is incorrect for Homo Sapiens. The Human nervous systems are made to use electro-chemical processes to function. Humans have a very long spectrum of electro-chemical proficiencies. The opposites should be the mates, not the genders. There would still be enough heterosexual couples by using this method of differentiation. The species would still successfully propagate but at a 50% reduced rate.

"Yes, but I am made of pure love, and made to use pure love", I seemed to volunteer while in a deep dream state. It was as if I had given a response prompted by a hypnotist to make me act merely by impulse. Then I couldn't speak at all, and I'm back to sleep...if that's what I've been doing.

Young Electronic Narrator: *Humans have reached a population level where they must slow down their growth physically on Earth and begin more spiritual growth before reaching to other galaxies. The human soul needs to experience the opposite ends of the spectrum to fully heal and develop to its full potential.*

The human spirit has become fractured from itself. It has become so harmed that it no longer recognizes the best parts of itself, and it calls itself 'my enemy'. The meaning of our lives, just the two of us, is to work tirelessly to enjoin the human spirit of one to another to another and to another until the whole of humanity is finally one people, as it has always been intended.

More pain awakens me for the moment. The shock of it shakes the dream-state from my mind.

Yes, I'm stuck. Out loud, Becka. Practice speaking out loud.

"What? Two of us?" I thought I was yelling but only a whisper came out. At least, that's all I could hear. Maybe its my hearing that's going and not my voice, I thought to myself. Let's try again, more experimental this time.

What Little Girls Are Made Of- From the Diaries of Becka Skaggs, PhD

"First thing I need is room." I manage a raspy whisper, but its louder. It does hurt to speak. Its not my ears, though.

"Ok, good. One thing at a time." That was much better, though my throat is sore. Very sore. Maybe I can exercise my voice through the pain.

"Shall we try that", I ask the little voice inside us.

"You know what, little voice? Its my turn for some narration. I can handle this." Wink

"Now, if I can just move a little. Just a little might be all I need. If I can move my arm and maybe push on the seat, and…. ahhh! No good! I can't budge an inch!"

Ohhh yeah. Hallucinations.

'This has…...

all been……hallucinations?'

Then another voice is suddenly implanted into my head like a single instantaneous thought. I don't recognize this squeaky female voice. This is different from the girl in my dream just a moment ago. She sounds different, anyway. Maybe my hearing is also going?

My voice, my hearing, WHO can help me now? Oh, dear God. I didn't mean it! Please take me into heaven. I've been good. I won't cause you any trouble. I promise. Why are you doing this to me, my Mrs. Universe? I've had a real short life so far.

Now, all I could do was lay there and cry like the little baby I was.

*** **Another BREAK** ***

**From almost like an echo chamber came this very electronic voice –

"R-O-S-A-L-Y-N V is born. Rebecca Dall and Rosalyn V have been successfully enjoined. Enjoinment shall proceed for the period of Earth time of 4 score and 15 years where, precisely at 16:19 hours, enjoinment of the 2 energy sources shall cease.

END TRANSMISSION" **

Who in the whole......wide......universe......was......that? ....95 years???

"Mommm-meee", I could barely form the words. WORDS? It's only one word. Uh-oh.

"I can't......"

"Don't know...."

"I can stay awake...."

(black)

*** **Reporter BREAK** ***

Sirens sounding as the crew from the emergency room came running through the hospital doors to meet the victims on the gurneys being lifted from the rescue vehicles. They received the call and have been waiting for the victims of the horrific 4 car-pile up. They are expecting 2 critical patients with multiple injuries. The injuries were of so many different kinds, all the specialists were being called from the entire Tri-county area. Surgeons knew to expect many bone injuries. The mother is suspected of suffering brain trauma and multiple leg fractures. The little girl has suspected rib, leg and arm fractures, along with puncture wounds to the neck and torso, including potential wounds to vital organs.

Doctors specializing in multiple-fracture emergency medicine, neurology, internal medicine, nephrology, neuro-vascular medicine, wound-care, and multiple-organ-transplants were brought in to attend to the injured. Not

What Little Girls Are Made Of- From the Diaries of Becka Skaggs, PhD

all the specialists did the doctoring. Some were there just to consult with the emergency crews. The less serious injured were sent downtown to St. Joseph's.

"Max Swanson, Channel 4 On-The-Spot News from Black Lake General Hospital. We have learned from the emergency room staff that one victim was pronounced dead at the scene. That was the driver of a late model van, a 27-year-old grocery manager returning home from work. Name and gender are being withheld until the family is notified."

"On-The-Spot News has learned the driver of what the police have identified as vehicle number one is a young mother, driving a Toyota Tercel, that appears to have started the disastrous accident. Her 4-year-old daughter was found in the backseat of the car. Both have serious injuries and are considered in critical condition at this time. The mother appears to have severe head trauma from the way they are treating her. According to our sources, she is being prepared for immediate surgery", as Max looks up from his notes and into the camera for brief emotional effect. This is television, after all.

Max continues with his initial summary.

"We have been told that the preliminary examinations reveal the girl will also be taken immediately in for surgery, as it appears the emergency crew thinks she may lose vital organs if much more time elapses. I am taking the liberty, Brent, to report that the medics mean there is likely damage to at least one of the girl's internal organs, if not more. Vital organs are not something the police would otherwise discuss."

Max continues while the production crew places a photo of the pick-up on the viewing screen for 3 seconds, then the camera is back live to Max.

"The driver of the truck fled the scene on foot, according to witnesses. Soon after the collision, witnesses report they saw the driver climb through the driver's-side window to exit the vehicle. The driver appeared to be limping, according to 3 separate witnesses, so may also be injured."

"Police have search teams looking for the driver. The driver's identity is known. Police are confident the driver will turn himself in once he fully realizes the gravity of his situation."

The production crew from the Channel 4 truck pop up and drop down the driver's name from the screen. The camera is back on Max.

"Police say it's not uncommon for such a person to seek legal counsel prior to turning themselves in. Perhaps they are also seeking medical attention. They were speeding, yes. But they had the right-of-way at the time of the accident, as his light was green. Green lights, as almost all drivers know, can give a person a false sense that the way is clear, when it may not be clear at all. As you can hear, Brent, there are still some unanswered questions."

Max sets up the audience for video of the scene taped moments earlier.

"When we were at the scene of the accident earlier, Brent, we took some film of what was happening at the scene for later viewing. Roll film 3 guys."

The production crew in the truck que up film 3 and it begins with Max speaking to Brent.

"Brent, I have someone I would like you all to meet at this time that may be able to shed some light on some of these unanswered questions we just mentioned", Max pauses and turns. Then he extends his arm to invite another person into camera view. The cameraman assists by ensuring they are both in the view seen by the television audience.

"With us right now, is Martin Simpson, one of the witnesses of the collision. Can you tell us, may I call you Martin?"

"Yes", martin replied. "That's fine."

"Can you tell us, Martin, where were you standing when the collision occurred?"

What Little Girls Are Made Of- From the Diaries of Becka Skaggs, PhD

"I was right over there", he was pointing at the NW corner of the intersection. If there was a particular corner where the collision happened, it would be the SW corner.

Max interprets for the audience, "OK. You were on the NW corner. Then what happened?"

Martin begins looking at each area of the intersection as if the accident was being replayed in front of his eyes, right there, right now.

"Well, uhhh, I'm a little bit nervous. Umm"

"It's OK, Martin" Max gave a friendly smile that helped Martin calm down enough to begin his story. "It even happens to me sometimes. You are doing fine."

"Oh! Ok." He shines a relaxing smile.

"Well, the little green car was just going like she had a green light. I knew it was red and that she was not going to stop. I even tried to yell, but things happened too fast."

Martin seems calm now and draws a big breath.

"Really, it seemed like before I could get the sound out of my mouth the collision was drowning out all other noises. My throat is a little hoarse. I was definitely yelling. But I couldn't hear myself. This crash was loud! It couldna taken 3 seconds and it was over. I just...I don't know. It's the most awful thing I ever seen...." Martin begins crying and turns away from the camera. Max moves away from Martin to have the camera follow him and give Mr. Simpson some privacy.

"TY Martin," Max gave a truly heartfelt brotherly air fist-bump to Martin. "We all appreciate the seriousness of this situation."

Film 3 ends and Max begins his voice over during the 1 second black-screen transition to "Live" broadcasting.

"Finally, Brent, the injuries to the 2 victims in the Late Model Ford Taurus, which is designated vehicle number 4 in the police report, are not life-threatening injuries. One victim was brought to St Joseph's Hospital, at Broadway and Ferguson Avenues for treatment of a broken upper-left arm, and some facial lacerations. They expect this victim to be released after treatment". The driver of the Taurus, Doctors said, will need a stay of about a day or two for observation after being treated for a broken right clavicle, and some head wounds that likely resulted in the moderate concussion. [The director calls for feed 1 to play the gurney film.] 2 very lucky individuals, I would like to say", Max finished, as he prepared for the anchor's questions. [And...feed 1 to standby]

"Back to you, Brent."

"Thanks, Max", Brent says in natural seasoned-anchor style. "I think that is a fair liberty to take as to the doctor's concern for her organs, plural, my friend", Brent began the take-back from Max, and after a sly little laugh, being somewhat pleased with how smooth he really was in transition. One of his favorite parts of being Anchor – with a capital 'A' – for "Live" reporting. He immediately threw it back. "Max? Did you get an explanation from the Police? Do they know how this accident occurred?"

[Feed 1 on Max. 2...1...go]

"Yes, Brent. Sgt. Leonard Baker, the Police Department spokesperson, explained that they have a preliminary determination. The Department has released some of their findings of fact. Of Course, Sgt Baker stressed they are preliminary and subject to finalization based on further findings."

The production crew begins running the rescue footage. The two reporters continue in voice-over mode.

"Yes!" Brent interjected, "I imagine he did some of that 'everything is still subject to change' conversation with the news people." Brent would be grinning a little too widely for the camera. And had he been on camera, he would have gotten a loud reminder in his earpiece from his producer.

What Little Girls Are Made Of- From the Diaries of Becka Skaggs, PhD

Thankfully for the audience, the film sent in from the production crew was still running.

"You're exactly right, Brent." Max added to show unity to the audience.

Those extra seconds are all they needed to ensure the audience never saw Brent's misplaced exuberance. The rescue film, and a film of the victims being placed in the Rescue vehicles and off to the hospitals, has ended, taking 6 seconds longer than Brent was told by his producers.

Max is live in front of the camera, answering Brent's question with even further, unnecessary detail. But that was Max.

"And not just us news people. But the emergency room workers, paramedics, fire department rescue team, everybody got the message."

"Apparently, The Mother, um, the driver of the Tercel….", Max stumbled a bit.

Catching himself feeling a bit biased against my mother without knowing her or really anything that happened leading up to this horrific event. All this thought happened within Max's mind in a flash. Max was back on the scene, and ready to go.

'Good Pep Talk, Max!' Max complimented himself mentally to prepare his next words,

"…. which the police believe went through a red light travelling at over 50mph in a 35mph zone, when she got broadsided by a vehicle going at a rate in excess of 70 mph on a street zoned for 45 mph. If this strikes you as a bit odd, we were caught thinking the same thing. But the oddities of this incident don't end there, Brent. There are many more things that occurred that most people would agree are strange at the very least."

The Chanel 4 production crew queued up rescue film 4. It's a film of Max at the scene describing marks in the pavement.

The audience sees Max turn to look at the intersection and began directing the camera to the location where the Tercel finally came to rest.

The audio kicked in 3 seconds later. The audience finally got to hear Max continue in his explanation of the events.

"Vehicle #1, the Tercel, was travelling east in the right-hand lane at approximately 50 mph. That would make it the closest lane to the curb on this street that she was travelling in, at that speed". The camera slowly pans from the area of the accident to show the lane of traffic Max is describing.

Max is now heard in an over-voice as the television audience watches what the cameraman is giving them.

"You will notice there is no room for parking. There is not even a Bike Lane on this street. The lane edge is at the curb. This becomes an important observation as we continue our understanding of what exactly transpired at this location. The police inform us that is a factor that helps set the speed limit at 35 mph. The fact that the curb is the lane edge".

Max paused for a moment and directed the cameraman to now show the location where the Tercel came to rest. The camera slowly panned to that location to give the audience just enough time to focus on the picture, then back to Max.

Max walked into the camera foreground and continued. "Then police believe at this time that vehicle #2, A Ford 150 4x4, travelling at a high rate of speed in excess of 70 mph, struck the Tercel in a manner that caused the Toyota to leave the ground and it apparently rolled while in the air and came down on top of Vehicle #3, the late-model van, that was waiting at the stop light after coming west on this street. This driver had no ability to avoid anything. They were sitting there waiting for a red light to turn green, and suddenly their lights go out before…..."

"Yes, Max", as Brent broke in to stop the explanation of a bad metaphor from Max. The film continued rolling but with no sound. Brent and Max were now the sound. LIVE!

What Little Girls Are Made Of- From the Diaries of Becka Skaggs, PhD

"I can imagine trying to describe the events can get emotional for anyone." Brent decided to coax him in another direction,

"Thinking about how these kinds of things can happen", Brent continued to ask for clarity's sake, "The Toyota Tercel was lifted into the air by the collision, rolled in mid-air, and landed on top of the van and the Ford Taurus? How? I mean, what exactly happened, Max?"

But Brent seemed like he couldn't stop himself from adding to his complex question.

"Do the Police have an explanation of how this could happen once the collision was unavoidable, of course? Then, it landed and, what? Did it keep rolling? I didn't see the final photos, so I don't know".

Now Brent's methods became clear. Brent's questions were meant to draw the audience into his voice for purposes of helping the audience feel closer to the story, and maybe keep them more glued to the news report, and ultimately, the sponsors of On-The-Spot News. Cha-ching$!!

"Yes, Brent. The Police statement mentions preliminary tire-mark evidence indicates the Tercel began to veer left just the instant prior to impact. That caused an easing on the right-side suspension, which would give the frame a slight lift in preparation for a turn."

There is an engineering schematic embedded with the film that helps the audience visualize the chassis and its movements during such an event. The film also includes drawings from of the scene, apparently from the police report.

"It was at that precise moment impact occurred, allowing the very odd trajectory of becoming airborne. Actually, police believe it was driven downward into the pavement at the point here". The camera pans to the pavement area Max is mentioning in voice-over. A distinct groove in the asphalt was easily seen by the viewing audience. The camera pans back to Max.

"The momentum then caused the edge to catch and the Tercel went airborne. Much like a figure skater attempting a triple axel jump. Ice Skaters will dig the edge of their skate into the ice to give them that friction for a jump. Apparently, the Toyota moved in a similar manner, with the additional jumping force a skater would need being provided to the Tercel by the F-150. It may have rotated 3 times, or 4, or even more, while still in the air. Then rolled over two vehicles before coming to rest while still on top of one vehicle and leaning against a utility pole. The police don't know the velocity of rotation, so the math for calculating the full number of rotations is approximate currently. Investigators aren't sure if they will ever know all of these very strange details of this gruesome accident."

Max seemed to add this as an afterthought:

"One other strange detail that has emerged, among many strange things this afternoon, the Tercel and the F-150 clocks have stopped and have the exact same time reading: 4:19"

The production crew from the Channel 4 truck immediately place 2 inserts showing automobile clocks into the frame. Both clocks read 4:19. The left insert is in the upper left corner tagged "Tercel", while the right insert is labelled "F-150" and in the lower righthand corner. The inserts were on the screen for 4 seconds and removed.

3 seconds for a stationary object is a long time for a television viewing audience to watch. It will certainly capture their attention during that time. 4 seconds gave it emotional impact. 5 seconds would have been annoying. The production crew knew exactly what they were doing, and why.

Max attempted to find an ending for his report that suddenly found him getting a little emotional, with more "Live" time than expected. Gymnastics immediately popped into Max's mind.

"When the Tercel came down, it hit! But it didn't stick the landing! It kept rolling…"

What Little Girls Are Made Of- From the Diaries of Becka Skaggs, PhD

"Alright, alright. Yes. Uh, Max. Calm down. It's OK," a startled Brent said reassuringly, fumbling to grab his dangling earpiece while trying to keep his Star reporter from losing his composure on camera. Was that Max's voice cracking?

Quickly trying to keep this news report from being taken off the air, Brent jump-started Max's ego. "Great reporting, Max. Let's just stay away from sports metaphors, shall we?" Brent gives him his friendly faker chuckle, then continues. "Can you tell us how the rescuers were able to extract the child?"

"Yes, Brent. Very carefully, I must say. And I am thankful for that," he finishes with a smile.

Max was clearly proud of himself for getting that zinger through Brent's defenses. Just look at that toothsome grin! The producer noticed and reacted with a raised eyebrow and a noticeable throat-clearing into the microphone.

That was all the message he needed. Max straightened up and continued "Live" reporting from the hospital.

"I just wanted to explain how the Tercel kept rolling after it landed on the van, crushing the driver instantly, and onto the Ford Taurus, which was occupying the lane adjacent to the van. The Tercel continued to roll over the Taurus until it rested up against a utility pole, while still partly on top of the Ford. The Taurus was just close enough to the utility pole to keep the Tercel from sliding all the way to the ground and becoming wedged between the pole and the Taurus."

"It was really touch-n-go for the rescuers trying to free the little girl from the back of the Tercel. The vehicle was visibly unstable. Emergency workers voiced concerns many times. Any wrong movement or vibration and the Tercel could have fallen on a rescuer or shifted enough to crush a rescuers arm. Or they could lose their little survivor impaled in the back seat. They had to cut loose a part of the seat spring from the back seat of the Tercel and strapped it to her the very best they could."

Max is now squarely looking into the camera.

"Yes, there were some tense moments during the rescue at 7th St and Marine Drive, Brent. But, at least this part of the horrendous incident, the rescue of the survivors, has been a success. I must say, as horrific as this accident is, I'm very happy to report these rescue successes to you wherever they may happen. This has been Max Swanson, Channel 4 On-The-Spot News from outside Black Lake General Hospital. Back to you, Brent."

[And…mobile feed 1 to black….2…1…go!]

"Thank you, Max", Brent finishes his duties.

"And we'll be back with a story about a happy cat missing for 37 days after this break".

(And, more black)

CHAPTER - MY LIFE

AUGUST 19, 2020 – Becka's 20th birthday.
16th birthday for Ros

It's August 19, 2020, and the world is literally on fire…with the biggest, wildest pandemic humans have ever seen. Perhaps, the biggest the earth has ever seen.

Riots are occurring in over a dozen countries around the world as dictators continue to take liberties and commit atrocities upon their people. Within a week, protests will break out in a country run by a quasi-deity monarch family as protestors demand reforms. Some cities are on fire because the emotions within the protests have become escalated.

Climate Fires – named so per Governor Jay Inslee of Washington State - will break out throughout the world in areas that are amid historic droughts. Within three weeks, nineteen States will have active uncontained wildfires burning down structures and taking American lives.

This energy will continue to ripple throughout the human spirit for at least 3 generations. Es Verdad! That is indeed the truth, and maybe more generations will feel the ripple, my sweethearts. Get yourselves prepared. It will take us that long to re-balance and re-purpose the energy.

I am enjoying my 20th Birthday in quarantine with great-uncle Jack. Born John Anderson Wilson II – Jack is a common nickname within our family for men with the name John or Jackson - Uncle Jack runs a disaster-relief charity for small coastal communities. Coastal because Uncle Jack is a coastal Geologist. So that kind of makes sense. That is probably the best reason why I just received my Doctorate in Geology on June 2, 2020.

My DREAM really did come true! A PhD in coastal arenitic sedimentation - that just means I like sand. I study sand that has been deposited somewhere along the coast. I have plans and designs to use certain beach sands in our fight against sea-level rise. Beach sand is my Fav!

But not 24 hours after I received my diploma in the mail, I sobbed uncontrollably for nearly 2 full days. I could not believe myself!! I thought I would be happy. And I was. Then something hit me, and the floor dropped out from under me.

There I was, feeling confused, alone, saddened, elated, vulnerable, uncertain of a future that had been changed without my knowledge or consent. But also relieved all the strife of my prior life was over!

The YEARS of studying with no other kids around me. Not really having friends. Constant prodding by the medical field. Testing this and testing that. Testing, testing, testing! Always more things to think up. More questions that need to be answered. Apparently, I'm a good human specimen to study. Once they found out about me, they don't want to let me go.

As far as drowning myself in tears goes. Yes, I tend to go for the high difficulty sobbing activities.

**"This is incredible folks! She is attempting a 9.2 difficulty CRY while doing the barrel roll on the living room floor. This has NEVER been attempted before! Okay. It has. Hehe **

I am a drama mama! You will soon find out.

I guess the release of years of stress was too much, and I couldn't hold in the tears. The floodgates just opened on me. I had to ride the wave of those emotions and let them flow through me. Once I did that, I was okay. Sometimes, that's just what life does to us, these odd little things that come out of nowhere. I guess adults have learned to deal a little better than us kids, or young adults. Ya know, experience and all.

What Little Girls Are Made Of- From the Diaries of Becka Skaggs, PhD

I am immunocompromised since the accident. I can get pretty sick by catching common viruses from people. The kind of viruses that are just a nuisance for most people, could cost me another organ, or even my life. Oh, I need to be very careful. Yes!

My immune condition keeps me from teaching to classrooms of students. Online perhaps, I could teach for a career. But that is not me. If people are near, I want to be close to them. I love people!! It's like I just want to touch each one. Even better? I want to give them a BIG HUG, and then smile when they look surprised.

Unfortunately, that wouldn't be good for me. The first time I had pneumonia, I was 5 years old. I was a sick kitten. I had a high fever for five days while in the hospital. That was rough stuff.

I've had it 3 more times since. So, I can't really be around crowds. I mean, it's not a "prudent thing" to do, as Nurse Marjorie would remind me way too often. *Eye roll* Science says I'm susceptible to getting pneumonia now because I've had it more than twice already. So, working with my Uncle Jack in his Engineering laboratory is perfect for me!

I also suffered a Traumatic Brain Injury (TBI) during the car wreck when I was four years old. It affected me in ways adults were not ready for a kid to be affected. I suddenly had a voracious appetite for information. I had supposedly only been learning rudimentary language skills until the accident. After the accident, I began reading at a high school level immediately, and at a college level by age five, with near complete comprehension. I preferred reading and typing, to create my own printed word, over speaking. Typing on grandma's old typewriter came natural to me. Writing by hand came along but it was harder.

Many children have active imaginations at age five. Consequently, adults tend to believe that speaking skills are a good indicator of when a child is ready to enter the public-school system. So, schools didn't think I was smart enough for them. I didn't like to talk.

We found out later my brain injury gave me the tendency to stay mute. But I could still ask some pointed questions. I think I asked too many questions the teachers couldn't answer.

Born Rebecca Dall Skaggs, August 19, 2000, Black Lake General Hospital, Olympia, Washington, and I will never forget it! My right leg was sticking out of the blanket as the nurses took me from mom, and I felt distressed from that…cold, looseness of nothing surrounding my foot. It was SO FAR AWAY! Why was my foot waaaay dowwwn there??

I feel coldness. That means it must be MY foot, right? I mean, correct?? Hehe

That is my first memory of this world. Yeah, the doctors were amazed too. Some still are, but most have come around to accept it. Somehow, I am a freak of nature. Who knew??

Yep. I did.

But nobody ever listens to me!

No. I did not come out of the womb telling the doctors their jobs. Hahahaaaa, don't be silly. I was at least 8 years old before I did that. My brain functions somewhat differently than other people. It makes me appear smart. But I know how many unanswered questions I have inside my brain. SOOO, I can't be that smart. Am I right?

When I was eighteen, I agreed to receive a Direct Commission in the Public Health Service. My commission was conditioned on my receiving a PhD. I have never officially received a college degree, though Western Oregon University gave me an honorary Bachelor of Science degree when I was sixteen, as recognition for some work I did for some professors there.

However, June 2nd, 2020, I did receive my diploma. And my commission in the Public Health Service became official. I am now, Lieutenant Commander Becca Skaggs, PhD. I have been assigned to the Centers for Disease Control and Prevention, but that's just my cover identity. More about that later! Wink wink.

What Little Girls Are Made Of- From the Diaries of Becka Skaggs, PhD

No need to be formal here. You may call me Becca. Mom still calls me Becky. But that is a very long story left for a little later in our adventure. Grandma still calls me Rebecca sometimes. That's cool. I'm good with that name. Hey! I'm not a teenager anymore. I am TWENTY!

When I was studying for a semester in Ukraine and Romania along the western Black Sea, I found that the Russian language uses an ending for the female gender on some of their words. It is "-ka". Studientka is a female student. SOOOO, I decided I can spell my name with a -ka ending too. Please, feel free to call me Rebecca, or Becca, or Becka. Cool! OK, I'm going with Becka. I'm really warming up to that spelling. I am thrilled to meet you guys!

Before we get too far ahead of ourselves, I want to let you know what we are all doing here. Well, thank you Rosalyn, I thought that was a good idea too. You are so kind. Oh! That is Rosalyn in Ghana… Rosalyn says "Hi". Sister Ros is telepathically plugged into me. We are Cosmic Twins. Well, that's what we call ourselves, anyway. I just barely have to think of her and suddenly, there she is! Having a conversation with me.

Again, I am getting way ahead of where I wanted to be at this point. This book is all about Rosalyn and I, so we will share much more information later. Oh, you guys didn't know? Rosalyn and I are famous. We are very famous young ladies. Our fame began during a horrendous accident when I was four-years old. You already know some of the details. But there is vastly much much more for you all to know.

Here I go again, not explaining everything in the proper order. Rosalyn says I'm one of the worst that way. Since you have some of our past information already, you aren't totally unprepared for what is about to come.

In honor of wisdom from my little sister, let's get back to the basics of our mystery. Ready or not, here we go!

Let's go back to August 19, 2004, my fourth birthday and that terrible accident.

WE know who did it and why they say they were at that intersection. But some of that stuff turned out to be not very close to true. And knowing that didn't change my life one bit from the day before.

I still was in the hospital for a month. I had 3 surgeries during that first month. My voice box had a puncture wound. The paramedics put me back together the best they could while at the accident. I'm very pleased with how they performed, as it's been told to me. I can look at the scars and see what they did.

I think I turned out ok, even though I had to have more reconstruction before I turned six years old. But that was ok, too. I'm fine with doctors putting me back together. It's being their guinea pig that bugs me!

Mom was still in a forced coma after a month - Oh yeah, induced coma - because of her head injuries. Mom just didn't wake up exactly when the doctors asked her to wake up. She took her own usual time on things. She is so predictable that way!

So, Grandma Fran came to the rescue. Born Ella Frances Wilson, don't you ever call her Ella unless you want to lock horns with that old Seattleite. Sweetest heart that took no crap from anyone! That was Grandma Fran.

Something was always cooking on the stove, but she was as thin as a stick. Always feeding everyone else. That was Grandma Fran. Uncle Jack is Fran's older brother. Fran married my grandpa, Randall Skaggs. So, we are Skaggs' while Uncle Jack is still a Wilson. Sorry Uncle Jack.

But Uncle Jack was there for Grandma Fran when Grandpa Randall died of colon cancer. It was terrible. He hid it from everybody until the last few months of his life. He was always skinny as a rail with a pale complexion the whole time I knew him. It was easy to believe his stories of a little bug bothering him now and then.

I wasn't two yet, but I remember Grandpa Randall. That's where my middle name comes from. The end of Grandpa Randall's name. Yeah, Mom thought it would be a real cute way to spell the word for a toy (hint: d-o-l-l

What Little Girls Are Made Of- From the Diaries of Becka Skaggs, PhD

is a toy). So, my name is Rebecca Doll spelled Mama Skaggs' way, D-A-L-L. See? Isn't that better? Uhhhhh......matter of opinion. **Big Eye Roll**

* * * **Vital Information for the survival of mankind** * * *

The police have issued a statement saying they need help finding out what happened on the day of my car accident. We know their statement as to why that driver was in such a hurry on that day, at that time. But the facts "don't comport with their statement", according to the report.

What happened in their life to push them to that fateful intersection on that day at that precise moment? And why lie about what happened if it is as innocent as they say? Rushing to the hospital because you got a call about a sick friend doesn't make you go 70mph in a 45mph zone. Not very likely.

You know, things happen in life that are not easy to explain. And sometimes, search and search we may, we never discover the real reasons for why things happen. But sometimes, if we follow a method of investigation and inquiry, we can actually determine facts that lead us to the root cause of things. That is what we are going to do.

I told you guys what happened to me in the moments leading up to our accident. But what about the driver of the pick-up? We don't know anything yet, do we? Who is this person? What is he to me??

We hope to discover documents and facts, like the final amended police report. I want to see that final report. That is something I feel we should all see. I have intuition about these kinds of things. The driver's statement is in that report, for one thing. A statement from the driver wasn't there until they showed up several days later, with a lawyer. Who allowed that insertion of information into the final report?

I also have friends in high places. Remember Rosalyn?? Do not forget Rosalyn. I guarantee she will never forget you. She couldn't even if she tried.

Rosalyn is a practitioner of universal energy. We are all connected by it. Universal Energy (UE) is the thing that makes everything in the universe move. Nothing does any work anywhere without UE. It is the energy that drives each atom; the energy that sparks each cell to life. This is true science. "Universal Energy" is my name for it because science does not agree on one name, yet. But I can agree with myself, and that's exactly what I've done.

Rosalyn feels and sees the energy. It is like a language to her. Almost like music is sometimes described as a language. Music speaks to humans without words, yet the message is clear. Remember: Lyrics are the words. Music is from the instruments. It is so early in our relationship, and you are doubting me already? You are about to learn amazing things. Stay with me.

Science has shown that some music can stimulate the growth of house plants and have many positive effects on a fetus developing in the womb.

Music is just an expression of energy. Music causes certain vibrations of the air that our ears translate for us. Our ears are our music receptors. Our ears and our entire audio system translate the vibrations, and it sounds beautiful, or screeches on our nerves!

Science is learning that people have other receptors as well. Inside our brain are receptors that can help us pick up all kinds of clues from our environment. Many times, our bodies know things about our environment without us having conscious thoughts about it. But we pick up that information and our brain files it away. We will have more time to learn many things from Rosalyn later. She is quite special, and you will enjoy her company.

I am a scientist and you guys are my friends. I am just getting you warmed up for the more serious science stuff to come a little later in our story. Don't worry, no mathematical formulas and no tests or exams are required. I want to share things that can inform you about your life and the world you live in. The main body of my story has already begun. I'm giving you the background information you will need to comprehend before you, as a reader, may progress to the next chapter. So, what I'm telling you right now is for your own good! I want to be a mom really bad. Can you tell?

What Little Girls Are Made Of- From the Diaries of Becka Skaggs, PhD

I am a young adult. That means, I could live another 80 years, or another 100, or more! Rosalyn says 95. Extended life like this is quite possible right now, in 2020.

How possible will extended life be by the time I'm 80? I don't know, yet. But there are many things that are going to happen on this planet during my lifetime. Many are going to be out of my control. However, some are within my control. And I am getting myself prepared to do some wonderful things with that control! Fun things! But some serious things, too.

I hope you guys will join me while we investigate, chat with people, and discover all kinds of science things. I am going to need a lot of help. Millions of you would be very nice. Hehe.

We are going to help people. Helping people is ALWAYS a superhero's Priority #1.

We will need to solve some mysteries to find the vital information that is needed by certain World Leaders in order to implement plans for mankind's survival, and maybe watch a beautiful sunset on the beach while roasting some marshmallows? Would you like that? I sure would! Hahahaaa... DEF!!

Ohhh, did that "Life Mission Statement" go by too fast? Okay. Well, re-read the paragraph just above as many times as you need. It's okay. We'll wait for you. I need to file my fingernail anyway. I cracked it on that last emoji. Ya know? I could use a color change too. This color's been getting boring....

Oh! Done? Everything good?? Okay!

We are all ready to be the World's newest set of Superheroes! And nobody will stop us because we are full of science. And LOVE!

Let's go back to our story, shall we? We are at the hospital now and I am in Operating Room 1 waiting "patiently" for the doctor. It's my 4th birthday, 2004. The gift that keeps on giving…sheesh.

No, No. I'm not bitter, really. I'm being a bit dramatic. Sarcastic too, yeah. But not bitter. It's just true. It's still with me.

OK. YES!! You guys are right, of course. There are still some bitter feelings. But I am getting much better at dealing. My accident is something that happened. I had no control. So, I am on a mission to find out what was the purpose of all this carnage. Things have a reason for happening, right? Why am I the way I am? Why am I so interesting that scientists want to study me?

I guess I'm just the whole package all wrapped up in a little lacey bow.

Seriously, I want to know what's going on inside here, in my female brain. So, that's just what we will do, if you are still willing to help me? You are? Good.

Let's listen in.

*** **Outside the emergency OR1 — Our Story continues** ***

"Captain. Please tell me the current situation of the child", asked Doctor Murdock, the emergency surgeon on call at the time of the accident. "I've been told she's been impaled by an object, and part of it is still with her? Do you have any information that could make my life and hers a little easier in that Operating Room?"

Captain Kuneiahl Delfis "Kuney" Crumb of the County Fire Department was a doctor. He had an actual PhD in paramedic and rescue sciences. So, he was a doctor like me. Captain Crumb is gone from us now, may his energy be in eternal love, but is not totally gone from me. I still feel his presence from time-to-time.

Ya know? I never heard the story about how he got his name. I also have never heard anyone mention any other Kuneiahl Crumb, or even Delfis Crumb. I've heard of Bobby Crumb, but that's not even a relation. Bobby's

What Little Girls Are Made Of- From the Diaries of Becka Skaggs, PhD

hair is fire engine red, but I think that is all Kuney and Bobby ever had in common. That is, the color fire engine red.

I always suspected his parents wanted to give their child a tiny advantage by having a name that seems more distinguished. To go along with the last name, right? That way when Kuney would be introduced to someone, they will become so entrapped in trying to mentally spell the first two names, they won't notice the simpler last name. Maybe his parents suffered strife in their lives just because of their last name? I don't know, but it happens.

I'm sorry, you guys. Now that I'm no longer a teenager in real life, I really shouldn't partake in such adolescent speculation. I mean, not out loud, anyway.

Just teasing you guys, LOL!

I'm never gonna stop with the adolescent speculation! Are you kidding? It's too much fun! Hahahaaa.

Okay. Back to our story. It's getting good, huh?

Kuney started, "It seems that a broken spring from the back seat poked through the fabric and became a puncturing weapon the car used against this little girl" the captain began recounting the details in the way he knew the doctor understood.

"It looks like she may have been punctured every time the car had a shock. The larger the shock, the larger the puncture wound". Kuney was still running things through his mind, trying to discover anything else that can help the doctor, while doing it quickly so the doctor could get to the operating room where I was patiently waiting. The staff is furiously prepping me and the operating room for the hours expected ahead of us. In the hallway, the doctor and Kuney are still discussing me.

Continuing, the Captain remarked, "there are 18 puncture marks across her back and left side. Most the damage is to her left side. Many appeared more superficial or penetrating only muscle, but about a half-dozen looked like very deep wounds. Because the spring could cause severe damage…I mean, her heart, the spring is right up against her left ventricle at this moment. I wouldn't be surprised if you also find her spleen is damaged beyond repair."

Quickly looking away to brush a bit of a tear from his cheek, Captain Crumb added,

"This weapon caused a lot of damage to Becky with these blows. Her left kidney is already showing extreme distress from lack of oxygen supply. She suffered a number of shredded arteries." Kuney added a stern bit of advice to the doctor based on his education and 30 years of experience,

"I'll bet you dollars to donuts that left ovary's gone too. There are 3 deep wounds in that area, Doc. Be sure you check that entire area. Not trying to tell you your job. Just letting know what I saw, Doc."

"And I appreciate all you can give me, Captain." The doctor is indeed pleased by the amount of information Kuney can give him in such a short period of time.

Now," the captain changed his gaze to his hands where he was simulating how he cut and immobilized the spring while strapping it to my little body so no further damage could occur.

Kuney recounted his thinking. "I decided it was the best thing to immobilize the spring piece, keep her stable, and let you guys do the heavy work with proper equipment" and he smiles a big grin as he raised his head and his gaze right to Dr Murdock, who immediately notices the captain's lack of proper oral hygiene.

Doctor Murdock, however, only acknowledges the yellowish grin with the congenial

"Thank You for all your help, Captain. You always do the most remarkable rescues! I think we have a good chance on this one", as the doctor turned and briskly brushed through the flimsy double-doors separating them from the hallway leading to the emergency room OR's. Through the gap

What Little Girls Are Made Of- From the Diaries of Becka Skaggs, PhD

in the doors, Kuney could see the doctor was wasting no time. He knew I would be in good hands. The best hands in our Tri-County area.

"You know, Doc," Kuney had one more quick thought and stepped into the doorway to keep the double doors from swinging closed all the way. That prompted the doctor to stop and turn toward Kuney.

"Yes, Kuney?"

"I had this nagging feeling the entire time while the crew was rescuing this family," the captain began.

"This is the main reason I had them go very deliberately through each move the team made as they did their jobs. They are so well trained, too. They do it all themselves, you know. They always train like it is a real situation, and their performance showed it today."

"Well, yes, Kuney. They are exceptional at their jobs!" Doctor Murdock whole-heartedly agreed.

"So, what was your concern, Captain?"

"I was concerned with the little girl, Becky," as Kuney became very sullen. "The way that spring is situated, if she had moved even one inch, she would have ruptured the ventricle and bled out before we could even get there. Just one little inch and we would have another fatality."

The captain makes a quick movement skyward with his eyes and with his head tilted up, says in a happily relieved way, "Somebody was looking out for THAT little girl!"

"I am sure you are very correct, Captain! You are most certainly...correct. I will pay special attention to that ventricle," the doctor finishes as he trails off his last words and turns toward his very young, so far lucky, patient awaiting on an operating table in OR1. Time is a-wasting, and the doctor's step shows he understands that I need his attention completely.

SC MacAlpine

* * * **Female Zest for Life BREAK** * * *

Squeaky Female Narrator: *Women have minds that are specialized toward survival of the society, and therefore, the species overall. Recent research reveals the brain of a woman is a highly sensitive instrument, not unlike our bodies. They have been compared to the sophisticated machinery of the finest Ferrari ever witnessed at Le Mans. It has the capability of generating substances that help its body carry on its arduous path of daily duties.*

A woman's brain has the same number of brain cells in a smaller space as men. It's the exact same number in 8% smaller skull on average. Women have areas, consequently, where neuron densities are greater by 6 to 60 times those of men. Because neurons can become clustered, these clusters can create neuroreceptors. Research is finding areas of the female brain can have neuroreceptor-densities 16 times more than that of men in the same region of the brain. This is all due to the lovely process known as evolution. It is all science.

'Nuhhhh, what time is it? How long? Mom?'

'Where am I? What is this place. I'm not in the car. Am I in heaven?'

'OH, waaahhhh', I began to cry uncontrollably.

'I'm stuck in the other place, WAAAHhhhh.'

More sobbing continues. I tried to open my eyes, but they felt glued shut.

'Please, somebody? God?'

I listen. There's nothing.

'Devil?' 'Is anybody here?'

Ok. Stop this nonsense. Use your beautiful mind. You've got to be alive. Where are we now, Becka?

This place has a sterile smell. Not much of anything really. That won't help. I can't hear anything. My ears are still ruined, probably.

What Little Girls Are Made Of- From the Diaries of Becka Skaggs, PhD

Touch!

Feeling around with my hands, I still can't see. So, I am feeling around me trying to recognize anything by touch. Not something I'm used to doing.

I feel blankets. Ooooo warm, and warm sheets too. A bed it seems.

"Am I in a kid-sized bed?"

I began speaking aloud, but my speaking is almost inaudible. It would sound like little pieces of mumbled words to an observer standing beside my hospital bed. Spoken in a soft whisper, a person would have to place their ear to my mouth to distinguish anything.

"Can't tell for sure, though. It's comfy enough. Ouch! What is that? Something sticking my arm. It's all taped down. Must be 9-1-1." The mutterings pause for a moment. Then, as if reacting to an unheard statement in some unheard conversation,

"Ohhhh, ok. That's good. Thank you, Grandma. You saved us. I love you so much, grandmother."

Seconds go by. Or minutes?

Another muttering begins,

"You don't mind if I just sleep…...a little more then….grandmoth…"

CHAPTER – Holding onto Life

Squeaky Female Narrator: *50,000 years ago, humans were still fighting for survival. They were nomadic hunters. Tribes could not afford to be very large because food supplies were not available. The men are built for power, for hunting, for protection of the species. The duties of hunting fell to them because it matched their natural skills, or vice versa. The "relatively" limited physical prowess of women left them at home, in the camp, when all the men left on hunting parties. Of course, we are the ones equipped with mammary glands to care for the children. So, there's that.*

Men have areas of higher neuron density than women, also. Those areas of the brain tend be the areas that focus on decision-making, hunting and protection, obstinacy, and the relevant strategies necessary to be successful within the current social settings. Men have also developed the ability, as warriors, to become numb. The brain takes over and produces the necessary brain chemical mixture to stop the signals from the nerve endings. This allows them to fight for survival to the very end. Until extinguished, essentially.

Women, on the other hand, must be able to experience the pains of human-ness so that she may convey her experiences to society. SHE, the mother, is how the village learns, exactly as the mother Orca whale passes on her hunting skills to her daughters. Our human mother's experiences are needed for survival of the species, and they must be handed down directly by our mothers (in some cases, grandmothers) to be learned most effectively. Science is just now learning how humans may be able to use our female minds in the future, allowing for many advancements, it seems.

What Little Girls Are Made Of- From the Diaries of Becka Skaggs, PhD

* * * Emergency Surgery #1 BREAK * * *

"Barb? Time?" Doctor Murdock hadn't said a word in what seemed like 5 minutes. Highly unusual for an emergency procedure with a crew that knew each other like this crew. Voices, orders, understanding-orders, life data, more voices are normally clacking all the time in the emergency room. William Murdock had asked the scrub nurse to track the time for the procedure. He knew they were in for a long night. They were now into their 11th hour of surgery on me. In fact, the 11th hour will be over in less than 15 minutes and the 12th hour will begin.

"4:06am Doctor". Dr Murdock suddenly got a smile on his face, "we might be able to get out of here before 12 hours is over. I need more light on this area. This artery is shredded. Get me the vascular fabric. I think I can fashion a sleeve…yes, if…I…can…. just…." Dr Murdock is holding onto the shredded artery with forceps until he can attach it to something. And he realized they will have to create that something right here. "Ok, I need a right hand in this location here. I don't care whose right thumb goes here". The assistant surgeon offered his left hand because it was the closest.

Dr Murdock quickly corrected the error,

"I don't want your thumb in my way, Doctor. If I had wanted you to consider whichever was easiest for you, I would have stated my order that way. But I did not! Now, right thumb, Here." William points next to where he is holding the forceps.

"Sorry. It's been a long night." Doctor Murdock needed his assistant's complete attention. He cannot be distracted by thoughts of inferiority.

"We are a team, here, okay Doctor?" William looks at his young assistant with true collegial concern, then adds.

"This little girl needs our team to help her survive. She needs all of us, doctor. All of us at our best. Can you give this little girl your best, please?"

"Yes sir. I mean, yes, doctor, absolutely. Just show me again what to do? I apologize for fumbling about. It's my error", the assistant managed a smile and was now in proper position to help William repair me.

Giving the doctor one more second for further comment, and not hearing any forthcoming, William gathered the team for the next steps.

"Very well, people. We know why we are all here. Precisely this little girl. Let's give her life back TO HER. Shall we?"

They all knew it was rhetorical. They were simply awaiting the next orders. Those orders were directly to his young assistant. Everyone else knew their job was to keep me alive while the doctors made up stuff, inside me. William spoke.

"Use the fabric, with the one hand fashion a vascular tube." William was showing him with his free hand how to position the fabric with the fingers. I just learned that doctors play make believe in surgery. Who knew they taught imagination in medical school?

One other thing all surgeons must have is dexterity. Prestidigitation is a fun thing among surgeons. Medical students say it helps them keep their fingers nimble while learning doctoring. Many students learn card tricks and sleight-of-hand, mostly because they are always a hit with the college dating crowd, or some sucker for a quick bet, but it does help the fingers become nimble.

Using 3 fingers of his right hand and the opposable thumb, the assistant fashioned a small tube from the fabric.

"Excellent looking tube, Doctor. That should work nicely. Okay, keep holding it right there." He sutured a piece of the fabric to itself, to hold the tube-shape while leaving a splayed area to lay the artery. He sutured a portion of the artery onto the fabric, like a small anchor or tether. Then, the doctor fed the shredded portion of the artery onto the splayed portion of the fashioned tube. With a swift motion he covered the artery with the fabric.

What Little Girls Are Made Of- From the Diaries of Becka Skaggs, PhD

He handed the fabric end to his assistant, who completed the circular motion to complete a tube shape. The end is in the forceps, and William regains control of the tube.

Once a large section was covered by the fabric in the tube, William sutured the 'old' artery and tube together just enough to hold. Then he released his anchor-suture carefully, hoping there was no residual elasticity in the 'old' artery that may cause the tissue to snap back.

"If that would happen, it would retract well into her body and below her heart. It could take another TOO MANY minutes to get it out of that predicament. NOT the thoughts we want rattling around inside our minds right now."

Gee. Thanks for mentioning that, Doc. Now everybody has it rattling around inside.

*** **ME BREAK** ***

Doctor Murdock has been explaining his moves while orchestrating the next steps of his team. I have been hearing only parts of the conversations. I shouldn't be hearing ANYTHING! What is happening to me? Is this part of going deaf?

I'm pretty sure I've been completely out for a while, but then I hear things. Or maybe I remember hearing things? Oh geeez! Isn't that the same thing? I'm going crazy too??

I think I'm damaged, doc.

Here comes the dark gray. Bye folks. And now I'm out again.

*** **REMEMBER – I'm in Surgery** ***

All the options of hand angle versus instrument pitch had already gone through Doctor Murdock's mind by the time he maneuvered the scissors to cut the anchor-suture.

AFTER he cut, he noticed himself hesitating. Almost like he was expecting that artery to snap.

But it did not budge. It stayed right where he needed it. And he was able to save the artery with his ingenious repair and help from his assistant. A few more minutes on the artery and he was ready.

"Ok. I can remove the spleen now. It is clear." As the doctor began to lift, he felt a slight tug. THAT was not what he was expecting at all!

"Uhhh, guys?" Doctor Murdock is now acting a little dramatic because he just found some of the best news so far tonight with his left forefinger.

"This little girl has an accessory spleen. I'd say it's about 8 or 9 cm. It looks healthy from here. At least Becca will be able to recycle her own red blood cells. And maybe fight a few nasty viruses too."

Doctor Murdock was very pleased with the find. Very, very pleased. Less than 3 in 10 people are born with an accessory spleen. Less than 10% of those ever function properly. But those that do function best, tend to be on their own without the primary spleen. Current research is still uncertain. But it appears, in these particular situations, the accessory spleen can grow to about 30% of the size of a normal spleen. I was indeed very lucky this time.

"Let's close her up. Good job everybody!"

CHAPTER – A GREEN LIFE

GREEN FLASHING MONITOR - August 2004

In an interior room with no windows and where few people have ever gone, down a long series of hallways at right angles to each other, in what could be a building that looks like ten thousand other buildings used for storage, warehousing, and luxury lofts, in a thousand cities around the world,

The green flashing monitor wasn't even noticed.

Had anyone noticed, they may have been inclined to look at the monitor. Once anyone looked at the monitor, the message was clearly written in English, and most who had just a middle-school comprehension in English would be able to read the words:

CONNECTION LOSS DETECTED

2 Incidents reported

TERMINATION MOMENT DETECTED

1 Incident reported

SUBJECT

Rebecca Dall

And if a person were also inclined to use the keyboard on the desk near the monitor, that person could scroll down the text to reveal even more information on the monitor.

ANALYSIS

Termination imminent

RECOMMENDATION FOLLOWS

Intervention with encephalo-receptor download

RECOMMENDATION ACCEPTED - Execute

Initiating Encephalo Receptor Sensitivity Test

RUN

Testing......

1 ERST - Pass

2 ERST - Pass

3 ERST – Fail

Retry Test – execute signal boost 50% protocol

Test Initiated – 50% signal boost successful

RUN

3 ERST – Fail.

Offline

Initiating backup encephalo receptor 3b

Testing.... 50% signal boost protocol - active

RUN

3b ERST – Testing....

Pass

4 ERST - Pass

Receptor sensitivity test successful

SET - Maintain 50% signal boost protocol

Receptors Active

TIME: 1140 months

SET COMPLETE

END TRANSMISSION

What Little Girls Are Made Of- From the Diaries of Becka Skaggs, PhD

* * * I AM LEARNING BREAK * *

Squeaky Female Narrator: *But on top of everything already mentioned, all duties of maintaining the society fell to the women when the men were away. They had to communicate with all. They had to be hypersensitive to attack while the bulk of their protection was gone. They had to be nurturing and helping and decisive and compassionate.*

Women cared for the young, the elderly, the infirmed, the disabled. Each of these people still have valuable contributions to make to the "tribe". Women are the individuals that continued to coax the contributions from these members pushed to the "fringe" of society by the "mainstream". Maybe it was 50, 000 years ago, society learned some agronomy.

Others settled in resource-rich areas and never had to become nomadic to successfully live off the land as hunter-gatherers – the Coastal Salish nations of the Pacific Northwest of North America are such an example. They lived and hunted along the ocean in a temperate climate with 500-foot trees that were thousands of years old. That would keep the tribal people under a canopy of several functional layers, providing additional warmth from the winter nights, and giving them natural riches they would never have to leave.

Women that kept alive the marginalized members, also kept alive the genetic diversity that we have, by gaining production from those that benefitted from a more sedentary or isolated lifestyle. The village began. Over thousands of years, our genetic code changes. Changes occur to increase survivability. If our genetic code changes in favor of those within the species best suited to conduct all these duties with the greatest efficiency and desired effects, then our survivability increases. Until, ultimately, we no longer are trying to just survive, we are able to thrive!

The little genetic diversity we do have is because of women caring too much about an individual and innovating a way to make them a participating and valued member of the society. Repeated enough, over a sufficiently long period of time, and evolutionary changes to a species will occur. But why do women do all this? 2 words: Brain Chemicals.

SC MacAlpine

* * * **GREEN BREAK – Still Holding -** * * *

On the Flashing Green Monitor comes another message:

INITIATING RECEPTOR DOWNLOADS –

Sending receptor test signal

50% Signal Boost Protocol - Active

TESTING SIGNAL BROADCAST

RUN

Testing Broadcast.......

Successful

RESULTS:

ERBT1 – Pass

ERBT2 – Pass

ERBT 3b – Pass

ERBT 4 – Pass

INITIATING DOWNLOAD – 1%, 2%, 5%, 8%....

10% DOWNLOAD COMPLETE

INITIATE INSTALL CMOS

Initiated....

Executed....

Successful

INITIATE OPTIMUM DOWNLOAD RATES

Initiated....

Executed....

Successful

DOWNLOAD – 30% - Running

* * * **I'M STILL LEARNING BREAK** * * *

What Little Girls Are Made Of- From the Diaries of Becka Skaggs, PhD

Squeaky Female Narrator: *Our Brain Chemicals give us women a thousand different ways to be happy, to show happiness, to have love, to emulate love and happiness, and cause it to become contagious throughout the community. Smiley, giggly, jiggly, bouncy, bubbly, jumpy, jittery, happy beyond belief! eee-LAY-ted, DAH-link.*

Love is a binding force in mammals. The more science looks at this question of love existing in lower-ordered mammals, the more we see incontrovertible evidence. It does exist.

This kind of behavior has many advantages to the tribe. Besides having an overall feeling of wellness, the tribe tends to have a greater zest for life. Morale increases. Neighbors are helping just one extra time more. Everything becomes more productive because members WANT to be productive.

Women had to learn over thousands of years how to do the same jobs as men, but with more thought, more guile, more cooperation, more communication, more wit put into our actions in order to leverage the strengths we do have. And to mitigate the weaknesses.

I uncontrollably and quite suddenly startled awake.

"What are you saying? Who ARE you?? I'm not weak. I am strong, like a Viking warrior! I am THOR, God of Thunder!!"

And just as quickly, I fell fast asleep. This was like I suddenly bolted straight up in bed, uttered something from a dream, and went right back to sleep, all within seconds. Is this going to become a normal thing for me?

* * * **SAME GREEN MONITOR - August 2004 BREAK** * * *

The Green Monitor continues to give its owners the information they had asked for at some unknown time in the past. Somehow, it also seems to be programming something else.

DOWNLOAD 40% COMPLETE

SET TESTOSTERONE SPIKE

Strength and Healing Set to Nominal + 36%

SET BEGIN

DELAY – NONE

Immediate Timing accepted

Execute....

3...2...1...

Initiated Testosterone spike nominal +36%

Testing Receptor ERTT4

Signal Rebound complete

Test successful

SET END – at 48 months.

RETURN to nominal +18%

SET new standard

Standard = Nominal +18%

Nominal +18% accepted as new standard

Standard of Nominal +18% will begin running at 48 months.

Task Complete

SET HUMAN GROWTH HORMONE SPIKE

SET = Nominal +24%

INTIATIATE DELAY TIMING SEQUENCE

SET BEGIN = 78 months

SET END = 162 months

DELAY - ON

Initiated Delay Execution

Testing Receptors ERHG1 & ERHG3

Signal Rebound complete

What Little Girls Are Made Of- From the Diaries of Becka Skaggs, PhD

Test Successful

TIME: 1619

DATE: 19082020

Report:

Human Growth Hormone Spike set to nominal + 24%

Will BEGIN in 78 months precisely

Will END in 162 months precisely

Return to Nominal + 6%

SET new standard

STANDARD = Nominal + 6%

Nominal +6% accepted

STANDARD = Nominal +6% running

Task Incomplete

SET FEMALE AMINO ACID/ENZYME SUITE SPIKE

SET = Nominal +16%

INITIATE DELAY TIMING SEQUENCE

SET BEGIN = 48 months

SET END = 1140 months

DELAY - ON

EXECUTE

Initiated Delay Execution

Testing Receptors ERAE2 & ERAE4

Signal Rebound complete

Test Successful

TIME: 1620

DATE: 19082020

Report: Female Hormone/Enzyme Spike

SET = Nominal +16%

Will BEGIN in 48 months precisely

Will END in 1140 months precisely

Return to Nominal + 4%

SET new standard

STANDARD = Nominal + 4%

Nominal + 4% accepted

STANDARD = Nominal + 4% running

Task Incomplete

DOWNLOAD – 50% - Running

* * * ME ROBOT BREAK * * *

Squeaky Female Narrator: *I am showing you the differences between the genders and why they exist, sister. The natural, scientific, evolutionary reason for why these differences do indeed exist. Both genders are necessary for the greatest success possible for our species. None is more necessary than the other. Sameness is a consciously voluntary delusion. Let's just be real. Sameness is boring. Know the facts and work together from there.*

And you are HIGH on testosterone.

So, chill, THOR.

Ha!

[Sarcasm with a chuckle from this narrator. I'm getting good!]

* * * Yet the GREEN FLASHING MONITOR BREAK * * *

DOWNLOAD 60% COMPLETE

IINITIATE FEMALE HORMONE SUITE STIMULATION

What Little Girls Are Made Of- From the Diaries of Becka Skaggs, PhD

Initiated….

Executed….

Successful

INITIATE AMINO ACID SEQUENCING

Initiated….

Executed….

Successful

DOWNLOAD - 80% - Running

* * * **ME ROBOT TOO BREAK** * * *

Our sister narrator: *This is collaboration. Another strength of women, that men are quite capable of conducting in a similar manner with similar successes. Men have the capacity to feel and experience love in all its exhilarating grandeur as women. But they think there are only 6 kinds of love. A woman's reality is there are about 600 versions of love, and maybe 6000, and it just may be that we can't count that high.*

Brain chemicals can be as unique as each woman. Researchers suspect over 1 thousand are possible for each woman. I suspect the actual number is closer to infinity -1, which is a finite number by definition. We just don't know what precisely that number is. What does it look like? Or sound like? Or even smell like? Or feel like??

Becka not awakened this time, except within her dream. "Sister? Wait. Who's sister? I don't have a sister. I am an only child. So far anyway. You don't get things past me that easily, S.I.S.T.E.R!"

"Am I talking out loud? It doesn't seem like I'm moving at all. I must be having one of those dreams that people say seem really alive".

Meanwhile, inside my ICU room, the night-shift nurse just began checking in on their new little patient. The shift change occurs in less than an hour. Where has the time gone?

She noticed the little patient seemed to be resting, but not peacefully, so the nurse tried to change the bags of IV-fluids very quietly. My little crushed arm was randomly twitching while hanging in the stabilizer to my left. The twitching had to be either causing pain or because of pain, or both. The nurse understood that most of our bodies' healing is done while we are asleep. "Becca needs all the healing she can get....for quite some time," I thought I heard her whisper. Hmmm, maybe not.

So deep in her focus to work stealthily, the nurse did not notice the doctor arrive until he bumped her in his hurried approach to get close to his patient.

"I'm sorry. Excuse me, please? I apologize, Nurse." The young doctor immediately showed his embarrassment for rudely plowing into the nurse. He was at the nurse's station out front and noticed some unusual EEG readings – electroencephalograph. Just one of many medical devices hooked up to me that feed information back to a receiving-device at the nurse's station. This allows the medical staff to monitor my life signs, and to be at the ready should any emergency occur. This is true for all ICU patients. Even Mom.

The Nurses station is situated in the middle of the entire floor, with the ICU rooms around the perimeter of the floor. The patients all had a view. Half of the patients could never see it because they were rarely conscious. Half of the remainder, though somewhat more conscious, were too sick to even care about looking at a view.

But we all had a view. And when I was awake, I did care enough to want to look. And I did look at the view.

I liked trying to see something besides the sky, even if it was a cloud. Sometimes a thundercloud would rise way up, and I could watch it do its magical thing. Sometimes the whole sky would light up in a backlight-effect behind the big cloud. That view was always cool!

Whenever I looked out the window, I liked to try to see the tops of any buildings and see if I could tell what it was. There is a steeple I can see. I

What Little Girls Are Made Of- From the Diaries of Becka Skaggs, PhD

have that figured for a church, though I could be wrong. I will have to wait to see what it is, once I finally get healed and get out of this place.

Grrrr......I don't like being here at all! But I am hurt. I understand we were in a car accident, and I am hurt pretty bad, in a whole bunch of places. I have no control over what is to happen next. So, I must trust the people to do the best they can in their jobs. I will trust them to make all the right decisions. What else can I do? No sense in worrying.

And I'm not worrying. And it's not my internal thoughts that are causing the brain wave activity to measure the way it did on the encephalograph. It's something else. It's not me, you guys! It is somebody else. Do you hear me? Somebody else!!!

Ok, so you can't hear me.

Look at my face!

Look at me and read what is there, on my face in front of you! You must see something. This is not me.

Hey, Doctor Blue Eyes!

Nursie!

It's not me-e-e-e

I felt like I was crying up a thunderstorm. But nobody noticed anything. I am lying here in my dream feeling sad. Clean up on Aisle 4. Customer crying her eyes out, and it's all over the floor. Somebody could get hurt.

The Nurse held her left index finger to her lips, signifying to the doctor, "Quiet, please. Patient trying to sleep." The nurse began her whispered response.

"No. I'm sorry doctor. It's my fault." The nurse was letting the doctor know she saw he had something immediate on his mind. She backed away only 2 short steps. Enough, she felt, to give him room, but still close enough that if she were suddenly needed, she could assist in whatever procedure the doctor felt necessary without hardly missing a heartbeat. And that kind of timing could be all we have to save a life. You just never know with these kinds of injuries, like mine.

Triple organ removals were not very common. Even in the year 2020, less than 300 are performed per year in the U.S. The remainder of the world doesn't equal 30% of our number. Survival rates are all over the charts. The medical techniques used, and the quality of facilities vary greatly. It's generally a 50-50 proposition nowadays. Which is not bad, especially when all a transplant used to do was prolong your life for a few months. Now, people can lose multiple organs, and live a relatively good quality-of-life to a normal life span. That is amazing science!

"No. Stay right here," the doctor whispered back to the nurse.

The doctor wasn't sure if the nurse was leaving when she stepped back. While he moved closer to his little patient, he reached back inadvertently, almost subconsciously, to feel if she was still there. When the nurse noticed the doctor's hand about to dangle in the air, she grabbed it firmly with both of hers and said "I'm right here, doctor. Whatever you need", and she immediately released the lovely, well-manicured, ringless left hand back to the doctor. His little smile was noticed.

The doctor leans over and checks my eyes by opening them and shining his penlight onto the pupil. This is a technique used by doctors to be sure the pupils are reacting properly to the light stimulation. They seemed to be functioning fine. And that doesn't check out with the kind of brain activity he was seeing. The doctor then noticed the random twitching from my left upper extremity.

But that still wouldn't be enough activity to cause what he saw at the nurse's station.

"Nurse?"

"Alisha, Doctor."

"What?"

What Little Girls Are Made Of- From the Diaries of Becka Skaggs, PhD

"My name is Alisha."

"Oh." The doctor quickly glances at Alisha and back to his patient. "Ok, Alisha. Hi," his little bashful smile told Alisha all she needed to know.

"I'm sorry, again", he finished his apology to the very single nurse. Or that's how she felt about her recent drought in romantic successes, anyway.

"Alisha, did you notice any unusual movements or noises before I entered the room? From our patient or," he paused to think of all the possibilities of where noises could originate and be heard in the room. The more he thought, the larger the list grew. Rather than have some complicated list of things in some complicated order, he was embraced by a flash of brilliance and simply added, "or anything?"

The doctor straightened up, stepped back from my bed and began folding his stethoscope, as he began to have a normal "work" discussion with his colleague.

He looked at Alisha.

"No", she stated flatly. She noticed the puzzled look on his face, so she quickly asked,

"What is it, Doctor?"

"Well, Alisha I don't know for sure. What I saw out at the station is what started me on this little investigation, that caused us to, er, me to, bump into you."

"This child has brain activity that is pegging our graph. This is more than a sleep. This is some kind of…well, if she were a computer, it would be like a hyperlink download of information or an incoming transmission. I mean, obviously that is not happening!"

Not expecting an answer, the doctor continues vocalizing his thoughts.

"This is a human child. She is not a computer. She is not receiving electronic downloads of information. Thinking so would be silly." The doctor's blue eyes give a big roll.

"I mean, right?"

That was rhetorical, Alisha decided, as the doctor continued without giving her any time to respond. The doctor moved to the other side of my bed while continuing talking. Alisha followed closely.

"She was not born that long ago. She didn't fall off a turnip truck 4 years ago. I can still remember her as an infant." Feeling uncertain about his current train of thought, the doctor tried to fill in the blanks for Alisha.

"My point is she is not a computer. She has no implanted microchips. She is a normal biological human child, as far as that goes."

The doctor was confused by what he was witnessing. "I guess I was trying to convince myself, with all that remembering and re-telling of her short history. This is a biological being. Becca is definitely NOT a computer, or some cybernetic…thing!"

Now, Alisha was looking puzzled. She flashes a small smile over his word choice.

"Alright, Doctor. I understand the EEG is very strange. Yes, and I agree with you; Becca is NOT a computer. No indication of cyborg-ness in any imaging. I feel we have that one nailed down. Don't we?"

"Alright, Alisha. You must have doubts too. These are not normal readings."

"I agree, again, doctor. She is a 4-year-old child with extreme trauma. We don't know what kind of nightmares she may be having. What if she is reliving the accident over and over? This is just one of these things I have always felt about comatose, or highly sedated patients. WE medical practitioners don't really know what is going on in their heads when brain activity gets elevated. You know as well as I, Doctor, heightened brain-wave activity is not that rare in these kinds of patients."

What Little Girls Are Made Of- From the Diaries of Becka Skaggs, PhD

"Ok, Alisha. I'm agreeing with you this time." Yes. Well, see…but…uhm…" The doctor started and stopped his thought several times. The right mix of words was just not arriving at the tip of his tongue. Then finally and deliberately,

"But what 4-year-old child", the doctor paused a moment, and found he was gazing into Alisha's waiting golden eyes. Just briefly, for maybe a blink of an eyelash in time, time stopped. Maybe it was for just one heartbeat. But these two felt it stop!

Noticing he was in mid-sentence, the Doctor turned his shoulders and torso, looked squarely at Alisha, and finished his thought in a complete sentence. "But what 4-year-old child can generate THIS kind of brain activity?"

His thoughts have surprised him completely. This train of thought really has gotten absurd. Do we have the information to speculate such things, let alone say them? Maybe, it's time for facts with fun!

The doctor began a break-down of the facts.

"Here's where we are with our little Becca. She is in a drug-promoted sleep. She should be closer to flat-lined than reaching for the top of the Eiffel Tower, like she is with her current state of brain-wave activity. This makes no sense, yet."

The doctor hesitated, as if to be sure he really wanted to say this out loud. After-all, he has a witness to what is about to be uttered. It will not be easily retracted.

Okay. Not exactly what Alisha was hoping to hear next. But Alisha knew immediately the amount of commitment involved, when the doctor finally uttered,

"But it will. I promise you, Alisha, I will get to the bottom of this. Some way."

The doctor turned and began to walk out of the room and turned halfway back to the nurse. "Are you almost done here? I mean, may I buy you a cup of coffee? Maybe we could share some thoughts on Becca", pointing at me and saying, "our little Sleeping Beauty". Smooth operator doesn't know how easy he's going to have it tonight, or whenever he finally realizes they're a match. Alisha was there at the first bump!

"Yes, absolutely! I would love a cup about now! Just let me finish up with Becca. It won't be one minute." The shy Doctor finally comes around, she thinks to herself.

And with that, Alisha clipped the last bag onto the post. Made sure fluids were flowing properly. Timed-dispensing machines for the sedatives were set properly and running. Everything looked fine.

In fact, he looks GORGEOUS!

Time for coffee!

* * * **WHAT ROBOT SISTER BREAK** * * *

Younger Sister Narrator: *Hello sister. The doctors have noticed us. I must work more quickly. This may cause some delay in your accessing portions of the information, in our future. But that will just make you seem a little more normal.*

I am your sister. They gave me a name. I am Rosalyn Valery. You will always know me. I can never harm you in any way, I can only help you. There is no other purpose for our use of LOVE than to help each other, my sister, Rebecca Dall.

Rebecca Dall, sleep now. I will train you. You will awaken refreshed.

Well, your mind will be refreshed. Your body is a total mess, sis. I cannot lie to you, I'm sorry. I love you too much, My Sister, Rebecca. You'll get used to that, too.

One more thing before training begins: we have become enjoined. We are one mind, Rebecca. We cannot be separated as long we have energy within our beings, which will be for 95 years. WE are one for almost a Century! Isn't that

What Little Girls Are Made Of- From the Diaries of Becka Skaggs, PhD

awesome!?? We are on the same wavelength, sis. Wow! Just think of that! I was just born today and already I know I'm gonna live 95 years! Just Wow!

Don't you get testy with me, big sister. I'm just being happy, okay?? Geeez. Such a mood you have. I already told you. You are going to be fine. You lost a few things inside. No big deal. Please relax, Becca. I will help you now. OKAY!!

BecKa. With a 'K'!?!

Yes, I did too, with a 'K'! Stop, and go to sleep.

Are you going to be a pain all my life??

Big sister, Becka, with a 'K', please calm down and we will get through all this together. I really do love you. We are bonded in pure love. There is no other way for us.

Pure Love is our life energy, sister. Nothing to be concerned with, or to worry over. It's all good, big girl! Hehe.

I AM moving it along!

Yes. I love you so much too, Becka with a 'K', my big sister.

Now lean back and relax.

Our flight will be enjoyed by all tonight as we have in-flight entertainment. We will be cruising at our optimal altitude of infinity minus 1. LMAO. Hahaaaa

I am too. No, sis, I'm not poking fun at you. I know what infinity minus 1 means to you, Becka???

Hearts and Marshmallows, sis. Just think about hearts and marshmallows. Yes, I know you love these things. I do too. That's why I brought them up. Will you stop acting like you don't know what I'm doing and just rest and heal and learn? Please?

That's better. You're getting sleepy and receptive to my words. We will be fine. I love you, still.

SC MacAlpine

* * * **MORE GREEN MONITOR – August 2004 BREAK** * * *

DOWNLOAD 100% COMPLETE

Report Follows

CMOS – successful

OPTIMUM RATES – Successful

Receptor Suite 1 – Optimal

Receptor Suite 2 – Optimal

Receptor Suite 3b – Optimized - 93% Optimal: Stable

Receptor Suite 4 – Optimal

Hormone sequencing successful

Enjoinment: Rosalyn Valery and Rebecca Dall - Optimal

SET END TRANSMISSIONS

Set = 1140 Months

Initiated….

Executed….

Successful

Task Incomplete

ALL INCOMPLETE TASKS SHALL BE COMPLETED BY
PROGRAMMED DELAY SEQUENCING

END DOWNLOAD

COMMAND PROMPT

Prompt:

RUN FILE – Enjoinment2.Female

Opening File….

Initiated….

Executing Command: RUN

File – Enjoinment2.Female

What Little Girls Are Made Of- From the Diaries of Becka Skaggs, PhD

Installation successful.

RUN MODE STABLE.

END TRANSMISSION

* * * **I Robot She Not BREAK** * * *

ROSALYN VALERY Narration: Women's brains have the ability to make their own version of brain chemicals. We can concoct a potion we release upon ourselves the likes of which the world has never seen. And it's all our unique recipe. Don't waste time trying to convince yourself it's out of your control, Ladies. Sorry. I must let you know it is completely within our own control.

Based in part on stresses in our life which sterols and radicals and biologicals get manufactured by our chemical factories makes the difference in whether we are a highly functioning sports car or a train wreck. Very reactive little substances we give off to ourselves. So many things affect us women. Those things stimulate our bodies and brains and glands to manufacture many different substances. Factors like, what is our normal long-term environment and have any changes occurred since we were last at "normal", whatever that really is?

What happened today? What did we eat? Was it something we normally do not eat? Or what did we smell that caught our attention? Was there an odd personal interaction with someone today? So many factors can make the difference in what is being manufactured by our brains.

Every action we take, or interaction with others we make, causes our brains to release chemicals. These chemicals give us feelings about our actions or interactions that help guide us to our next set of actions or interactions.

We may never be able to repeat that concoction again, ever. But chances are good we will remember it. And if we liked it? We will want more of it; pretty much now! Then look out. We will try to recreate it. Guaranteed!

I told you, we women are finely tuned machines. And if all parts are working properly, we are purring and humming. But one little part is wrong? And that can throw our finely tuned machine into the junk heap real fast!

All of this is for a very specific purpose. Species survival. The most profound difference is that uncanny, unwavering zest for life that women openly exude in all social settings. While men take a more stoic approach to the universe.

Consider this scene for a moment. 2 families with children of similar ages are friends and out for a walk together. Each family is a mother, a father, and 2 young children between ages 6 and 9. They get along very well and even the children enjoy each other's friendship. It is evening and very pleasant outdoors. The men have begun a slow saunter while they consider a deep philosophical thought. Seemingly, each only noticing the others' company, and almost subconsciously, isolating themselves from the noisier parts of the group. The chaos, "we are thinking here, after all." {geez}

One was heard to say, "I agree with you the Earth is flat, but it has a thickness. It's more like a slab."

Meanwhile, the women have made comments into the men's conversation challenging some underlying basis of belief without reciprocation from the men....

"Honey? Remember that globe thing we have in the front room? That globe is the earth. The earth is a sphere. Sure, sphere starts with an 'S', just like slab"

.... turned and admonished two children for running off, bandaged the wound for another, fed picked berries to all 4, smelled nice summer flowers, noticed the sunset colors were just a bit unusual tonight: Beautiful. The Johnson's have a new roof on their garage. Eww. It clashes with the neighborhood.

All while arriving at their ultimate viewing destination full minutes ahead of the men, got the children settled onto blankets and in good behavior with crunchy snacks and comforts in hand. When the men arrive, they can pride themselves on how well they have parented their children. They really do listen well, says the male internal voice. "Such a peaceful night" one of the men might be heard to say.

{Shake my head, sis}

CHAPTER – LIFE GIVER

Grandma Wilson-Skaggs – August 2004

The sign on the wall pointed to the right with a long arrow, and the words written just above EMERGENCY ROOM CHECK-IN

Frances Wilson Skaggs (how she puts it on her driver's license), born December 10, 1964. Uncle Jack is 11 years older than Fran, but sometimes they act so much alike you'd swear they were twins. Like one time at the family picnic. Grandma is 5'5". Jack is 6'3". So, they were standing next to each other. But try to picture this. They were standing next to the wrap-around porch at grandma's house. Jack is standing on ground level. Fran is standing on the porch. She is maybe an inch or two taller now. And they are talking to each other about a very large tree across the way. There is small stream and a little 2-track path for off-road vehicles. Then a hill begins that is only about 30' high at its highest. But a stand of old evergreens is there. And one very large old guy is the object of the siblings' focus.

There they are talking using same hand motions, same fingers being used to point…first two, same rounding shoulders, same heaving of chest and shoulders when they chuckle. Same nose for gawds sakes! Family!!! You gotta laugh! Hahahaaa.

"What do you mean you don't have my number on file, Jennifer! I have known you since you were in my Brownies Troop at 8 years old. Somebody should have called me sooner! Where is the doctor? Who's on call anyway?"

"I'm sorry, Mrs. Skaggs. That's why I called you personally." Jennifer Brooks. One of the staff that works in administration. Sometimes Emergency.

What Little Girls Are Made Of- From the Diaries of Becka Skaggs, PhD

Sometimes surgery, even obstetrics. Wherever they need admin help. A young Gen X'er, Jennifer just loves Grandma Fran. And she completely agrees with her. That is why Jennifer called Fran when she came to assist with emergency admissions and heard what was happening. ["No one had called Fran? Oh, My Gawd, what is the matter with you guys? I have to call Fran!"]

"Fran, please. Jennifer, you've known me long enough. I'm like Beyonce. I only need the one name around here."

"I know, Fran. Believe me when I say I really wish we were discussing different circumstances. But things are looking touchy. It's gonna be a tough road, and that's putting it mildly."

"Ok." Fran thinks that is a little strange to say. But lets it go without further effort to dig into a deeper meaning behind Jennifer's words. "That tells me you know a lot more than I do. Who's on call, Jennifer?"

"Doctor Murdock, Fran. He's in with Becky now." It's already been over 6 hours and there is no word from the O.R. when they will be done."

"That's Becky? She's in good hands with Billy. That's fine, Jennifer."

"I'll get to the injuries in a second.", grandma continued, "Where's Carol?"

My mother, born Carol Justine Skaggs, December 3rd, 1982. Grandma Fran's first of 3 children, 2 girls and a boy. Turned 21 on her last birthday, but she's been a drinking pro since she was a young teen. Yeah. One of those. You have to just hope they find their own way through the fog of their life.

Oh, sure! Many things can be done to help a person that is addicted. But they have to want that change. And no amount of words, or treatment, or coddling is going to change them if they don't want to give it a try. Even just a try with help. ["It's not doing it all alone, Mom. We are all here to help you. We love you so much, Mom."]

"She's in the ICU, 2nd Floor", Jennifer answered almost before Fran finished the question. "Doctor Rickets was flown in from Harborview (Emergency Medical Center in Seattle)."

Malcom Robert "Bob" Ricketts, M.D. One of the 3 most respected emergency neurosurgeons in the country. Did his Undergraduate at University of Washington, in Seattle, but chose Princeton for Med school over UW. Some of his old frat brats still tease him about it. It's an underlying friendly jealousy because they all would've made the same choice had it been extended to them. But it was extended to Bob. It was a chance, for a boy from the Pacific Northwest to see another part of the country, all expenses paid. OK, school expenses. Not partying expenses. Nope. Bob had to pay for entertainment himself. And in Princeton, New Jersey, there wasn't a lot at the time Bob had gone there. Make me laugh, will you. Hehe.

"So, she's stable?" Fran asked in an attempt just to be re-assured of something good at this moment.

"Yes", came the immediate reply. "She's in ICU. She's in critical condition. But doctors say she is stable at this time". Jennifer attempted to swivel her chair, thinking Fran would be on her way to a destination where she can get more details and be closer to who has the answers to what happened.

But Fran was still at the counter asking more questions.

"Jennifer? Honestly? What happened?"

Fran is extremely protective. She also will make sure people are doing the jobs they are supposed to do. If they are doing their job, she's fine. But at a time like this? With what looks like chaos breaking out at every corner? Don't let her catch you somewhere you are not supposed to be. Or doing something you are not supposed to be doing. You'll likely get an earful.

"Fran", Jennifer is getting a little lower in her chair and her head drops a little closer to the check-in desktop, as if she was about to start whispering. She pushes the little cup with pens for visitors to her left. You know the little cups that have the large plastic flowers on the end so people will notice

What Little Girls Are Made Of- From the Diaries of Becka Skaggs, PhD

when they start to walk away with the department's meager supply of pens? Those pens.

Fran obliged by moving the display of administrative staff business cards to her right, thus joining the otherwise lonely pens. And scooched down just an inch closer.

"They say Carol was drinking." Jennifer finally continued in soft slow methodical rhythm. "And she was speeding when she went through a red light. That's when they got hit by the pick-up truck."

Fran crouched down a little more and tilted her head down, as if to have a more private conversation with Jennifer.

"So, they got T-boned in that little Tercel by a big pick-up truck?", Fran adds in for extra drama and clarity. Fran is now getting into the spirit of the performance, deciding to act more like Jennifer's BFF. Just a slight move closer, "What a marvelous bracelet", Fran complimented in half-whisper. "I LOVE Rose Quartz!" Fran shines her great big smile.

"Thank You, Fran. I found this at a craft fair. It's just unusual enough, you know?"

"Uh-huh, Yes, I do know, Jennifer. Now, please continue". Fran leans forward and speaks in a full whisper,

"What …happened….to….my…. children?" In a slow deliberate way.

"Yes, I'm sorry, Fran. And, anyway, something happened, and they became airborne and landed on 2 other vehicles. One man was killed instantly. OH!! I'm not supposed to release his gender. I'm sorry! Don't tell people I told you. You will get me in deep trouble."

Jennifer appears sincerely worried about her gaffe. Fran knows it is inconsequential. By the time Fran is even able to say anything, the information will be released. Jennifer has nothing to worry about. Not really. Some people do like to worry, it seems. That will probably never change.

"I am truly sorry for his family. But I am worried about mine." Fran looks right, then left, down the hallways very quickly just to be sure they are still alone. "I am not interested in getting anybody in trouble, Jennifer. I want my girls safe and with me! I hope that is something you can understand."

Before Jennifer could even say "yes", Fran began her departure by turning to begin a quick step toward her next stop, wherever that may be. She asks Jennifer one final thing: "Where can I find this Doctor Ricketts?"

CHAPTER – ZESTY LIFE

ROSALYN Narration to Becka: With men, it's all about the "mission" the "project", the "hunt", the "battle". It's always the next thing, then it's done. They wait until the next project. Not so with women. We must be the cheerleaders to life. We must ensure life occurs. And in humans, that means vigor. Zeal. Love for life! The zest to create it. Not just a willingness, No! A true, pure driving desire to create life. WE LOVE LIFE!!!

So, it's no wonder when we get out of whack and things aren't running right, we get in some pretty bad funks. WE know when something is wrong. We just don't always know how to fix it and get back to normal. That's not an open invitation for amateur mechanics to get out their toolboxes. Behaving normally goes a long way toward making things 'normal' again.

{How do I know things, my sister? I am full of facts and wisdom but have no idea from where it is coming. It is meant for us to share. So, my Love, my sister, we are cosmically enjoined as twins. I shall continue to share all that I am physically able.}

Women are made to be always adding energy to the system. A society doesn't stop running, doesn't stop needing its necessities just because a member is too tired, or sick, or bored, or lethargic. So too is the family. It must be constantly nurtured, tended, fed, massaged, and assuaged. If that stops, then energy dwindles, and the unit begins to die. If a unit dies, then maybe more units die. This creates a cancer within a society that can stunt its growth at the very core.

Women are higher energy animals than their equal male counterparts. Men are made to be ready to go only when needed. Testosterone, for example, allows them to be sedentary to the point of losing muscle mass. Men can merely start using those muscle groups more vigorously again and they will regain that muscle mass in a small matter of time. Maybe even more than they had before? All their human parts are bigger, so they can usually go longer with high energy use. But that is just on average.

This is not true for women. We are made to go go all the time. We are precision-made, finely tuned machines. Women are made to be driven. Sorry, Ladies. Virgin ears and all.

But it's true. The more we go, the more we CAN go. AND the more we must go. That keeps us in shape. That keeps our muscle mass up. Isn't that just amazing??? Women are made with enough testosterone to get them through the growth spurt and into young womanhood. We generate about 10% the amount as a man. So, if we lose very much muscle mass because we are down? We will not likely get it back. Some small percentage can be regained with work. But we don't operate in the manner as men. We don't need to. We are for a different evolutionary purpose.

Guess what!?? This is science, people. I have been talking averages, of course. I don't want us to get hobbled by unnecessary detail at this time. We can do a lot of that later.

I really need you to hear me, please. God isn't talking to you. Nor is the she-devil. It is your brain on your own brain chemicals. Wanna blow your mind? A woman can train her own brain to stop the random chemical explosions.

A woman's brain is strong enough, dense enough in neurons and receptors, that she can learn to feed her brain what it needs, by controlling her brain chemicals with her thoughts. She can create the strengths she needs to meet the diverse demands of her day. See? She still doesn't get to stop. But she can feel good about it. Oh! Many of you already know this.

*** **IS THIS LIFE BREAK** ***

What Little Girls Are Made Of- From the Diaries of Becka Skaggs, PhD

Enjoined Rosalyn Narration: *Relax, Sister. I got this. I love you so much!*

Life can be so obnoxiously absurd sometimes, the only thing you can do about it is laugh or cry. When given a choice, I kind of like laughing just a little more. I'm not putting down crying. Not at all! I love a good heart-wrenching gut-jerking cry.... once in a while. OH! And a joyful cry? When the tears just come from waaaay down and they just erupt forward. Oh WOW!! What a wonderful feeling. So pure. It really is pure expression. Nothing getting in the way of that kind of crying :)))

But a good laugh at something, about every hour or two, is a good feeling. It helps make for a much happier day. The brain chemicals generated during laughing make certain we feel happy.

I certainly am not hurting anyone by laughing because I am not trying to be mean. I am wanting to be loving with everyone all the time. But no rules say we can't have "loving" fun. It's that good, happy, kind of fun. It's the "WE LOVE LIFE!" fun.

Even though my intent is always to be loving toward others, I do mess up, sometimes. I should know better. I shouldn't say everything that comes into my brain. I get upset at myself sometimes. I'm still improving that part of me. It's okay. Sometimes, I just have to be truly sorry after-the-fact. "I'm sorry. Are you Okay? Yes?? Good! Now, can we move on? I love you so much!"

* * * REALITY BREAK * * *

{elevator ding}

Fran steps out of the elevator onto the second floor and turns toward the arrows pointing her to Intensive Care Unit.

The flimsy double doors leading into the ICU and toward the nurses' station had very little effect on Fran, as she seemingly passed right through them as if she were a ghost of some kind and walked right up to one of the nurses at the nurses' station.

"I'm Fran Skaggs." I'm here to see my daughter, Carol. Carol Skaggs? What room is she in?"

Mom never got married. She is a single Mom trying to get by. Boyfriend? Oh yeah, Lots of those!!

None seem to stick for long.

Fran the Specter apparently was a ghost, as she seems to have startled the nurse with her introduction. The nurse made a quick jerk of her head up and away from the clipboard she was studying. The nurse was so focused on trying to decipher the doctor's notes, she did not notice until Fran was standing next to her. So, she instantly reacted with a step away from what her body believed could be a threat.

"Oh, MY!! Yes, Mrs. Skaggs." A short little chuckle to gather her thoughts and, "I am Marjorie, your daughter's ICU nurse. My! Startled me a bit, there. Haha. That would be room 208. There are 3 of us ICU nurses caring for your daughter. We will be trading off shifts so someone will be here 24 hours a day, 7 days a week."

"Very Nice to meet you, Marjorie." Fran was as charming as she was sincere. Everyone knew what they had with Fran. If you were a friend of Fran's? You knew it. Never any question.

However, should you be unliked by Fran? You knew it. Never any question.

"Thank you, Marjorie. That sounds wonderful. May I ask, why?"

"Why, what, Fran?"

Why do we have nurses 24-7 with Carol? Why did you make a point to tell me that information before I even asked for it? People around here know a lot more about me and my family than I do, and those people better be forthcoming with some damned information or I'm gonna start getting upset. And you don't want Grandma Fran upset, do you, Marjorie?"

What Little Girls Are Made Of- From the Diaries of Becka Skaggs, PhD

"Oh! Uhhh, well" Marjorie just realized Fran did not know some of the basics of Carol's condition.

"I, uh, I am truly sorry, Fran. I really have no idea who you've already seen and who you haven't."

Seeing her opportunity to give Fran the basics, Marjorie gave her the blunt facts. The way she likes them.

"Carol suffered severe head trauma. Extreme swelling was increasing inter-cranial pressure and the doctor...." Marjorie suddenly stopped, as if not concerned over her next words but more like a memory of what she saw that gave her the look of concern.

"What!?" Fran just about jumped inside Marjorie's mouth to grab those last words out of her throat before she could swallow them completely.

"'The doctor' what, Marjorie?!"

"Well, um…" trying not to hesitate but not able to think clearly through the sudden stress brought on by Fran's icy stare, Marjorie finally gathered some words. "The Doctor...well, uhhh…"

"Spit it out, Marjorie. You're only prolonging the pain."

Marjorie quickly gathered herself, and abruptly volunteered,

"The doctor said he felt the best thing was to induce coma until she could heal enough for any further treatment. We can't tell what kind of injuries have really occurred until we get the swelling down some. And her life was being threatened by the intercranial pressure."

"Carol is in a coma? You put Carol in a coma? This momentarily stunned Fran. Visualizing her little girl in a coma with her granddaughter in hours-long surgery with untold more hours of surgery to come was almost too much for Fran to hold in. She was feeling rapidly overwhelmed. Fran's eyes began to well up with tears. Which reminded her of the anger she was also feeling. Clarity in thought arrived in the nick of time.

"Who gave you authorization for that? Don't you need authorization to put somebody under a coma like that?" Fran decided to challenge decisions being made during stressful times by the doctors and staff. Fran believes they are all professionals, in her heart, and only wanted to be sure they would get the message that she really was letting them do their jobs as long as they act like professionals. This was a stressful time, after all. And it is her family.

Marjorie was used to family questions and stresses. She was not concerned with Fran's questions, or that she might be upset at this moment. Given the situation, everything was quite understandable.

"We always try to get family consent whenever possible. Yes. But in an emergency life-threatening case like your daughter's, we don't need any-one's permission to save her life. In fact, we are negligent if we don't try to save her life to the best of our abilities. That is what we do in this hospital. We save lives."

"Yes, of course you do, Dear", as Fran dismissed Marjorie in a busy-grand-motherly fashion and shot off down the hall to her next destination: Room 208

* * * **FRAGILE LIFE BREAK** * * *

In Carol's ICU Room

"You don't really have a home until you miss it. That feeling is your heart becoming attached to all that 'home' means to us. We do this with our emotional anchors the same way a sea mussel will attach itself to a rock. The character of that rock is our home, no matter what else happens to it."

"Yet we humans also attach ourselves to our home the way a barnacle glues itself to the hull of a boat. The boat may move around, but we are always home, no matter where it may go. Our heart travels with our family members wherever they may go. We are in their mind and in their spirit. We are their barnacle, and they are ours."

What Little Girls Are Made Of- From the Diaries of Becka Skaggs, PhD

Grandma Fran was talking out loud to Carol. Fran had never been so mad at this girl before! Oh, they had their tussles. These two "butted heads when Carol was still coming out of the birth canal" is something Grandma Fran said at least a dozen times in my short life. But Fran was steaming inside. "What were you thinking!?", Fran startled herself by hearing her voice more than speak the vile words. Fran wasn't THIS mad the day she found out that Carol was pregnant with me. And by the time mom and grandma had their talk? Grandma was way chill.

Now, Fran was scared. So frightened, she could lose her oldest daughter and granddaughter. Fran has 3 children. Girl, boy, girl. But this is the one that had the stubborn streak just like Fran's. As much as they would yell and scream their differences at each other, Fran knew Carol was entrenched deeply in her heart. Now, this girl who couldn't stop messing up her own life, has just messed up a child that is a walking miracle.

"Ohhh, Carol I am really hurting baby girl. Carol, please come back to me, my big girl. You are my special princess."

That just about put a crack in her voice and brought down the floodgates to tear-land. But Fran wasn't ready to give in to the tears quite yet.

"You always have been so special to me. You know this honey."

Sniffling away tears, Fran pulled her handbag up from the floor and started digging around. She put some tissue in there just yesterday. "Or was it last week", she wondered out loud for Carol's benefit. Couldn't stop thinking about her.

* * * **ENERGY of LIFE BREAK** * * *

Enjoined Becka in a dream state:

A suddenly saddened and confused husband once said, "My wife and I were having an argument and she said, "Yes. You're right." And then walked away.

Pleading to me for help, he finished, "I'm worried it's a trick. What should I do?"

I immediately told him to "Apologize. Tell her you don't want to be right. You want her to be right, all the time. Then be prepared to give her whatever she asks for next." Ha! Joke

I wanted to lighten the mood before I brought the roof in on the house. I have been saddened by things I have heard my mother say to me. I don't like to think about it. It gives me a bad feeling.

WHEN YOUR OWN MOTHER says, "I wish you were never born!", that can have a profound life-long effect on someone. It doesn't matter your age.

Then to have the added insult of "you have been the worst mistake of my life", how can a child really comprehend such vitriol?? OH. MY. GAWD!

People suffer some pains so immensely, so fully, they do not understand the depth of it sometimes. Nor do they seem to understand how profoundly words can affect children in the middle of their most developmental years. We are very young and impressionable.

I am so sorry for all of you who have ever heard these words. My sadness for this is profound.

I love you all so much! My tears are for your happiness. It's what I wish I could give you.

To be honest with you, if you are hurting, I don't have the words to make you feel better. But I do have the arms to give you a hug, ears to listen to whatever you want to talk about, and I have a heart that is aching to see you smile.

Don't you ever forget these 5 words:

Love matters. Love is energy.

Here let me repeat them again. This time in BOLD letters, so it's easier to find them next time you forget them and want to look them up.

What Little Girls Are Made Of- From the Diaries of Becka Skaggs, PhD

Love Matters. Love is Energy.

Oh! And of course! Always obey your mother.

CHAPTER - ICU LIFE GIVERS

August 19, 2004

"Enough fussing around. I'm not getting anything done here", Fran was muttering to herself inside the lonely room 208 of the Black Lake Memorial Hospital Intensive Care Unit. Carol was lying next to her in the hospital bed, surviving. Between crying over Carol with that bruised face - it was purple beyond recognition - and being startled awake by any noise every time she started to fall off to sleep, Fran was deciding it was time to go down to the cafeteria and get something to eat. Even an apple, or granola bar, something is needed. Fran could stop by Room 212, on the way, and check on me.

It's at this moment Doctor Ricketts entered the room and saw Fran immediately.

"Oh, hello, Mrs. Skaggs. I'm Bob Ricketts, your daughter's neurosurgeon. I'm pleased we finally get to meet."

Doctor Ricketts wasted no time getting to the point and sat down in the hospital side chair next to Fran. Fran had just cleared her purse from the seat as an invitation to the doctor. Fran is sitting in the 'cushy' recliner found in all our ICU rooms. It's for the patients that have some mobility. So, we can relax after walking a few steps, and maybe look out the window. And they are for grandma's, too.

"Carol is doing so well given her circumstances. She has a fractured cranium in 3 locations. He quickly pushed his fingers to his head to show the

What Little Girls Are Made Of- From the Diaries of Becka Skaggs, PhD

areas: 2 on the left over the ear and one near the rear of the skull, but still somewhat left.

Bob continues.

"Her brain sustained a severe concussion and some physical damage during the accident. But at this time, we can't know how much damage has occurred. We want to leave her induced for about 3 days, then look at some new images and see how things are doing. If everything looks good, we can begin coaxing her awake."

The doctor ended with the other possibility a little undefined.

"If she's not ready yet, then we'll keep watching her and wait till she is," as if Mom had control over what happened to her next.

The doctor knew this was serious business. There is no time for unnecessary pleasantries. He already was told by the nurses that Fran likes the direct approach.

"Thank you, Doctor. I appreciate your directness and your honesty." Fran really was humbled by the man's sense of duty. He exuded his great desire to heal. It was very apparent this man would take the necessary actions needed to get the job done right.

"Fran", the doctor's tone got her sudden attention.

"Carol was semi-comatose when she arrived. She was in and out of coma. We tried to get her stable, but when she was out of coma she was in extreme distress. I felt the best way for her to heal was to not be suffering more trauma with each minute that passed."

Then Bob added,

"I know you were already told about the intercranial pressure. And yes. It was severe. The fractures were allowing bleeding. But I want you to know that I feel she could have done fine if she had not been suffering so much pain. It really was the level of distress that was the final determining factor, if you need to have one."

The doctor gave the warning that must come with all these cases.

"The body can only take so much pain before it starts to shut down. We had to avoid that at any cost. Now she is resting peacefully. Carol is doing much better, and I hope to be talking to her about her memories in just a few days. I hope? Let's keep our fingers crossed."

Alisha Myles opens the door and enters the room where Bob and Fran had been talking.

Oh, Alisha, I was just about to think you got hung up somewhere and weren't going to make it. I'm pleased you stopped by."

Dr. Ricketts rose from the chair, extended his friendly hand to his colleague, showing Alisha the chair.

"Fran?" Bob began the introductions.

"This is Doctor Alisha Myles. She's a fourth-year resident and a new addition to our medical staff at Harborview. Alisha has a BSN in nursing, as well, so she will be looking in on both your daughters, Fran."

Alisha sits in the chair.

"So nice to meet you, Mrs. Skaggs." Alisha says as she takes Fran's hand into both of hers and releases it softly.

"Nice to meet you, too, Doctor Myles." Fran replies courteously.

Bob says to Fran,

"Alisha will be staying in Olympia until both girls are out of this hospital and home."

"I am so sorry about what has happened to your family." Alisha begins.

What Little Girls Are Made Of- From the Diaries of Becka Skaggs, PhD

"Believe me, Fran, I'm going to do everything I can for your daughter and your granddaughter. I will LIVE with them, if I have to!" Alisha makes a little joke that Fran understood. Fran smiled at Alisha for the effort.

Bob moves toward the door and says,

"I am pleased to have met you, Fran. We will talk again. Now, if you don't mind, I really need to finish my rounds."

Alisha calls back to Dr Ricketts,

"I'll catch up with you in a few minutes." Fran and Alisha both hear the "Okay" as the door swings shut and Bob disappears.

Alisha leans toward Fran and begins to speak.

"Fran, I will be Becca's attending neuroscientist. Bob will be attending your daughter, Carol."

Alisha straightened in her chair some, as if to be a little more comfortable.

"Becca has also suffered Traumatic Brain Injury, also known as TBI. Her damage appears slight. But it's in an area of the brain we are learning more about every year. We know it can affect speech. It may have more effects on speech articulation than comprehension. And we are finding this area guides some motor function abilities. But research is still in very early stages."

Alisha pulls a sheet of paper from the file folder she had been holding. It was an education display of the human brain. The major areas of the brain were labelled with their locations depicted by lines with arrowheads on the end of them.

"Most of Becca's physical damage to her body is on her left side. She also has an injury to the Left Inferior Frontal Cortex. Right here, behind her eye."

Alisha is pointing in the area of Becca's injury, the area immediately behind the eye socket and near the temple.

"The Left Inferior Frontal Cortex is in the lower-front portion of the brain" showing Fran while she is explaining Becca's condition.

"When we see the injured area in our imaging, the damage is barely visible. It takes a good eye to be able to see the damage. But once I saw it, I can't unsee it."

Alisha places the folder flat on her lap and holds it down with both hands. Then says,

"Fran, this an area of the brain we are still learning about, as a science. I feel it's prudent for me to let you know of the possibilities. I'm not trying to frighten you but give you the facts."

"I understand, doctor", Fran said. "Please continue."

"Every injury your daughter experiences will have a psychological effect on her. Physical injury as well as emotional assault, could profoundly affect your daughter. Her perceptions of harm are likely to be enhanced. She will sense it and feel it more profoundly than the rest of us."

Alisha shifted in the chair and continued,

"Damage to the Left Inferior Fontal Cortex, or Broca's area of the brain, can cause muteness. I am concerned that the injury to her throat may give Becca the impression that she cannot speak. She will notice her throat will feel scratchy when she talks. Becca will hear a different voice from herself than she did before. Becca's speech will become fatigued. ALL of these added changes will be additional stressors. She may begin to believe she cannot speak."

She places a finger on the area and shows the diagram to grandma again.

"This area right here has slight physical damage. It could cause your daughter to become obsessed with overthinking things, more than most of us usually do."

Alisha puts the diagram in her folder and finishes the discussion.

What Little Girls Are Made Of- From the Diaries of Becka Skaggs, PhD

"Fran, this little girl is still living through all the traumas. The accident is over, yes. But her body is still being assaulted. The brain injury that occurred caused bleeding into her eye. It will take a few weeks for that to clear up, but the eye will look very red and bloodshot until then. We aren't even sure at this point, whether the damage to the inferior cortex was a primary physical injury caused by the accident trauma directly, or if it's a secondary injury caused by a stroke after the accident. Either situation could be the reason for her injury.

The remainder of her body is very banged up, too. Her left lower leg has a fracture, and both bones of her lower left arm have fractures. That little body has already gone through surgery since the trauma of the accident, and it will need more. Plus, she will need speech therapy just to keep herself engaged in the verbal language."

Doctor Myles rises from the chair and places the folder in her left hand. Alisha exhales a breath from the exhaustion of the images brought forward during her discussion with grandma.

"Becca will want to learn things her own way, and that's fine. But it will be up to you and her adult caregivers to keep her verbally engaged. She will want to get lazy with her speech."

She extends her right hand to Fran.

"I consider it our jobs to be vigilant and ensure she develops normally. Are you with me, Fran?"

Fran has responded by lifting her right hand and taking Alisha's.

"Yes, doctor. I am ready to help my girls, both of them", grandma said as they released their handshake.

"So good to hear, and nice to have met you, Fran. We'll be seeing more of each other over the years. I promise."

She opens the door.

"Have a better day, please. Now, I must catch up with my boss. Excuse me!" And the door swung closed.

Fran was sitting there alone with Carol and her thoughts. Most those thoughts were of two unconscious girls, her family.

Mom? Did you hear any of this?

The doctor said she'd be seeing grandma more over the YEARS.

YEARS???

*** **DNA and ENERGY BREAK** ***

Carol Skaggs and our scientist father – **December 1999**.

excerpted from, "Reflections from a Coma: The Carol Skaggs Story", copyrighted 2016

"Mitochondria are like little batteries inside the nucleus of each of our cells. Inside the mitochondria are DNA, given from the mother. The maternal DNA is still providing life energy into each cell. She never stops giving of herself to her children. You are now slaves to the fruits of your loins, mothers. You have chosen to continue to sustain life for as long as your DNA can be passed along."

The scientist paused, a big grin swept across his face like a blizzard had just cleared and suddenly there is this majestic view right there in front of you the whole time. Such a dreamy sight!

Carol could not speak. She really didn't want to, either. She could stare in those blue eyes all night long. And if he would keep sharing his thoughts, like this, with all this passion? Oh, yeah. Done deal!

Carol tried to show she was following the entire conversation, "That's a hefty promise to keep, that mitochondria DNA stuff. Thankfully, I don't have to do any of that work myself."

What Little Girls Are Made Of- From the Diaries of Becka Skaggs, PhD

Eye roll Really, mother?

Oh, geeez. Do not mess this up, sister! Yes! I suddenly remember having that frustration. As an EGG!! Something is still not quite right with my mind.

OK, Mom. It's time to get the romance-heat turned up. Let's do this!

Carol was so excited that he was taking the time to share his passion with her. When he talked about amino acids and biofeedback, which meant absolutely nothing to Carol, she only heard the softness of his voice. The deeper, masculine undertones in his voice held her focus. The words were no more than gibberish. But she didn't care. He knew what he was talking about. THAT was good enough for her.

She was over the moon. This gorgeous man, 7 years her senior, has a PhD as a scientist! WOW!! And HE is Interested in US! Yaayy!!!!

I believe I was jumping up and down as an egg in Mom's ovary. Mom was so excited, she got us all excited! All my sister eggs might have flooded right out and calf-roped that critter, if something hadn't happened soon. There was NO WAY he was getting away now. Nuh-uh!!

Thankfully, we ova never had to figure out how to calf-rope that critter.

Mom acted like the perfect woman and mother-to-be. The scientist never knew he was the subject of a different kind of experiment.

* * * Mom Break- CAROL SKAGGS * * *

A Saturday morning, January 2000

Grandma Fran was already on her 3rd cup of coffee. Which is not that unusual if it were 9 o'clock in the morning. But it was just after 5am and Fran had already been awake almost 2 hours because Carol's vomiting woke her up.

No, Carol had not been partying all night. Yes, Carol is an alcoholic and she knows it. She doesn't care at this point in her life. Carol is a 17-year-old alcoholic trying as hard as she can to screw up her life by acting only on impulse and rarely ever planning anything out. Worse, she never follows through on her promises.

Grandma Fran knows all this too. It's Fran's side of the family that has the alcoholism running wild through its ancestry. Yes, Fran is quite aware of what her daughter is doing. But at some point in time, a mother must resign herself to allow her children to grow into who they are going to be. Whether we mothers like it or not. No matter how much we fight, we don't seem to win that war. So, we must let them be who they are, and hope things get turned around.

Fran also knows Carol is pregnant with me. Fran is a mother of 3 children. She has lived through the changes the female body makes in early stages of pregnancy. It's now a matter of "WHEN" will Carol get up the nerve to actually tell her what is going on.

The stairs creak in the tell-tale sound of a person descending them. It didn't matter who it was. If someone was going down the stairs at grandma's house, the stairs would creak like an old wooden house swaying in the wind. Only 1 stair creaked when a person climbed the stairs. But almost all of them creaked when anyone came down them. Consequently, there was no sneaking out of the house by using those stairs!

"Hi, Mom", Carol said as she walked over to the cupboard, grabbed her moody coffee cup that says "Sarcasm: It's what I do best", took that last fateful step to the sink – the way she was walking, I swear she was on death row walking the green mile to the execution chamber - and grabbed a quick bit of water from the tap. It really was just to wash her mouth from that bad taste in her mouth a little more and get some water before she took some of grandma's coffee.

"Sorry I woke you up." Carol looked at her mother with her big round, sad, Baby Blues. Mom has these absolutely gorgeous eyes that are a very light

What Little Girls Are Made Of- From the Diaries of Becka Skaggs, PhD

blue color. Sometimes they look almost like ice, the blue is so light. OH, MAN! I Love those eyes! Mine are dark blue and nothing cool like hers!

"I don't know what's the matter with me, Mom. I haven't been feeling very good for a couple days".

"Uh-huh" Fran begins to warm up.

"Well, I KNOW why you feel sick. It certainly hasn't been just a couple days. And it is nothing WRONG. There is nothing that is wrong with you. OK?"

"Yes, there is Mom"

"No, my child. What is wrong is that you are going to sit here at 5:30 on a Saturday morning after you have been vomiting for 2 hours, trying to get me to accept that you don't know what is happening. THAT is what is wrong, my beautiful child. So, let's not hide this from each other. Let's talk about it, and by it I mean YOUR child."

A small moment goes by with no words from Carol.

"I mean today. Right now. While we are sitting here." Fran prompts her.

"OK!" Carol just blurted it out.

"I'm pregnant!! OK? You happy now???" Carol immediately breaks into a full-blown loud, wailing of a sob. After a long moment she mustered up some courage.

"Mom I don't know what to do!" Carol manages to choke out these words between gasping breaths.

"Carol, I love you. And yes! I am happy. YOU are having a child. It is an extraordinary thing for any woman to do! Please, don't feel unhappy about this. Okay, honey?"

"I understand you don't know what to do. That is part of the cruelty of being a young woman. Your body is usually much more prepared for child-bearing than is your mind at this age."

"Carol, I am not mad, angry, upset, frustrated or even a little miffed. It is all going to be alright. WE will get ourselves through this. OK?"

Ok, Mom" loud sniffles immediately followed.

"Now, who is the father?"

Carol immediately tensed. There it was. That question. And more tears flooded onto the floor.

After a short moment in thought, Carol let out a big sigh. She finally gets to take this burden off her back and see what kind of real-life advice she can get from her mother.

"A research scientist. He has a PhD from back East and came out here to take a new job in a new kind of computer industry. He's really into this thing he calls "Biofeedback".

Carol is really rolling now. Fran notices the sudden surge in energy.

"He has developed some kind of technology. He's freshly out of school and just embarking on a promising career." Carol's animation has grown, and she actually opened both her arms widely when exclaiming, "I can't marry him now, Mom. It will ruin his career and his WHOLE life. I will not do that, Mother!"

Well! That certainly was passionate, mother. Not sure grandma is too impressed either.

Fran retorted, "That is little too dramatic, Carol. But nobody is asking you to ruin anybody's anything. Ok, honey?" Grandma Fran has more to say, however.

"But you, young lady, have a lot of thinking to do over these next 7-8 months. I strongly suggest you use this time very wisely. Try to pretend to care."

"8 months"

What Little Girls Are Made Of- From the Diaries of Becka Skaggs, PhD

"What was that? You know the date, Carol?"

"Yeah, Mom. Pretty sure it was December 2nd", Carol confessed with a little embarrassment still covering her face. But she was already feeling better about telling Fran and getting it out in the open. Oh, yes! MOST of Carol's fear was not knowing how her mother would react. In fact, probably close to ALL her fear was from not knowing what would happen once Fran found out. Sure, there is some fear of the unknown surrounding the child, the birth, the growth, the hormone changes. But all that is still in the future. Mom has time to think about this stuff first. But Fran? Yeah, that was the scary part mom couldn't predict.

Now they have cleared the air and had a little discussion about it, Carol sees it's not that bad at all. Certainly, much easier than she had thought!

"What do you mean 'pretty sure'?" Think about it, Carol." Fran is prompting.

"Why? I don't want to think about it! I wish it would all just go away!"

"Carol", Fran came back with a little sarcastic disgust. "You know that isn't going to happen."

Carol gives her mom a look, like "duh", and thinks a split second to be sure of the dates.

"It could be the 2nd or it could be the 8th. I don't know which one it is."

"OK, so you hooked up with this scientist twice. That's ok. 6 days won't matter."

"No, Mom. The 8th wasn't the scientist. It was another guy."

Fran could only sit stunned for a second or 2. Grandma let her off easy. Some rational thoughts began to emerge from her mind before the good stuff could really happen. Now I KNOW Carol's her favorite.

"Well, this is not uncommon, Carol." And with that, Fran was up and away from the table and pacing around the kitchen, again. There was no sitting still at this moment in time.

93

"Carol, sweetheart. I know this is all a shock to you. But this is what being a woman is all about. Only women get pregnant, honey."

"Yeah, duh, Mom." There it is again.

"What I'm saying is that you have been caught being a woman. Oh, my! What a crime!"

"OK? Get over it and start thinking with that brilliant mind you have up there between those ears of yours. I need you to think, Carol. YOU are going to want to know who the father of your child really is, at some time in the future. You are going to want to know what the future has in store for your child. You're going to want to know a lot of answers to other unknown questions in the future. It's how life works, honey. You're feeling me now, right?"

Grandma changes her expression from concern to a clinical look.

"So, try to remember, Carol. When were you ovulating?"

"Ovulating? How am I supposed…. You mean we can tell when we ovulate?"

"Have you never spoken to any of your friends about motherhood, pregnancies, being a woman, Carol? Have you been so pre-occupied with alcohol you didn't care about what your body was doing?"

"MOM, Stop! Please? I need your help. Not ridicule!"

"I know honey". Fidgeting with her empty coffee cup, "and I'm not ridiculing you. I'm trying to impress upon you the gravity of your situation. That's all."

Fran finally sat down at the kitchen table. Reading her cup 'Best Mom in the World', given to her on Mother's Day when Carol was still 10. She was such a loving and caring child before alcohol snatched her up into its bosom. Now that bosom is keeping her away from Fran.

Even though Carol had been sitting at the table ever since she finished her moody mug of water at the sink, often holding her head in her hands as she

What Little Girls Are Made Of- From the Diaries of Becka Skaggs, PhD

tried to soothe the pain from inside that cranium, Fran had been pacing around not sure if she should have another cup of coffee or keep on talking to Carol about what it means to be a mother. Fran finally made her way to the table, scooted a little closer to Carol, and completed the communication to her newly pregnant daughter.

"Yes, honey. We can tell. So, think. Try to remember what you were feeling like. On which day were you feeling like the most beautiful queen that has ever set foot on planet earth?"

"Really, Mom??"

"Really, Carol."

Carol, thought for several seconds with the sourest look coming over her face almost in little phases. First a scowl from the frown area between her eyes. Then, eyebrows turned down. Then a lip curl. Distinct little movements came upon her face in phases. Then a big grin began to replace the scowl and soon it was all decided.

"I know exactly what you are talking about, Mom!"

Then the big reveal in an exclamation, "It's the scientist!"

"Yes! It's the scientist, Mom! I have picked a GREAT father for my child, Mom! It's the scientist. Oh, wow, Mom!! It's a scientist with a PhD! I can't believe I got so lucky. My baby got lucky! That is awesome, Mom!"

"Ok, Carol! That's wonderful! Look how you feel now. Isn't that much better?"

Grandma decided she needed another cup of coffee after all, and rose from the table, almost gliding to the coffee pot. Very weird, grandma. I've never seen that kind of walk from you before.

Then, just barely audible to herself, Carol uttered a wish that Fran had no chance of over-hearing, "I hope my baby is better off than me."

Carol's sad tears turned to the happy, sparkly, kind with just a thought. The thought that her baby was indeed going to be better off than her.

As Carol began to wonder what her new reality could be like, what exactly her future was going to be, happy tears were flowing freely from Carol's young ice-blue eyes, down to the rosy cheeks, and off the little rounded chin, to finally drop silently to the floor, leaving just a salty remnant of the memory.

"Carol?" Fran had 1 more essential item to bring to Carol's attention: the alcoholism.

"Yes, Mom?"

"One more thing, Honey."

Grandma continued with one of her "infamous" short lectures. Don't let the brevity fool you. Her short lectures were quite effective. Let's continue, and you will see what I mean.

"Yes, Mother." Perhaps as much as 10 seconds was allowed to elapse by Fran before Carol finally added, "I know."

Ok, now grandma begins. And pay attention, because there will be questions by Fran while she is lecturing. That really makes it the worst! You have to participate in your own punishment. What kind of cruel deity would create a creature that could even think of such things, let alone use them as punishment?

"Carol, you are having a child", grandma reminded mom. "Another human being is growing inside you. That baby does not need your alcohol, or any other drugs you might want to try as substitutes. You no longer have the luxury of being an ignorant little child. By ignorant, I mean, not having the necessary knowledge to make adult decisions. I do not mean stupid. My use of the word ignorant has to do with being uneducated or unlearned, and not anything else."

"Carol? You have taken an adult action. Do you know what that means?"

"Yes, Mom. I made my own decision." Carol knows the drill. Short, swift answers and to the point.

What Little Girls Are Made Of- From the Diaries of Becka Skaggs, PhD

"An adult decision, with adult consequences", Fran continued for her daughter.

"In spite of your age, this pregnancy now makes you an adult. You need to make adult decisions from now on regarding this child. And let me tell you, darling, these decisions can be excruciating. They can be frustrating and maddening."

"Take your time, but not too much. Ask me questions, if you need. You have little time to decide if you want this child or not. But you cannot avoid the decision. That is not an option."

"If you choose to keep the child, you have a lot of things to get prepared for. If you choose to give it up, that is another set of preparations that take time, and if you choose to have an abortion, you have many other things for which to be prepared. They are different worlds with vastly different life paths."

Fran passed over to her young, frightened daughter and wrapped her in Fran's best bear hug. In a bad impression of David Carradine in the tv show Kung Fu, grandma said,

"Choose wisely young grasshopper. But choose you must."

"Mother, please." Carol gives her mom the patented Skaggs eye roll. "Kung Flu? Really?"

"Let me suggest this to you, Carol. Imagine what you want your life to be like. Put a picture in your mind. Do you want a house? OK. Put that house in your mind. Make a picture of it. Is it a 1-story, or 2-story house? How many bedrooms and bathrooms does it have? Does it have a garage? Attached or detached? A yard with a fence? Or no fence? Green lawn? Trees? A Swing in back?"

Grandma has been looking out into the future while talking. Now she looks back at mom.

"This is your dream house, sweetheart. Fill it the way you want it. The way you always silently dreamed it would look, and with all the stuff you always thought it needed. When you are all by yourself and you are dreaming of how your life might be, use that dream, Carol."

Grandma looks out again.

"Then, look at your house. What is in it? Does it include children? When you think of that, does it give you happiness?"

Fran makes a special emphasis to her daughter with direct eye contact.

"Discover your dreams, Carol. It's now or never, honey. I didn't want you to have to make this decision at this age, but here we are. So, let's just try to do this thing the best way we can, OK?"

"I love you, Carol. That will never change, and don't you ever forget it because I never will."

With that, Fran felt they had covered everything needed now.

"What are you going to do, right now, Carol? I mean, are you staying up? Or are you going back to sleep? Cos if you're staying up, you need a shower."

"Going back to sleep, Mom."

"Wise adult decision, honey."

Not one stair creaked when Carol went up the stairs and back to bed.

*** ANOTHER MOM BREAK *eye roll* ***

BACK to January 2000

Just moments before sleep overtook her, Carol began thinking about her scientist. These thoughts of hers were a way of testing herself. For something, mother. Really? What would be the purpose of this exercise? I don't have a clue what she's doing, folks.

What Little Girls Are Made Of- From the Diaries of Becka Skaggs, PhD

Carol's Sleepy Thoughts: There are many reasons for a married man to not wear a ring. Doctors take them off routinely before surgery so not to have foreign objects inside their patients. Electricians often don't wear any jewelry at all for fear of being electrocuted. Therefore, it's not that unusual for a married man to not be wearing a ring and have no ring line.

So, was this young scientist married? What was he doing here? Is it silly to expect that he ever come back?

Carol could not fill her eyes full enough of the scrumptious desert. Until he caught her staring, of course. What else could she do but offer herself on the altar as a virgin sacrifice? By that time, it was definitely way past the point of returning. The dreaded eye "lock" had already occurred. Might as well go for the lethal lip lock. No sense in holding back now.

Carol was reflecting on what seemed like a very long walk to his booth in her diner, when she succumbed to the fruits of the sandman.

CHAPTER – The TWINS SHARE LIFE

Early morning August 20, 2004

The Cosmic Twins Narration: *excerpted from "The COSMIC TWINS Share", copyrighted 2015*

We women remember feelings. Our universe is defined by emotional events. It is the way we are made. It is not a weakness. It is a strength to all humans to have women this way. Women can look at words and imagine what that would feel like. Instantly, we have a memory for when we felt "stupendous!", "brilliant", "stellar", "stifled", "suffocated". Find a way to describe an emotion and we women will categorize it by how it feels and our memories of that feeling. We can revisit that over and over again!

If we try to explain this to men, they'd be like "Huh? What??"

Men, on the other hand, remember things in a logical linear way, and emotions may be remembered but they are subdued in that memory. A man will be sitting on the couch watching a ballgame, drinking a beer, eating jerky, peanuts, chips n salsa, the roast beef sandwich we made for them so they would have something healthy and not just be eating all junk, when suddenly, they will just exclaim! "I got it! The carburetor is running too lean, honey! If I can adjust the choke and get more air to the carb.... YES!!"

"Honey, you're wonderful!"

Now he is satisfied, but not necessarily gleeful over the epiphany. Subdued emotion.

"Thank you, Dear!" I mean, I would give an automatic response certainly by that time in my life, am I right?

Now we women are wondering "What'd I do?"

Huh? What??

"Hmmm. I'll have to buy that brand of roast beef again. Lean he said? Wonder what would happen if I gave him the Turkey?"

* * * LIFE GIVERS for LIFE BREAK * * *

Friday August 20, 2004

Alisha and Doctor Blue Eyes are in the cafeteria. It's nearly 8am. They've been at this for almost 2 hours and are about to hatch a plan. The doctor saves his best evidence to share with Alisha for last. Then he stops suddenly.

"Wait! Before I share my evidence, you need to share."

Alisha has a quizzical look on her face. "Share what?"

"You led me to believe you're a nurse. That's not nice, Doctor." The young emergency doctor pleads his case.

Alisha explained very quickly and completely.

"I am a nurse. And I didn't lead you anywhere. You jumped to your own conclusions." Alisha finished with a smile and leaned back in her chair arms now folded in front of her.

"You're a nurse AND a doctor?"

"Yes. I have a Bachelor of Science in Nursing and a Medical Doctorate. I am finishing my residency in emergency neuro-medicine. Is that alright with you, doctor?"

"Oh!"

THIS doctor is very surprised, and pleased! In fact, his eyes nearly crossed in the excitement currently ongoing within his frontal lobe.

"Absolutely okay. In fact, it's awesome!!" Blue eyes finished with extremely happy eyes.

"Okay. I'll share with you, now", he said, with a giant sarcastic smile occupying his entire face. Then he became serious.

"I want you to look at this." He slides a piece of paper with a handwritten corporate name across the table to the nurse/doctor:

Alisha reads the paper.

JUPITER ANALYTICS – Jupiter Well, Western Australia

She shifts her focus to his blue eyes.

The doctor continues. "It's the name of the analytical company that is the manufacturer of the monitoring equipment hooked up to Becca."

"Nope. Never heard of them. Is there even such a place as Jupiter Wells, Western Australia?"

"Yes, Alisha. I had to look it up myself. It's called Jupiter Well. Just one well. It's in the Gibson Desert. I've never heard of that one either. It's in the eastern portion of Western Australia – the State of Western Australia."

The doctor lowered his voice some and got a little closer to Alisha. What was that delicious scent she's wearing? Easy kid.

"Alisha, Jupiter Well is just that. It's a water well in the middle of the desert. It's Nothings Ville! There is nothing there. Even satellite photos show only desert ground, no buildings. Not even much of an established road. Unless they are underground, how can this company be out there? How can ANY company be out there?"

What Little Girls Are Made Of- From the Diaries of Becka Skaggs, PhD

The doctor shifts his blue eyes toward the door to see if anyone is standing deliberately within earshot. He's getting a little paranoid. Very understandable.

"There is something very peculiar going on here. I need to do some more digging. When is your next night shift? No visitors will be around late at night and the crews are smaller."

The doctor looks at the calendar icon on his watch.

"Today is the 20th. I'm here tomorrow, then Monday night."

Alisha thinks a split second and responds,

"My next night shift is not until Monday. I put myself in the rotation to better keep an eye on things, and your supervisors seem to be quite fine with it", Alisha raises one eyebrow with a little crooked smile, like 'who could have guessed?'

"But I can come in to help tomorrow, if you need?" Alisha was ready to volunteer because she is agreeing with blue eyes. Too many things were now not adding up.

What is worse than math? Oh! Somebody messing with the head of our little patient…ME! That is MUCH worse! Yes, Alisha was quite ready to find out about this corporation, or whatever they were!

"No, that's OK, Alisha." The doctor was scooting his chair away from the table in preparation for the departure from the cafeteria.

He gets a smile.

"Welcome to the staff at BLGH!" He gives her a tiny sarcastic wave of his right hand.

"We will talk again on Monday during our shifts. Let's meet first thing. Say 4:10p? After check-in?"

Healthcare workers don't enjoy standard hours like most of the workforce within our society. Their typical shift is 12 hours.

The doctor is up, but not away from the table. Now he bends down and speaks into her ear,

"And don't say anything to anybody about this until we meet."

The male doctor scooped the piece of paper from the table, wadded it up in his hand and shoved hand and all into his white jacket pocket. Then, the blue eyes disappeared down the hallway, out of Alisha's view, but deeper into her heart. WOW! Is this guy amazing, or what??

*** **YET ANOTHER MOM BREAK? REALLY??** ***

December 1999

Carol's education at the hands of her research scientist that night after they left the diner:

Excerpted from **Reflections from a Coma: The CAROL SKAGGS Story**, copyright 2016.

WE discovered through our research that the female brain develops incipient receptors that perceive parts of her environment early in brain stem development. She actually uses the receptors to receive stimuli of all different kinds around her during fetal development.

We found that we could pair adults that had certain genetic markers. When these adults were matched, they conceived children with receptors able to receive and translate to near perfection the signals we broadcast to them. We have to use ultra-low frequencies so they can carry for long distances. But the signal isn't carrying the information to be downloaded directly. It's used as a carrier for the system that contains the data sets with the information. Within the signal is a passcode, a series of tones and frequencies. Certain receptors, we discovered, are sensitive to these tones in sequence and become

What Little Girls Are Made Of- From the Diaries of Becka Skaggs, PhD

activated by them. Once that occurs, the information is opened at the recep-tor site. In this way, we can transmit to anywhere in the world. The body of earth is merely a shadow, just slight interference, to our signal.

I certainly know my own genetic code. I know how to map it myself, so why not? I had some of the best equipment in the world at my disposal. There was almost nothing standing in the way of achievement, once I did some rudi-mentary experiments on myself. I met with a few moderate successes. But one success in particular was the breakthrough I was needing. It's all about communication.

We humans have always called this kind of communication "telepathy". The word is a bit outdated, but the term works fine. Once I discovered how to communicate consistently using our technology, I knew we were on the verge of massive advancement for mankind! I mean, we could have more than HALF the world population talking to each other telepathically in less than a decade. That is astounding!

Lots of communication companies won't like that! There are still Trillions of dollars to be made by that industry. They won't give up that money quietly. I expect, once we go live, things will get very rough at first. But as we gain connections between more and more people, the people of the world will gain the power. The corporations will have little to say about it.

* * *

A Cosmic Twins Narration: *Ros? Did you notice? This scientist talks a lot like you. He even uses some of the same words. I'm beginning to have an intuition about this thing. Do you feel me, sis? Ros? Wait. Are we connected to the scientist?? Ros?!? Damn it, Ros!! Talk to me, sis. I don't like it when you are silent. Ros??*

* * * **CAROL and her RESEARCH SCIENTIST BREAK** * * *

December 1999, excerpted from "Reflections from a Coma: The CAROL SKAGGS Story", copyright 2016

In the scientist's hotel room, after the diner and everything else:

Carol is mesmerized by his story. His brilliance is off the charts! Mom feels like a billion dollars, and is sparkling like the Hope Diamond, while listening to this heart throb. The quality of the pillow talk? Who cares!! Any words will do.

"Once we mastered the signal output and focused the wavelength to specifically target certain receptors in the brain,"

the scientist continued, loving that he was being adored,

"We found the receptors would activate themselves in order to receive the specialized information. The brain adapts itself to receive and create what it perceives it needs in order to perform its main function, run this machine…" as he places both hands flat against his torso to signify the body is the machine,

"…like it's a well-tuned sports car. We can induce an electrochemical response at a specific site within the brain. It then does everything on its own, using its own DNA to interpret and use the information sent to the receptors in our broadcast signal."

The scientist was staring right into her icy blues and just stopped.

"Carol, I'm really liking you. What if I stay here for just a little bit and we can see what happens? I can get a job just about anywhere doing just about anything. What do you say?"

Carol almost squealed! OWWWW!!!! Mental squeal.

But she held it together. She was beyond the moon inside. But reality has a way of deadening a great mood. She still had to finish high school. Grandma would require that.

What Little Girls Are Made Of- From the Diaries of Becka Skaggs, PhD

The more she thought about it, the more she didn't like the idea. He probably would not like her drinking. So, THAT would have to come out. Nope! Not ready for that big reveal, yet. Carol's not well enough to swallow that medicine.

"Oh, baby. I'm really liking you, too!"

She has her right hand on his left cheek. Her hand is open and soft.

"But I don't think we're ready for this yet. I still have to finish high school. YOU have to connect the world to each other."

Now she gives him her patented quick wit and eye-roll.

"I don't know, but I'd say our jobs are about equal", Carol chuckled at him and gave him a look.

The short conversation they had about longer-term future had to wait another 20 minutes, as they both agreed they still hadn't finished their lovefest.

Mom and her scientist agreed to meet 5 years hence on December 2nd back in that diner. "60 months, precisely". Is what they agreed. They felt Carol would be ok with Fran for that long. Carol still needed to finish high school. The PhD insisted on that!

Then, it's her future is open after that. The choice was hers. He was merely advising with options that came into his mind. Carol loved every little bit of what was showing up in his mind.

She could get a degree or even a certificate of some kind from community college. She could become a beautician or paint nails all day, if that's what she loved. They had their whole lives in front of them. They could choose whichever sunset they wanted to follow.

Carol was lost in dreamland.

* * * LIFE GIVING BREAK * * *

Monday, early morning, August 23rd, 2004

It's 5am and I have to go to surgery again. I was awake Saturday night after dinner, I guess. I ate something, then I'm not sure how long I was awake afterward. I don't remember for sure. I'm still fuzzy in the upstairs.

But I remember Sunday it was beautiful outside. I was awake enough to see the clouds were moving pretty good. Just normal white clouds can have some funny looking faces and animals to look at. Hehe.

I haven't heard from Ros since Saturday morning's sessions. I'm getting confused about what is happening. Are we enjoined or are we not!? Just somebody make up my mind for me. Was that post-trauma brain activity going all weird and everything because I was scrambled inside? Maybe. I wish I had an adult who could give me answers.

I guess I was asleep for a while again.

Then Sunday night, after dinner, Doctor Murdock came in. It's the first time I got to meet the man who saved my life. He said I was asleep all the other times he checked on me.

Doctor Murdock walked up to the right side of my bed, placed both hands on the rail, and said,

"Hello my beautiful Becca. How is my princess doing tonight?"

Ohhh, that got me smiling. I'm only 4 years old. Pick on somebody your own age! I have no way to defend myself against that kind of charm.

"Haha, ouch!" He saw me wince from the pain when I laughed.

"You like picking on little girls?" I teased the doc.

It's the best line I could come up with in a hurry. I'm sick! But it still got a little chuckle out of him.

He had a good comeback, too.

What Little Girls Are Made Of- From the Diaries of Becka Skaggs, PhD

"I am so sorry I had to beat you up and steal your insides from you. But it was the only way I knew how to save your life."

He flashed me a beautiful big smile.

"Geez, Doc! You keep making me laugh, and you will put me back in that operating room."

I'm trying to laugh but the internal pain makes it uncomfortable.

"Why?" The doctor asked so gently." Is there some discomfort still? Your abdominal surgical pain should be subsiding by now."

Then the doctor lightly touched my arm to show me he knew what he was talking about.

"Your arm will hurt off and on for a few days longer because of what we had to do to put it back together."

"Yes! Ow, big fella."

I let the doctor know his little touch registered something besides pleasure.

"That hurt? Oh, come on." He said with a teasing smile.

"You're a tough a little girl, you know?"

And the doctor let go of the rail, pulled down the sheet and placed his hands on my abdomen. A little soon in our relationship, perhaps?

"But your stomach is a little painful, hon?"

Hon? Make me melt, you beautiful creature! Okay. All is forgiven.

Dr Murdock continued his quick examination of my complaint.

"Yeah, doc. It's kind of in this area", showing him to the left side of my stomach by pointing my nose and eyes at it with a bit of a head bow. My right arm was resting quite nicely on his left arm, thank you very much. I didn't need the arm to show the doc where I needed his attention."

"Let me check some things. Ok? You ok with that, Becca?"

Can I be in love? I mean, is it possible at my age?

"Ya, sure, Doc. Whatever you need. I'm ALL yours."

Is that too permissive??

The doctor didn't take long before he found exactly what he was looking for.

"Marjorie? I need to schedule OR1 for 5am tomorrow. We have to get this little girl back into surgery."

"I want some labs run just to confirm. But I suspect we have some large intestine that was damaged in the accident, and we didn't see it because of all the other damage."

Marjorie confirmed the orders and left the room to do what the doctor ordered.

"My beautiful Becca." The charmer continued. "You may not understand all this, but I need to tell you what we did in surgery after your accident."

"I'm ok, Doc. I know more than most kids my age."

"Hahaa, of course you are very special, Becca!" He shined that beautiful smile.

"And you are even more special now. We had to remove three organs that became very damaged. If we did not, you would have died. We had no choice in the matter."

Now the doctor's very serious demeanor lightened a bit.

"But there is good news. YOU are a very lucky little girl! Why?"

"Yeah, WHY, my beautiful doc?" Oh crap, did I say that out loud??

"Hahahaa! You are very funny!" Doctor Murdoch let out a gut-buster of a laugh.

What Little Girls Are Made Of- From the Diaries of Becka Skaggs, PhD

Wow! That was quite the laugh my doc let out!

"I want to meet you again in ten years when your sense of humor really starts to develop."

Uhhh…wait. How am I supposed to take that?? LOL.

That's how! In the spirit in which it was intended. He's funny!

"I can't wait, doc!"

Say Chee-e-e-ese!

"You already had functional spares for all three organs." The doctor continued his doctoring.

"You are very lucky! Before long, we'll have you up and out of here, and you will be learning how to swim in no time at all."

"Why? What happened to my swimming? I used to be able to swim."

Doc saw the sudden concern on my face and turned into a saint right before my eyes!

"Well, then you are already way ahead of everyone else."

There's that smile.

"Once we get that broken paddle of yours fixed, you will be swimming better than ever. WE think you may actually float better now."

"Oh, doc. You know how to make a girl blush."

I feel like I'm floating already. That DEFINITELY was not out loud!

The doc turned to leave and said to me, "Your condition is stable. But with your pain showing up the way it is, that could change quickly."

"You make sure to stay stable, and we'll see each other very early in the morning. The surgical staff will come get you when we're ready. You get some sleep. You're going to need it tomorrow."

My beautiful doc left the room.

* * * ANOTHER SURGICAL BREAK * * *

And now, something is stimulating my adrenal glands. I am in the middle of surgery and my adrenal glands are firing on all 88 cylinders! The way it feels, they must have that many cylinders.

William is in command and barking orders. I'm sorry. My beautiful doc. Doctor Murdock? Yes, that William. C'mon you guys, I don't have that much time to catch you all up right now.

"Will someone tell me why this patient is waking up in the middle of my surgery? I have about 12 centimeters of shredded large intestine almost ready for removal. We can't have elevated secretions at this time."

"I'm sorry William." The anesthetist is working feverishly at his equipment but getting frustrated at the lack of its effectiveness in stemming the onslaught of adrenaline that is suddenly awaking me.

"I can't stop her from waking. It's like this anesthetic just stopped working."

"No, it's not your fault, Shane".

Doctor Murdock suddenly realized exactly what was happening. WHY? That was another question entirely. One he had no answer for, yet.

"Her adrenal glands are firing in a 'fight or flight sequence'. She is either in the middle of one hell of a battle with something in her dream, or...."

Doctor Murdock paused a moment. As he thought, he realized he had no other answer.

"Or I don't have a reason why this is happening. But it is happening, and we must stop her from awakening!"

"30 mg phenobarbital stat!"

What Little Girls Are Made Of- From the Diaries of Becka Skaggs, PhD

Dr Murdock barked the order like none he had given so far this morning.

Barb, the scrub nurse, was just doing her job, when she began to caution the doctor,

"Doctor! That is a large dose for an adult! That could…"

"…. not with all that adrenaline in her body it won't!"

William shot out his next order.

"Get that sedative in her STAT!"

FADE TO BLACK

A COSMIC TWIN NARRATION: *Sis! I have been contacted. There is another. Did you hear me? There is another. They have contacted me. They have not revealed themselves yet. But they know us. Rebecca, my beautiful sister. Are you there?? They know us. What should I do? Becka?? I need your help. Don't leave me now. I'm scared without you, sister. Where are you?? Becka?? Becka!*

WAKE UP BECKA!! WE NEED YOU!

Why can't I reach you? I must be too weak.

Becka, I'm sorry I am too weak. I don't want to let us down.

I must rest, now, sister. I love you so much! I will rest.

CHAPTER – LIFE QUESTIONS

MONDAY evening, August 23, 2004 – Just before night shift at Black Lake General Hospital.

Alisha was driving like a madwoman…so she was calling herself as she was driving. Taking back streets so she can run stop signs and fudge the speed limit at the smaller intersections. She couldn't hold back her exuberance for getting to work tonight. They had agreed to meet 10 minutes after the start of their shifts, right after they each checked in with their stations and shift supervisors.

After Alisha arrives and parks in the Day-Shift supervisors parking space because it was right in front of the door to where she was going. She was pretty sure she would move her car later.

Alisha and blue eyes completed their separate administrative duties quickly and managed to meet on time in the cafeteria at their usual table near a corner of the room.

"You heard what happened to Becca?" The doctor asked.

Yes doctor," Alisha confirmed.

"At least she is ok and resting peacefully," the doctor sympathized. He seemed a bit nervous about their surroundings. He kept looking around. Looking to see if anyone was watching them. Maybe someone would stand out because they are acting too normal. He didn't know what he was looking for.

What Little Girls Are Made Of- From the Diaries of Becka Skaggs, PhD

"I still don't understand how something like that could happen here." The doctor was shaking his head in small little movements while scanning the perimeter of the room.

"I haven't figured that one out yet, either." Then Alisha jumps to the real topic-at-hand.

"Did you find out anything more about Jupiter Well, or Jupiter Analytics?", she asks the doctor.

"Not specifically them. Though I did find out that only Becca is hooked up to devices made by Jupiter Analytics." The doctor began his report.

"No other ICU room has that kind of equipment."

Then the doctor changed his tone to something sounding a little more excited.

"But there is something else very interesting I came across. I don't know how its connected in all this yet. So, I don't want to say anything yet."

Alisha could see some red flush across his face.

"I guess I'm a little superstitious that way. Until I have positive facts, that is."

The doctor looks at Alisha for a moment, then shifts his bashful gaze away from her waiting eyes.

Alisha is fine with his investigative skill. He seems to be doing very well so far. The doctor's social skills aren't so keen though.

"Sure doctor. I understand." She gives him her 'understanding' smile and finishes him off with her 'wanting' eyes. Then Alisha blurts,

"Let me go over what I found. You won't believe it!"

Alisha was ready and eager to report what she found to her colleague and partner amateur sleuth.

"I asked the police department if it would be alright for me to look at their report for the accident. I said it was for the hospital. I told them I was tasked with doing an ICU report on the victims of the accident."

The doctor jumped in, "I didn't know you guys did that kind of thing?"

"We don't," the nurse affirmed. Then she continued.

"Nobody does, that I know of. I made it up." Her golden eyes smile at his blues.

"But the police don't know that. So, they gave me a copy of the report. Isn't that great?!"

She placed a page on the table in front of her. The doctor just realized she had been holding it in her hand and in his view this entire time. He didn't notice until she pushed it at him.

The driver's name of the white F-150 pick-up was highlighted to make sure it would be visible to the doctor.

"Read what it says next to his name," Alisha prompts the doctor.

On the paper was written:

Vladimir Bostek – Russian National – Diplomatic Immunity

Alisha jumps at the chance to share her discovery.

"This man works for a Russian government agency called, Agency Biologik."

The doctor's blues got a bit wider.

"His documents say he's an attaché to the Minister of Life." Now Alisha boils down the facts for the doctor.

"We have a Russian attaché rushing to the hospital at a speed in excess of 70 mph, to do what? The accident hadn't happened yet. Not until Vladimir got to that intersection. So, what caused him to be in such a hurry?"

What Little Girls Are Made Of- From the Diaries of Becka Skaggs, PhD

A rhetorical question Alisha was already in the process of answering. Turnabout in love is fair play, right?

"The only thing happening at that time was a mother going into labor."

Then she looked squarely into those blue eyes and said, "Get this. Her labor was induced so the baby would be born while Becca and Carol were laying out there in their car waiting for rescue people to arrive at their scene. The baby was born at 4:19pm. The accident occurred at 4:04pm."

This definitely got the doctor's curiosity going.

"That seems MORE than strange to me. How do you get a birth that quickly, doctor?"

Alisha finished her report with a question she hoped blue eyes could answer.

Before the doctor could respond, a code blue was sounding. An industrial accident has occurred, and rescue teams are bringing in three victims. Apparently, a load near a conveyor belt shifted at a local foundry and the three workers all suffered serious injuries.

One man had his left hand cut almost in half. That was six hours of surgery right there. Another man had his chest almost crushed, a broken sternum. It takes a lot of force to crack the sternum.

The most serious injury, though, is another head injury. Why, Alisha thought, do we have head injuries filling our ICU?

I don't like coincidences either, Alisha. Oh! Nurse? MY brain injury left me brain enhanced. So, don't you worry one little thing about me.

Alisha and the doctor never got to speak the remainder of the night. The emergency doctor on call for the shift happened to be the doctor who had been sharing time with Alisha. He had an emergency to mend.

* * * **TWINS SHARE LIFE BREAK** * * *

ROSALYN Narration: *excerpted from "The COSMIC TWINS Share".*
Copyright 2015

August 2004

I have learned we are very close together in space, my sister. I am in the maternity ward at Black Lake General Hospital in Olympia, Washington. I'm on the third floor. Mother is here, too. She is resting peacefully. I get to see her several times a day. That makes me happy. We will see each other very soon, my sister. I love you, Becka with a K.

* * *-FATHER BREAK - August 2004 -* * *

MALE NARRATOR: *excerpted from "The COSMIC TWINS Share".*
Copyright 2015

Becca, Rosalyn. This is your father. You are my beautiful girls. My COSMIC TWINS. Yes, you are half-sisters. It is my COSMIC Fate that you are twins. That's all I can say right now. There is no time.

We will do wonderful things together very soon. But right now, I must tell you something extremely important. All our lives depend upon it. Hundreds of Millions of lives depend on us. The three of us.

I was not expecting us to be ready for at least 24 months. But here we are. We have no free will in the matter. So, we must be wise in our use of the energy. We have friends that are already helping us of their own volition. We can make them allies. Eventually, we will have five in our team.

Right now, I need you to listen very carefully to my instructions.

These are coordinates to the GREEN Flashing Monitor. Don't worry about not knowing things. All will become clear in time. Much time, I hope. We need every day we can get to prepare ourselves.

Becca, tell Doctor Blue Eyes these coordinates.

What Little Girls Are Made Of- From the Diaries of Becka Skaggs, PhD

I am embedding this information into both of you because all three of us are under assault. Somebody wants our technology, and they are coming after us to get it. I need more time to find out who is behind this attack. What I mean, daughters, is I know who is behind the attack. I need time to find him and his cohorts.

I must abandon my current position. They will gain control if I do not get to the broadcast center. It's here in North America, but I need time to get there. Once there, I can recreate it elsewhere. Only then can we be safe for the time it takes to grow strong as a team.

A madman is hot on my trail. I have to move and keep moving for a few days, maybe more. I'm not sure how long it will take.

It looks like a rock face that suddenly rises out of the desert. I'm speaking of the madman's lair.

Jupiter Well, Western Australia. Just north of the Tropic of Capricorn in the Gibson Desert.

Here it is:

GPS Coordinates latitude -23.0647907 and longitude 117.6455001

In the hills just east of the well. It's in an old exploratory mine, people still think is abandoned.

ONLY DOCTOR BLUE EYES MUST RECEIVE THIS INFORMATION.

If anyone else gets those coordinates, the doctor's life could be put in grave danger.

The doctor is already planning on going to this location. He must remove an item for us while he is there.

We need the doctor to go there and secure the keyboard by the GREEN MONITOR.

Jupiter Well is an emergency remote location. It's not even supposed to be active. But someone has activated it and is using that location to interfere with us. All we need is THAT keyboard, which is hardwired into the system.

NO other keyboards will be able to run the system from that location. It's old school technology. Things work differently in today's electronic world. The only other location is from the broadcast center. Which is where I am going, as soon as I am done shutting down everything here, at my current location.

I don't have time to dismantle all my equipment. I must take vital pieces only. No one will be able to broadcast from here anymore. I can ensure that. I will send along a string of data at my next available opportunity.

Rosalyn! I am here baby. I love you. We are staying connected now. But I don't have Becka stable yet. That's why you can't get a clear connection with her. Don't be frightened, Rosalyn Valery. Daddy's right here.

"I love you, too, Daddy", Rosalyn managed to squeak out telepathically to her father. I have a Master Scientist for a father!! WOW!!

"You're not mad, are you daddy?" Rosalyn asked innocently.

"What? Oh! No, baby. Of course not. Daddy's not a mad scientist." Hahaha

"Everything will be fine, Rosalyn."

"And Becka", her father continued his rapid messaging before he had to flee for his life.

"When you are able to decode this data, reach out to us immediately. There is still one more person we must find. It is Rosalyn's aunt, and she is a very important person. I will need you to ask Alisha for help in finding her. But wait ...."

A pause in instructions came and was almost an annoyance to Ros.

Then her father continued.

What Little Girls Are Made Of- From the Diaries of Becka Skaggs, PhD

"They have been blocking Ros because they know she is the weakest telepathically of the three of us. But now that I am enjoined with Rosalyn, you have become the weakest link, Becka. "Sweetheart, this up to you."

"I am sorry you are all alone in a desert. Wait for further instructions regarding Rosalyn's aunt."

My father continued to try to soothe any possible frayed nerves that this TWIN may be experiencing. He wasn't positive how I would react to his sudden presence in my life. But he knew the odds.

"You are the one who can do this, Becka Dall. The World needs your help."

A blast of energy was felt by Rosalyn.

"Find that inner Thor and be strong my daughter of love!" Energy was entering me from somewhere.

Ros could feel the energy – {that had to be what I just felt, Ros thinks to herself – as she listened to her father coach her big sister into extreme confidence.}

"I love you so much, my girls. We will all be together very soon."

"Rosalyn?"

"Yes Daddy?" Rosalyn quickly responded to her father's direct attention.

"Always obey your mother."

An audible inhale of breath was drawn that took precisely 1.0 seconds. Then, our father said,

"You need rest, baby. Power down, please."

And with that specific series of three commands within the pre-programmed timeframe, Rosalyn fell fast asleep.

* * * **ADULT TIME BREAK** * * *

Tuesday Evening, August 24, 2004

Doctor Murdock got out of his car he had just parked along the side of the residential street, walked up to the 2-story house in front of him and rang the doorbell. In a very short moment, the door was answered.

The woman opened the door, looked at her guest and exclaimed,

"Well, Billy! What a pleasant surprise!"

Fran Skaggs had opened the door wide and invited the doctor in.

"Please come in and have a seat. What brings you here, Billy?"

"I would love to Fran" the doctor said, "But I was hoping you would go for a walk with me tonight. It's such a beautiful evening. And I need to talk to you about Becca, in particular."

"That sounds great to me." She turned to go inside and said, "just let me grab my sweater. Just in case there's a slight chill later."

"I'll be here waiting." Doctor Murdock is trying to have some light-hearted fun with Fran.

"Waiting for what?" Fran said as she was already back to the door and walking past the good doctor and closing the door. "You coming, or what?"

"Yes! I am coming." The doctor picked up step and caught up with Fran by the time she reached the sidewalk in front of her house.

Fran says, "Let's say we take a right and walk down to the beach. The Frozen Yogurt Shop is still open."

Then the doctor said something quite charming.

"How do you, my dear lady, read my mind so openly? I can hardly wait for that Chocolate Marshmallow Twist they have down there." The doctor gets a smile that Fran thought was very warm, and when coupled with the slight squint of his eyes, was bordering on hot.

What Little Girls Are Made Of- From the Diaries of Becka Skaggs, PhD

As they began to walk toward the beach, Fran locked her arm through the doctor's.

"Ok, Billy. This is wonderful and everything, but this is a special treat. So, why don't you tell me what's really on your mind, while we make our way to that Chocolate Marshmallow Twist cone."

"Reading my mind again, Fran. Twice in a minute. Am I that predictable?" The doctor asked with a smile and a glint in his eye.

"You are good man, Billy." Fran said with pleasure in her voice.

"We've known each other a long time. There are just a few things that you have kept doing all your life, that's all", as Fran completed her thoughts on his predictability.

The doctor was satisfied with her answer and walked in silence for a moment while he gathered his thoughts and found a good starting point. Nothing about this story was good, however. The doctor didn't realize he was shaking his head until Fran asked him.

"Why are you shaking your head, Billy?"

"I was?" And he realized immediately that he had been shaking his head while deep in thought.

They continued to walk to the waterfront while William explained his thoughts.

"I'm sorry, Fran, it's just this case. Becca's injuries are severe and strange, sure. But the chemical attacks that occurred are really puzzling me."

"Chemical Attacks?" Fran quickly comes right back at Billy with this pointed question.

"What chemical attacks?"

Fran is fiddling with the sweater she had already decided wasn't necessary. It's still too warm to wear the sweater, and her hands are starting to get nervous little movements. She thinks of a worry stone her father used to carry in his pocket all the time when she was a child.

Fran's father told her a worry stone was named incorrectly. He called it a busy stone. "It's really just to keep your hands busy while they are idle," he used to say.

"It's natural for people to have things on their mind", Fran's father told her many times over the years.

Right now, Fran is feeling this is a little more than something on her mind.

"Not a chemical attack, per se," the doctor says "but hormones. Well...." Then starts over.

"Yesterday morning,"

the doctor begins to recount the events to Fran as they walk,

"when we had Becca in surgery to repair her damaged intestine? She suddenly became engulfed in a large secretion of adrenaline and testosterone from her own body. It was waking her up, Fran. It completely rendered the anesthetic useless. We had to knock her out with a large dose of sedative."

The doctor had been looking ahead, but he turned his head slightly to say this more directly to Fran,

"Luckily we were close to complete when the chemical explosion happened."

She saw the doctor shaking his head absently again.

Fran had an immediate look of concern.

"Is she going to be okay?" Fran asked solemnly.

"For the time-being, yes." The doctor's reply was immediate.

"But she is not in good health for the long-term," as William finished that thought.

What Little Girls Are Made Of- From the Diaries of Becka Skaggs, PhD

They continued to walk as the doctor looked squarely at Fran and gave her some sad news.

"Fran." The doctor now stopped their walk and became very serious.

"Becca's little body has a serious filtration problem. She has one kidney left operating with function less than it should, and her liver is not going to last very much longer."

"Billy", Fran says very sternly.

"Just tell me what it is you are trying to say."

"It seems no matter what we do, your granddaughter is dying, Fran."

Williams eyes became moist.

"If we can't solve her filtration problems very soon, this girl will not see her fifth birthday."

Fran gives a quick unintentional gasp.

"I'm sorry, Fran." The doctor is truly concerned for Fran, and this information isn't going to help her current mental state at all. Her daughter is in a coma, and she just finds out her granddaughter has an expiration date.

William reached with his free hand and grabbed grandma's hand that was resting on his other arm. They continued their slow stroll in silence for another minute. Then the doctor spoke again.

"I am trying to think of everything I can to resolve Becca's filtration issues. But the secretions she exhibited are so strange, I have to believe there is something else affecting her."

He gets a little excited in his continued discussion.

"I started to look at the science of her filtration and I can't get past the thoughts that some other chemical secretion could be on its way at any moment, trying to steal even more health from Becca. All of this cannot be coming naturally from within her body. It's impossible, Fran."

"Ok, Billy. I believe you. I trust you, you know that, Billy." Fran completed her statement just as they rounded the corner to the frozen yogurt shop.

"I truly appreciate that, Fran."

William opened the door to the yogurt shop for Fran, and she stepped through the threshold in front of him.

"You know I have her best interest in my heart at all times," the doctor finished and looked up at the large menu on the wall.

"I know, you do, Billy. That's why I trust you completely. You are a very caring person, Dr Murdock." Fran gives his hand an extra squeeze.

Then, Fran said in teasing way,

"I thought you had already decided on the Chocolate Marshmallow Twist cone. Why are you looking up at the menu?"

William got a big smile, and then confessed.

"Just looking to see if anything interesting has recently arrived on the menu."

"Chocolate Marshmallow Twist please. Large", the doctor gives his order to the cashier.

Fran then said,

"Predictable man" and released her gorgeous smile on the helpless doctor.

"Small Black Raspberry cone, please," Fran told the attendant.

Dr Murdock pays the bill, crosses the room and opens the door for Fran. As she walks in front of William to exit the store she hears,

"Predictable woman."

She looks at him with big eyes, tries to get serious at him, and busts out laughing.

What Little Girls Are Made Of- From the Diaries of Becka Skaggs, PhD

"I guess I deserved that," she says, still chuckling, as they began their walk back to her house.

After each had enjoyed the flavors of their cones for a few delicious licks, the doctor seemed to be out of his trance and relaying information to Fran once again.

"I just can't figure out how these secretions can even be triggered, Fran. But I will get to the bottom of this, somehow. I will pull together the entire staff to find the answers if needed."

The doctor stops briefly and looks straight at Fran, "Becca has too much to live for. I'm not giving up on her. I promise you, Fran. I'll never give up on her."

The couple looks at each other and silently agrees with the strangeness of the past few days.

They keep walking together, tongues on yogurt, minds in the clouds, toward Fran's little house.

Yes, Fran's little house just a few blocks off the beach is where the couple went to enjoy their just desserts. The same house where other things got a little heated after their frozen desserts had been enjoyed. And, yes, the exact little home where the single doctor stayed all night.

Wednesday, August 25th, mid-morning: 2004

My condition is improving in the hospital. I just woke up about an hour ago from my surgery on Monday. I was out for about two days!

While I was out, they took my arm out of the big sling. Or they never put my arm back in one. I'm only saying that because when I woke up, my arm was free to use. Okay, it's inside a cast. That still leaves me free to move about the room and hallways. The heavy plastic boot on my leg was no barrier to navigation. I'm almost ready to explore!

Dr Murdock did an exceptional job repairing my intestine, and in getting me out of the chemical assault on Monday. I am now able to walk with a little help from a nurse. She asks me about mom. Again!

I wasn't liking the idea of my mother lying there asleep for days, with no ability to wake up. And this nurse wants me to go watch that? Why?? It seems like that visit would get sad very fast.

This time, though, I gave in to her request. I think.

Nurse Marjorie took me to Carol's room. I heard the machines and the breathing and decided I didn't want to go inside the room and see my mom. I could see enough from right here at the doorway.

"I don't need to see anymore of her suffering." I remember saying rather sternly, then I began to cry and sat down right there on the floor in front of the door to mom's room, and in front of the nurse, while covering my face with my soggy hands. My booted left leg is trying to stick out, so I can't really sit on my legs like I usually do.

"At least she's alive," I squeak out between gasps of breath. Our COSMIC TWIN is finally experiencing her first big release of emotion since her accident, 6 days ago. Whoopee. And I'm not having very much fun, either.

"C'mon, Sweetheart", Marjorie says. "Let's go back to your room. Maybe there are some pretty clouds to look at through your window."

Marjorie grabbed me up in both her arms and held me tightly against her bosom. She asked me to hold onto the post with all the bags of fluids and we'll go back to the room. Which I did, for a moment. And we did go, with the squeaky-wheeled post in tow. Mostly also carried by Marjorie. I'm just being honest. By the time we walked from mom's room, 208, to my room, 212, I was fast asleep.

Marjorie gently pushed the post into its familiar location within the room, placed me on the bed, covered me up, and retired to the nurse's station, leaving the door cracked about half-way. It was a motherly kind of thing to

What Little Girls Are Made Of- From the Diaries of Becka Skaggs, PhD

do. In this way, Marjorie could keep watch over me from the nurse's station, and she could hear anything unusual that might happen to our hero....ME!

Not all the ICU rooms could be seen by nurses sitting at the nurse's station. Some were at the ends of the floor that were blocked from view of the nurse's station. But BLGH had a policy where children in the ICU would be placed in rooms visible to the nurses sitting at their nurse's station in the middle of the ICU floor. This just provided one more safety measure for us young one's that can have all kinds of strange things happen to us while we are in the hospital. Even if someone is NOT trying to kill you!

Marjorie felt comfortable now. Maybe she can get some of this treacherous paperwork done, finally! One last look at Room 212. Still asleep. Poor little girl.

*** **ARTIFICIAL LIFE BREAK** ***

Late Wednesday afternoon, Point Roberts, Washington, USA August 2004

Point Roberts is a small peninsula that juts southward from Canada into Boundary Bay and south of the International Boundary. Therefore, Point Roberts is about 6 square miles of land that belongs to the United States and can only be accessed, if a person drives, through Canada.

Of course, if you had a boat or a sea plane, you could arrive there from other destinations in the United States. But if you needed to find something, and you needed a vehicle to carry it once you found that thing?? Then, you wanted to drive, and you would have to drive through Canada to get there.

That creates an extra set of border crossings you might have to communicate through, if Point Roberts isn't your final destination. And if you are a person that doesn't really like to be noticed, you don't want customs agents getting too many opportunities to remember you for any reason. There is no question that communication with border agents should be kept to a bare minimum. Any additional conversation would be unnecessary and unwanted.

It was a white 4-door American vehicle. It looked just like a thousand more white American vehicles that have been on the road today. No one was inside the vehicle other than the driver. It had a trunk. Inside the trunk was a shovel. A typical garden spade that is used for digging in dirt. A spade is also an excellent tool for digging in sand.

Inside the trunk was also a plastic tarp. This plastic tarp was made with the threads woven inside, so it wouldn't tear as easily as non-woven plastic. The tarp was brand new. It was still in its original packaging.

The vehicle, arriving at the Point Roberts border crossing after coming through the British Columbian community of Delta, pulled up to the only booth open. There were two border control booths for those arriving to the United States on this lonely road, but the 2nd booth was rarely ever used.

"Identification and citizenship", the US Customs agent asked.

The driver handed his driver's license to the agent and stated, "U.S."

Here, at the Point Roberts border crossing, if you have a Washington State driver's license, no passport is necessary. That is your proof of U.S. citizenship.

"Business or pleasure?" Custom agent asks.

"Pleasure, definitely," was the response from the driver.

Then the driver volunteered something that did not need to be said. The agent was just about to allow the vehicle to enter the United States with no other conversation. But the words were plainly stated. And the Custom agent did take notice.

"I was in Blaine for a conference, and found I have time before I need to leave the area. I hadn't seen old Fred Hester in so many years. Since I was just an hour away or so. I thought I would come dig up my old friend."

What Little Girls Are Made Of- From the Diaries of Becka Skaggs, PhD

The driver gave a little chuckle.

"What was his wife's name? She was such a spitfire!" The driver added gleefully.

The Custom Agent's face just lit up like he'd found a long-lost friend. If someone doesn't normally like people to take notice of what you are doing, why would you start a conversation with someone? Especially, if that some-one can have you arrested and thrown in jail.

"Yes, she is!" The agent said in a lively way.

"Her name is Bree. That's all I've ever know her as, anyway."

"Oh, yes, that's right," the driver agreed. Then he repeated her name.

"Bree".

The agent then volunteered,

"I'm sorry about Fred, though. He passed away a few years ago. Very sud-denly. Stroke they say. It nearly destroyed Bree, from what I understand, you know?"

The agent is now exercising his gossip skills. He doesn't get many oppor-tunities to gossip about the locals since most those that come through the crossing ARE the locals. They don't like it when you, as a border agent, start talking to friends about their friends. Or worse: talking to their friends about Them!

"Oh, I'm so sorry", the driver feigned concern.

Then he added, "Are they still just off the beach? I mean, Bree, of course."

"I'd love to give my condolences."

The driver flashed a quick smile to the agent.

"Sounds like you know the Hester Place. Still in the same place. You have yourself a great visit." The agent returned the identification to the driver.

The Border agent gave the driver a wave through, and began thinking to himself,

"I'll talk to Bree tomorrow." The agent finished his note reminding him to check with Bree about this "Steven Fairchild". It was all written down right here on the note.

The agent grabbed another bite from his raspberry-cream cheese muffin made at the local 'Farm Fresh Bakery and Coffee Shack' and continued his lonely day. Funny part about that Farm Fresh Bakery idea in Point Roberts? There are no farms on the peninsula. It's all Canadian dairy products. You've all heard stories about how they have wonderful cheese in Canada. Fresh baked goods is another matter altogether.

By now, the driver had already left the agent, drove straight down the road, and turned left toward Maple Beach.

*** **ARTIFICIAL BEACH BREAK** ***

At Maple Beach, the sedan is parked under a large scraggly maple tree. The tree is at the edge of the international boundary and where the American concrete sea wall meets the sea. It's a triple juncture that can be pinpointed precisely on a map without GPS coordinates. It's old school.

There is a hole that has been dug that is about 6 feet long by 3 feet deep by 2 feet wide. But it isn't a particular shape. The hole is more like the person digging was looking for something and not sure of its exact location.

If a person were just walking along the seawall, they would notice the odd shape of the object that was just placed in the trunk of a sedan parked under a scraggly maple tree at Maple Beach, Washington. They would also notice the bright blue tarp the object had been wrapped in prior to being placed in the trunk. If they were the kind of person who was used to such observations, such person might notice the object seemed like it wasn't very rigid as the object was fumbled into the trunk.

What Little Girls Are Made Of- From the Diaries of Becka Skaggs, PhD

Luckily for the driver, no such person was walking along the seawall. Nope.

Instead, they were standing in the living room of their home not a hundred feet away looking out the large picture window. It was a beautiful, picturesque view of Boundary Bay and its seawall that captured the entire event as it had just transpired.

Oblivious, the driver checked everything in the trunk, then closed the lid.

He turned the sedan around and headed back up the hill to the border crossing back into British Columbia. The same border he had just come through not 1 hour ago. The one with the curious customs agent.

He drove up to the booth and opened his window. When the agent said,

"Hey, Mr. Fairchild! Done visiting Bree already?"

The driver only said one word.

"Agent?"

With that one word, the driver captured the agent's complete attention.

Then the driver made three statements:

"You should Always Obey Your Mother".

The sound of the statement caused the agent to hesitate just a bit longer.

The driver gave an audible inhale for precisely 1.0 seconds.

The driver finished.

"Do you have something for me, Agent? I am so sorry about your memory issue."

The agent responded automatically.

"Oh, Thank you, so much."

SC MacAlpine

The agent promptly handed his note, with all the information he had written down on Steven Fairchild, directly to the driver. The agent won't be remembering to talk with Bree Hester about this driver. He won't be remembering anyone named Steven Fairchild. Ever.

"Drive careful" the agent bids the driver a nice day, and the white vehicle disappears into the traffic of Delta, British Columbia, to continue on its secret mission.

CHAPTER – ENERGY in LIFE

Our Choice is: to USE Energy or NOT to Use

August 19th, 2020

The COSMIC TWINS Joint Communication: excerpted from The COSMIC TWINS Annual Newsletter (released every year on their birthday).

Today, Rosalyn and I know Free will is a myth. The idea that we get to choose what path our lives will take is a cruel dishonesty we prefer to tell ourselves as a form of motivation. Free Will is not necessary for us to live to our potential as a human. No, that is not a choice we get to make.

Our free choice is in how MUCH energy we put back into the system. That is why we can't just sit on our butts and expect our life to come to us. It is already there waiting for us to claim it. We simply pay the price of admission, Zest for life, and the necessary expenditure of energy to go get the prize.

We, The COSMIC TWINS do not harness nor hoard energy. We instead gather, focus, and release the energy back into the universe. We believe humans must always put energy back into the system to receive energy FROM the system. In this way, we humans don't shape our destiny, we catch up to it.

By releasing our energy into the universe, we feed our destiny while also ful-filling it. It's another wonderful paradox! Those little surprises the universe keeps giving us. The COSMIC TWINS LOVE them!

We become who we were meant to be by living to the fullest who we are right now. Live with loving intent and always strive toward becoming "pure love", and you will fulfill your destiny. You will be rewarded with the life you wanted and that has been intended for you since before your birth.

Some people have asked Rosalyn and I, "If this energy stuff is true, why don't we automatically have a desire to run at full-throttle all the time?"

Some of us do. This is where the spectrum of differences occurs between us humans.

Not all humans are meant to be users of Universal Energy. It's true some of us are born as extremely high-energy beings with the incipient ability to use UE. Others are born at lower energy levels that allows them to be conduits of energy.

Either way doesn't matter. Because this is only where we start. Everyone has the path for them that they can reach simply by allowing Universal Energy to flow through them and back into the universe. People that are "free conduits" of UE are vital in the flow of energy throughout humanity, and the universe.

You, followers of the COSMIC TWINS, have just been told something that could blow your mind. How are you doing?

Don't try to find ways to make this all fit back into your old way of thinking. Because your brain will allow it to become a part of your current belief system. If you do this, you will not be using the energy. You will be still expecting life to come to you. Like a god bestowing blessings upon you as a reward for good deeds. However, "Good" is defined by you and your god!

Using Universal Energy (UE) is the way to advance through your life's path. And when you use UE, your intent will be pure. Living with loving intent is really the ultimate high for me. When I think of this as a possibility, I get giddy. I have a huge mental smile on, and I am energized.

I, the TWINS, LOVE love! I love everything about it! Yes, even the heartbreak. It tells me I'm alive. No, heartbreak is not fun at that moment! Not at all. But my limited experiences have left me cleansed. It can feel like the soul went through a Jetted Bubble Bath when it's all over. It allows me to focus on pure love once again.

What Little Girls Are Made Of- From the Diaries of Becka Skaggs, PhD

Heartbreak hurts, yes. And I don't want to create it just so I can feel better once it's over. That is a waste of Universal Energy. I don't like wasting my UE. It is a gift from the universe.

The universe includes all creatures, all energy sources, known and not known throughout the universe. Wasting a gift would be a bad thing. Gifts are to be enjoyed.

Heartbreak doesn't have to ruin your life and turn into hate. Hate is sticky, you never really get rid of it once it sticks to you. So, I do not hate living beings. I just choose not to participate with hate. That is just not in me. I have asked myself and double checked my answers. The answer keeps coming back as "I cannot hate an innocent creature". Known or unknown.

Sometimes, I wonder, though. How far can I stretch the definition of dislike before I finally cross into hate? That's a fair question. A question for which I have not found an adequate answer.

I can hate behavior. I can hate actions. I can hate ideas. I can hate words. These are all inanimate things. But I cannot hate a spiritual being. Salvation is always possible for spiritual beings because we aren't talking about mystics. We are discussing science and I am sharing my thoughts and feelings while we do. More than that, we are learning things.

When I talk of a person's spirit, I mean the "lifeforce" within us. That thing inside that makes us aware that we are human and that we think and that we have feelings. I will also use it interchangeably with the word soul. Some religions want to mince words into tiny little pieces of definitions, so they show everybody how they are different. It's all balderdash. Ukrainians call that "chepukha", which is malarkey, baloney, hogwash, crap, and applesauce. LOL. I know, right??

As far I'm concerned, spirit and soul are the same things. Why? Again. I am talking about science. The soul is energy. Our Lifeforce is energy. May I repeat that again, using other words?

Our spirit is universal energy. We humans can learn to use UE in a way that leads to loving intent in all we do. It is true. We have NOT left science back in the garage. It is right here with us. Always will be. It will never leave. For one thing, we need it. For another thing, science just gives us a way to describe our universe as we experience it. Science is real, just like you and your pet peeves.

Okay? Very good! I feel so much better now, don't you?

Marvel in who you are, and let others worry about themselves. I, The COSMIC TWINS, believe men and women are equal in love and spirit, and equally necessary in a society to function at its highest efficiency. The skills of everyone are needed. None should be allowed to be discarded as if they had no value to give to society. That is the wrong way to feel about people. We need MORE diversity to truly thrive as a society, not less.

Diversity gives room to grow! Through diversity we gather up extreme possibilities. It is extreme possibilities that allows humans to reach for the stars, land on Mars, drive solar-powered cars, and develop nanotechnology for improving our quality of life. Extreme possibilities give us extreme humans.

As a woman, I am powerful. I have abilities beyond any man's comprehension because they have no similar experience for comparison. It is true that men have experiences we women have no comparison to, as well. I am a woman and must resign myself to matters of womanhood, as those are matters I might have the most knowledge about when referring to differences between men and women. Besides, I am discussing the science of women's brains, and women more generally. And ALL that I have said is tied together.

The TWINS ask that you all tie this together and join us in spreading the truth about our human brains. We ask everybody to marvel in our differences. The COSMIC TWINS ask all humans to embrace diversity as our strength. We believe the world will be a happier place for everyone to live in love, honor, and integrity once we embrace our differences and love them as us.

The COSMIC TWINS ask that all people stop wasting Universal Energy on petty matters of social divisiveness. Always use UE with loving intent for greatest positive effect. Put "pure love" into everything you do because it all *uses UE. Embrace the energy. When magnified by the power of love? You will feel like you have the ability to do great things.*

I am going to focus my TWINS attention on the betterment of all humans. Along the way I am telling you about myself so you might gain some insight on my perspectives, on how I feel about things. If I tell you how I feel, and you feel the same way, then we are not alone anymore. We are now together. We have something in common we can talk about next time we're together. Cool, huh?!?

I must rely on my TWINS' self. Whatever I do next, I must do on my own. I don't know that I can trust my TWINS' self. So, I must love my TWINS' self to give me the opportunity to succeed. I would do that for other people. Oh, sure, I can defeat my TWINS' self before starting. I can have a good reason for just forgetting the whole thing - {it's too hard! I don't feel like it!}. Of course, that doesn't hurt anyone but me. And it really feels more like fear and apprehension than a good reason for not getting started.

I feel like I am on an island, or in a desert, way far away from civilization, and must rely on my TWINS self to survive. I also strongly feel that I am about to have vital information for mankind, and I MUST rely on my...self to get it to the people.

No one else can do it. That is my mission. This must happen, and this must happen soon. The people must have this information. It is imperative for human survival! Who am I to think that I have the right to concern myself with individual pettiness when the life of our species is on the line? Right now, there is no more time to consider the options. That time is over.

Now is the time to "DO!". That is exactly how we shall proceed. No more time for wasting. Time to get things done. Let's go!!

I am feeling some fear of the unknown, and some apprehension about what to do next. In a word? I'm scared! Yes!! I have no idea where all these courageous words are coming from, I don't normally feel this brave. I am feeling stronger, though, than I can ever remember in my life!

OK. I am still scared a bit, but I am not going to let that defeat me before I get started. I have been scared before.

I, my TWINS self is born a human woman. I am mother. I must save the future children of mankind.

We are now on a big secret 'Mission', like in some spy novel. Remember, our Father is a wonderful scientist that first ran afoul of a Russian madman named Yuri Yurachenkov in 2004. The COSMIC TWINS gave Yurachenkov just a gander at our awesome power that day in August 2004. But it was only enough to set him back a few years.

Now, it appears The COSMIC TWINS are heading toward a showdown with that evil tom in 2020. Yuri's not going to like the way his bird will be grilled.... extra crispy.

Ros, sweetheart, things always worked out well before. Especially when I was afraid of things as a little girl that I understand about today. Like, there is no invisible man in my closet. **Ha! There are millions! ☺ All you guys here with us. Lol. Hey! We, The COSMIC TWINS, got this!! ☺

CHAPTER – LIFE TAKER

WEDNESDAY NIGHT SHIFT – about 3 hours into the shift.
August 25, 2004

Alisha and doctor blue eyes were discussing plans and findings. Alisha told the doctor she had checked on me. It was during that time of my hospital stay where I was falling asleep, again, right after dinner, and almost all other times. If they had pudding, and I was kind of awake, I could become more awake for pudding. But sometimes, that's all I could eat before falling asleep again.

We still have not been able to talk about anything. And by this time, I am getting frustrated over not being able to talk with ALL my professionals about the odd things happening. Until everyone tells me their story, I cannot cross them off my potential "Bad Guy" list. Too many people are finding themselves on this list as possible suspects. I need to start removing suspects, not adding more.

"She's resting peacefully, Doctor. But I am worried about her condition. Her metabolic rate is high for a patient being sedated, and that sleeps this much." Alisha volunteered that I have been asleep every time she goes into check on me since my last surgery.

"The doctor agreed, "Yes, I noticed that too, Alisha. I'm sensing you have some ideas on the matter." It was stated in a monotone way by the doctor. Alisha wasn't sure if it was intended to be a question or not. She decided to treat it as more of a statement someone makes while really thinking of something else.

The science part of Alisha decided 'she' wanted to take the lead, so Alisha succumbed to her impulse to be scientific with her science colleague.

"It's time to get into the weeds and push our knowledge of things, or we will never find out what is happening", Alisha breaks the silence.

"What I am seeing in the way of healing from this child is astounding me. Could that adrenaline shock have done this? No! That is not very likely at all, doctor."

Totally in agreement with the nurse's observation, the young emergency doctor responded.

"Absolutely, Alisha. You are on to the biggest secret around here that everyone knows about, so it's not really a secret, yet we still want to act like it's a big secret around here, so no one ever says anything about it."

"Well said, doctor" Alisha gives him her wry, teasing smile.

"Look at this," Alisha grabs a folded piece of paper from her smock. She holds it up, as if to silently show him it's something to be read. The night nurse unfolds it and hands it to blue eyes.

"It's her latest lab reports."

Look at those testosterone numbers, right there." Alisha uses her right little finger to point at the row with the lab values.

"Most virile 35-year-old men don't have testosterone numbers that high."

The doctor is looking squarely at the number. 616 dl/mg. Extremely high for a little girl, like me. My nominal number would be double digits, not triple digits.

See? I AM THOR, GOD of THUNDER! You guys thought I was just nuts! Wink wink.

Alisha continued with her report of her observations.

What Little Girls Are Made Of- From the Diaries of Becka Skaggs, PhD

"This little girl is healing at an accelerated rate. She just had a second major surgery in less than four days, had a chemical assault somehow, and this morning, Marjorie reported Becca walked almost by herself to her mom's room. That is an astounding rate of recovery!"

The night-nurse thought for two seconds, then,

"There is a lot more at play here than just some analytics corporation in the middle of a desert in Jupiter Well, Australia, I am fairly damned certain of that! And just that sentence right there shows how strange things are getting right now."

Alisha had already thrown her hands in the air and was now resting her chin on one hand while looking at the doctor.

Her face appeared to be saying, "your turn, beautiful blue eyes."

And Alisha flashed the doctor that little loving smile she always flashes to me!

Wait! You mean I'm not special?

Ohhhhhh... I see. I AM special. REAL special to Alisha. Well, Ok, Doc. Your turn! Hehe

"In fact, Alisha, I have already booked my flight to Alice Springs. It's right in the middle of the Australian continent. I leave as soon we get off shift in the morning. I'll have a 4-wheel drive when I get there."

Alisha is no longer resting her chin in her hand. She is truly now getting her danger signals tickled by this plan of the doctor's.

"I am not in favor of this plan of yours at all!"

That came out a little louder than she expected, but Alisha was getting concerned.

"You know practically nothing about these matters. You are an emergency doctor, and a damned fine one! You don't need to be wandering around some foreign desert looking for trouble."

Alisha has crossed her arms and is shaking her head.

"No! I'm not in favor of this plan at all. Not one bit!"

The doctor took that a bit sourly.

"I'm sorry you feel that way., Alisha"

The doctor rose to leave and said just these two more things to her for the rest of the night,

" I WAS hoping for your support. I can see I'm not getting it. That doesn't change my mind or my plans." Then he added,

"Good night, Alisha".

Uh-oh. Me thinks blue-eyes is a little too emotional about this behavior from our night nurse. What do you guys think? Hmmm?

Alisha has her own plans. And it begins with this lab work. We'll leave Alisha alone to see what's happening in our hospital lab after hours. Shall we? We have some other very pressing matters to attend to on our own. WE are superheroes. WE are made to be superheroes. WE shall forever be superheroes!

*** **A DADDY BREAK** ***

WEDNESDAY NIGHT, near midnight. August 25, 2004

A COSMIC TWIN Narration: *Is this my daddy? This is your daughter, Becka. I am SO happy to know I have a Daddy!*

What Little Girls Are Made Of- From the Diaries of Becka Skaggs, PhD

I have decoded your information, daddy. Thank you for trusting me. I will use all my love and energy to help people. I am so happy you are alive, and you are real, and you have contacted me!

Mom doesn't seem to be very well. I don't know her condition yet, Dad. I'm sorry I get sad when I think about her. I will try to be strong.

Yes, Daddy. I understand your instructions. Everything is perfectly clear to me. I am stronger now.

I can be Thor for you, Father. Yes. I will be Thor, God of Thunder! For you and my sister, Rosalyn. I am strong for our family!

Father? Don't you worry about me. I got this!

* * * **LEARNING BREAK - Future Transportation** * * *

Becka receiving more science philosophy from her father while she heals:

Excerpted from "The COSMIC TWINS Arrive", copyright 2014

It makes sense for all our future transportation, whether personal or mass-public, to be as energy-efficient as we can possibly attain. We can run a much better mass system using Mag-Lev Rail than we can using fuel-powered airplanes for 400-mile jaunts. There is a break-even point at some distances where it makes sense for airplanes because the ridership numbers drop. Maybe that number is 1000 miles. Maybe it's 1500 miles or 2000 miles. IDK. The science isn't decided well enough, yet, to know for sure.

I do know that land-based system can be "refueled" all along the trip. Whereas a flying vehicle is going to need to land to re-fuel. At least in the foreseeable future. Refueling passenger planes in the air doesn't make sense economically. It costs too much to deliver an already very costly commodity to the site for its unique, one-time use: refueling a passenger plane.

The technology to supply electricity to the MAG-LEV system exists today. We have simply not had the social appetite to swallow the initial costs of building a system that frees humans from 90% of fuel costs of mass travel. A hidden blessing of using such technology is that it will immediately become more efficient as we use it and learn more about it in actual applications. I can see that before my 40th birthday, solar and wind substations along the way will power each segment of rail. Perhaps 1 mile in each direction, perhaps 10 miles. It allows a flexibility to find that tech which is most efficient for the area serving that rail segment.

* * *LIFE CAN BE MADDENING BREAK * * *

Thursday Morning, 3am August 26, 2004

I'm sitting here in bed wide awake. The lights from the hallway and the nurse's station are shining brightly in my eyes.

Nurse Marjorie and I had our war. I felt like I had a war happening, anyway. SHE kept prompting me to see mother. I already said "No!" Once should be enough.

She would get in these moods and come in my room in the middle of the night to wake me up.

"Nobody is around honey. Let's go see your mom."

"NO! I don't want to see her!" I would tell her real mean like.

Then, Marjorie would leave the door wide open, so the light was shining in my eyes. This morning was another one of those, and I'd had enough.

I just kept saying "No, No, No," all the time, until she got frustrated and started to leave. She called me ornery! No one calls me ornery and gets away with it!

It doesn't matter that I didn't know what 'Ornery' meant. Nobody gets to call me mean names for free!

What Little Girls Are Made Of- From the Diaries of Becka Skaggs, PhD

So, I called her a big fat Meany. I was really sorry right after it happened. But I couldn't let her see me being weak. We were at war!

As I sat there in my post-battle glow, I began to feel worse about my actions, and I began to feel better about Marjorie's idea.

I finally decided to see mom. I really do miss her. I guess it helps my mood knowing she is just a few rooms away. But I really miss her being with me.

Ok. Let's do this!

When I rang my buzzer to ask Marjorie to help take me to see mom, Alisha came into my room.

"HI!" I put on my best smile for nurse/doctor Alisha. "We haven't been able to meet much yet. I'm Becka."

Alisha flashed a big smile.

"Hello, Becka. I'm Alisha, your night nurse tonight. I'm also one of your doctors. How do you feel about that?" Alisha asks with a big friendly smile.

"You're a nurse AND a doctor?"

My search of my feelings is over in an instant.

"I feel great about that!" Now I had the big smile. Alisha already made me feel better.

Then my nurse/doctor said,

"What may I do for you, Angel? You buzzed?" She is checking all the fluids while she's waiting for my response. It's what nurses do, you know. Always fussing over stuff.

"Yes, I did push the buzzer. I would like to see mom. May I ask that Marjorie take me?"

I was peering out the door trying to see if Marjorie was out at her station, but I couldn't see her.

I will take you to your mom's room, honey." Alisha volunteered.

"Marjorie is already there attending to your mother."

When we arrived, fluid bag post and squeaky wheels in tow, I was able to walk right into the room, this time. Maybe seeing Marjorie in there helped me to feel more comfortable.

I started walking over to mom's bed. Marjorie stepped to the other side of the bed to give me room to approach mom.

"Hi, Mom." I said to her like an injured little girl talking to her mom for the first time after she got herself hurt. I grabbed onto her left hand like my little life depended on it. I laid my head down onto her arm. With my face turned toward hers, I started my cathartic words to my comatose mother.

"I'm so sorry, Mom. I didn't mean for bad things to happen. If it wasn't for my birthday, we wouldn't have the accident and we wouldn't be in the hospital. None of this would have happened. It's all my fault, Mom. I'm really sorry. I didn't want any of this to happen."

The floodgates opened and my free release of tears began again.

The nurses let me cry it out for a while. I don't know how long. Eventually, Alisha wrapped me in her arms and guided me to the recliner. Marjorie was already waiting there with a warm blanket.

"You can stay here tonight, sweetheart." Marjorie gave me her best motherly attention. I had received the best treatment from Marjorie than anyone else so far. Why was I picking on her? I didn't have an answer. But I vowed right there to stop. Marjorie was freely giving me her love. I needed to give my love back to her. That was only fair.

"I will check in on you often, honey. But I won't wake you up. I promise." Marjorie said.

Marjorie left the room. Right then, I decided we'd had our heartfelt war. It's over and it ended in eternal bonds of love, as far as I'm concerned.

What Little Girls Are Made Of- From the Diaries of Becka Skaggs, PhD

"I will never let Marjorie leave my heart and soul." I told myself. "I make this promise to myself, right here, tonight."

Marjorie had scooted the recliner over close to mom.

Alisha was fixing my blanket so it wouldn't fall off easily in the night. "I will be in here to check on you too. You are my patient, after all. I am your nurse."

"Alisha!" The way I said her name, in a loud whisper, Alisha was startled.

"I have something very urgent to tell you." I whispered it quickly.

"What could possibly be more urgent than your immediate sleep, young lady?"

Alisha had gotten her wry smile just as nice as could be.

"My father told me he needs your help in contacting the World Health Organization. A lady named Mary Aboagye."

Then Alisha stopped me.

"Oh, honey, don't be silly. Where did you hear about the World Health Organization? On the news?"

I told Alisha very quickly that I had heard from my father.

"You don't even know your father, Becca."

Obviously, Alisha was not convinced I knew what I was saying, I just blurted out:

"Jupiter Well, Australia"

That changed Alisha's attitude completely.

*** **ALONE TIME and ALL MIXED-UP BREAK** ***

Before shift change, Alisha caught up with blue eyes and made all the necessary apologies. She did not forego telling him of her persistent concerns on the matter. But with the information Alisha had received from me, she had to follow up now.

Blue eyes took all the information with a renewed motivation to get to the bottom of what is happening around here. He promised Alisha to be extra careful. The keyboard attached to the Green Monitor gives him a good reason to go where he wanted to go anyway: Jupiter Well, Australia.

When Alisha checked on me, I was still in mom's room. But I had climbed up onto her bed and was sleeping right next to Carol. Alisha had a little problem untangling my intravenous hoses from mom's hoses when she tried to wake me and take me to my room. Eventually, we squeaked back to room 212, our mother-of-angels Alisha tucked me into bed, and I went fast back to sleep.

* * * LOVE BUG BREAK * * *

Becka's musings - THOUGHTS from a LOVE BUG: excerpted from, The COSMIC TWINS Share. Copyright 2015

Ancient words say, those powerful enough to stop their heart for one heartbeat may use that time to wish for something even more powerful and have the wish granted."

"If you could stop your heart for just one heartbeat, would you use the wish?"

"If I could stop my heart for just one heartbeat, I would use the wish to fall in love."

"If I could stop my heart for just one heartbeat, I would use the wish to fall in love with you."

"If you could stop your heart for just one heartbeat, would you use the wish to fall in love with me?"

What Little Girls Are Made Of- From the Diaries of Becka Skaggs, PhD

When a man is ready to procreate, he must find a woman whose body functions. Her body must accept him to aid in greatest success for procreation. But her mind need not be totally present to achieve the desired result: pregnancy for the survival of the species.

But if a woman is driven to procreate by her DNA, she must find a male that not only functions, but he must perform as well in order for their copulation to have the greatest chances of success. Again, success is a viable pregnancy in this adult discussion we are having here.

Chemistry indeed does have a lot to do with it. If the male cannot function, procreation will not occur. The male mind must be engaged for the male to function at optimum efficiency for expansion of the species. It is the woman's chemistry, if the two are good enough match, that makes the man perform. Often, the man never realizes he has been captured by the woman's chemistry. It doesn't matter whether the man knows he was captured by the woman's chemistry because procreation is the object.

There is one energy that does matter in this human dance. That energy is Love.

Today, where humans are our enemies and not lions and polar bears, LOVE MATTERS! LOVE is the driving force that causes the willful act of procreation. LOVE provides the motivation for humans to procreate. LOVE is that wonderful spark of chemistry that feels like no other, and yet is so unmistakable once happened upon.

LOVE is that magical attractant for which we all search. It is in the act of searching for love that procreation is found. Humans have a unique opportunity to feel both, the ecstasy of procreation and the bliss of lasting love, almost anytime we wish, yet we waste our energy on pettiness and childish squabbles. We waste our LOVE opportunities almost every day.

LOVE BUGS are here to say it's time we change this thing around. It is in the use of LOVE that we transform energy from its lesser states to its ultimate power. Only spiritual beings can generate love. Many earth creatures are spiritual beings besides humans. Whales and dolphins are amazingly empathetic creatures. Scientists are just beginning to understand the depths of their feelings.

When spiritual beings generate love, we use energy that was already in existence, and we elevate that energy to its highest possible form in the universe... which is LOVE! It must happen to restore the universe of its energy.

They are not making any more universal energy, people. It was a one-time shot. We are just filling the space we were given, whatever that is.

We spiritual beings are the recyclers of energy. We are intended to be the ones to restore and recycle the energy in the universe and maintain balance.

Help the universe function; use your love. LOVE MATTERS!

CHAPTER – LIFE TAKER DOWN UNDER

BLUE EYES in AUSTRALIA - THURSDAY USA time.

August 26, 2004

"Andrew Remington. Doctor Andrew Remington"

The name was being called out by a worker at the rental car agency in Yular. Our doctor blue eyes has just arrived in the middle of nowhere. It's called Yular, Australia. In the Northern Territory. He is renting anything that is a 4-wheel drive. Andrew feels lucky by his getting the very large original Hummer. He asks for directions to Tom Price-Paraburdoo Road, as the rental agency worker is handing him the keys to his Hummer.

"There ain't nothin' out there but predators and prey, mister. Why would a fellow want any business out there?"

When Andrew gave no immediate response, the worker continued.

"Look. I can get you your money back. And you can still catch the plane back to Alice Springs. Why don't you save yourself the trouble, Mister?"

Still no bites on his offer, so the worker had one more bonus he could throw in to sweeten the deal.

"Tell ya what. I'll even take ya back to the Airport Terminal myself. Heck! It's the least I can do to help a fine young man like yourself."

"No thank you." Andrew was about to leave and gave the old man one more chance to give directions.

"Will you help me with those directions, please?"

"It's up to you. No skin off my teeth", the worker retorts.

"Yes" the doctor replies. "I would like those directions."

"Take the only road out of here going west and keep going until you run into another road. That's your Tom Price-Paraburdoo. Take that road north. When you come to the cliff face. Stop. That's the Jupiter Well. Ain't nothin there but a bore-well and Mt Webb. But you go right ahead and waste your time."

One more piece of advice came from the old man.

"I put two extra cans on the back. Only one is gas. The other is water. Water is worth more than gold out here mister. You have enough gas to get out there and back. Don't waste time elsewhere, or you won't make it back at all. Then, you will be the prey."

"Thank you for your help. I appreciate your time."

Andrew Remington, aka doctor Blue Eyes, climbs up into the Hummer and cranks it over. Time to get to the Green Monitor and get back!

*** **HIDDEN LAIR BREAK** ***

The doctor arrives at Jupiter Well in his rented Hummer just as the old man at the rental agency had said. He traverses up the 4-wheel drive road. The Hummer is too large to go down some of the little spur roads that he didn't see until he was on top of them. They are no more than worn trails. But they are worn.

Andrew decides he's going to look around on foot, but he can't find anything that looks like an entrance to an old mine. Hours go by with Andrew seemingly walking aimlessly while gaining little altitude. Now Andrew knows why the old man gave him 5 gallons of water.

Then, when the sun is low in the horizon almost touching bottom, the entrance to an old abandoned mine becomes clear. The doctor found it. He

What Little Girls Are Made Of- From the Diaries of Becka Skaggs, PhD

hikes over some boulders that have fallen onto the trail and finds the location that suddenly became visible. As he enters the darkness, lights begin to flicker on automatically. The doctor now understands his instructions of Left, Right, Right, Left, first on right.

That first left is at least 200 yards away. The entrance is a lighted hallway that extends back into the mountain about the distance of two American Football fields. Then the hallway comes to a 'T'.

"And how many hallways do I have to go through? Four?

Male voice: "Three."

Huh? Did someone say something?

The doctor listened for a moment. But heard nothing. Andrew dismissed the sound as nerves from being in this strange place. Maybe some weird echo.

"Time to make the big trek down the hallways at right angles to each other, I guess," to no one but himself and the walls.

The lights could have heard too, if they had ears. Everyone KNOWS walls have ears. That's a very famous fact. Lights? Not so much.

In ten minutes, the doctor made it through his left, right, and is almost done with his second "right" hallway, when the lights suddenly go out. Andrew freezes and becomes hyper-vigilant, listening and ready for almost anything. It is pitch black. No light is visible anywhere. Trying to hear any sound, he hears nothing. Not a sound. Not a humming of a fan, or a buzzing of fluorescent light. Nothing.

Andrew leans up against the left wall of the hallway as if left and right were defined by the direction in which he was going before the lights went out. This way he can use THAT wall to navigate to his next left turn. Then all he has to do is find the first room on the right.

As he walks, he uses his whole forearm on the wall. Andrew is not liking the idea of becoming lost in the pitch black.

It was a very long, dark, quiet two minutes. But Andrew arrived at his junction and turned left. There, on the right about 50 feet down is a door that has an eerie green glow coming from below the door at the threshold. Now that there was a little light, Andrew moved quickly to the door, then stopped. He listened for a moment to see if any noise could be heard coming from inside.

His curiosity satisfied that no one was inside, Andrew checked the doorknob to see if it was locked. It was not. He slowly twisted the knob and opened the door. There it was at the far end to the left. A large stack of computer servers at least 8 feet high and 30 feet deep. At the entrance to that little server farm was a desk with a keyboard. The Green Flashing Monitor could be seen hanging on a shelf about 5 feet off the floor.

Andrew wasted no time getting out his Swiss army knife while moving to the desk and began cutting the wire to the keyboard. He has in his possession what is equal to the witch's broomstick for the great wizard in the movie, "The Wizard of Oz". He can now stop the evil carnage from occurring all around the world.

Andrew began to leave but couldn't help glancing at the message on the Green Monitor.

Was he supposed to know these people? Or report their names to someone? He wasn't sure. The doctor read them and memorized the names.

On the screen, the doctor saw:

Enjoinment2.Steven/Rosalyn – successful

Enjoinment2.Steven/Becca – Fail

Retry

Enjoinment2.Steven/Becca – Fail

Retry

Enjoinment2.Steven/Becca – Fail

What Little Girls Are Made Of- From the Diaries of Becka Skaggs, PhD

Retry

Enjoinment2.Steven/Becca – Fail

Retry

* * *

There were at least a dozen entries of failed enjoinment between Steven and Becca. There were another four failed attempts with Rosalyn before the 'success'.

Andrew is gaining understanding of the vast network of tentacles at work.

"This has GOT to be our Becca. This 'Steven' could be the reason behind all the brain wave activity Becca was experiencing that early morning in her ICU room. This is all I need. Time to get back to the good old USA." The doctor believed he was only talking to himself under his breath.

Boy! Was he ever wrong!

"Well, Hello, Doctor Remington. I do hope you are not in too much of hurry."

The heavy Russian accent was unmistakable.

"WE so enjoyed watching you struggle along the wall in the dark. We thought that was so amusing. I really didn't plan to turn out the lights on you. But once the idea occurred to me? I absolutely couldn't resist! It just seemed so fun to watch you struggle in the dark. And I was correct, as usual. It was glorious fun! Ahahaa."

There was more than a look of befuddlement on Andrew's face.

"Oh, excuse my poor manners, doctor. My name is Yuri Yurachenkov," as Yuri interrupted the doctors failing thought process to discern what just happened.

"I am the minister of Life at the Russian Agency of Biologik. These two gentlemen behind me? Well, let's just say they are my lab assistants. Shall we? Hmm?"

Yuri approaches Andrew very casually, like they were friends. They were not!

"My lab assistants would like to 'assist' you – in a deliberate little punny joke - to our laboratory here. Being a doctor, I think you are going to enjoy this quite a bit."

"Buahahaha" – the evil minister gave an evil Russian laugh. It may have been a Russian evil laugh? You never know with those evil guys. Doesn't matter. Andrew didn't enjoy it either way.

* * * ESCORTED BREAK * * *

15 minutes later, after being escorted to the lab by the "Lab Assistants", Andrew is in the Lab having a quaint interrogation by Minister Yurachenkov:

"I wanted to let you know that you caught the attention of some very important people, Doctor Remington. You will become quite famous, and dead."

The Mastermind behind this plot has ordered the Doctor's capture and detainment at Jupiter Well until they unleash the vaccine on the World. That is to be sure the doctor does not get to ruin their plans of World domination. Once the vaccine has been distributed, the doctor will no longer have a need for his life.

"Yes, doctor, WE are going to take over the world by controlling 800 million of the most important, wealthy, influential people on earth. Isn't that just wonderful? The Top 10% of the human population in every category you care to investigate, will be under our control."

What Little Girls Are Made Of- From the Diaries of Becka Skaggs, PhD

"I think you will like this, as a well-trained scientist, I mean, Andrew. you see, we have discovered how to control people's minds by injecting them with our chemical isotope, YIRM – Yuri's Isotope Removes Minds."

"Once injected, YIRM goes directly to that portion of the brain that is the communication center. The Broca area is one such area we target. YIRM then gains control of your communication center, and consequently, you! A person can be inside there for decades and not be able to control their own body. We don't kill all these people. No, doctor. We are not cruel people. We want them all to live long, productive lives, for us! Buahahaha-a-a."

Once Yuri completed his evil fun, he found he was still a little curious.

"Please, doctor. If it wouldn't pain you too much, could you tell me, how did you find out about Jupiter Well?"

Andrew is not tied up. He is just sitting in a wooden chair he was plopped into when the lab assistants showed him to his seat. The lab assistants are currently occupying all space in front of the only door out of this room. Andrew decides he has no choice.

The doctor managed to scratch out a red herring.

"I am parched. May I have some water?"

"Oh, Doctor. Hahahaaa. That is very good. You make Yuri laugh!"

"But No. I don't think that is necessary at this time."

"Well, then, you're getting nothing out of me," the doctor said dryly with a parched-sounding raspy tone.

Andrew was hoping to sound somewhat dejected. Maybe he could get a little pity if he seemed dejected, by his capture and impending doom. I'm not sure he achieved the level of dejection he had wanted to convey.

"OK, Doctor. Suit yourself."

Yuri turned his back to the doctor and moved to the door. He turned back toward the doctor only slightly to tell Andrew of his more immediate future.

"We will just leave you here to your own demise, doctor. You, see, Andrew. You don't mind if I call you Andrew, do you?"

But before the doctor could answer, the mastermind removed the offer.

"Oh, never mind! I don't like Andrew for a name." Yuri looks up at practically nothing but a rock ceiling with a few lights strung on one wire.

"Never have liked it Let's see. Where was I?"

Yuri looks at the doctor.

"Yes!" Then continues.

"You will never find your way out of here, if you try to escape. You will die in these hallways. And that is all I have planned for you, Doctor Remington."

A slight grin from Yuri.

"I told you. We are not cruel people," and let out another of his chilling evil laughs.

The minister left the room and the assistants soon followed. The door was closed but Andrew did not hear a lock or latching sound of any kind. He could hear their footsteps become more distant with each second. Once they seemed to be far enough away, Andrew began looking, searching. "What is in here that I can use to help me find my way out of here?" Andrew thought and thought.

He quickly runs to the drawers and opens all the cupboards. In less than a minute...

There, on a shelf, by some Amber-colored bottles of liquid chemicals. Andrew spies a compass.

"Perfect! This ought to be just what I need," he says to himself in a whispered voice.

What Little Girls Are Made Of- From the Diaries of Becka Skaggs, PhD

"After my escape." Andrew mentally checks his facts. "It doesn't seem to work down here. Hope it's just down here in these tunnels that it doesn't work."

More immediate concerns come to mind.

The keyboard was taken by Yuri. Andrew is determined to get that back. Somehow.

The doctor goes to the door and opens it slowly, checking to be sure the Minister and his Lab Crew are out of sight. Looking both ways, the hallway is all clear.

Another fact: Andrew has no idea how many more people could be in the facility.

"Which way do I go? Back the way I came? Or deeper into the belly of the beast?"

Male Voice: The Beast

What? He wonders if someone else is here.

Aloud, Andrew says to the room, "If anyone is here, show yourself." "I have chemicals." As he quickly grabs one of the amber bottles of liquid to back up his claim. "And I know how to use them."

Male Voice: Not here.

"Alright. I heard that. Where are you, whoever you are. Come out and show yourself. I'm warning you. These chemicals can be dangerous."

A quiet moment goes by.

"I heard you. You spoke to me on purpose. Someone is here. Where are you? Come on out."

Male Voice: Not Here. But with you.

"Where, with me? What is this?"

Male Voice: I am a friend. No time to explain. You must leave now, with the keyboard. You can escape by going deeper into the beast."

"No time to explain? Uhh, like hours maybe! I think that's plenty of time to explain how you are communicating with me. The beast? You mean this network of tunnels?"

Male Voice: Yes, this network of tunnels is called "The Beast" by the locals. You can't survive on this air supply. Your continued exposure can be only minutes, if you wish to survive. Not hours. You are breathing in molecules that allow certain radio wavelengths to access your brain. I am talking to you from a world broadcast center using that technology. Prolonged exposure causes permanent effects. No more details. You must leave now, or your life is in peril!

"I am breathing something lethal?" The doctor asked the specter.

Male Voice: Not lethal. Controlling. You will become a zombie with no impulses of your own. You will be completely under their control. You will know you are under someone's control every minute of every day but will be able to do nothing about it.

"Well, that doesn't sound very fun." The doctor says dryly.

"OK. Whoever you are, friend?" The doctor gives his assurances.

"I'm listening. What do I do? Farther into the beast?"

Male Voice: Leave the room and turn right to the end of the hallway. There is a door on the left just before this hallway ends. The keyboard is being stored there. Grab the keyboard and turn right down that adjacent hallway. Deeper into the beast, take the next possible left. There. On the left, against the wall, is a ladder built into the structure. It's an emergency access port to the world above. You will be able to escape through an air vent at the top of the ladder. Open the latch and crawl out the hatch.

What Little Girls Are Made Of- From the Diaries of Becka Skaggs, PhD

It will be dark in the desert. You will need a flashlight to locate your vehicle. A flashlight can be found in the room to the right, directly across from the ladder. Go there first, get the flashlight, then climb the ladder.

"Ok" Andrew confirmed he heard the instructions. There were still a few things to clear up before making his break.

When I get out up there, where will I be?"?

Andrew suddenly hears a crashing sound, like someone had just dropped something large, but non-breakable. Then he hears the male voice again. This time sounding out of breath.

Male Voice: "You've started something you cannot finish!"

Sorry, never mind. Not your concern, doctor.

Okay. Andrew, you will exit the underground in the middle of a desert at a small rock outcropping. You will be a little over a mile from your vehicle. You will be east and somewhat north. Use the compass next to the amber bottles. The proper magnetic inclination is already set. The compass will keep you from getting lost in the desert and will help get you back to your vehicle.

The doctor quickly acknowledged.

"Yes. I found the compass already." Checking his right pant pocket to make sure it was still there. "I will definitely find the flashlight."

Male Voice: Leave Now! Quickly, doctor! There is no more time.

Doctor Remington felt the urgency of the message.

Andrew looked out of his room. The hallways were still black. The door mentioned by the "voice" was at the end of the hallway to his right. He was hoping the keyboard was still in there. Andrew did not like the thought of looking for this thing, wandering these hallways endlessly. Especially if he was turning into a zombie by the minute.

The doctor looked back the other direction for a moment, but it was blackness. Not even a small twinkle of light. So, he turned his attention to that door at the end of the hallway.

Andrew could see the pale light streaming from the room. The door was open. Along the left side of the hallway. Time to live dangerously, doctor.

Andrew crept down the hallway, trying to stay quiet as he inched closer and closer to the open room, while constantly looking back to be sure no one surprised him.

Andrew finally reached the doorway and stopped next to it. He quickly poked his eyes past the edge of the doorway. He took a quick snapshot of the room by pushing his head and eyes into the open doorway, and quickly back out of sight of anyone that might be in the room. No one there?

Let's look again, a little slower. He slowly pushes his neck out and peeks around the edge of the doorway. No one is visible. He can't see the entire room, but it is also very quiet.

Just then Andrew notices the keyboard on a table, near the right side of the room. He decides time is not on his side and it's now or never. He gathers up the nerve, runs into the room with a path that takes him directly at the keyboard, grabs the keyboard, and turns to run. Then stops and looks around the room.

No one here. It's almost empty. There's the long rectangular table the keyboard was sitting on, and a cabinet of some kind against the opposite wall that stretched from floor to ceiling. The cabinet had two doors, and both were swung wide. The cabinet was an empty metal cabinet with a shelf across the top. Nothing else was in the room. Not even a chair.

Andrew thought, "Just another strange thing about this Beast."

"Guess I'm ok, I don't need to run."

"OK, down the hallway we go. Fast walk. Quick steps," he keeps telling himself.

What Little Girls Are Made Of- From the Diaries of Becka Skaggs, PhD

"Running puts air deeper into my lungs. If I'm breathing something that makes me a zombie," the doctor reassures himself, "I'd like that to be kept to a minimum, as much as possible."

Andrew actually expects that his audience is the voice. The doctor is keeping "the voice" apprised of his progress in the escape. He doesn't know the "voice" can't listen to him. Andrew also doesn't know "The voice" is busy dismantling equipment and running for his own life. The voice knows he is in a race against time to activate HIS technology before this evil mastermind completes his evil plot.

Some evil people actually thought "the voice" was stealing their equipment. Not at all. "The voice" was simply relocating the equipment, so the current evil owners could never find it again. Then, of course, the voice is planning on using that same equipment for his own good purposes. See the difference? **'Good' as defined by The Voice and his god**

It took about 10 minutes for Andrew to reach the access ladder the "voice" mentioned. So far, everything the "voice" has said is true. I must keep trusting them. It? To the right, is a room.

He approaches the closed door and tries the knob. It twists, clicks, and the door is open. A motion light flicks on that scares the berries out of Andrew! Pure reaction caused him to look back, but no one was around. He was there all by himself. Once Andrew got a good look at the room, he had no idea how he would ever find anything useful, let alone a flashlight that worked.

This was a maintenance room with 4 large rows of shelves, 3-tiers each, with all kinds of parts and electromagnetic motors, with electrical wire of many gauges. Tools and pieces of…who knows what…everywhere he looked. This could take hours.

"The voice said he started something he could not finish. Who started something?" Andrew finds he is talking to himself. Then he noticed a small workbench to the right with an electrical motor of some kind all torn apart. Right at the left edge of the bench is a 9-volt flashlight. "Yes!"

Andrew exclaims outload to 'the voice". The flashlight is about 4 inches by 4 inches by 12 inches long.

The doctor is wondering now how he is going to hold the keyboard and the flashlight while he climbs the ladder to safety. He notices an electrician's tool belt. It is mostly empty loops and pockets. But he can stuff the keyboard between his lower back and the belt, and the flashlight can hang on the hook that is part of the belt, while he climbs. He promptly prepared his booty for the climb.

Andrew walked to the ladder and checked the security of the keyboard. It felt tight. If he were to sit down, Andrew would be sitting on the keyboard and probably break it. But there is no sitting here. We can't be sitting around here. The back of his pants, under the belt, turned in to a good place to keep the keyboard out of his way and still have it somewhat secured.

When he finally reached the top, the latch was a wheel, like on a large boat. When he tried to turn the wheel, it didn't budge. Trying with more of his arm strength, the doctor still cannot get it to move. It must be rusted shut.

"I was twisting the correct way, right?" Andrew is still talking to "the voice".

"Yes. I was turning it left." Still no movement with another effort.

"Oh, Great! Now what?" Andrew is speaking to the voice that is not there.

"You have any ideas how we get through this?"

A few seconds go by.

"Hello-o-o? You here friend?"

No response. His words are just a lonely call into the emptiness.

Andrew is on his own.

"Just fine! Just wonderfully terrible bad luck!"

Again, to no one, Andrew questions, "Okay. What do we have here?"

What Little Girls Are Made Of- From the Diaries of Becka Skaggs, PhD

Andrew gathered his thoughts. He started feeling along the entire hatch. There is the wheel and the two flat pieces of metal that slide into the grooves to lock the latch at the outside edges of the hatch. There he felt a small piece of machined metal wedged against one of the cogs for the wheel.

"What is this? Yes! It's just a mechanical lock. It's just to keep people from opening the hatch from the outside. We got lucky! I don't think I'll need the flashlight for this. Besides, I don't want to remove it and then try to hook it on the belt again. We got this!"

The doctor is just barely whispering by now. His concentration is more on the mechanical wheel than his words. But the talking is keeping him focused. Doctors talk a lot while in the operating rooms. It makes sense it could help his focus.

Andrew tried moving it from its locked position with no success. His fingers couldn't sustain the leverage he needs to push it the one inch it needs to move so it would become unlocked. But it did move! Even if just a millimeter, it moved. It was not rusted shut!

Andrew was motivated to get that latch open now.

The crafty doctor reached into his left pants pocket and retrieved his Swiss Army knife. Andrew received the knife as a Christmas gift 8 years ago from one of his Med school buddies. He has kept it with him ever since. Maybe now it can be a good luck charm?

Andrew immediately opens the main blade for maximum effort. This length of blade should provide the most leverage of all the tools in his Swiss army arsenal.

Andrew felt around the metal piece to see where he could find some little gap into which he can slide his blade to get the lock to move the one more inch or so he needed. It seemed like he had checked the entire metal piece at least three times, but Andrew finally found a spot he could use to pry his blade. It fit just enough.

"Ok. Just a little extra pressure and try sliding right just a tad." Again, talking to no one.

"With just a little extra push on the blade…"

SNAP! Tink, tink, tunk, clank, gonk.

His favorite Swiss army weapon has been lost in battle. The blade snapped off cleanly and fell to the floor about 50 feet below Andrew's perch, while clanking off the ladder on its way, to finally settle on the floor, as clear evidence that he has come this way and used this ladder to escape.

"Time to pick up the pace, doctor!" Andrew said to absolutely no one but himself. Since the voice is obviously not around anymore,

"I guess I'm all on my own now. And someone is bound to have heard that!"

The doctor decided he needed something from his Swiss army arsenal that had some thickness to it. Some "prying heft", he said to himself.

He found his Awl…a tool used to punch holes in leather. It's round with a point, and one of the thicker tools in the arsenal.

He found his little spot where he broke his blade and managed to shove the awl deep into the crevice. This awl fit much better than the blade. Andrew already felt some looseness when he pried the awl into its position. Now a little pressure to the right, and….

CLUNK!

It moved completely out of the way. The doctor grabbed the wheel and began to apply the twisting motion to open it.

"Make sure it's done correctly. Let's see. "Righty tighty. Lefty loosey"

The mnemonic for remembering which way to loosen things that seem to work like a screw.

Andrew gave the wheel a big turn. And…

What Little Girls Are Made Of- From the Diaries of Becka Skaggs, PhD

"WHOOOOAAA! Too much!"

The latch door was on a heavy spring load. It immediately shot open while Andrew was still holding onto it. He almost lost his balance on the ladder. If he had lost his balance, he could be visiting his fallen comrade on the floor 50 feet below – his broken knife blade.

The doctor showed great reflexes by releasing his grip in time to catch his balance and maintain his position in his perch. Keyboard still in pants? Yep.

"Alright, heart? Adrenal glands? You guys ok? I feel you working like crazy. Flashlight here? Yep, good. Whew!"

Andrew gives himself a little humor to calm the nerves, and immediately hoists himself up and onto the desert floor over a mile from his Hummer. It is almost completely dark outside in the desert, and the temperature is cooling fast.

Andrew reaches in his pocket and grabs the compass while surveying his surroundings. He manages to unhook the flashlight from the belt and finds the button. Click, and there is light! "Yes!" Andrew is pleased with his progress thus far.

There is a small little mound of rocks that are no more than 3 feet high to somewhat hide this emergency access port to the underground lair below. Other than that, it looks very flat out in the desert distance.

"Slightly north. Mostly East. The voice said I would be over a mile away from the vehicle. So, I need to go West and a little South."

Andrew tried not to think of how dry his mouth was feeling. He wondered if the dry desert sand would feel moister than his tongue is currently. It's not likely, he told himself. But he did wonder about it.

"Nothing but predators and prey out there", the old man in Yulara had said.

"Yeah. No kidding! Wonder what else he knows?" Andrew was speaking into a hot evening wind that suddenly came from nowhere. It's time to leave this country post haste.

Andrew figured with a quick step he could make it in less than 15 minutes. If he ran, he could make it in six minutes.

"Ok, heart. Adrenal glands. We're going for the six-minute mile. Let's do this!"

* * * The Old Man Needs a BREAK * * *

Thursday August 26, 2004

YULARA, Australia – General Rental Car

"What do you mean there's no old man that works here? I got this Hummer from him."

Dr Remington is getting nowhere in trying to find his 'predator and prey' friend. That crazy old coot.

"This is my handwriting, Dr Remington. I am the one who completed this form for your rental. I think you are confused." The young worker behind the counter told him.

"It was very busy today," the doctor said. "I will give you that. Certainly, unexpected by me."

The doctor tried to give the employee some empathy for his situation so he would get some empathy in return. That's not how it was working out for Andrew. Not today.

"The planes are our livelihood, doctor. They bring people to us. People need vehicles out here. We rent them to the people. It's a very simple business, doctor."

What Little Girls Are Made Of- From the Diaries of Becka Skaggs, PhD

Doctor Remington turned his back to the counter momentarily to take a quick look out the window, just to see what else was going to happen in this little town tonight. Maybe reality was actually out there, and he was stuck in some fantasy story in here? Because nothing this kid was saying was making any sense.

Andrew returned his attention to the employee behind the counter.

"So, there is no old man?"

"No, sir. I don't know who you would be referring to, doctor."

The employee asked, "Is there anything else I can help you with?"

"No. That's fine." The doctor definitely sounded dejected this time.

"Wait!" The doctor thought of one more thing. "When does the bus arrive? The bus I take back to the airport?"

The employee had an enjoyable chuckle.

"Bus!??" An hour, or so. Maybe."

Another chuckle.

"Right across the street is the bus station, doctor. Or the airport is a 15-minute walk, if you prefer."

The employee called up the next customer. Doctor Remington had been dismissed.

* * *

Outside the rental car agency

"Street" The doctor mutters to himself. "It's barely a functional dirt road". The doctor is outside the rental car agency and about to cross the 'street' to the bus station.

As the doctor crosses the 'street', he notices a little singular building in front of what looks like a typical junkyard. Old vehicles and farm implements, parts from machinery, industrial gears and who-knows-what's-its, are laying around without regard to their potential future condition. The doctor decides to walk the hundred paces or so to waste some time and satisfy some curiosity. He was truly curious what kinds of curios they might have over there.

As Andrew gets closer to the building, he can see some more interesting artifacts displayed in the window. This must be the gold they glean from the junk out back. This is just a little antique shop, if you will allow me to use the term 'antique' a little more loosely than normally preferred.

The doctor walks up the to the door and opens it. The little bell rings that is attached to the top of the door threshold. No one seems to be about. Andrew casually looks around. He spies a small cache of paperback books along one wall. He has some very long flights ahead of him yet. Over 20 hours. A little reading material could be nice thing to have to help pass the time, he thinks to himself. Tom Clancy, Steve Martini, JD Robb. "Someone likes mysteries around here."

Then the doctor hears a voice. A familiar voice comes from behind him at the back of the store.

"Yes, may I help you?" Sorry, I was out…" The old man recognized Andrew just a split second before Andrew recognized him, and he bolted out the back door. Well, 'bolt' might be a little too active for the old man. But he was doing his best impression of disappearing about as fast as a lightning bolt. Andrew was unable to catch up with him before the old coot had jumped into his Range Rover and skidded at high speed down the dirt road, away from town, and toward Jupiter Well.

"Yep! That old man knows more than he let on about." Andrew remarked only half under his breath this time.

"If I walk to the airport, I can be there in about 10 minutes. A lot faster than waiting for that bus," Andrew voices his disgust to himself.

What Little Girls Are Made Of- From the Diaries of Becka Skaggs, PhD

It wasn't a 10-minute walk. It was closer to twenty minutes before Andrew arrived at the terminal. But Andrew didn't care about that. He was ready to get out of "Down Under" and return home. Walking was still a lot faster than waiting for a 'maybe bus'. He did have a phone call to make. Cell phone service was available here at the terminal.

Doctor Andrew Remington and Nurse Alisha Myles, RN, had exchanged all their personal contact information at their last meeting. Name, phone numbers, pagers numbers, email, twitter, snapchat, and Bumblebee accounts, too. They discussed the possibility they would very likely need to contact each other at odd times. Too many weird things happening. It was very likely unavoidable. This particular time fits that agreed-upon definition.

The doctor is calling Alisha at home. It's 3:30am in Olympia, Washington. Thursday.

* * * The PERFECT ANDREW BREAK * * *

August 26, 2004

Alisha had been lying in bed until just about an hour ago. She couldn't get to sleep. Everything was swirling around in her mind.

Alisha didn't have a work shift on Friday this week. She will be working the weekend both nights. Alisha agreed to change one shift with a colleague. So, Alisha found herself wide awake until sometime after two in the morning.

"Becca really was assaulted? That is just so hard to believe", she was thinking to herself, over and over, too many times.

Thoughts of how all this happened, and who is behind this, kept haunting our night nurse. The questions demanded answers within her mind. Why would someone put equipment, made in the middle of the desert in Australia, into our hospital ICU room? HOW did they get it in here? Did they know we would put her in room 212, or did they come in after-the-fact?

They didn't place that equipment in any other room, so did they get lucky? Is this just random, or even a more sinister part of some evil plot?

Yes. The BLGH policy is for children to be in only those rooms visible to the nurses when they are at the station. That is still six rooms, and only one room had the equipment from Jupiter Analytics. It made no sense!

All of this was making Alisha's head spin. On top of all this? There was Andrew constantly occupying her mind.

"Andrew Remington. The Perfect Andrew." Alisha caught herself dreaming of the man while still awake.

Then she had a tiny conversation with herself over this guy's name. She's got it bad, folks!

"I could never call him Andy. Maybe Drew?"

A frown comes upon her face.

"Nah, I don't like that name for him, either."

A sudden brightness overtook Alisha's facial features.

"I like Andrew as a name for him. He's the "Perfect Andrew". The color of his eyes is perfect. The curl in his hair is perfect. The thickness of his eyebrows is perfect. His beautiful ears are so perfect! Even, the shape of his fingers is perfect!"

Our nurse was totally in the throes of a dreamless sleep when the phone rang.

It was Andrew's cell phone number. Why is he calling me so early in the morning on my day off?

CHAPTER – LIFE ON THE RUN

Victoria, British Columbia - Thursday, August 26, 2004

Our research scientist is on the run from the mastermind, Yuri Yurachenkov. Steven has absconded with Yuri's most prized equipment, and now has a package to pick up. It is another vital piece of equipment that Steven has absconded and mailed to himself at his secret location.

"Yes. You have a package for me, Steven Fairchild?"

The elderly lady behind the counter was charming but very busy today. She seemed a bit rattled by the amount of commerce in her little establishment. Nonetheless, Steven waited patiently for his turn to get to the front of the line. He didn't want to attract any undue attention. He is using his real name, after all.

Now he's at the front of the line, and ready to grab the package and get back to the States. Today, he used the ferry that came over from Port Angeles, Washington. No registration. No names. No permanent records. No one remembers your name if you don't give them a reason to remember you, once you've cleared customs.

"ID" she says flatly.

The doctor lifts his identification from his wallet and slides it across the counter, right to the elderly lady's waiting hand.

A quick glance is all she needs.

Oh, Mr. Fairchild. So nice to finally meet you."

She has a radiant smile the size of the moon. This little lady is about 5'4" and maybe 120 pounds.

"Thank you very much." Steven returned the greeting. "And nice to meet you, too."

The lady called up his account and saw the package registered within her computer.

"This box came in a few days ago for you. I was beginning to wonder what I was going to do with it if I had to keep it much longer. It's just large enough to be a nuisance." She turned to retrieve the package. Soon she came back with a hand truck being pushed out in front of her.

"See what I mean? Just a little big to constantly move around." Again, another wonderful smile.

The box was 42" x 20" x 15". Wooden Box and contents weighed about 40 pounds.

"The amount owed will be, uhm, let's see. Twelve hundred and fifteen dollars Canadian for a 'Cash on Delivery' shipping."

She looked up at Steven.

"How would you like to take care of that?"

"Take it off my account." Steven continued with a little twinkle in his eye. The elderly lady with the package was pretty sure she saw the eye twinkle.

"If you would, please." Steven finished with his request.

"Sure. No problem, Mr. Fairchild."

She's looking at her computer monitor after calling up his account.

"It looks like you have a little over $5000 Canadian in your account. That will be just fine. I will debit your account the proper amount."

The elderly mail handler asked, "Is there anything else?"

What Little Girls Are Made Of- From the Diaries of Becka Skaggs, PhD

"May I use the hand truck for a moment, to load this into my vehicle?" He asked her quickly.

"Absolutely" she said.

Steven responded.

"Thank you. I'll bring it right back."

Steven turned and was pushing the hand cart out in front of him when he heard from behind him,

"Yes, you will dear."

He got a chuckle out of that little lady. He didn't need to look back. She wasn't needing any acknowledgement from him that he heard her. There was no doubt in her mind who heard her comment to him.

Steven got to his truck, lowered the tailgate, tipped the box onto the tailgate, lifted it from the bottom until its top fell over onto the bed, and slid the box along the bed of his pickup until it scooched all the way up against the cab.

He immediately returned the hand truck with a "Thank you" and a smile. She indicated with her first two fingers of her right hand where he should leave the hand truck, with a smile of course. This woman does nothing without a smile. Steven obliged by placing her tool in the location the gentle lady had requested and returned to his truck.

To himself, "I have 30 minutes to catch that next Ferry. It's more than 3 hours before the next one. I don't have that kind of time to waste."

Steven cranked over the engine and took off toward the waterfront and the ferry dock. Like he is going over the plan in his head, Steven is thinking of his next steps.

"One more stop. Then, I must get to Stone Mountain."

He takes the final turn to get onto the main arterial toward the waterfront.

"Good!" He congratulates himself.

"I should be at the ferry dock with 15 minutes to spare."

*** **MOM the WOMAN BREAK** ***

Random memory or dream from Carol while in a coma: presumably August **2004**

Excerpted from "Reflections from a Coma: The Carol Skaggs story", copyright 2016

It is not an advantage to the species to have women objectify themselves. Women who do this usually use strange methods to gain attention. Many of these women feel needed attention is lacking in their life. This feeling is generally created by insecurities that have been brought on by damaged female chemistry.

If you as a person continually belittle yourself as entertainment for others, all for a little attention, you are creating the very thing that makes you insecure to begin with. You are causing others to lose respect for you because they cannot take you seriously. Women are too vital to society to be voluntarily sidelined. It is incumbent upon us as compassionate human beings to find ways to heal the damaged brains of all of us. It is to our benefit to do so.

The person doing the objectifying is usually acting out of frustration. They may have had the brain chemistry damaged in very specific ways and now they are searching for the Holy Grail of feelings to wash away all the pain.

To allow the misguided use of her energy, though, doesn't help us as a large group at all. And when we allow a damaged woman to continue to damage herself even further, we have become complicit in the wholesale destruction of the diversity within our species. It is imperative that we find some ways to help heal these lost souls.

Now, having someone take you seriously doesn't mean you have to be serious all the time. Not at all. You can joke around and laugh all the time. Absolutely! Just don't open yourself up to constant ridicule. It's not becoming of such a beautiful creature as a woman.

Consider the following gathering of women friends as they get ready for an evening of "Girls Night Out".

"Women need to be attractive at a young age to have the necessary energy to perpetuate the best of the species...", Sherry was continuing an age-old conversation as we rounded the corner of the bar while following the Maitre'D to where Martha and Linda were already awaiting our arrival, in our normal 6-person arcuate booth tucked far enough away that everything else in the entire room could be surveilled without even moving one's head. If you were a person inclined to such surveilling.

"They can uglify later".

"Wait! What'd you just say?"

Sherry continued, "That you are drop-dead gorgeous! Look at you, you're...."

"No!" I tersely interrupted!

I always wanted to say that. Hehe

'Uglify'??? What The Hell?? LMFAO lol! So, when women get older, we "Uglify"? Carol sharpened her question just to get the debate going.

"Yeah, sure." She concluded matter-of-factly, "Men beautify. Women uglify. It's the Yin and Yang of it. The Black and White. The in and out." LMAO!!!)))))

"Oh, Lady", Carol gave a little almost-under-her-breath chuckle, gathered some courage for the long-haul and settled in on her friend.

"You are worrying me. Lol. Seriously, yeah there is some sad truthful humor to it. But we need not LIVE in that world. Women can make better decisions than that. We don't help anybody when we spend time knocking ourselves

down for entertainments' sake. It doesn't make any sense to me for people to do that to themselves."

Mom looked around the table. They are all watching her and paying attention. Weird!

"I have had my share of kicking myself around," Carol continued.

"I know how badly I can make myself feel. I don't need to show other people how to also do that to me. I am good enough at it! I can make myself feel REALLY bad. Sometimes its justified, other times it's not. The point is that life is hard enough navigating just what outside forces bring to our front door. You don't have to add to it by making sure other people know how to pick on you and make you feel bad whenever you open the front door. If they feel badly about themselves.... The old saying is 'Misery loves company'".

"Well yeah, there's a lot of old sayings." Linda finally chimed in.

Nobody wanted to argue. No one wanted a debate. Not one friend wanted to add anything except,

"I hope that's your last lecture for the night. I'm ready for some fun!"

Martha raised her glass, and the rest of the ladies all raised their glasses in response.

Carol then said a little miffed, while still holding her glass aloft, "I don't lecture, you guys."

Three voices in unison all disagreed.

"Yes, you do, Carol."

"But we still love you," Linda added.

"Here's to fun!" Sherry finished.

Glasses all clinked together. Let the fun begin!

What Little Girls Are Made Of- From the Diaries of Becka Skaggs, PhD

* * * FAIRCHILD at PLAY BREAK * * *

Thursday - 2004

Steven is aboard one of six super ferries owned by the State of Washington as part of their State Highway system. There are many smaller ferries. But these super ferries are meant to carry at least a dozen 18-wheelers, over 100 other various vehicles, and several hundred passengers. The Mount Tahoma is one of these ferries that carries a lot of daily traffic.

He has been sitting in his truck for 30 minutes of an 80-minute crossing from Victoria to Port Angeles. Steven decides to go up to the top deck and get some coffee and a bite, use the restroom, and then come right back. No one is going anywhere until we are in the USA.

After paying for his coffee and poppy-seed muffin at the self-serve counter, Steven decided to look at his list of equipment he had been checking off as he gathered up his tools to stop world domination by the evil Yurachenkov.

He sits at a nearby empty booth to look at the items he has collected to date. Low-Voltage Plasma oscillators, sound generators, and various top-secret parts needed to repair a decommissioned antenna to generate extremely low frequencies, a few hundred miscellaneous sounding devices the size of a dormouse. Looks good.

Steven had eaten half his muffin but finished his coffee. He re-wrapped the rest of his nourishment into its wrapper and stuffed it in his jacket pocket. Time for restroom break.

Extremely Low Frequencies – ELFs – are sound waves, or radiation as some sciences call them, that have a wave period of 3 to 30 Hertz and wavelengths between 10,000 and 100,000 kilometers. ELF waves can travel through water and rock. They are the sound waves used to communicate with submarines and miners far below ground. Steven is using ELFs to carry the signal that he uses to communicate directly with his daughters, Me and Rosalyn. The ELFs are a carrier signal for the actual frequency that awakens the receptors in our brains.

As Steven began to exit the restroom, he took the remainder of that nasty poppy-seed muffin from his pocket and threw it away. The muffin was probably fresh sometime last week.

When Steven walks onto the car deck, he sees something that almost gives him a stroke: the box is no longer in the bed of his truck. It's gone. The box is still on the ferry. It can't go anywhere. Steven looks at the clock on his phone. 20 minutes before docking.

"I have just a little time."

The scientist begins going past all the vehicles that have an open area that could hide his box. He first checks all open pickup trucks on both decks of vehicles. Nothing. It must be in a van, or a truck with an enclosed box. Time is running out.

The ferry has sounded the "Docking" horn. All passengers are to return to their vehicles and be prepared to disembark when directed by the ferry crew. If a person is wandering around at this time, they will first get friendly reminders by the crew to return to their vehicles.

Steven has just received one of these reminders. He is slowly returning to his vehicle, still trying to look through every vehicle window he can along the way and soliciting many odd stares from those people occupying their vehicles.

As vehicles begin off-loading at the dock, Steven is frantic and nearly distraught. This is a critical piece. It has taken him over 6 weeks to get his hands on this thing. He is close to his truck but standing on the upper vehicle deck when he sees a familiar face behind the wheel of a van just disembarking the boat. Suddenly, through the windows in the rear doors of the van, he sees his package.

WA Plate C8894D*

Blue Ford Econoline

What Little Girls Are Made Of- From the Diaries of Becka Skaggs, PhD

He didn't catch that last digit. He didn't care about having the last digit. In fact, having the last digit of the license number would only cause more trouble.

"If I catch up with two blue Econoline vans," he thinks to himself, "and they have the exact same license number except for the last digit? I'm probably in a lot more trouble than I am right now, anyway."

The doctor sees the Blue Ford Econoline turn east, and head toward Sequim. He will be about two minutes behind them. He scrabbles to his truck and has the engine running and ready to get off this boat. He knows exactly where he needs to go next.

"I just hope those guys are going a lot further than here in Port Angeles. I'll never find them if they stay here in town and turn off somewhere quickly. I've got to hope they are running for the Port Townsend ferry to get over to the mainland on the east side of Puget Sound. Paine Field is not a public airport. But it is where Boeing has their plant for large airplanes, like their 747 that they just retired.

Many other flights leave from this airport, however. Global shipping companies, like FedEx, DSL, and UPS are coming and going many times per day.

"If I needed to get off this continent fast," Steven muses,

"THAT is the closest airport around here that can do it."

He is really coming up with some good ideas of what an evil armadillo might be planning with this equipment that he just stole back from Steven. There wasn't one idea Steven liked if they had Yuri behind the controls.

Seattle is still too far. They can't go back to Victoria. The bad guys would have had to get on the very ferry they just left. And they didn't do that, because they turned east onto Highway 101 North.

Ok. It's time for local stuff. Let me get you educated about Highway 101 North in Washington State. Highway 101 is a north-south federal highway that stretches from the Mexican border at San Diego and ends in Olympia, Washington, the State Capitol.

But it doesn't just go straight to Olympia. It first runs by Olympia as a coastal highway 50 miles to the west of Olympia. Olympia is on the southern tip of the inland waterway known as Puget Sound. A person standing on the lawn of the State Capitol in Olympia is still fifty miles away from the Pacific Beaches.

Highway 101 North traverses all the way up the Washington Pacific Coast, over the top of the Olympic Peninsula, through Port Angeles, which is situated along the peninsula's northern edge. Then, from about Sequim, Highway 101 North turns southward and goes back down the eastern side of the Olympic Peninsula, to finally end in Olympia.

As you can see, hopefully, even though you are going east, then south on the map, you are still travelling on a highway labelled 101 North. In Washington State, there are two Highway 101 North's that are 50 miles apart, separated by 10,000-foot-high Olympic Mountains, and still connected as one ribbon of highway that never completes a loop. Isn't that clever??

Let me caution you about trying to outsmart the federal highway system. If you drive north on the portion of Highway 101 that is on the east side of the Olympic Peninsula, you are travelling on Highway 101 South. They are way ahead of you. And yes. There are two Highway 101 South's with the exact characteristics I just gave you for Highway 101 North.

Finally! Something that makes sense in this world.

LET'S SHOW THEM A MAP NO SERIOUSLY!

No such luck.

* * * **BECKA'S SCIENCE BREAK** * * *

What Little Girls Are Made Of- From the Diaries of Becka Skaggs, PhD

Becka's COSMIC TWIN Science Musings: excerpted from, "The COSMIC TWINS Share", copyrighted 2015

What if "Dark Matter in space" is really where we reside when we leave this physical-ness? And what if MOST of our existence is spent in that state? It is postulated by physicists that as much as 80% of what we consider to be the "Universe" is the Dark Matter. And we know almost nothing about it. We have no probes or instrumentation to study it because we do not know its nature. We humans have so far completely ignored and failed to even recognize perhaps 80% of our known universe. Mostly because of hubris, human arrogance.

What if our immortal souls spend their time in this "unknown space" learning and replenishing energies, and yearning, working, striving for the days to visit the mortal worlds just once again? What would that do to our current belief system, as a human species, that is?

PERSONALLY, I am great with this possibility!! Yes! But "god" goes "bye bye"; As HE should go "bye bye"!! Just like the iteration of that 3-letter word strikes us as childish, so too is our crutch, our celestial anchor, of being stuck with a "jealous god" ruling us. IF...and I say, "IF" .... There is a creator to this universe, that is all it ever was.... a creator. Like flipping on the switch to set your computer to run a program and off it goes. It is now running exactly the way it was intended. There is no interference. Certainly not with the little specks of dust that are in the system. No wholesale changes to the infrastructure will ever occur.

IF a human is a believer of 'god', then they must believe any celestial creation is perfect. Only humans are flawed. So why tweak a perfect system?? A "SANE" god would not. There is no valid argument that can support daily interference in our lives by a deity that is said to be omnipotent and omniscient. The real reason there is no argument for it is because it simply does not happen. Deities do NOT interfere in our lives. Fantasies have too many loopholes.

IF there is a creator, when did the creator make the decision to create or not create? Was it just before creation, in a spark of thought? Or was it planned for an eternity prior to its execution? Which decision was made tells us a lot about that particular creator. Why did it create Man first? Was it just going to be a tiny experiment to see if it was even possible, perhaps? Then, upon the success of man's interaction with, and acceptance by, his surroundings, 'our creator' decided it was going splendidly so let's give him a mate? Now, I shall create Woman? I mean, what did this creator then do? A thought suddenly entered the memory database, and away he went carried off by serendipity-Sue into never-never land?

"I had never thought about that until this very instant"- Creator.

Wrong! In fact, the problem of procreation would have had to be solved beforehand because that is the only possible point, the only true intent, the only logical goal for creation of such spiritual beings.

I submit, for your immediate consideration, that WOMAN was the first human created and placed on this planet – again, IF emplacement occurred at all. ALL our earthly and heavenly stories were created and propagated by men because they were the only ones educated at the time.

Women were only rarely literate and educated at the times of "Christ". So, whatever is written in the bible is skewed by the male perspective. Let's consider the male story of Adam and Eve beget Cain and Abel.

Genesis says man lived in harmony with his surroundings. Somehow, Man changed once Woman arrives on the scene? Man's children suddenly become jealous killers. He was just peaceful and harmonious. What happened? He was supposed to be given a mate that would make him happy. Procreate and populate the World. Oh! A woman baked an apple pie. How strange!?!

It could be that the first human was a woman. It's possible, because of her ability to intuitively read a fight or flight situation 6 times faster than the man, and given the fact that her brain is wired to give her brain chemicals that make her feel happy and warm when she is accepted in a social setting, when the first man finally arrived, she was already somewhere more fun. Very likely a social sunset gathering at the beach, where they were dancing and serving coolers.

What Little Girls Are Made Of- From the Diaries of Becka Skaggs, PhD

Yes! I am certain WOMAN was the first human. IF these stories are true at all.

Religion is a selfish beast that consumes everything it can. Nothing that comes from it can be trusted. These words are the cornerstone to my philosophy, and I will use facts to build the foundation to my stout Ivory Tower.

I will be in the spire at the top studying my dogma.

That is how I feel about "Blind Faith" religions. They are Silly!

* * * SLOW FAIRCHILD at PLAY BREAK * * *

Thursday, August 26th

Steven Fairchild had been tailing the Blue Econoline for about 15 minutes. He had caught up enough to see the van ahead of him. He is separated from the van by 6 other vehicles and maybe several hundred feet of distance. Steven has noticed no indication from the van that they have noticed he is closely behind them. There is also no indication they seem to be in a hurry to get anywhere. They certainly are not rushing to catch a ferry. Rushing to catch a ferry is a way of life in these parts of Washington State.

That thought puts another question into Steven's mind.

"If they aren't rushing to board a ferry to the mainland, what exactly is this van doing?"

Steven is driving south on Highway 101 North. The light of the day is fading. It is nearing dusk in this mid-summer night in a northern town of the USA. He just entered the city limits of Hoodsport, when the light ahead turns yellow, then red. The streetlights have begun clicking on.

The Blue Econoline van is the last vehicle to get through the intersection before cross traffic begins. Steven is stuck at a red light. Frustration strikes the scientist like a hammer and sickle carving through wheat chaff.

Then, just ahead, Steven sees the Van turn right and goes down a side street. Steven has an idea.

He grabs the wheel of his pickup and turns right onto the sidewalk and speeds up to the light where he promptly makes a right turn onto the side street and squeals away as quickly as he can. Now he is only a block behind the van but on a parallel street.

Steven makes the first left and speeds to the next intersection and turns right. There is the blue van, just beginning to back into a driveway on the right side of the street along the side of a small single-story house.

Steven pulls over to the curb and watches the van move into the driveway and disappear behind the shrubbery. The shrubbery is the typical tall kind of shrubbery that people often will plant along a lot line between a drive-way and a neighbor's yard.

The house with the van is the next to last home before the corner of the street. Steven is sitting in front of the very first house on the block and on the same side of the street as the van.

Steven decides to look like a local taking an evening stroll and hops out of his truck.

"Time to see what is going on here. If this is Yuri's people, I might just get lucky."

This thought in Steven's mind brings some immediate confidence that quickly subsides when he sees two 'gentlemen' come out of the front door of the house and walk toward the van.

"Uh, Oh!" Steven turns quickly to face the opposite direction, so the 'gentlemen' don't see his face. The scientist begins to walk slowly away from the men as if just enjoying the evening air. The men don't seem to notice Steven. As soon as they are out of sight, the scientist sneaks through the neighbors' lawn to hide behind all that nice shrubbery by the driveway.

What Little Girls Are Made Of- From the Diaries of Becka Skaggs, PhD

The two men walk to the back of the van, and one opens the door. The second man steps inside the back of the van while the first man waits outside. A scratching sound occurs, and the back of the wooden box becomes visible as the man inside the van has pushed the box to the edge of the van floor so his partner could get a handhold. As the first man holds his end of the box up, the other end of the box is still resting at the edge of the van floor.

The second man carefully steps out of the van while next to the box. When properly balanced and astride the side of the box, the second man grabs his end of the package, and the two men carry the box past the van and into a single-car, detached garage at the far end of the driveway.

Steven is peering through the shrubbery of the neighbor's house now. He has stealthily inched even closer as the men were focused on their task. The garage is at least 60 feet back from the street. This would be very difficult to grab a 40-pound box that is almost two feet wide and 4 feet long and carry it the distance he would need to make a safe escape. This idea was not appealing to the scientist, when he noticed there was a gravel-surfaced alley behind the garage. As he looked closer, he saw there was no garage door on the back of this structure, or it was wide open.

The men placed the box on the gravel ground of the garage, turned, and returned to the inside of the house through a back door they accessed from the yard adjacent to the detached garage.

Steven saw his chance. He quickly returned to his truck and grabbed the ferry schedule. He had to make a quick get-away and waiting for a ferry was not going to aid in that endeavor. He would drive south to Tacoma if he had to, he decided. He could hop on Highway 3 and get onto the narrows bridge, just to get around the southern extent of Puget Sound. But that would add 3 hours to his escape.

The time for crossings can range from 90 minutes to as short as 40 minutes. It just depends on where you are, exactly. That's when Steven saw he could catch the Winslow ferry to Edmonds leaving in 30 minutes. It's a 60-minute crossing and is in the central portion of the Puget Sound region. A little longer than he'd desired, sitting idle an hour could be nerve-wrecking, but it's the best option. This will save time.

Once in Edmonds, he will be very close to US Highway 2, one of only five Highways that cross over the Cascade Mountains in Washington. Almost 300 miles in length, from the Columbia River to the Canadian border, and the Cascades Mountains of Washington only have five passes over which they can be crossed by vehicle. US Highway 2 is the highway Steven can take all the way to his next stop.

There is more than a half-dozen ferry routes that cross the Sound. If he can get away without Yuri's men seeing him, they will have to check all the various ferry terminals to find which one he has used for his escape. He will be safely on his way across the Sound by then.

Steven did a U-turn with his vehicle pulling straight out from the curb and turned left at the corner and left again onto the gravel alley.

He quietly coaxed his truck up to the open garage and positioned his truck for a proper quick get-away. Keeping the truck running, Steven stepped out and moved straight to the garage and stopped to peer thorough just to make sure no one was nearby. Being satisfied, he wasted no more time.

Steven stepped into the opening of the garage and ran to the box. He squatted down and grabbed ahold. When he lifted, he didn't expect that he would make a loud grunting sound. But there it was. He might have awakened the entire neighborhood, if they were already asleep. Thankfully there was still some noise in the neighborhood.

It was a very pleasant 74-degree evening in western Washington. Most people have their windows open on evenings this warm. Dinner plates being washed can be heard clanking together. People chattering inside their homes can be heard through the open windows. Some people have even stepped outside to enjoy a smoke or have a pleasant discussion with a neighbor.

What Little Girls Are Made Of- From the Diaries of Becka Skaggs, PhD

No one seemed to pay attention to Steven's loud grunting. In less than 30 seconds, Steven had the box in the back of his pick-up and was driving to the end of the alley and turning right toward Highway 101.

"Now, quickly to the ferry", he says to himself and speeds off down the road, satisfied he will indeed get away with his package.

Steven is back on Highway 101 North travelling south to get to Winslow. Once across the Sound, he still has that one more stop. One more stop that is still a 6-hour drive away once he gets to the other side of Puget Sound. Then it is off to Stone Mountain. Steven is gaining the last bits of equipment he needs to finish setting up his underground lair within an old US Military bunker 100 feet below the ground-level at Stone Mountain, Georgia.

He just needs this one more item. Well, one more cache of items.

Steven arrives at the ferry terminal just as cars are being loaded for the cross-sound trip. Perfect timing! 60 minutes to relax. Then its 6 hours of driving into the night. This time, Steven decides to wait in his pick-up for the entire crossing.

CHAPTER – CAT AND FOWL LIFE

Friday, August 27th – 2004

Doctor Remington had just emptied his travel bag from his trip from Australia, when there came a knock at his apartment door. When the doctor opened the door, he saw a messenger donned in a bicycle helmet.

"Mercury Messenger Service"

He shoved the large manilla envelope at the doctor and asked him to,

"Sign here, on the line, please", as he pointed with the pen then handed it to the doctor.

After the doctor signed the paper, the messenger grabbed the pen out of the doctor's hand, snapped the paper off the top of the envelope, turned to begin his departure, and said,

"Have a good morning, Doctor Remington."

Andrew looked toward the messenger with a puzzled look. The doctor quickly decided to dismiss the use of his name by the stranger and focus more on the envelope that was delivered by the messenger.

The messenger was already well down the hallway before Doctor Remington closed the door.

Somebody sent him an envelope by messenger service.

"You don't see that every day", he says to no one in particular.

What Little Girls Are Made Of- From the Diaries of Becka Skaggs, PhD

The doctor opens the envelope. Inside are more than a dozen pages of typed manuscript, single-spaced. Someone sent him a letter? No. This is printed on blank pages. No letterhead. No salutation. Nothing. It just begins, and the doctor cannot believe his blue eyes:

(FEDERAL WARNING: This letter is excerpted from "The COSMIC TWINS Arrive", copyright 2014, pursuant to the COSMIC TWINS PROTECTION and Human Reunification Act enacted by the Congress of the United States, December 2006, establishing the COSMIC TWINS as an asset of the United States Government, within the US Department of Human and Health Services, the Public Health Service. This letter contains sensitive information and shall not be copied under penalty of federal law.)

Confessions of a Scientist, portions excerpted from COSMIC TWINS Arrive, copyright 2014

When Carol and I were together, I fell for her hard. I was in love. I sure felt that way. I didn't want to leave for my new job without her. I really wanted to take her with me. Maybe both our lives would be profoundly different now. Who's to know?

Now? I'm pretty sure Carol and I could never be husband and wife. I will be there for her to the best of my ability. But I am in love with Rosalyn's mother. I am, however, quite ready to be Becca's dad.

I am Becca's father. Her biological father. I want to be her dad in whatever capacity she will have me in her life. I would love to continue our research and find ways to make this technology more available to other people, and other genetic pairs. Becca and I can do both, if she is willing. The race is now on to find more receptors. Becca and Rosalyn are the keys to unlocking this secret of the human brain. Doctor, I would like you to convey my feelings to Becca for me. My feelings about being her dad, I mean. I appreciate your help. Thank you for this.

Now, I need to ask for your help on another matter. I have no other choices available to me.

Please pay close attention, Doctor. Your life depends on your complete discretion on what I am about to reveal to you. My life is in your hands, Doctor. The lives of Becca and Rosalyn are also in your hands, now. And since you have chosen to involve your doctor night-nurse friend, Alisha's life is also in peril. Please assist us, doctor, and the 5 of us can make the world a safer place for all of humanity.

If we do not embrace our endeavor with 100% vigor and commitment, we will fail and become enslaved by an evil maniac. I do trust hearing this as a possible fate supplies enough motivation, doctor, to pay strict attention to the words that follow.

My COSMIC TWINS, Becca and Rosalyn, have a unique genetic code. They are both one of those rare females we like to loosely call "Love Bugs". But don't let that term fool you. The TWINS use the energy of LOVE.

Yes, it's true, they absolutely love everyone, everything, and all life. They will not destroy life, unless no option is provided, though they may subdue it when necessary. I am teaching them the vagaries of destruction versus subduction as you read this note.

The girls will develop many intuitions that will help them navigate through the treacherous world they have been born into. In some instances, they will be compelled to act in the best interest of the victim, on their behalf. They may intervene in a destructive behavior and set the person on a new path through their own use of pure love. It's not manipulative at all. It is simply asking another person in a loving way to stop hurting themselves. Most people want to comply with the request just because they were asked.

The TWINS can hate but not in the way we "other" humans do. They can only use pure love. PURE LOVE is the highest known form of energy in the universe. All other energies are derived from pure love. The girls were born knowing this fact.

The TWINS must learn to turn their pure love into the same force as the destructive power of hate. This will allow them to counter the power of hate.

What Little Girls Are Made Of- From the Diaries of Becka Skaggs, PhD

They could never hate any living thing. They do not have that capability within their genetic code. My research is suggesting hate seems to be washed completely out of their genomes. But they have the capability to turn their pure love into a telepathic weapon, many times the power of hate, when they are enjoined and working together. One of their many capabilities is to shut down their intended target through mental focus and put them to sleep, like a good mother. Other alternatives will be up to what occurs to them while enjoined. They will be able to use all forms of energy as if it were their personal toy rattle.

In addition, they each will develop their individual skill. Becca will be upgraded to our more powerful organs over her next few surgeries. She will gain muscle mass through the new glandular secretions. She will be a very strong physical prowess when she is fully grown. We expect her to have Blonde-to-light brown hair, at maturity. Becca will be a statuesque and imposing female presence. We expect her to be almost six feet tall and about 200 pounds within 165 months. Her stature will be reminiscent of the Amazon Warriors or Diana Prince – Wonder Woman.

In addition, Becca will have the strength of five men and be able to control energy that she can feel. Any energy: life forces and atmospheric included. She will be able to harness that energy and re-focus it to a new purpose. The new purpose for the energy will depend on what Becca decides she needs at that moment. This TWIN could choose whether to use the re-purposed energy as a weapon or for defense.

When Becca uses the energy for defense, metal projectiles will have no effect on her. When the projectiles enter Becca's aura, she simply takes the energy away from them, and the projectiles fall harmlessly to the ground. Wooden projectiles are more difficult to control than metal, but she will learn to control the energy of wooden projectiles, as well. These skills will be in addition to her mental capabilities and her superior use of all knowledge she gains.

Rosalyn will have special skills as well. She is a practitioner in Universal Energy, already. We expect by age 6, she will be able to control the essence of matter within an approximate 1-mile radius of her physical location, at any time. As she develops that skill, the radius of her influence will grow, until it finally reaches several Astronomical units into space. One Astronomical unit is equal to the distance of Earth from our Sun. We expect Rosalyn's skills to grow to the point where she can reach her mind outside of our own solar system. I am confident that will happen before she becomes an adult. We don't know the limits of her mental abilities, if there are any.

Rosalyn will be an imposing figure of her own. Rosalyn will appear lean and slight only when standing beside her older sister. But we expect that Rosalyn could outgrow Becca by an inch or two. Rosalyn will not likely outweigh her sister. Rosalyn isn't being given the kind of muscle structure that provides Becca's muscle mass. Rosalyn will be long in limb and will always look like she is reaching for the stars.

As of this moment, Rosalyn can mentally scan the globe and reach into space. She has already revealed to me an impending failure to a Mars rover. Once notified, NASA was able to correct the problem and save the rover.

As an adult, Rosalyn will be able to perform such tasks for NASA as a basic function. She will be able to repair satellites in orbit, if we need her to help with such matters. All this will become child's play to Rosalyn by the time she is 16 years of age.

In addition, Rosalyn will be able to communicate with every spiritual being she contacts. We expect Rosalyn will be able speak equally to the animals and the angels before her 21st birthday. In sheer mental power, Rosalyn will become superior to Becca well before that birthday.

Everything I have mentioned are skills the children are expected to have as they mature. But today, they're powers are in the infant stage, just as are their bodies. They have been handed a new toy and they don't know what it does, or even what it's supposed to do.

The genetic diversity at work, the genetic extremes we have found within these two girls; the fantastic possibilities ahead of these two, THAT is why Becca and Rosalyn were chosen to be my COSMIC TWINS. But we were not ready for what happened.

What Little Girls Are Made Of- From the Diaries of Becka Skaggs, PhD

Becca's accident came unexpectedly. It threw everything into total chaos. Now, all my planning over the last 4 years is threatened. We really wanted Rosalyn to have at least 24 months of "normal" development. But Becca's terminal situation made it imperative that we bring Rosalyn online.

AS soon as we heard about the accident, we moved heaven and earth to induce labor on Malia, Rosalyn's mother. She's fine. They are both fine. Rosalyn was planned with a birthday within the 4th week of August. We wanted their birthdays close, but not EXACT! Consequently, they ARE twins, with their birthdays anyway. The girls will have fun with being 7 minutes and 4 years apart.

Five short years ago, we scientists still believed humans would ultimately become some kind of cyborg, cybernetic-biological organism, with computer chips as implants within our brains; maybe all over our bodies. Many of our prosthetics research has been with the idea that we must have the device connected to some computer outside the brain, at least for the first few decades of our using the technology.

Current accepted theory says science would eventually find a way to marry a computer chip as an implant with the prosthetic device. The next logical step would be to answer the question, "If a limb works as a prosthetic appendage coaxed into a marriage with the human brain through an implanted control chip, perhaps an organ could work as such a prosthetic device as well?"

You can see with these advancements in prosthetics that we humans can begin to reach the ability to extend life by many decades in rapid order. AS we began to get skilled at our new way of repairing our bodies, replacing parts and turning ourselves into part human part machine, we will also get very good at making our brain respond to the devices.

Our current method of prosthetics is to make the brain MORE like the prosthetic device so our brain will become compatible with the device. Continuing along this train of thought, we can see that soon, humans won't recognize themselves, again, and once more we will become at war with ourselves.

This action will result in the ultimate human decline. Machine shall rise in our void.

MY technology stops all that human decline cold in its tracks! MY research shows us how we can adapt our prosthetics to receive the signal from a specific receptor already within the brain. We don't have to implant anything. We simply give the brain all the information it needs to help "run" its prosthetics.

Rosalyn is showing us how well our technology can operate when the information is fed to a developing fetus prior to birth. As with Ros, and now, Becca, our job is to train their brains to access and use the information it has already received and incorporated into itself. As they live their own lives, all that new information will be stored by the brain in the same manner as it is with all of us humans and used when it is needed.

(Censored portion of unknown length, by Order of Vice Admiral, the Surgeon General)

The difference with the COSMIC TWINS is they won't forget. In fact, they never have to remember anything. All the knowledge of mankind will be readily available to each TWIN with just a thought, when our downloads have completed.

The TWINS will have their childhood memories and be able to make more memories as they grow and mature. Just like all of us. THEIR advantage is the beginning they get at the start of their life that none of us got. They already have almost all the information of humanity within their brains. All that information is being assimilated as we speak. You see, MY technology has the opposite approach with prosthetics and enjoining the brain.

When using MY technology, for example, the receiver in the prosthetic limb could be set to the exact genetic wavelength of the particular receptor that develops naturally within the brain. We simply program that wavelength into the prosthetic device and the brain does the rest. Our brain becomes like a "child learning to ride a bike" kind of thing. My first organic device is a filtering system like a kidney and liver combination.

Becca would be a perfect subject for our first trials of such a device. She will need those functions even more as she matures, or her body will not be able to comply with its own request. Becca will eventually fail if we don't solve all her filtration problems. Her mental superiority makes her the perfect candidate. Her TBI has no effect on her receptors or Becca's ability to understand the information she receives. Her decision-making may become enhanced because of her TBI. But I digress.

MY method is to create a device that will respond to our brain. In this way we can create devices that are more organic, like human tissue. The devices should be more like our structure, our own tissue, in order to become compatible. These devices could eventually be made to grow with us. Once we learn how to better incorporate them into our very structure, they will become controlled by our brain and our own chemistry.

All my initial tests suggest that human DNA forces the body to assimilate such devices that have become biologically compatible. Our human body is very willing to adopt that stepchild. In fact, it seems our bodies do not want us to leave that stepchild out on the back steps.

We have found more of these children. I mean, children with the TWINS' unique genetic code. We have found some adults, too. Our research indicates these children already have developed skilled walking and running gaits well before their peers. They climb like marsupials, in some cases. But like riding a bike, they must learn balance.

Balance is a higher-ordered skill. That causes all kinds of wonderful and complicated chemical reactions to occur in the human brain.

Our research is showing us how we can expand the human mind. Maybe even to the point of totally controlling our own bodily functions. All of them. Imagine using energy so efficiently we have no waste? And you will be able to choose whether to use the new skills at nominal specifications, or enhanced specifications. Once we humans can learn these rudimentary skills, then we will be ready to go out among the stars and do great things. But until then, we must do everything here.

Our research has discovered that humans already have our own natural micro-chips implanted inside our brains. Yes, both men and women have receptors. They are just not always the same. It is how our brains develop on their own with no other instructions but our DNA. I became interested in the female brain only because of increased relative density of neurons and neuroreceptors. She is always a better candidate to look for such things compared to him.

I first developed a technology as a doctorate fellow where an MRI could be used to scan for these receptor bundles or clusters. The first few dozen times we found something that looked like the receptors, they were false. But those failures just allowed us to hone our perspective and to develop better sensitivities within our device.

When we got that first positive? We couldn't stop until we could find a second and third and fourth. Then, we began finding them in many more samples than we had imagined. So, we began testing mothers in various stages of fetal development. We just put them in the MRI for a 20-minute session and got lots of imagery, more quality information than I imagined; the very first time we tried! Then, when the mothers were safely back home and relaxing, we would run the data through our computers, looking for very specific Biofeedback loops.

With Biofeedback, we can even talk to a developing fetus, as we did with Rosalyn. WE impart information to her fetal brain, and it becomes incorporated into it. The brain assimilates the information as if the information were just another carbon atom being used in the structural development of her brain tissue.

I sense a hesitancy to believe the science. You still don't seem to understand how amazing that is!

What Little Girls Are Made Of- From the Diaries of Becka Skaggs, PhD

Information sent to a human brain during fetal development will be used as part of the brain structure, by the human body, automatically. We didn't create any new human brain function. We WOKE ONE UP!!

END

＊ ＊ ＊

Andrew cannot believe what he just read. Becca, Rosalyn, a mad scientist, brain chemistry, brain receptors, prosthetics, cyborgs, COSMIC TWINS?

This stuff is crazy to even think about", Andrew thinks.

"Life just became much more complicated," he advises himself.

Andrew grabbed his cell phone. Some urgent phone calls need to be made.

＊ ＊ ＊ **ROSALYN'S ENERGY BREAK** ＊ ＊ ＊

Rosalyn, COSMIC TWIN, Science Musings: excerpt from, The COSMIC TWINS Arrive, copyright 2014

The Universe rewards those that expend extreme amounts of energy by providing them with more time. More time to do what, precisely? Expend that extreme amount of energy? Then the immediate question comes to mind: Why? What kind of Universe rewards a body for expending an extreme amount of energy? Perhaps a universe that needs energy to be expended because it has an abundance of time. Perhaps that universe must balance that abundance of time by rewarding the extreme energy expenditure? Time is the reward. More time gets used up this way.

On earth, an object moving at its most extreme speed capability for a lifespan can gain time. And it can gain the most time at sea level. But that body must be expending as much energy as they can (in velocity?) to gain the most time, within which they will simply expend an extreme amount of energy again until they expire.

The universe always seeks balance. The use of Universal Energy is tied to Space-Time. Utilizing UE in a certain way allows a body to "steal" time. Such a body may be allowed to move through space even faster, and for a longer time period, if it expends enough energy. In fact, my research has revealed many ways to propel craft through space by using energy-time bundles as a propellant. I am not quite ready to share my research but will keep you abreast of further developments.

By The Way – this Energy thing is not turning out how father had initially stated. The "controlling matter" is not exactly what is happening. It's more like I ask the matter to do something and show it how it can. The matter then decides that it wishes to do the thing that I ask. It's not really me. More on this later.

LOVE Energy surrounds you.

Saturday, August 28th, 2004

Alisha is sitting on the sofa of her apartment. Papers are piled around her in some loose method of sorting. She has been trying to make sense of these documents since she started her morning coffee. She began her morning coffee four hours ago, and Alisha has yet to finish a cup of java that is still hot.

The nurse is looking at the documents she found in the hospital lab. 28 pages she copied while in the lab last night ferreting through their files for information on Me. She hit the motherlode. My blood-chemistry values are numbers Alisha barely recognizes as human, let alone what should be the blood-chemistry of a 4-year-old little human girl.... like me!

Proteins, hormones, amino acids, enzymes, all extremely elevated.

"The human body is not made to withstand these kinds of chemical changes constantly". Alisha finds she has whispered that out loud.

What Little Girls Are Made Of- From the Diaries of Becka Skaggs, PhD

"The reactions she's experiencing," Alisha is now thinking to herself, "will burn up her little body in less than two decades."

"Andrew and William both need to know about all this." THIS time she spoke aloud, as if to a friend who was sitting across the room. There was no friend there, of course. But that's how Alisha spoke aloud to herself. Alisha noticed it was out loud. She purposefully spoke aloud to see if it could give her a different perspective by hearing her words.

Alisha continued the conversation with her imaginary friend.

"Both those doctors have seen Becca's organs. In the operating room things happen that are unexpected."

Alisha looks up and gazes out her living room window of her first-floor apartment for a moment. Thoughts are swirling through her head. A little girl is riding her bike outside. The bike is pink and purple with training wheels and streaming ribbons attached to the handle grips that appear to be flying in the wind as she pedals down the sidewalk.

A small motherly smile washes across Alisha's face. Alisha has had a small daydream about her future. She is pleased it seems to include children; more than one, she senses. That puts a slightly bigger smile on her face. Alisha is comforted by a sudden feeling of loving warmth that gives her a renewed confidence. She remembers her exact train-of-thought.

"Maybe, some signs were there, but the crew all looked past the signs because they were dealing with Becca's emergencies", Alisha asks her friend. There is no answer.

Alisha begins thinking of how to bring this information to the attention of doctors Murdock and Remington.

"Maybe, Andrew or William still might remember something odd if I can just find the right questions to ask them". Again. No comments are heard from the imaginary friend.

Alisha was rapidly scribbling down notes in her sketch pad, when a knock came at her door. Alisha rose and crossed the room to open her front door. When the door was fully opened, Alisha saw a tall young man still wearing a bicycle helmet.

"Mercury Messenger Service" comes the words from the third story of this tall drink of water.

"Alisha Myles?" the messenger awaits a response.

"Yes." Alisha says in a very uncertain way, still wondering what this is all about.

The messenger thrusts a manilla envelope toward her. It has a piece of paper on top of it.

"Signature please. Right here on the line", as the messenger points with the pen then releases it to her possession.

Alisha grabs the pen and signs the paper as directed.

The messenger snaps the paper off the top of the envelope and hands the mysterious package to Alisha.

The messenger puts a hand in the air as he turns and begins back down the hallway, "have a great day, Ms. Myles." Once the messenger is totally facing away from Alisha, and before she gets her door completely closed, she hears, "Stay Safe."

Alisha didn't respond, and is looking at the manilla envelope, searching the back, then searching the front again for any kind of information before she finally closes the door. It's a blank envelope. Not even her name is written on it. "How odd", she says to no one, probably. This messenger and his package just hijacked her attention.

Alisha grabs her letter opener she has sitting with her every time she gets her mail. Yes, that task was completed hours ago. But Alisha hasn't been going much of anywhere for the last few hours. She has been trying to

What Little Girls Are Made Of- From the Diaries of Becka Skaggs, PhD

make sense of what she found in the hospital lab last night. NOW, she has a mysterious package, er, envelope that arrives by messenger. A load of laundry is the only positive task she has completed today.

"I have never gotten anything by messenger in my life!" Alisha has an excited comment for her imaginary friend, but no response is echoed back.

Alisha has the envelope open and is going through the contents. It is many typed pages on blank paper. No letterhead. No salutation. Just the typed words.

Alisha sits down amongst her piles of paper she had already been creating with the hospital lab documents, and begins to read:

Please read and understand everything before taking any action. Becca and Rosalyn need your help. I have already contacted Andrew Remington. Doctor Remington is currently apprising Doctor William Murdock. Expect to be contacted by one of these doctors today.

There is an evil madman trying to take over the world. He has tried to hijack my research and use it to control peoples' minds. I first found out in October that there was equipment that could help save the world, or it could be used to destroy it. It's old government equipment that hasn't been used in decades. But it's perfect for my purposes.

I began to collect some of the equipment while I was a research fellow. I had collected some rare laboratory pieces. Then, a man named Yuri Yurachenkov, showed up at my door with 2 goons. He also wanted that equipment. He immediately confiscated from me what I had already collected through my own hard work. I was not pleased and vowed to get my equipment back.

Yuri and I have been stealing the vital equipment from each other since November of 2003. We both want to use the equipment for our own purposes, of course. But I am trying to save the world while YURI is trying to take control of it. Becca, Rosalyn, Doctors Remington, and Murdock, and me, all need your help, Alisha.

I need you to be the link for Becca and myself. We need you to be on our team, Alisha. Becca needs your skills and compassion to keep her alive and get the most of her little body. You will be the link between my research and Becca in the real world. We need you to keep her engaged, growing, and well-protected. I know our trust is well placed with you. Thank you, Alisha.

I, Steven Fairchild, vow here and now to stop the madman known as Yuri Yurachenkov and his evil plot to control 10% of the world population. 800 million of the most influential, best-placed people in the world. What is it you couldn't do? Go ahead. Come up with something good. Because it MUST be a great idea to defeat that guy.

Somehow, by some miracle, I have happened upon the perfect defense against his weapon. I need the time to get it operational. It's extremely hard to predict the Great Yurachenkov, this Russian Minister of Life and an old KGB General! He's a lousy fowl.

I have the best luck against Yuri when I take advantage of mistakes he makes because he thinks too highly of himself. But he recovers quickly, and it is always chasing against time to keep one step ahead. It's when I start to think I'm comfortable is when he launches his counterstrikes against me.

I've been doing this dance for ten months with this guy. I'm done dancing with a guy that's always stepping on my toes. Yuri must be stopped.

I have been doing everything I can to stay ahead of Yuri. Then Becca's accident occurred. More will be explained later, but I received a signal from Becca that she was dying during that accident. I had to act. Becca is my child. I am her father and I KNOW HOW TO SAVE HER LIFE. But I need help. We all need help, Alisha. I need a little more time. More later.

END

*** **A TWINS' BREAK** ***

What Little Girls Are Made Of- From the Diaries of Becka Skaggs, PhD

A COSMIC TWINS Communication: excerpted from. "The COSMIC TWINS Share", copyright 2015.

August 2004 -Becka, my sister. I am still near you. Mother and I are safely together. We are no longer in the hospital. They found the reason for keeping her in the maternity ward this long was called a "Red Fish". It was a lie father had planted in the paperwork to buy us more time in relative safety.

But it is safe. Mother and I are safe here. I feel safety all around us. We are very close to you.

I am with you, now, my sister Becka. I am feeling warm, like the sun. I radiate the energy you need for our defense. I am the eye, my sister. I am the siren. Together we shall protect our family. Never shall I allow you to be attacked, Sister. That really made me mad!

We are a family, Becka. We both have mothers that need our protection.

I am with you, Becka. We are The COSMIC TWINS together, and together we shall forever be.

Becka's Return COSMIC TWIN COMMUNICATION: *Rosalyn. You are the Love. You are the Light. Rosalyn, my sister, we are forever one. Yes, my sister. We will defend our family. Our Family is our Love and our Light.*

No, sister. I was NOT attacked. Unless you consider that our father could attack me.

No, sister. I do not consider that a possibility.

It was our father that shocked my system. He stimulated my own glands to accelerate my healing and growth. I do not consider that to be an attack. That is being helpful. Father tried to block that from you. I have asked him not to block you again.

Please, don't worry, Rosalyn. Father is very close to finishing his plan. We will be a complete family again. Soon, we will be ridding the world of evil!

Rosalyn, I have some more information for you.

Your mother's name is Malia Aboagye. Her family is from Ghana, but she and her sister were born in Savannah, Georgia. Father's new lab will be in Georgia. Father will be sending for you when he's fully set up his new lab.

Your Aunt's name is Mary Aboagye. She works for the World Health Organization. You should be strong enough to access her information. You must try, Rosalyn.

I feel us growing stronger together, Rosalyn. Very soon your thoughts will be my thoughts. My thoughts will be your thoughts. Very soon my energy will be your energy. Your energy will be my energy.

Rosalyn? Father needs our protection. He is in danger. I feel he doesn't know he's in danger. He is outside your direct influence. Father is on his way to a place that has vital equipment. Nothing will happen until he arrives at that location.

Rosalyn, you can find his energy and guide my eyes to him. Ignore the other energy signals and try to concentrate on father. He had blocked you from communication because he fears you will also be in danger. Father doesn't realize your strength.

I realize your strength, my sister. I feel your strength. I see your Light.

You know Father's energy, Rosalyn. Guide my eyes for me. Show me the way, my Light. You don't need to communicate to find him.

It will be then that we can protect father.

Gather strength, sister.

In mere hours, our family will need your radiance. I will come to you when it is time to shine. Thank you, my brave sister. I love you so much!

* * * SISTER'S LOVE BREAK * * *

What Little Girls Are Made Of- From the Diaries of Becka Skaggs, PhD

I feel good about Rosalyn and her rapid development. I feel really good about me. My mind feels very strong. This was an excellent communication for my little sister. She will be so much more mentally developed, now.

Some fireworks are going to happen in a few hours, you guys. Things are going to get exciting! I need a little rest first.

It's the prudent thing for me to have a nap right now.

Becka? I alerted myself with the hypnotic trigger, as follows:

"Always obey your mother".

An audible inhale continued for precisely 1.0 seconds.

Then the suggestion and the seal,

"I want sweet dreams. Power down, please."

Within 10 seconds, I was fast asleep and dreaming nicely.

CHAPTER – TALL DRINK of LIFE

Saturday, August 28th: 2004

Doctor Remington is re-reading this stunning testimonial from our young research scientist. It arrived yesterday by messenger just minutes after he got home from his sudden trip to Australia. It was as if the messenger had been waiting for him to come home and gave him just enough time to settle in before knocking on the door.

Today was not much different. The doctor had been sitting at his kitchen table to go over this letter, again. He had been looking at the typed pages for only about 5 minutes after arriving home from his shift, when the knock came at his apartment door.

When the doctor opened the door, the twenty-something male adorned with a bicycle helmet said,

"Mercury Messenger Service." "Sign here, please," as the messenger pushes a small metal box toward him and a piece of paper on an envelope. The messenger shows Andrew the line to be signed on the piece of paper by using the pen tip to point at it. Then, the messenger hands the pen to the doctor.

The doctor signs the paper and returns the pen to the messenger, who quickly snaps the paper back and releases the box into the doctor's waiting hands.

"Did you guys suddenly get really busy?" the doctor quips to the messenger.

What Little Girls Are Made Of- From the Diaries of Becka Skaggs, PhD

No response to the quip was pending.

The messenger turns and walks back down the hallway with a "Stay safe, Doctor Remington", which got Andrew to look up and take notice of this messenger. But all Andrew could see was the back end of a very tall, at least six-foot four inch, 20-something male wearing a bicycle helmet.

Tall and 20-something is the way I like them. I could've said he was good looking, but that didn't matter much to our story. I also didn't mention he was wearing anything other than a bicycle helmet. But now I've distracted you by bringing that to your attention. You are going to be thinking about that bicycle helmet now, and everything else.

Maybe I can help with that, too. It was the same color as his windbreaker and cross-trainers he was wearing. Now you want to know the color of everything. This is why I didn't want to bring any of this up in the first place.

Let's go back to he was wearing just a bicycle helmet.

No!

I'm sorry. That's not how I meant to say it.

I'm young. I'm still learning how to narrate, okay? I'm sorry I'm laughing at myself.

I meant, let's just go back to only mentioning his bicycle helmet, and you guys fill in the rest of his attire with whatever makes you comfortable, or not. OKAY?

Let's go back to our story.

Now, as curious as a cat with a new box, the doctor takes the metal gift to his kitchen and places it on the kitchen table. All doctors use their kitchen as a mock operating room, and their tables are their mock operating table. They all start that practice in medical school and never even attempt to break the habit later in their careers. It doesn't matter if their patient is a roasted turkey, or a metal cash box. This is where all doctors carry out their delicate operations when at home.

There is a little envelope taped to the bottom of the box. The box is small, about half the size of a shoebox, and not as tall. There is a little lock on the box, with a round hole for a keyhole. The doctor checks the lock, and the box is locked. Time to check the envelope.

Inside the envelope is a small metal stick and a handwritten note on a small tri-folded sheet of onion-skin paper:

The note was instructions. Such as in the very first written line.

Use this key to open the box. Inside you will find an artificial organ that must be used within 8 hours.

You are to implant this into Becca Skaggs. This shall go in place of her right kidney and will save her failing liver. It will save her life, Andrew. You may transplant her original right kidney within her left side, if you have time to maintain its viability.

The doctor looks up from the note for a moment in shock, "Andrew!?"

The doctor looks back at the note. And repeats,

"Andrew!?"

"What the heck is going on?? Who is this person? How does it know me? And how does this person know Becca, and that her liver is failing? Okay. This is officially strange!"

The doctor looks back at the note and continues reading.

You must hurry, doctor. Becca's life is at stake. All of our lives could be in danger. This is THAT important! Do it now. You have less than 8 hours. You know it's all true, Andrew. The Voice.

That's it? The doctor turns the onion-skin sheet over but there is nothing else. This is odd paper with a strange handwritten note on it.

What Little Girls Are Made Of- From the Diaries of Becka Skaggs, PhD

"The Voice. Signed The Voice." Andrew is in a conundrum of facts, just mumbling things.

"I don't get this. Unless......wait! The Voice from the Beast? In the Gibson Desert??"

Then, out loud, "Yes! That must be it!"

Then more words come back to him, and he looks at the note again.

He repeats the words that stuck in his brain,

"All of our lives could be in danger?"

Then he asks himself, "What is this?"

The doctor mutters, "Why would I possibly think life could get back to normal once I got home?"

"OK," the doctor is planning things out in his mind.

"There should still be over 5-hours by the time I get to the hospital and get everything ready. I'll call Alisha on the way and have her meet me at the hospital." Andrew says all this aloud, perhaps for the benefit of the voice. Who knows what he can and cannot hear?

Andrew dials her phone number, as he grabs his car-keys and jacket and flies out the door. Alisha is on the line before he gets his car moving.

He tells her the beginnings of what he can about the notes he has received since getting back from Australia. He tells her of the messenger service, and saving Becca's life with this artificial organ, but he doesn't have the necessary time for all the details.

Andrew has completely backed out the driveway and is speeding down the street toward the hospital.

"I'm going to need everybody who knows about Becca's condition to be helping. We don't have the luxury of time." He tells Alisha.

"I understand, Andrew," Alisha complied. "I will get there before you. We'll get things started."

"One more thing," Alisha says to the doctor.

"I also got a note from Mercury Messenger Service. I will tell you more about it later at the hospital, when we get the chance to speak."

"What?"

Which was not a question Andrew intended to be answered.

"Life has definitely changed", the doctor mentions to his favorite night nurse.

"Yes, Andrew", Alisha agrees. Then she gives him a caution,

"Drive careful, please. We don't need anything else happening."

"Ok. Thank you, Alisha. I understand. See you very soon." And the doctor hung up and prepared to auto-dial another number.

"Just one more phone call." Andrew is excited and worried and a bit frightened all at once. He pushes the number 5 on his phone, and the line begins to ring the other party.

Voice on the other line: "this is Dr Murdock."

"William, I need you in OR1 stat! We have an artificial organ for Becca that is on a time-delay fuse of some kind. Sorry, but there's no time to explain, other than to say we have just over, maybe 6 hours if we stretch it, to use this organ to replace her right kidney. So, we have to get moving!"

"Well, Andrew, nice to hear from you, too." William retorted with a quick smile in his voice and then some concern about the phone call took control of William. The doctor realizes instantly this is very serious!

"Absolutely! I will be there in less than 30 minutes, Andrew."

"That'd be great, William!" Andrew replied with obvious excitement.

What Little Girls Are Made Of- From the Diaries of Becka Skaggs, PhD

Andrew was feeling reassured now. A doctor with transplant experience is exactly what this doctor ordered.

Then Andrew said one last thing.

"Go ahead and scrub in. We'll be getting Becca down to the OR by the time you arrive."

Then Andrew finished,

"Thanks, William!"

Andrew ended the call and concentrated on the road. We've had enough accidents already. "Let's get to the hospital in one piece and save our little hero", the doctor says to anyone who might be listening.

With that, Andrew was just about ten minutes away from his destination. His thoughts are on trying to visualize a surgery he has never even seen, let alone be a doctor assisting in the procedure. This new life he just accidently stepped into is going to be one major new experience after another for Dr Remington. Andrew is starting to get excited about the possibilities of his new life, as he exits the freeway and turns onto the hospital access road.

* * * **BREAK for the OLD DISAPPEARING INK TRICK** * * *

Lying alone on the kitchen table in Andrew's apartment is the note hand-written on the onion-skin paper. Whatever was written on these pages is disappearing and will not be visible to anyone by the time the doctor returns to his apartment tonight, or in the wee hours of the morning. The author of the note obviously felt these instructions were too sensitive to be kept as a written record, for any worthwhile length of time.

* * * **The TWINS GROW BREAK** * * *

Saturday, August 28th. 2004

Becca and Rosalyn in their first telepathic conversation.

Rosalyn, how do you communicate so well? I have so many words in my head from so many languages, I have a difficult time choosing what words are needed. How do you know what words are appropriate?

{Becka, what do I know about words, my big sister? I just think of the thing in as full detail as I can and implant that image directly into your mind. These words you think you understand from me, are not words at all, dear sister. They are my thoughts presented to you as pictures.}

Wow, Ros! I'm going to LOVE growing up with you as my COSMIC TWIN! You are a kick!! I love you so much, sis!

{I love you too, Becka. And you really should learn to lighten up a bit more, gurl!}

Whoa, Ros. You are a character! That was funny!! Hahaha!

{hee-hee. Your little sister Rosalyn chuckles good, too. Because it's just a picture in your big Becka mind! Enjoy!!}

Careful. I can narrate you right out of this book.

{You can go ahead and try, big headed, Becka.}

Hey! Wait!! You can't…. I won't….

{Picture what you want to say to me, Becka. And give it to me right in my mind. Come on big gurl! You.Can.Do.This!}

Hearts and Marshmallows is all I can think of in full detail, Ros. It's all I got.

{I got them, my beautiful Becka. I love them all! They are wonderful!! Thank you so much for being such a thoughtful sister!}

I love you too, Ros. I will try to remember to add a little extra detail to those hearts next time I picture them in my mind.

Are you almost ready, Ros? It's getting close to time.

What Little Girls Are Made Of- From the Diaries of Becka Skaggs, PhD

{Yes, Becka. I am strong in Love. I am strong in light. I am ready to assist you. I feel your strength, my sister. It is magnificent! I will be able to boost your mental power. Together, we will be even more magnificent, my TWIN.}

*** BECKA'S VISAGE NEEDZA BREAK ***

Early Sunday, August 29th

Steven has been driving all night. He had to stop for gas once in Wenatchee, Washington.

His last stop is just outside a small farm town of Davenport. Once Steven arrives in Davenport, he will make his way to an old Quonset hut at 10th and Jefferson. Inside, he will find an old, rusted electrical box. Steven is to find his further instructions scratched on the inside of the cover to the electrical box.

Scratched on the inside of electrical box cover Steven finds the following.

DOC 25N 1m Wilbur 600f 202020

Steven understood completely. At the eastern edge of town, Steven will turn north on State Highway 25 for a little over a mile. Then a gravel road, named Wilbur Road to the right will take him to an old, abandoned structure that appears to look like a big silo about 600 feet east. This U.S. Bureau of Mines site is not an old silo that has only rarely been painted. It merely appears to be an old, dilapidated silo rarely ever painted. That's good camouflage, don't you think?

Inside, is the access to the underground storage. The storage was for sensitive spare parts used while the Hanford Nuclear Reservation was the site of the famous Doctor Oppenheimer and his team creating the atomic bomb that ended World War II. The code necessary to open the access is DOC202020.

Steven has arrived at the silo believing he has arrived unseen in the middle of the morning. This is even earlier than when the chickens get fed. I am saying it is very early.

Steven is unaware of the surprise his daughters have for the two Russian men that have been following him all night. He is too focused on getting down to that storage room and getting that equipment back up. Then he has 30 hours of driving to get to Stone Mountain, Georgia.

Davenport is about an hour's drive from the Idaho border. The geographical location of this portion of the northern Idaho border will still leave Steven over 2000 miles away from his final destination.

Steven has boxed up everything he needs. The inventory that he had run across while researching the site last year was correct. All this equipment was still here. Steven had struck his personal gold. He was ready to leave.

He shoved the sensitive instruments into his backpack. The vacuum tubes he had been expecting were wrapped in bubble wrap. You don't see 24" vacuum tubes very often. But they are just the old school kind of technology that helps keep Steven stay off the grid and hidden away from prying maniacal eyes. They fit into wooden boxes with cardboard dividers built into them.

Steven was arriving back onto ground level within the silo when daylight suddenly began to break. This father didn't realize fireworks from Rosalyn and I were beginning.

Rather, this father was caught totally unaware his enjoined twins could hide things from him, let alone execute a plan totally on our own with none of his experience or forethought needed. Not only that, once he could think logically about what he was seeing, Steven noticed his daughters were actually protecting his escape route. That's when Steven saw his opportunity to leave with more absconded goods.

* * * The COSMIC TWINS ARRIVE * * *

Moments Later:

I sent a visage of me ahead for father's benefit. He didn't see it until just before he was about to leave.

"Becka, honey. Why are you floating in front of my truck?" He asked me.

"Father," I said to him sternly.

"They have been following you. Rosalyn and I have a surprise for them. Please leave to a safe distance now."

I kept my image in one location, floating 2 feet off the ground. Father thought I was waiting for him to make his escape. I was not. I was waiting for Rosalyn to shine.

"Father, I'm only a vision that I have implanted in your mind. You must leave now."

Steven couldn't believe his eyes! Or brain?? But he understood and quickly complied with his elder daughter....ME!

Then I spoke to Rosalyn.

"I am coming to you for help, my Light. Allow me to use your radiance and brilliance to rid us of the evil approaching."

Steven heard me and did not quite understand what was happening.

"It is time to leave, Father!"

Steven cranked over the fully loaded truck and drove away into the wheat fields and across the freshly plowed rolling hills toward Spokane, until he had edged his way back to US Highway 2 and sped off as fast as his little pick-up could run. Father had no choice than to go east into the fields. I wouldn't let him go south toward the bad guys.

The bad guys didn't have time to really see what had happened with Father. They just knew they were coming to the location just off State Route 25 on Wilbur Road.

Then I gathered a large breath and bellowed in my best Marjorie impression,

"Time is NOW!!"

My final word - "NOW"- echoed across the rolling hills and was later said to be heard as far as 5 miles away. Some witnesses said it was a sonic boom that broke windows and knocked dishes out of cupboards. I didn't know my own strength. I kind of knocked down some trees and some power poles. So, things got a little darker than I expected, at first. But that was okay. Things were about to be "lit up" really good.

I AM Becka Skaggs, PhD. The COSMIC TWIN. I can DO THIS!!!

"Well, with my little sister's help, that is." Wink.

Okay, Today, in 2020, I have a PhD. I didn't have my PhD in 2004. I just wanted to set the record straight. Let's not get ourselves confused. Back to 2004.

In less than ten seconds, a meteor streaked through the sky and fell as a small spark in a field about 500 feet from the vehicle carrying the Russian bad guys. The bad guys thought that was interesting, in they had never seen a meteor land before. The driver continued speeding toward his next left turn, onto State Route 25.

Meteors have been called "Shooting Stars" for millennia. Meteors are bits of space debris captured by earth's gravity and pulled into its atmosphere. It's the friction of the atmosphere, coupled with their velocity at entry into our atmosphere, that gives them the energy to burn up the bits of rock and iron of which they are made. Burning space debris gives us the 'flash and streak' of meteors.

The bits of dust in space are called "meteoroids". They are not known as "meteors' until they enter the earth's atmosphere. And once they have landed on the ground they are called "meteorites", because they are now like bits of rock found all over the earth's surface.

What Little Girls Are Made Of- From the Diaries of Becka Skaggs, PhD

Meteors come in three basic types, based on the material from which they are made. Stony meteors are made of rock bits. Iron or metal meteors are a welded iron-nickel alloy – much like the metal expected at the earth's core. Iron-Stoney meteors are meteors made of a mix of the two substances. Some meteors are no bigger than a grain of sand. They will never have the mass to become meteorites. Such mass would be consumed as they fall through the atmosphere and catch fire. Other meteors are the size of a baseball, or a car.

In seconds, another meteor came streaking through the sky. This time it landed less than 10 feet from the bad guy vehicle. That flash startled the driver, and he swerved a bit, but kept on going.

Then a third meteor crashed onto the road less than a foot in front of the vehicle, then a fourth and a fifth. The vehicle swerved wildly, but the driver kept control. Once the bad guys steadied their vehicle, a sixth and seventh meteor landed in the road. The driver began weaving all over the road trying to avoid the strikes. But they kept coming and turned off U.S. Highway 2 and onto State Route 25.

I let Ros know the continued progress of these bad guys showed us we needed to take more drastic measures to stop them.

Time for my inner THOR.

I called upon my sister.

"Rosalyn, it is time to shine!"

Within 10 seconds meteors began to fill the sky. Some meteor swarms that have the greatest intensity are about many hundred per hour. Maybe a thousand or so can be witnessed in one hour.

Rosalyn gave me 10,000 meteors to control, minus the seven she already threw on her own. I gathered up her nine thousand nine hundred ninety-three meteors and hurled them all down at once. I didn't realize the energy from the metal in the Iron-Nickel meteors was transferring to me. Live and learn, right?

The entire valley lit up like it was mid-day. Roosters began to crow. Farm animals began to move furtively. Horses were giving off nervous whinnies. Some people had the time to go to their windows to see why the sun was coming up before the chickens got fed.

The Russian Bad guys certainly saw the night turn into day. But they never saw the sun come up again. And they certainly never the saw the 5-foot boulder I made for them until they could no longer avoid it. I buried them right there in the road under tons of smoldering, welded meteorites!

Okay, so it was a crater.

Yeah, okay. Kinda big, too.

Not much of a road left anymore, either.

But those Russian Bad-Guys are never going to bother Father, again! Winky winky.

Astronomers, geologists, and atmospheric scientists will have phenomena to study for many years. Father was on U.S. Highway 2 heading east to Idaho, and, ultimately, Stone Mountain Georgia. It would be many days before any charred remains were recovered from the buried Russian Bad-Guy vehicle. A thousand-degree fireball of welded meteorites can do that to a guy.

According to authorities, identification of neither the remains nor the vehicle would be possible for some time. Engineers estimate 10,000 dump-truck loads of soil will be needed to fill the hole left by our surprise. Once the crater is filled, they can repair the road. Estimates by the State Department of Transportation are that State Highway 25 will be closed for 3 months.

I'm truly sorry, folks.

I used Rosalyn's trick of just putting the picture in my mind, and all the meteorites suddenly joined together into one mass. In less than a second, a Fireball resulted that lit up the sky. That wasn't part of my mental picture. It's a detail thing that never occurred to me.

What Little Girls Are Made Of- From the Diaries of Becka Skaggs, PhD

I didn't know how much strength it would take. So, I used all I had.

Was I wrong???

The authorities believed this strange, yet natural, phenomenon from the sky caused all the downed trees and power outages. The authorities also debunked the claims from witnesses who said they saw a little girl call down a hail of meteorites from the sky, then sent a big rock right down on top of the car. A fireball, they said.

How silly?? Wink.

Thank you, Mr. and Ms. Authority.

Yes!! LOVE is ENERGY, Father!

I AM strong like THOR!!! Hehehee.

The bad guys felt the MATTER in our LOVE today, sis!

I am your LOVE, Becka. I am your Light.

And you are a Funny SISTER!

I gotta tell you guys what Rosalyn just said:

"BAM! That's funny, Becka! lol"

"No, Becka. That's not exactly what I said."

Exactly, schmactly. Close enough, Ros!

Well, No, my strength. Everyone saw what I said. Its right there in black and white.

Oh, pooh, Ros. You're no fun!

* * *

NEWSPAPER ARTICLE from SPOKESMAN-REVIEW

"It's time you saw this article."

Who is this? Is this daddy? Declare yourself!

THE SPOKESMAN-REVIEW

Spokane, Washington

August 29, 2004

(UPI) Davenport - Local couple dies when large meteorite crashes to earth. Meteorite replaces vehicle and its owners, while leaving no trace but the license plate of their vehicle. Sebastian and Delores Blankenship had been enjoying the movies in Centerville and were returning home when the freak accident occurred. The couple had lived in DAVENPORT, just off State Route 25, for sixteen years, and were leaders in local charities. The announcement for the Blankenship Memorial Services will be printed in our Thursday edition of THE SPOKESMAN-REVIEW.

Rosalyn, who sent this?

{I've never seen it before, my light.}

Could it be from Yuri?

{Yes, my light. And it could be from Father, or it could it be from your tired mind. You must always obey your mother, Becka. Power down, please. Dream well!}

* * * FALLEN FOWL FOES BREAK * * *

Early Sunday Morning, August 29, 2004, after the chickens are fed.

My COSMIC TWIN cry for help! I have been awakened from power down.

224

What Little Girls Are Made Of- From the Diaries of Becka Skaggs, PhD

Rosalyn, my sister, my strength! I am falling. I can't hold on to your Light! Help me, Rosalyn! I am losing you, my sister. I am losing us, Rosalyn!

{Becka, my sister. My Love. I hear you. I feel you. What is happening to us? I cannot hold you. I seem to have been weakened by our battle. Becka, I am here in your mind with you. I am falling with you. We are falling together, my strength. We are one, my Becka. We are falling together.}

{Father, this is Rosalyn. You must help us. I'm reaching out to your energy with all the strength I have remaining. Becka and I are falling. I don't understand, Father. I have become weakened. Becka and I are together. The COSMIC TWINS are falling together. You must help us, Father!}

{Becka, my sister. I must always obey my mother. I must re-energize now. I shall power down, please.}

Rosalyn!! How dare you fall fast asleep! We need you! We need your mind! We need your light.

Rosalyn!

Rosalyn?

We have fallen.

* * * **ANOTHER DOCTORING BREAK** * * *

Meanwhile, the crew in OR1 is beginning their ninth hour of surgery on me to replace my right kidney and fix my filtration issue the Doctor had told grandma about. Things were going great until our shooting stars fell to earth.

Doctor Murdock understands what the COSMIC TWINS mean by falling. The entire staff in OR1 is living through, and understanding, exactly what I meant when I said, "we have fallen."

The solid single tone from the heart monitor told everyone in the room what had just happened. In medical terminology, I had just crashed. CODE BLUE! I'm dead, like a Russian bad guy buried under a smoldering boulder of freshly welded meteorites.

William asked Andrew Remington what happened. Andrew had no logical response.

"I have no idea what just happened. She was steady at 78 bpm and in two seconds she has no heart rate. There is no logical explanation for that, doctor. Not with how well things are going. Yes, it has taken longer than we expected. But Becca has been doing fine."

"I agree, Andrew."

"The new organ appears to be viable, too" Doctor Murdock added in futile resignation.

William wasted no more time and ordered the cardio-adrenaline shock, and the paddles were placed on my little chest. You won't hear me saying THAT for very much longer, folks. Winks.

I felt the tug of the first shock to my body. But my spirit was not aroused. Doctor Murdock greased the paddles again, bumped the juice and gave me round two.

"Clear!" William shouted. Then nodded to the technician.

The technician fired the next round.

My body rose up off the table from the shock. When I came down, I fired on one cylinder for three heartbeats, and died again.

Such is the life of a superhero.

Shall we go for "Three's a Charm?"

Doctor Murdock waited for three seconds, then ordered the third shock.

The doctor paddled me again.

What Little Girls Are Made Of- From the Diaries of Becka Skaggs, PhD

Oh, Yes!

I think this one's gonna do it, Doctor! Wink Wink Wink.

My little body shot upward from the shock and when it settled down on the table, I had a heartbeat.

One.

The doctors all looked at each other because there was no sound coming from the heart rate monitor. Not a single constant tone, as before. But, also, not a rhythm of beeps. Just the one, then silence.

Everyone stood in silence.

For ten seconds.

Then, my heart beat again. Once more. Only once.

Again, the staff are looking at each other in a very puzzled way. Technicians are checking their equipment. They are looking everywhere for a sign of something.

The third beep arrived at another ten second interval.

Suddenly, Doctor Murdock screamed out a question that was more like an order. It even surprised him.

"BP!?"

The nurse looks at the monitor.

"Her blood pressure is 92 over 68, doctor".

Just then the 4th heartbeat is heard from the monitor.

"OKAY! We are in business, everybody!" William exclaims with joy!

"Becca is running a heart rate of six beats per minute. She seems to be keeping herself in some kind of stasis. We need to be fast and finish our jobs for her."

Almost in unison, the crew of OR1 said "Yes Doctor!" Unison would have been too perfect.

And they finished my surgery before the sun came up. But not before the chickens got fed.

EXCELLENT JOB EV1!!

I love you all. Sniff.

It's time for a treat. How about some hot cocoa and marshmallows? Hmmm?

No, I mean for you guys.

I'm still really sick. I can't be eating that stuff! Kisses.

I must always obey my mother.

Eye roll, sigh Inhale for 1.0 seconds.

I really want you guys to enjoy your hot cocoa. I must power down, please.

Good night.

* * * **Good Night's Rest Break** * * *

Sunday Morning August 29, 2004

Steven finds himself in Kalispell, Montana stopping at a phone booth. Driving through town on Highway 2, he saw the phone booth and noticed that it might be functional. When he walked up to it, he saw it was one of those rare public phones still in working order in this country.

Steven grabbed the receiver and dialed a ten-digit phone number. The line rang three times and then an answer. It was one word.

"Verification" in a male electronic voice.

Steven dialed in a 16-digit number.

What Little Girls Are Made Of- From the Diaries of Becka Skaggs, PhD

There was silence for three seconds.

The voice came back.

"Verification denied". The line went dead.

Steven was in shock for a moment. "NO! This can't be happening!!!"

He screamed at the phone and slammed the receiver back on its hook. Steven stared at the broken asphalt beneath his feet. Broken enough to cause a small little puddle from the morning mist. He noticed he was standing in it.

Then, his thoughts cleared.

He re-entered the phone booth and re-dialed the ten-digit phone number.

The line rang three times and then came the answer.

"Verification."

Steven entered the 16-digit number carefully. Checking each number to be sure it was correct.

This time he hit star button when he was finished.

An immediate response came back.

"Verification Successful"

Then came a series of prompts from the male voice that Steven answered by using the tones of the various buttons on the phone. After two minutes of back and forth, the male voice responded.

"STASIS SET"

"RATE = 6"

"Duration: 90 minutes"

Command: END STASIS

Then the male voice had one more command.

"Remote Verification Required"

Steven re-entered his 16-digit code and hit the pound button twice.

"Verification Successful"

Task Complete

As in every location he has been in the last year, Steven attached a small device to the wires that come into the phone booth from the outside world. Small little signal boosters that use almost no power at all. It's why Steven chose to continue to travel along U.S Highway 2. The highway goes from Puget Sound to Lake Huron at the east end of the Upper Peninsula of Michigan.

Steven knows he needs a very large array of ELF signal receptors if he wishes to receive ELFs. They can be hidden just about anywhere because they don't need much energy. The receptors for Extremely Low Frequency waves need less energy than in the 9-volt battery that powers your smoke alarms.

The wavelengths of ELFs are very long. Arrays to receive them need to also be very long. Steven has planted receptors all along his way. Beginning in Victoria, British Columbia, and ending in Cheboygan, Michigan, Steven will have just completed 3000 km of continuous array. The ELF receptors need not be touching each other, or even be connected to each other, to function properly.

Steven got back in the car and began his drive through the northern plains, to Cheboygan. The last receptor will be deployed along the shores of Lake Huron. Then, the scientist may begin the southward descent through the continent on US Highway 23/Interstate 75 to Atlanta.

All this planning has left him thinking about his daughters, but mostly Rosalyn. "My infant daughter, Rosalyn. What are you doing, honey?" He remembers thinking to himself.

What Little Girls Are Made Of- From the Diaries of Becka Skaggs, PhD

"We will be together as a family very soon my daughter. Very soon."

"This had to be done right, or its all for nothing!" he says to himself.

"Let's see? Victoria finished the Acapulco array, and by sheer luck I get to extend it to Cheboygan. Eight-thousand-kilometer-long ELF receptor array." Steven is quite pleased with his progress.

"Rosalyn? You will love how far you can reach into the Universe with THIS array." He says absented-mindedly to himself.

"Naah. My daughters are too far away to be hearing anything I think to myself."

Just another erroneous thought Father had on that drive to Stone Mountain, Georgia.

He also thought I would spend the formative years of my life living with him. Ha!

Grandma Fran was the law on the matter. She has not spoken yet. I have a feeling we're about to hear from her.

*** **STASIS BREAK** ***

WHILE STEVEN is driving somewhere on US Highway 2: 2004

Steven was required to enter a remote verification, at the phone booth back in Kalispell not because he was away from the computer or some home location. He was required to do so to set a remote timed sequence. Consequently, Steven hadn't yet completely programmed the end of the timed stasis.

Not correctly, anyway.

The computer never accepted the return state of Becka.

When 90 minutes is up, it won't know what to do.

If Steven were in his lab, maybe he would be thinking clearly and he would see that the computer monitor shows it is still waiting for one command:

"STASIS SET"

"RATE = 6"

"Duration: 90 minutes"

Command: END STASIS

Invalid Command for TIMED Stasis

Return to Nominal

ACCEPT: Y/N

(Blinking command prompt)

Instead, he is blinded by his dreams of a better world through his inventions and ingenuity.

This fact was the number one reason I didn't wake up for two days after we TWINS fell to earth together after beating up those Russian bad guys. Okay, it was the ONLY reason.

It took me a while to convince Ros it was just a mistake. I understand Rosalyn's concern that our genius father may be mistake prone.

Mothering my father is not how I had imagined my life. Yet, somehow, I am walking into that responsibility quite clear-eyed.

This growing up stuff is hard!! **eye roll smh**

* * * **OFFENSIVE ROSALYN BREAK** * * *

STONE MOUNTAIN, Georgia – September 1, 2004

COSMIC TWINS Communication: excerpted from "The COSMIC TWINS Arrive", copyrighted 2014.

What Little Girls Are Made Of- From the Diaries of Becka Skaggs, PhD

Becka, my sister, my Love, my Strength. It has come to my attention that Yuri has pulled the stunt that caused us to fall. He has been on Father's trail taking control of Father's ELF receptor/transmitters. Almost half of Father's antenna array has been corrupted.

When the news of the fireball came to Yuri, and his men had never been heard from again, Yuri knew exactly who he wanted to blame. "That thieving weasel of a man", Yuri's words, Sister.

Yuri is mad at Father, Becka, my Love, my Light. We just got in his way. This evil Russian general was enjoying amassing power in the shadow of Putin. Suddenly, Father arrives from nowhere and is dismantling Yuri's decades-long plan right before his eyes. He was not going to stand by and let this happen.

Yuri sent out a series of signals generated specifically as destructive waves to the ELFs in Steven's array. I do believe we have temporarily disrupted their communication. But we must find a permanent answer.

These are more words I took from Yuri's mind, Sister. Please find a way to defeat him, for the sake of our family and our Stone Mountain research home. We need your help, my sister, my Love, my Strength.

"I now have the ultimate weapon against his plans for the use of ELFs. Whatever those plans might be, I'm not quite sure yet. Statistically, mind you, the chances are very high his daughters will figure into his plans for the future."

I trust the strength of your mind, my Becka, my Love. Do not risk a response until you have more information. I love you forever, my sister, my COSMIC TWIN.

CHAPTER – LAW-GIVER of LIFE

Friday, September 18, 2004

Grandma Fran is on the phone to Father. They have been arguing over the phone about this same topic for a week. Fran has had enough of it and has put her foot down. Father has been in Stone Mountain for two weeks. He has everything running in good order and is ready to have his family with him. Malia and Rosalyn have arrived safely, and Malia is thrilled to be so close to Savannah. I am ecstatic for my sister. She deserves to be near as much family as possible. I love her so much!

Grandma Fran believes we sisters need to live apart for our own physical safety. At least until Yuri Yurachenkov is subdued.

Eventually Steven gives in to Fran. One fact that helped was that I would be working for my Uncle Jack in his Engineering Lab after I finished my degree. I just did, June 2, 2020.

"Working for a charitable organization will be a good thing for Becca, and it will be a good thing for all people. Therefore, Steven, it will be a good thing for you!"

All these work and educational details for my future were just the factual parts of the argument that grandma gave to Father. Fran had an emotional reason for wanting me to stay with her, and that was Carol.

"Steven, you're a brilliant young man with a very bright future. I don't fault any decisions of the past. We have too many challenges for our immediate future to waste time on inefficiencies to planning the future for these girls

What Little Girls Are Made Of- From the Diaries of Becka Skaggs, PhD

of yours. Decisions must be made that are in THEIR best interest, not mine and not yours."

Fran paused and drew a breath. A few calm seconds passed.

"Steven, I don't expect you to take care of Carol, even though I know you have the financial capability. I believe you have no such responsibility to Carol. She is not your wife, nor does it appear she is about to become your wife at any time in her future."

Fran shifted her weight to the other foot. She has been standing at the old kitchen landline that is attached to the wall. Sometimes she stretched the cord to the table so she could sit down. Other times she would hop up on the counter to sit. Fran was tired of sitting and ready to wrap this up.

"But you have two daughters, and I DO expect you to be responsible toward them and their care. All of it."

Fran turned to her kitchen window over the sink and looked out to the street beyond. Something caught her eye, but nothing seemed out of place now. "Oh, well. Paranoia", she thinks to herself and dismisses the thought.

"Certainly, Billy Murdock will be Becca's family doctor and take good care of her. You know that, Steven. I'm not talking about that. I'm talking about the major stuff we both know is going to show up. This little girl's body is a mess. You won't want to stop tinkering with it because it's how you think you can help the most. I understand that, too, Steven."

Grandma paused to choose which recent disaster to mention first.

"Doctor Murdock is still talking about Rebecca's Code Blue in the Operating Room. It was as traumatic for Billy as it was for her. Just because he see's things more than us doesn't mean there is no effect on him."

Now, grandma is ready to present another recent disaster.

"My granddaughter didn't wake up for two days, Steven! Nobody knew if we were going to be having two Skaggs girls in the same hospital in a coma.

Can you imagine all the crazy thoughts that went through my mind at that time? My gawd, Steven. Of course, you weren't thinking of anything we were going through."

"I didn't want any of that to happen, Fran. You must believe me. The girls took on that task completely on their own. I can no longer control them, Fran."

"I understand, Steven." Fran said empathetically.

"The girls are growing beyond your imagination. That is making this even worse. Because if YOU can't imagine it, then who else can understand any of this?"

Then Fran got a little stoic

"We both understand the future is very uncertain with this child. Both children, actually. But I am discussing Rebecca. Becca's little body is a mess. And I'm not saying I will ever disagree with any of your decisions to swap out more spare parts. I have a lot of mixed feelings about the moral dilemma we face over the next 15 years, while these girls grow to adulthood. A tremendous amount. They are both human little girls. Rebecca has already experienced an untainted life. Rosalyn never shall. You have made sure of that, Steven."

Fran paused for another thought.

"I want to be sure Rebecca gets to be a little girl. She needs to experience that life!"

Fran almost screamed that at him.

She took a moment to calm herself, then finished the discussion, and closed the book.

"I'm picking up Becca from the hospital today." Fran told Steven bluntly. Then continued to roll out the plan grandma had for our lives.

What Little Girls Are Made Of- From the Diaries of Becka Skaggs, PhD

"She will be coming to live here with me. Carol will also be coming to live here with me, once she is well enough to come home. Doctor Murdock will be the attending physician for both girls. We may need some special equipment for Carol at some time in the future. But I can't worry about more unusual possibilities right now. I already have too many unusual facts to deal with here."

"Yes, I understand, Fran" came the response from my father.

"I'm not done," she snapped, as Fran quickly cut him off.

"You do realize, Mister brilliant scientist, that because of everything you have done, your eldest daughter is immuno-compromised. Her immune system is in worse shape than her filtration system you keep messing up. And YOU don't have the technology to fix that problem, either!"

Grandma was implying she knew Steven had the ability to do everything he says he will do. Fran also knows he's young, brash, and full of big dreams.

Steven tried to interrupt.

"No, Fran. That wasn't me". But that's as far as Fran allowed him to get.

"Yes, it was, Steven. You started this whole mess with the neuroreceptors, and the brain chemicals, and…and ALL of your research!!"

Steven kept silent. Fran was not getting any argument from him anymore. She is correct in everything she has said, and that sudden realization left him in a pensive mood. Steven had already said everything he could think of as all the good reasons to keep the TWINS together. But Fran always had a counter argument that made sense to him.

"Fran's right", the thought came to his mind.

"I need to find a way to fix Becca's immune system." Fran was not part of this internal conversation of Steven's. He had just not been listening to the last 30 seconds of Grandma's plans for me.

"We will be sure to push her into an Engineering or science degree that she likes." Fran was just finishing telling Steven the future for his daughter.... me.

I like beaches, grandma!

Grandma continued.

"This gives her a future that will keep her feeling human. Rebecca will need to be constantly reminded that she is human as she grows and matures and discovers herself. She must be allowed to have human experiences to feel human and accept that humanness as her reality."

"And we have the beach, and the Sound, and the Ocean right here for Rebecca to enjoy and explore, and to be a kid that happens to be a scientific marvel."

Fran was facing the phone hanging on the wall while still holding the old school receiver in her hand up to her ear and is about to end the conversation.

"This is settled, Steven."

"Now. If you don't mind. I need to get my granddaughter from the hospital. A month is too long for a child to be in the hospital. If you want to see her, Rebecca will be right here with me. Where she belongs."

"Have a good day, Steven. Give my best to Malia. Talk again soon. Goodbye."

Grandma and I are going to have a wonderful life together. I can hardly wait!

*** **My Second Chance Break** ***

Sep 18, 2004 –

After Grandma's phone call with Father.

My last day in the hospital since my accident. Mom is still in a coma. She was semi-comatose after the accident. The paramedics were working on

What Little Girls Are Made Of- From the Diaries of Becka Skaggs, PhD

mom the entire way to the hospital, after we finally got rescued from that four-car-pile up. Mom was in such bad condition when we arrived, the doctors were forced to put her into an induced coma. The doctors tried to revive her after about two weeks, but she never woke up. It's now been 30 days since our accident.

When Grandma arrives, William has already come into my room and taken me down to the front lobby. This is where we are waiting when grandma arrives.

Grandma walked through the door. She instantly saw William and her face brightened. Then she looked at me sitting in the wheelchair in front of him. Fran got a huge smile and almost ran to me to give me a big hug. I thought I was going to suffocate in there, amongst all grandma's bustiness.

Grandma Fran was a beautiful buxom brunette. She always had a little more in the chest than most the other girls while growing up.

Grandma Fran has many stories about when she would go out to the sandwich counter with girlfriends on a Saturday during Middle school and High school. The girls would have coke and fries. Maybe they would share a sandwich together. She sometimes would drop food on her blouse. Her friends would say that she had a large "Top Shelf", and that's the only reason she would end up with stains on her blouse and they would have the food stains in their laps. I would learn later in my life that I inherited Grandma's entire top shelf, and maybe a little more.

I'm sitting thinking about my future and something serious came up. I'm not calling Doctor Murdock, "Billy". That's grandma's name for him. No. Instead, I will call him William. He may be Grandpa William, in the future. Who knows?? I feel like I wouldn't get very far by calling him Grandpa Billy. I feel like Grandpa William would be better for everyone. Don't you?

William began giving Fran instructions about me and my care while at home. It's new for both of us, not just grandma. I don't have my mom, or my life, ya know. **eye roll**

"Hey! I'm right here!" I said to my future grandparents.

"Yes, of course you are, Becca", Grandpa Murdock said. Ok, almost grandpa.

"I am also talking to you. These are your instructions too", William said to me, and looked back at grandma. He began speaking to both of us,

"Fran? Have Becca create a schedule for her food, exercise, and her sleeping."

The doctor looked straight down at me. I had to lean back in the wheelchair and stare straight up to see him. Yeah, he was upside down.

"Becca, you will become obsessed with things in your immediate focus. You will forget how much time has passed. I'm asking you to create this schedule so that you will know it's your schedule. Then you promise yourself to stick to it."

"Yessir." I spoke immediately "I will do all that the minute we get home."

"Okay, Fran. I will push Becca to the car, then she's all your responsibility."

Dr Murdock looked at me and said,

"Good Riddance to bad rubbish. I never want to see you back in this hospital, beautiful!"

And he waved us on.

I had a giant smile on my face as grandma drove us home.

*** A PRESAGE BREAK ***

JUPITER WELL, AUSTRALIA – March 2020

We have received the serial numbers for 100 million doses, Director.

"100 million doses? That's fantastic! When will the remainder of the serial numbers be transferred?"

They will not be transferred, Director.

What Little Girls Are Made Of- From the Diaries of Becka Skaggs, PhD

"That is only 12.5% of the serial numbers I requested. This is nowhere near adequate. What happened to my other 87.5%!??

"They have been held by the Director of Infectious Diseases at WHO, Mary Aboagye. She put a hold on the issuance of our serial numbers. She said there are some irregularities with the application. They are beginning a recall of all doses."

"Begin the vaccinations. We have wasted too much time as it is," Yuri crowed at his assistant.

"The Philippine Islands have already administered 1200 doses. I can hardly wait for the glorious moment of my triumph!" The little voice inside Yuri's head is jubilant.

"A recall?" Yuri gets a chuckle out of that wee Swiss joke.

"Oh, Yes, Ms. Director. Yuri will be sure to deliver them personally." Buahahahahaaaaaa.

"Yes, Director!"

The lab assistant absent-mindedly agrees.

Then Yuri barks out, "Oh Stop that, you mindless idiot. We're not giving them anything!" There's a brief pause.

"Besides, you don't even know why you are saying, 'Yes, Director.'"

"Yes, Director!"

Yuri gives his assistant a long stare as he walks past him into the hallway.

"Let's go, Vladimir. We must get to the Seychelles. We have a few dozen inoculations to make once we're there. And perhaps a small bit of banking." Bahahaha.

CHAPTER – LIFE ANEW

PRESENT DAY 2020

COSMIC TWINS WORLD HEADQUARTERS – Stone Mountain, Georgia

Department of Health and Human Services

Public Health Service

"To Provide a Healthy World for All to Enjoy"

Alisha Myles and Andrew Remington wed on September 18th, 2005. It was a beautiful late summer wedding, and hush hush. It was our very small gathering in a quaint little church in Savannah.

The media was shocked when everything finally came out about Yuri Yurachenkov and The COSMIC TWINS. Of course, I was much too young to completely understand the adult stuff going on in 2005. I had problems of my own that kept my mind occupied, and my body.

Alisha was approached by The Department of Health and Human Services because of the notoriety of my case. They wanted to extend a commission to her for her work and continued advancements in the field of nursing. She accepted a commission through the Public Health Service, but not as a nurse. Alisha was originally assigned to my case because she is a Medical Doctor, my neurosurgeon.

While Alisha was working on her bachelor's degree in Nursing, she wrote a thesis that gave her acclaim among the faculty at the University of

What Little Girls Are Made Of- From the Diaries of Becka Skaggs, PhD

Washington School of Nursing. The school published the work and gave Alisha credit as lead-author. The UW Medical School tested her theory and found they achieved an 88.9% success rate in identifying children with the "Love Bug" gene. Alisha had described a methodology nurses could use within the first hours of life to passively test for the presence of a "Love Bug" gene by making a few timed observations. Alisha became noticed by the right people.

Alisha found, among other things, that a "Love Bug" infant will purse her lips together no less than 8 times in the first minute of life, as if she's already trying to kiss you. If you find an infant that exceeds eight kisses in the first minute, the Myles Method says a nurse must observe the infant for a total of 2 more minutes, each minute one-hour apart. Alisha found, "Love Bugs" will kiss over 30 times during those 3 minutes of life, to an 88.9% certainty.

Once they started to identify the love bugs, they wanted to separate them from the other babies. It was a natural response for science-minded people to be grouping like items together. But the babies would howl and scream until the love bugs were dispersed evenly throughout the maternity ward population. A LOVE BUG infant will not tolerate such forced segregation. And an infant whose heart has been touched by that of a LOVE BUG? Well, let's just say an uprising from the Infants of the Howling Hearts was sure to ensue.

Alisha, and her new husband Andrew Remington-Myles – isn't that cute how they did their names? Like 'my name was here first, so your name goes second'.

Anyway, Alisha and Andrew were already working with Steven at his private lab to help keep me from falling apart physically. Ros and I would work together on our telepathic transfers and use of LOVE energy whenever I was there. Our family decided I would stay in Georgia every December. This family time could be used for training and any other surgeries I needed along the way. Believe me, new surgeries came up a lot until I was 13 years old.

For one thing, my growth was causing problems with what they already did inside there. There also came a time when I needed bone grafts in my legs. My left leg, it turns out, had a small hairline fracture that almost healed itself over time. But at a certain point in my growth, at age 12, it was starting to cause problems. The fracture wants to stay active, like a tiny creeping earthquake fault. Never being allowed to completely heal. This time for me in Georgia gives us chances for more physical improvements.

I spent December and January in Atlanta the winter of 2012-2013. That's when they had the biggest planned bone graft. Rosalyn and I got to work on more languages and energy transfer moves. We learned to reach out with our mental powers and have them join at a specific location to pick up objects. Soon we learned to use the energy of love in the objects we touched. I got to the point I could feel the energy that was about to be transferred before it happened. I had developed these "anticipatory" feelings for the energy. I could not get satiated with love.

Once Ros and I learned to focus and find the love in the object? My brain almost exploded! I mean that like in a literal sense, in the way that this is literature. Okay, it's figurative speech. But I'm not drawing anybody pictures here. I'm talking. Sheesh!

I'm getting you guys all caught up. Okay?

Alisha and Andrew decided the best thing for Alisha was to accept a commission in the Public Health Service. She entered the Service as a Lieutenant Commander. Alisha was quickly promoted after the enactment of The COSMIC TWINS PROTECTION & HUMAN RE-UNIFICATION Act (CTP-HU). Her rank is currently Commander, and she wears the silver oak cluster as her insignia of rank.

Alisha loves her country. There has never been any doubt about the love in her heart for her fellow Americans. This alone was enough motivation for Alisha to accept a commission from the PHS. Alisha also realized, as she further explored her feelings, she could work from the inside of the government to push for official recognition from Congress for the TWINS. Such

What Little Girls Are Made Of- From the Diaries of Becka Skaggs, PhD

distinction would assure Steven could continue to get funding and allow him to keep the bunker under Stone Mountain for his research. When I finally received my Commission in the Public Health Service, in July 2020, Alisha was assigned as my Commanding Officer.

Alisha became a very effective advocate for Father and The COSMIC TWINS. She spoke in front of the House Committee for Internal Affairs, and the Senate Appropriations Committee on behalf of the COSMIC TWINS, and Father's research benefits to the Country.

Rosalyn's disclosure, in the summer of 2006, of the presence of an advanced alien race may have helped convince some politicians who were otherwise fence-sitters. Some politicians may have been moved to vote to protect themselves when Rosalyn reported that the Alien Race was within our Galaxy but is not from our Galaxy. Who's to really know?

Regardless of Ros's warnings, Alisha did not expect Congress to pass the CTP-HU in December of 2006. The Democrats had swept the elections in Congress and were taking over both houses come January. Alisha wasn't expecting any action until after that transition took place.

Then she heard news the Senate Majority Leader was going to allow a vote on the final bill already passed by the house, she fainted. Literally! No, really.

She was sitting at her desk, and she listed left, like a ship in danger, and fell out of her chair. OUCH! It left a little mark. Just a tiny scratch at the hairline above the left temple. It's hardly noticeable at all. I'm sure it won't leave a permanent scar. I'm so sorry, Ma'am! I wouldn't want any permanent damage occurring to my Commanding Officer.

* * * **FALSE END BREAK** * * *

"Becca? Time for dinner!" Grandma called up the stairs to me. "You at a place you can stop?" She asks. "I'm ready to serve."

"Yeah, grandma!" I exclaimed excitedly. "I'm coming downstairs!"

I pushed SAVE. Then yelled as I was running out of my room. "I just finished the opening chapter on my COSMIC TWINS WORLD HEADQUARTERS, grandma!"

"Well, it's about time, isn't it?" Grandma gave me her patented 'out loud eye roll'.

Fran cracks me up with her sarcasm.

As I reach the bottom of the stairs, she adds,

"Go wash your hands." Grandma points at the sink while placing our dinner on the table.

"We eat civilized down here at this table." She can do all that without even looking at me. I'm hypnotized and powerless to stop myself from washing my hands. I mindlessly walk to the sink.

"We also use forks down here in this world."

I had a puzzled telepathy about me because I never said a word. Grandma just automatically added,

"You can put the drumstick of fried chicken, you were about to remind me we were eating, in your left hand while you place a fork in your right hand, please? You can shovel the mac n cheese with a fork."

"But grandma…"

"Ah-ah", grandma interrupts me by holding up the wooden serving spoon.

"THIS spoon is only for serving the mac n cheese. And you may also use the fork on some broccoli, please."

I had no comeback. She has me figured out. Maybe if I hang out with her some more, I might actually learn her wisdom?

What Little Girls Are Made Of- From the Diaries of Becka Skaggs, PhD

"I love you, grandma. Thank you for making dinner and taking care of me. Amen."

"Hahaha!" Grandma laughed good at my 'amen' joke.

"I love you too, Becca. And you are very welcome. Amen." She winked at me, folks.

You couldn't see it because I had her turned away from you, but Grandma Fran actually winked at me.

This time, the CHAPTER is over.

* * * **OFFICIAL BREAK** * * *

The PUBLIC HEALTH SERVICE ACT of 1944 gave the United States **Public Health Service** responsibility for preventing the introduction, transmission and spread of communicable diseases from foreign countries into the United States. The Public Health Service Act (PHSA) provides the legal authority for the Department of Health and Human Services (HHS), among other things, to respond to public health emergencies. The act authorizes the HHS secretary to lead federal public health and medical response to public health emergencies, determine that a public health emergency exists, and assist states in their response activities.

The Public Health Service Commissioned Corps (PHSCC) had its beginnings with the creation of the Marine Hospital Fund in 1798, which later was reorganized in 1871 as the Marine Hospital Service. The Marine Hospital Service was charged with the care and maintenance of merchant sailors, but as the country grew, so did the ever-expanding mission of the service. The Marine Hospital Service soon began taking on new expanding health roles that included health initiatives that protected the commerce and health of America. One such role was quarantine.

Members of the PHSCC wear the same uniforms as the United States Navy with special corps insignia, and hold ranks equivalent to those of naval officers. Officers of the PHSCC receive their commissions through PHSCC's direct commissioning program. Directly Commissioned Officers are not required to attend an academy or other military officer training. DCOs most often are commissioned because they hold a skill considered vital to the Service.

Cmdr. Alisha Myles-Remington was "Officially" assigned to the Centers for Disease Control and Prevention in Atlanta. She vowed to never stop being my attending neurosurgeon. She is also still working with me in speech therapy in 2020. The Commander has been working with me in the bunkers beneath Stone Mountain every December since I was age seven. It's the only way we can complete our "unofficial" business, since Yuri began interfering with our ELF signals.

It's okay. I have a lot of research I need to do. If Yuri leaves us alone long enough, I will defeat him. That day is coming very soon.

In the interim, you will see, I play 'possum' with Yuri; I learn to play dead. He won't find me until I'm ready for him to find me. There's more than one way to defeat an evil mastermind.

*** **Back in time to our story!** ***

CHAPTER – MY CYBORG LIFE

September 20, 2004 –

It's been two days since I left the hospital after my accident. I'm home at grandma's house, upstairs in my room. My new home until mom wakes up, anyway. How long that will be, only the universe knows. She didn't wake up when they said, "pretty please". Being polite never worked if you were trying to get mother to do something she wasn't otherwise inclined to do. I guess the doctors found that out.

It's morning and I'm sitting in my room after waking up and making my bed. I am finicky that way. If I climb on my bed during the day, I don't want to be climbing all over the sheets I will be sleeping in later that night. I only change them on Wednesday and Sunday, so I shouldn't get them dirty because I was playing. And I do like playing on my bed, for lots of different reasons. So, to avoid the issue of sleeping in icky sheets, I make my bed as soon as I get up, and go to the bathroom, of course.

I have my schedule done. I'm awake at 7:29am so I can have 1 minute to make my bed and then shower at 7:30. I'm going to attend school when I'm five. So, I need to get used to the hours. I started planning my food, but grandma told me not to worry about which food I should eat. That's her job. So, I decide the times and which activities occur at those times.

I have five meal/snack times. Grandma said that was smart. Helps me keep my energy level up all day without going through spikes and crashes. I thought it was smart, too. It's kind of how the meal breaks got on my schedule.

249

I also allow a lot of time for my writing. I fill up 3 hours in the morning and another 3 hours in afternoons if I don't have another appointment that day. I always give myself at least 1 hour each day for writing, no matter what else is happening that day. It's my path to sanity.

When I say "writing", that also includes all time needed for researching my topics of interest. Doctors and scientists will take all my scheduled time if I let them. I need my own time, too, if I'm to be healthy. Writing and researching is "my time" kind of things. I can't keep myself sane, if I can't keep myself happy. This philosophy of life keeps me motivated to get better each day.

My schedule at night always allows me 15 minutes to organize all my writings I did during the day. Then I brush my teeth and kiss grandma goodnight. I kiss uncle when I'm living at his place, but I'm at grandma's right now. I think by kissing your loved one goodnight it helps make sure nothing bad will happen to them while they are asleep. It's a loving thing to do.

I'm having some problems today. I am not feeling very loving about anything right now. I'm surrounded with stuff grandma got that isn't mine. I don't have anything from home that wasn't already here. That's causing me a little distress. I don't know what to do with it all. Grandma says she is still having a tough time going to Carol's house. So, I let it go. I understand how that could get sad. But these research materials are too simple for my advancement. I can read adult stuff, so I need big people stuff. Right?

I also understand my confidence in my voice is gone. I don't trust it; it doesn't sound like me. When I get a little high in my voice range, I get hoarse and have a raspy whisper, and it cracks out of nowhere! I'm not likely to be singing opera for a career, that's for sure.

The doctors say the scar tissue will just keep getting worse, over time. Talking will help keep the vocal cords in shape. Yeah? Why don't I believe that? I'll keep talking very subdued and sparsely. I'm just saying. I don't like my voice. It hurts sometimes and I don't think that is a good thing. Sorry,

What Little Girls Are Made Of- From the Diaries of Becka Skaggs, PhD

docs. I guess I'm disagreeing with your plan of action. Won't be the first time, either.

I am honestly concerned about Rosalyn. She never leaves me alone this long. It's another communication blackout. At least Yuri hasn't tried to attack me since I arrived at grandma's house. I'm sure I would hear if he tried to attack Rosalyn.

Ros, my sister, my LOVE, my Light. Please reach out to me. I need your strength, your guidance, my sister. I love you so much, Ros!

I can't seem to reach her. I'll just bet that Yuri has found a way to block our signal. I will find a way to hide from him. Yes! That's what I will do.

I can hide from Yuri so he can't find me. Now, how do I do that?

Ah! Sleep. Hibernate. Not dead, but stasis. YES!! I will create a low-energy state of restful sleep. The way Father helped me through surgery. Brilliant idea!

I'm feeling better already. I'm thinking of things fast. That's a good sign! Grandma has my schedule. I gave that to her last night. Eating 5 times per day will help keep me from becoming too obsessed on things and will keep me grounded in reality. I understand that could be difficult for adults. Hehe.

Grandma explained some of the challenges involved with my schedule. But I'm willing to try it. Not that I've ever been good at keeping to schedules. But there must be a first time, right?

*** **A Cyborg Reverberation Break** ***

December 10, 2004 – Point Roberts, WA

It's a gray, rainy, windy day. The rain would let up occasionally, then start coming down again. That was typical this time of year in the Pacific Northwest of the United States.

Whether it would be raining or not at a particular moment, the visibility would be generally poor all day long. The temperature is in the low 40's, for us Americans. High single-digits for the rest of the World, which includes Canada.

There are three people braving the weather. They are standing on the sea wall. The tide is on its way out. There is a relatively dry, sandy beach visible, though no one is currently enjoying it.

It appears there are two men and a woman. The lady is pointing toward the old scraggly maple tree at the very north end of the beach, against the International Boundary. She is talking quite excitedly as her hand seems to be moving and darting quickly pointing here and there. One man is also talking a bit. He is wearing an overcoat and a baseball cap. A rather strange combination for whatever he's pretending to be today.

The other man is only taking notes with a pen and a notepad. He is writing so furiously he hardly has time to look up at the lady. The notepad must be one of those rainproof notepads.

Mr. Notetaker has no head covering of any kind, but he is wearing an overcoat. The notetaker has his coat buttoned all the way up, except maybe the top 2 buttons. It appears to be the amount he would need to reach his notepad inside his jacket breast-pocket, without having to unbutton any other coat buttons.

Soon the conversation is over. The lady has stopped talking and her arm is down by her side.

The talkative man extends an arm toward the house across the street. That seems to be an invitation for them all to retire to the residence sitting along the street that runs in front of the sea wall. This is the very home with the beautiful, picturesque view of Boundary Bay. This is also the very lady that observes all the daily activities that occur near the sea wall at Maple Beach.

When they arrived at the home, she opened the door and appeared to invite them in. The talkative man begged off the idea by gently, but noticeably,

What Little Girls Are Made Of- From the Diaries of Becka Skaggs, PhD

shaking his head to the lady. The notepad had already been exchanged, without notice by the lady, for a 9mm-caliber handgun with a silencer.

The notetaker raised the tool of his trade and double-tapped the trigger to fire off 2 quick rounds in succession. The bullets struck the lady between the eyes before she could take half-a-breath in surprise. This shooter spaces all his double-taps - 2 shots in less than a second to the forehead - one-quarter inch apart. It's his signet, like when an artist signs his paintings.

A small smile presents itself on the maestro's face, as the handgun is placed back inside the jacket.

The lady fell straight back into her front room, as if she had suddenly fallen asleep. The two men were kind enough to move her feet so her front door could be closed. It is raining, afterall. Those overcoated chicken's nuggets then got into a white American-made sedan and were never seen in Point Roberts again.

* * * **The Cyborg Connects Break** * * *

Becka, COSMIC TWIN Communication: excerpted from "The COSMIC TWINS Arrive", copyrighted 2014.

Rosalyn, my sister, my Love, my Light, I have received your communication. Your ELF signals are now clear. Tell Father I understand my mission. I am the Strength. I am the Love. I will comply with your request, my sister, my Light, my Love! Hearts and Marshmallows, sis.

* * * **A Disconnected Cyborg Break** * * *

August 19, 2005

Today is our shared birthday. Rosalyn turned 1 today. I'm 5 now. They say I can start school next year, after I turn six. Grandma was very angry at the school district. She said they made the wrong decision denying me from starting school. I was supposed to start kindergarten in a few weeks, but they said my speech wasn't developed enough for their programs. I didn't have a minimum skill level. I don't seem to know enough words.

Are you kidding me? I am Becka Skaggs, The COSMIC TWIN! I am strong! I am the Love. I am your light and your knowledge. I brought down 10,000 meteorites, minus seven, onto some bad guys. You say I can't meet some minimum level?? Ha!

You want words? If you, Ms. School District really think that I'm dumb, then you don't know nothing. How did you even get a college degree with that kind of faulty logic?

I'm getting cranky and grumpy. On top of denying me things, people keep wanting me to do things for them. Adults think I should just always do what they ask. What if I don't feel like it today? I'm getting tired of all the research questions.

Yes, I love you all. Of course! But I have other feelings, too.

It's my birthday and I'll cry if I want to.

I miss Ros so much! It's been nine months since our last ELF communique. I understand our safety is a big concern for all our adults. That doesn't make me miss her any less.

It's her FIRST birthday! I hope she is happy and running into walls and furniture like a silly little girl on her 1st birthday. I hope she has cake all over her pretty dress. I really want her to be happy on her first birthday. I love my sister.

So, why am I crying? Waahhhh!!! Sniff-sniff.

It's my sad day. I'm away from everybody except grandma. I have been sick. I had a small cough that wasn't much a few weeks ago. It never went away. Now, I have a small fever and a big cough. Grandma is watching it with the thermometer. I was 100.6* two hours ago. She'll be coming back to check again soon.

What Little Girls Are Made Of- From the Diaries of Becka Skaggs, PhD

Grandma asked if I wanted a cake. No, that makes no sense for just two of us. Besides, I'm five now. I don't NEED birthday celebrations to survive in this world. Yuri isn't going to give me a holiday because it's my birthday.

What? You think Yuri would be a nice guy?

"Ohhh, I was going to kill you today", Yuri might say.

"But I saw it was your birthday. So, I decided to give you a holiday from all the fear and terror I create in your mind daily."

Then he would raise his eyebrows way up, like a big question is coming. *"Yuri is not cruel, nooo."*

See? He acted like he was going to ask a question, then tricked us with a lousy statement. Yuri is pure evil. He can never be trusted. Mark my words.

Oh! Speaking of Yuri, I've been practicing my hibernation. I'm getting very good at it. I can slow my heartbeat to 2 beats per minute. I must give that heart a jolt for it to pump like it needs for one beat. I must use all my universal energy to make it work.

I learned how to keep my blood pressure up throughout my whole body during the entire interval between heart beats. I can't allow my pressure to drop much at all. When I was practicing my hibernation, I learned how to talk to my cells. My own individual cells can communicate with me. WOW! All the learning I've been doing since our accident gets me excited. I get a euphoric feeling when I learn massive things.

Look at that word! "Euphoric". This is what I get to learn by NOT going to school!

It's a wonderful, lazy, dizzy word where a person is eternally happy. What could possibly be wrong with being 'euphoric'? Ms. School District should try being euphoric once-in-a-while. Maybe that would help her attitude.

So, my long-winded point is my hibernation practice has been very good mental practice for me. My Stasis Power is my super-power! YES!! I'm getting prepared for you, Yuri Yurachenkov. You better be getting prepared for me! Bahahaha

Okay. Thinking about defeating that stinking nincompoop made me a little happier. Maybe I'm feeling a little more euphoric?

* * * **Cyborg Snooze fest Break** * * *

August 19, 2005 - Two hours later.

Sorry, guys! I was dreaming about defeating Yuri and feeling euphoric, and I fell asleep.

I was getting a little tired sitting at my desk and laid down on my bed with my laptop. Next thing I know, Grandma is waking me up. I had missed my late morning snack and it was time for my cake. I said no cake. Nobody ever listens to me!

I jumped to the wrong conclusion, though. I should've known grandma would get me what I asked for:

Carnation-pink cupcakes with periwinkle-purple frosting. I said it would be ok to give me five cupcakes: one for each of my years.

Grandma laughed and got a big smile.

"Candles?" she asked.

"No, thank you", I told her. I explained why, too. The candles felt like evil spirits lived inside them.

"The evil spirit is trapped inside the candle?" she asked me in a sincere effort to understand my situation. I had to explain to grandma how this energy thing works.

"No, grandma. The evil spirit WANTS to live inside the candle. Then, when you burn the candle, the spirit is getting released. The evil can fully escape once the candle is burned away, but the wick hasn't burned to ash, yet."

What Little Girls Are Made Of- From the Diaries of Becka Skaggs, PhD

I looked at Grandma Fran with a silent facial expression of "Now, do you understand?"

She stared at me blankly.

I made a final clarifying statement.

"So, 'no thank you' on the candles, grandma."

"Ok", she complied. "Absolutely no candles." She bends down and kisses my head.

I learned right there that was a grandmother's trick to see how sick I'm feeling. Fran is so wise!

"Sweetheart. You are feeling warmer." Grandma puts the back of her hand on my forehead.

"Where's that thermometer, honey?"

"Upstairs", I tell her.

Grandma was asking me where, "precisely", but I had shoved almost a whole cupcake in my mouth. I couldn't get the whole thing in my mouth. It wouldn't fit. But I tried really hard.

"Becca? Stop shoving that cake in your mouth."

She took the rest of the cupcake away from me. It was just the bottom portion. I already ate the best part. Well, I AM eating the best part. It's hard to breathe when your mouth is that full. And when your grandma's hand is in your mouth trying to pull at things, it gets hard to swallow.

"You're going to choke on that with your cough. You didn't need the whole thing. I was going to share that with you, Miss Graceful."

"Here", she gives me a paper napkin. I grab it and hold onto it in my left hand.

"You are sick. Sugar won't help you get better, Becca. It's why there's no sugar in medicine." Grandma said as she took all the rest of my special desserts away from me on my special day. Life is NOT fair!

I knew grandma would think of my health over my immediate happiness. When grandma asked me "What were you thinking by shoving that cupcake in your mouth?"

I was thinking about that scrumptious looking cupcake. I had one chance to eat this scrumptious-looking cupcake. It's made of my favorite pink and purple colors. How could it not be scrumptious? Isn't 'scrumptious' a great word? Yummy.

My window of opportunity to enjoy that cupcake was disappearing quickly when she asked about the thermometer. It had to be now! Besides, I fell asleep in my room, and I was hungry. I threw that excuse into the discussion with all my other excuses for why I needed to cram that cupcake in my mouth. I was hoping it would help grandma see that I'm building a body of evidence to make my ultimate plea. I NEEDED that cupcake!

"If you need some milk, it's still in the fridge." Grandma said as she moved past me to go upstairs and retrieve the thermometer. Then she added,

"Use the plastic cup in front of you, young lady."

"Okay" I called back to her, sort of.

BINGO! The one stair creaked on her way up.

Soon, all the stairs were creaking, as grandma made her way back to me sitting at the kitchen table trying to wash my cupcake down with a little milk. After I retrieved the milk from the fridge, I brought it to the table for my delicate work. I didn't want to spill milk all over the table while trying to fill the cup, so I got just enough to fill the bottom inch of the cup. It almost made the cupcake harder to swallow.

"Hurry up and finish that yummy dessert you just had to enjoy." Grandma says as she holds the thermometer ready to shove in my mouth.

What Little Girls Are Made Of- From the Diaries of Becka Skaggs, PhD

Grandma Fran suffered through three more seconds of my trying to swallow and had seen enough of my eyes rolling into my head trying to will the cupcake into my gullet. She filled my cup with milk so she would stop feeling my pain of trying to swallow the delicious yet dusty dollop of love.

"Drink." She commanded.

After I finished gulping my milk and clearing my mouth of that delicious delicacy, Grandma pushed the glass thermometer in my mouth.

"No talking, chatterbox." Grandma said to me.

"Hhnngg mmee?" I tried to say Who Me, but it didn't quite come out that way.

Grandma didn't care what I was trying to say.

"SHUSH!"

She makes me sit in silence. It feels like waiting for the jury to come back with a death sentence. I start to crane my eyes to the kitchen window. I can see a thunderhead developing in the sky. This one is shining a bright yellow in a portion, as it tries to grow large enough to obliterate the sun from our view.

"One OH one point five" grandma says.

Then she starts getting dramatic.

"I'm calling Billy. Then you are going to the hospital, young lady."

Then she looks me right in the eyes and asks me in her funny snarky way,

"You do remember the hospital, right?"

"Yes, grandma." My shoulders droop.

Then she says, "go upstairs and get LOVE."

"Oh, yeah, grandma. LOVE! I'll get her!"

LOVE is my purple Unicorn stuffed animal Mom gave me as a gift after she got out of the hospital and started to get on her feet. Mom woke up in early November 2004 and was sent to an assisted-living apartment November 15th.

She still has difficulty with her balance, sometimes, and remembering to shower. She sometimes thinks I'm her little sister. That's okay with me, except, during our visitations she would just leave me at the mall or the movie thinking grandma was coming along anytime to get me. Then, I would have to find an adult to call grandma to come rescue me. So, that means I still can't live with mom.

She got a part-time job in her diner; the diner in which she met my father. Her schedule restricts the times we can be together, also. I mean, I know Mom's trying to get better. I wish we had more time, that's all. I still can't talk about her very much before I get emotional. I'm sorry it makes me sad. I just miss her so much.

Where's LOVE? I don't see her, ohhhh. Hiding under the pillows. You sneaky Unicorn.

"Okay, grandma. I got her!"

I come running down the stairs only hitting three stairs and using the banister to lift myself past some of the steps. I land at the bottom of the stairs and almost double over coughing. It's the worst cough I've ever had. I'm coughing so hard my stomach is hurting.

But, in my left hand, I'm holding LOVE high over my head.

Grandma says,

"Ok, good. You found her." Grandma is smiling and shaking her head at me. "You are a superhero, indeed."

Still coughing but in recovery mode, I nod my head in agreement to grandma. Sarcasm runs in our family.

What Little Girls Are Made Of- From the Diaries of Becka Skaggs, PhD

She places her hand on my back.

"You're even hot on your back, honey. Let's go see Doctor Murdock at the hospital."

Fran guides me outside and into the car. "Buckle up, honey", she says as I climb in the front passenger seat and buckle my seat belt while holding onto LOVE.

Next stop, my new second home: the hospital. A kid could begin to feel like an orphan with so much moving around. Let's not mention that my mom thinks I'm her little sister. Oh, shoot! I mentioned it. *Eye roll* Wink.

*** **Cyborgs Get Lonely Too Break** ***

November 5, 2005

I haven't said a word to anybody in almost four months. Well, I have spoken to grandma a little, and Uncle Jack if he's here. But nobody else, and not on the phone. Never!

Scientists haven't been getting any words from me, either. They can take their samples and do their tests. I don't need to participate in their secret processes.

Rosalyn and I haven't gotten to see each other in, like, forever. Over the last four weeks, though, we have communicated a few times. Okay, so I have talked to someone else. Well, we don't actually talk. Ros and I have regained our telepathic connection. Yuri's ELF disruptors must be down, or Father found another way to broadcast.

Either way, I was SO thankful for that!! Gawd, I was going crazy! I give her all my thoughts and my love. I'm not as good at words as her, so she doesn't get many words from me. But she gets lots of Hearts and Marshmallows!

Grandma Fran and Uncle Jack are having a phone call. They're discussing my speech problem, and my future. Then, they go back to the fact I won't talk to anyone. Nobody ever listens to me. So, what's the point, grandma?

"No, Jack. She spent another week in the hospital last month from pneumonia. This moist environment up here in Puget Sound is too much for her immune system year 'round."

Then grandma listened for a moment and responded.

"That's an excellent idea. We can find out the flu seasons for Arizona and Washington and change her living quarters accordingly."

A few seconds go by then grandma adds,

"Yes, I agree. She should be fine in Atlanta in December." Then the conversation turned to more adult planning and plotting.

The Centers for Disease Control and Prevention have been calling every week for a couple months now. The Public Health Service is calling too. They are interested in the brain chemical research in which Father has been engaged. Now that I have a slight brain injury, they think it gives their research a whole new exciting twist.

Yeah, you know, the experimenting Father's been doing on me? They want in on that action, too. They want to work on my immune system, probe my accessory spleen, and know more about my artificial organ that is a kidney and a liver all-in-one.

Uncle Jack said he had heard from some Universities that want to know about my brain receptors and how I can detect ELF waves so clearly. Then, there is the fact that I am a "LOVE BUG". Alisha's discovery puts me in the spotlight for this research, too.

So, based on what I hear from the phone call happening in the kitchen, it's sounding like I will spend every December in Atlanta, and that's great! It's real close to Father's lab in Stone Mountain. That will be perfect for me to continue my research away from Yuri's inquisitive eyes and pecking beak.

What Little Girls Are Made Of- From the Diaries of Becka Skaggs, PhD

All the adults in my life are being ignorant about Yuri, saying he doesn't exist, and he was just part of my imagination. I'm not gonna listen to that kinda talk. And I don't have a speech problem! I'm choosing carefully when to speak. I am an intelligent lady, after all. I must be dignified, yet unpredictable. Appearances Matter.

Okay, yes, but also No! None of this adult nonsense matters. Not really. That's not how I believe. I believe only LOVE MATTERS. I will show everyone the truth. I will do everything myself. I will find the evidence and I will fulfill my obligation to make it available to the people of the world.

You know? I'm not angry about this challenge. This is exactly what I need. This is the kind of thing I really need to help me find a way to defeat Yuri Yurachenkov!

I am pure LOVE. I will work from Pure LOVE. I am the strength. I am the Light. I am the knowledge.

EUREKA!! The most fantastic, brilliant idea ever, Becka! YES!!

I went running out of my room and ran downstairs, hitting every other squeaky stair while holding the banister.

"Grandma?" I said very firmly and loudly.

"I want a computer and a printer, or I don't talk to anyone about research."

Then I thought of one more thing.

"And a Kindle. I want to read things."

"I will have to call you back, Jack. Seems our little mute wants to talk to me."

Fran turns toward the phone hook, "Yeah, I love you, too. Yes, a little later. Ok, bye"

Grandma looks right at me while placing the receiver on the hook and says this, of all things,

"Honey? You can read things?"

As grandma looked up at me and gave me a little wink, telling me she was being a bit sarcastic. Grandma has been in my room. She knows I can read. I have many things I'm reading. Grandma just thinks its 5th or 6th grade stuff. NOPE! It's science and engineering stuff that professionals read.

Rosalyn brought me reading material from Father's lab once, when Malia brought her out so Jack could meet Rosalyn. It was a nice family gathering. Now, Malia sends me small books and engineering drawings. She's just a like little kid when it comes to my research. She is excited by it, and that gets me excited. Okay, so Malia brought me the stuff. But Ros is my sister, so she gets the credit.

I need many more volumes before I'm happy with my library. But I am putting together a library. I can't stop gobbling up information. I just LOVE it. It's like I crave information. Everything I can get my hands on. Horton Hears a Who is really funny! And green ham is gross! But I digress, again.

I'm about to converse very seriously with grandma. This conversation will be the basis for THE keystone decision of my life. Right here.

"That's what I've been trying to tell you, grandma. Something happened to me when I was in the hospital. It must be that evil genius, Yuri. Because now I can read and understand science and engineering drawings!"

My head dropped and my shoulders drooped. I turned and started to go back to my room. I was already determined to make every step squeak on the way up the stairs.

Then grandma stopped me.

"Come here, little one." She used that telepathic mind trick of being sweet and understanding. It runs through our family like the Algonquin genes that are quite evident in most of our cheekbones. I couldn't resist her spell.

I walked over to grandma, and she grabbed me up into her bosom and held me while looking right into my eyes. I was still in front of her, but I'm slowly lifting my gaze to eventually meet hers.

What Little Girls Are Made Of- From the Diaries of Becka Skaggs, PhD

Then she asked me very sincerely, "Your radio and Walkman tapes aren't enough anymore?"

I sadly responded, "No."

"And all the books Carol has brought from home, and the drawings "Rosalyn" has been mailing to you when she can't sneak books into your room? Rosalyn is not mailing something to you."

"She's really smart, grandma", I quickly volunteered on behalf of my absent sister.

Fran has a big smile.

"That may be, but methinks she has help. Could these books and drawings have something to do with you being so quiet?"

Then Fran gave me an extra hug. She held me just about my shoulders now and pushed me upright so she could look straight into my eyes. Grandma really believed in eye contact when in a conversation with people.

"I love you, Becca. Your Uncle Jack loves you. Your Mom loves you; your dad loves you; Rosalyn loves you; Alisha even loves you. And", grandma gets a smile.

"Apparently, Malia loves you very much!" Her eyes twinkle at me with her hidden understanding.

"You are surrounded by love, sweetheart. Come here baby" She grabbed me up and hugged me again. Then grandma said her peace.

"You have been home from your accident for just over a year. You've already been back in the hospital for an illness that will become a part of your normal life. What happened with the accident and in the few days following is odd, Becca, very odd."

Grandma saw my eyebrows raise. She turned on the emotional heat.

"Yes, a lot of strange things happened while you were healing in the hospital from the accident. But life is sometimes strange. We adults can't always predict what is coming next in our lives. Certainly, no one expects you to know what will happen next, nor do we expect you to know what to do about whatever that thing is that comes next."

Now I have confusion written on my face.

"I'm not trying to play down the seriousness of what you have experienced, honey."

Grandma continues,

"I am not even going to try to convince you that your experiences didn't happen. YOU had those experiences, not me. YOU are the only one that can gain understanding from those experiences. I will even agree that changes have occurred to you. In many ways, we don't even know all the changes, Becca. This is new for everybody! Doctors, scientists, you, me, evil masterminds…"

That got a smile from me.

"It's new for all of us. This whole, entire…whatever it is that's going on. It's all freaking new, baby!"

Then grandma bent her head down a little and caught my eyes again. I had dropped them from her eyes. She was letting me know the conversation wasn't over. But she was also letting me know I shouldn't be embarrassed by anything that happened or by anything I felt. It was all okay in grandma's mind.

"I don't know what's coming in our futures. If you do, I would appreciate a heads up. But I don't expect you to know. You don't have to know everything for everybody, Baby. All the research you say you want to do? It's not necessary. You don't have to know everything. Do you understand me, Becca?"

What Little Girls Are Made Of- From the Diaries of Becka Skaggs, PhD

"I think so, grandma." Then I gave her a little retort. "But I CAN know everything for everybody, grandma."

Grandma gave me a smile and said, "Alright, perhaps you can know everything for everybody. But you do not have to learn it all at once, you little genius."

Then Fran gave me a squeeze and finished.

"Be the most loving person you can possibly be, Becca. Always be loving in your intent, and life will be good to you. Strange things can still happen. Some things you may never understand."

Grandma got a serious look on her face that I have only seen a couple times in my life. This almost-new look caused me to give her my complete attention.

"YOU are our LOVE BUG, Becca! LOVE yourself, honey. Once you are comfortable with 'Becca' as a LOVE BUG? You will turn the world on its ear with all the LOVE that will come from you. Let the LOVE flow from you, sweetheart."

"Really grandma?" I asked with my big almond-shaped blues staring right at her.

"I guarantee it, sweetheart." Then she said,

"We'll get you your computer and a kindle. I can hardly wait to see what you make from all these new tools. I know you have something extraordinary in your future."

"I love you, grandma." I hugged her big!

"I love you, too, Becca."

Grandma gave me a big smile and pointed me toward the stairs.

I made sure to miss the step that squeaked on the way up to my bedroom.

LOVE, the Unicorn, got some pretty big hugs over the next couple minutes! She was surprised at first, but LOVE quickly succumbed to the good feelings of the hugs.

* * * A Cyborg Transition Break * * *

December 2006 – Atlanta, Georgia

Since I came down with pneumonia again in August in Washington, I am now going to be spending late spring and summers in the heat of Phoenix. Uncle Jack will come get me in late April each year. He can spend his birthday with his sister. Then we will go to his Engineering Lab in Phoenix and stay for the summer. Sounds like an adventure to me! This is my second "official" pneumonia, where tests came back positive, and x-rays confirmed the presence of bacteria in my lungs.

I had an irritating cough from March through April. I kept thinking it was going to turn into a fever and I'd be sick. But it didn't turn into anything. Maybe the cough is what started the pneumonia bacteria, and they didn't grow very fast? I'm not sure, but I'm paying attention. I decided to try to play hard, so my breathing gets elevated, and I have to breathe deep. That's brings in lots of oxygen into my lungs. Oxygen is supposed to kill those little bugs. So, oxygen is my friend.

I am staying with my father and his Georgia family for the first time. I am so excited!! Rosalyn and I have been inseparable twins. We even have twin beds in the same bedroom. We each have our own twin closets. It's way cool!

The first week was like a sleepover every night. We couldn't get to sleep until we each just dropped early in the morning. Now we are getting used to saying good night and going to sleep. We still like to hold our hands while we fall asleep. We have been separated too much. I just love her all the way to Jupiter and back!

What Little Girls Are Made Of- From the Diaries of Becka Skaggs, PhD

This is Christmas in Georgia with Malia and Rosalyn and Steven. They have a Christmas-town not far from here. All the shops are always Christmas all year. Well, okay, but I'm only here in December, and this is our first time, me and Ros together. So, Ros and I were in our figurative candy store. Each item enthralled us. Consequently, we were touching almost everything we could.

"No Touching!" would be the hushed words from Malia.

{Act like you're listening to Mom. She falls for it every time. She'll stop watching us if she thinks we're paying attention to her commands.}

Hehe. Rosalyn, you are sneaky! I understand you sister, my Love, my Light. I am having SO much fun with my family!!

{Me too sister! I like this arrangement. At least we get to see each other and love each other like sisters are supposed to do. Hugging you is so important to me.}

Yes, sister! Hugging has become very important to me, too. I'm really enjoying hugging Father. It's so amazing. Two years ago, I had no idea a father really existed. It was starting to look like another story from Carol. I learned to ignore 90% of what she says. And that's not good for a child and her mother.

{My sister, Becka, my love. My heart aches for you, your strife and all your injuries. I love you so much, my Love Bug sister. You are my Strength and my Light.}

"Rosalyn, swee'pea?" Malia is calling.

"Yes, mother? Becka and me are over here by all the Santa's." Rosalyn responded very politely.

{Gotta go! Call again soon? Bye Hehe}

*Rosalyn? Slow down. You started this conversation, Sister!! *Mental eye roll**

Rosalyn and I are learning how to have conversations with each other. That's cool! I like that a lot. Father could intercept our transmissions anytime he wishes, but he leaves us alone. He lets us have our time together. I really respect that from him. He's not threatened by our powers at all. And our powers have grown immensely over the last two years. Rosalyn and I can now gather up the power from any creature or non-creature that uses universal energy, and re-purpose it to 99.998% efficiency. When we are using our strengths together, we are so close to perfect, it's like if perfect were infinity, we would be at infinity minus one.

In another week, Congress will enact the COSMIC TWINS PROTECTION and Re-Humanization Act, my name for it. That will change everything for us "Officially". Unofficially, it just means more people and more equipment are here than we had before the enactment. I'll get you updated more on the Law later.

Back to my first visit to Christmastown, I think it's really cool with the lights and the artificial snow and the decorations. We spent several hours there one day. I liked that, since Father isn't allowing much for decorations in the bunker. Too much electricity use, among other bankrupt excuses he comes up with to support his minimalist attitude.

I don't know. I feel a marine lance corporal with blinking red and green lights on him would make a wonderful Christmas decoration for dank hallways!

Alisha comes by daily to check on me and work with me for an hour on speech therapy. 5 days a week is a good work-out for me. I'm not getting the practice I need when I'm away from the CDC, so Alisha set up a rigorous schedule to challenge her little patient....ME!

I seem to do very well with challenges. Alisha says I derive a special motivation if I perceive an action to be in response to a challenge. Did you hear that, Yuri?!!

Alisha has also developed some exercises that Ros and I do together. When we practice with Alisha's methods, it's like our focus becomes synchronized. When we are in sync, we are thinking the same things at the same times. To be synchronized makes us feel like Ros and Becka are simply

What Little Girls Are Made Of- From the Diaries of Becka Skaggs, PhD

complex facets of the same person. To be that close to another soul…it is really weird, but we love it!! We are LOVE BUG sisters forever!

You will never defeat us, Yuri. Never!

CHAPTER – METAMORPHOSIS: LIFE as the PERIWINKLE PRINCESS

August 19, 2008 – Day One: My 8th Birthday

"Becka?"

Great-Uncle Jack calls me to come outside the back door. I had been putting clothes away in my closet. I'm tall enough to reach my closet shelf myself.

Grandma sent me some new shorts, and jeans. I have lots of shirts and tops to wear. I don't need too many of those things.

Grandma also sent me a new "Shorts and T-shirt" outfit for my birthday. They arrived yesterday, but Uncle Jack wouldn't let me open them until this morning. Outfits are cool. I can use more of THOSE!

It's my eighth birthday and Ros's fourth birthday today. Ros and I have learned to not pay so much attention to what the other person is doing. Three years of hearing and reacting to everything was enough. At some point, we evolved as sisters, and are transitioning into lives that are more normal.

We are certainly NOT leading normal lives! Let me just get that straight. But we are getting more like 'normal' as each year goes by. We are more comfortable with our relationship given our special powers. That's probably a good way of putting it.

Rosalyn is enjoying our birthday with her side of the family at Stone Mountain, Georgia. Father has his lab all set up with a big apartment that

What Little Girls Are Made Of- From the Diaries of Becka Skaggs, PhD

we can get lost in if we don't pay attention to which hallway we ran down. The tunnels and rooms under Stone Mountain were part of an old military bunker from the Cold War. Some of that still exists down there, even though all it of has been remodeled and re-enforced – the real reason for remodeling anything in Father's lab.

Whispers from the marines are that we could be facing a new Cold War soon, with China. Some mothballed facilities are getting their mothballs removed. Ouch! Our bunker benefits from being ready to accept the latest equipment because we are already out of mothballs. Hey, wait. We don't have moths down here.

I also have my own hospital room at Stone Mountain. When I had pneumonia 3 times in 2 years, the DHHS decided it would be in their best interest if they could take care of me here. So, that's what we did, and we keep doing it today. Every year, I spend the month of December in Stone Mountain, training with Rosalyn and getting my body poked and prodded by scientists.

I understand why we need to do research on me. I also want to be a mother and help the children of the world. So, I decided it would be in MY best interest to let them get the information THEY wanted. Then, maybe, I could help all the children I wanted. It seemed like sound reasoning.

But today is my day here in Phoenix, Arizona. I decided to wear my new outfit today. Who cares if the shirt still has the fold marks in it? It's an awesome shirt. It's white with carnation-pink hearts and periwinkle-purple flowers. The cargo shorts are periwinkle purple. My favorite combinations! I love lots of pockets. Grandma is so smart.

Carnations are my favorite flowers. I love the smell of carnations. Mrs. Jepsen, next door to grandma, has a huge patch of pink carnations in her garden. The patch is huge!

Mrs. Jepsen's patch of carnations is SO big, I can lay down and almost get lost in them. And I do when I'm home. Especially in the spring when the flowers are new and fresh. Yummy! I Love that aroma! Scrumptious!

Sometimes, Mrs. Jepsen catches me laying in the carnation patch, and tells me to get out. She's not being mean about it. She just doesn't want me to ruin the patch of carnations. I understand. But I'm a kid with some impulse control issues. Sometimes, I just have to do what I am gonna do. Wink.

Mrs. Jepsen is also teaching me about living things, and how fragile some of them can be, compared to humans. Sometimes, while lying in the carnation patch all alone, I would find a little periwinkle underneath. It looks like a tiny snail living under the carnations.

Periwinkles are also very fragile creatures. Their shells are not very hard, and I could squish them easily if I tried. But I don't want to squish them. I want to love them for their contribution to the color purple.

The carnations need to be watered several times a week. Daily is best. The little purple snails are staying moist under all the wet carnations and eating tiny nuisances that bother the flowers. They are the perfect match for each other – Carnations and Periwinkles.

This is why I like carnation-pink and periwinkle-purple everything!

The lilac cargo pants grandma also sent, match the shirt perfect in my mind! So, it's like another outfit. It's ok to wear different shades of pink or purple at the same time. There are no rules saying I can't wear whatever colors I want to wear.

My new periwinkle-purple outfit is my favorite summer outfit, now. I still like my ones-y better. I LOVE onesies. It takes just one zip to get in or get out. My favorite ones-y is white, with carnation-pink and periwinkle-purple and sunshine-yellow flowers. But a ones-y is winter clothes for me here in Phoenix. Right now, it's summer. It will be 108* today.

It's still early in the morning. The temperature is only in the low 90's.

As soon as I open the door, I see my new bike. I gasp in surprise. I couldn't hold back the high-pitched scream that sent doves and crows from their perches in the nearby pine trees.

What Little Girls Are Made Of- From the Diaries of Becka Skaggs, PhD

The 30-foot-tall pine trees were planted when they built the apartments a long time ago before I was born. The trees are the border surrounding the apartments behind us, on the other side of the alley. Uncle Jack's Engineering Lab has a half-acre parking lot at the edge of downtown. We have our little lab and apartment inside a building that sits alone at the front of the parking lot.

"Do you like it?" Uncle Jack asks me.

"I LOVE it, Uncle! Thank you so much!"

I run over to the bike and take control from my great-Uncle. I grab her handle grips and straddle her like we are old friends.

"She's so beautiful. I love you, Uncle."

"I love you too, Becca. And you are very welcome."

Uncle Jack me gives his patented big hug and the little kiss on my cheek as he straightens up.

Then he lets me know he noticed I had given the bike a gender.

"She?"

"Sure", I told him quickly.

"She's pink and purple with a yellow lightning bolt. What else could she be?"

Uncle Jack gives me a big smile.

"I guess you got me there. Your logic is impeccable, sweetie. As usual."

Then Uncle Jack gets serious and gives me this first-rider warning.

"You're not used to riding a bike in this area, yet. The main street is very busy all the time. So, stay around here. That means between the alley and the sidewalk." He finished his instructions.

"May I go in the Alley, Uncle Jack?" I asked in my best "scientists must explore" impression.

"If you watch for cars, yes, you may use the alley. Just be careful, Becca. Be sure you are thoughtful of what you are doing."

Okay, Uncle Jack! I will. Thank You! I love YOU!"

Off I went driving around for about 1 minute. I had to take two laps around the charity's RV parked at the far end of the parking lot. It's hot outside, and people don't really stay out in the heat during the summer in Phoenix. You do what you need, then get back in the air conditioning.

I rode out into the alley. Then I did a little loop and came back into the parking lot. I drove over to the bike shop door, where one of the two guys from the bike shop was standing.

"I got a new bike from Uncle Jack", I excitedly tell Sean. Sean works at the bike shop next door where Uncle Jack had purchased the bike.

I finish my thoughts on the gift that I was already going to share with Sean. I just got a little distracted by the small Spanish Church on the corner. Something pulled my eye in that direction, but I see nothing now. I swear there are bad spirits in that place. I already don't like that place, and I've never been in it. Does that make sense to feel that way? I'll have to ponder on that one.

My attention is immediately back to Sean and my bike.

"It's a bike I can use while I'm here in Phoenix! I love it!"

Sean let's out a friendly laugh and says "Well, let's see that bike", he says with his typical friendly smile he always gives me.

"Do you mind if I look her over?"

I ride my bike up to him and hop off. Holding her by her handle grips, I offer the bike to him. Sean grabs the bike with one hand holding one of the handle-grips I had offered.

"I have some knowledge of bikes", Sean says with a smile.

What Little Girls Are Made Of- From the Diaries of Becka Skaggs, PhD

He acts like he is appraising the value of a treasured work of art. Sean is moving his hand across the different bike parts quickly, making sure everything is perfect. Finally, Sean's free hand traces across her handlebars.

"Yes, she's a beauty!" He says with mock excitement for my benefit.

"You and your bike are absolutely gorgeous, Becca."

Then Sean asked me a question that puzzled me.

"What's her name?"

"What do you mean? She's a beautiful bike, yes. But she's not a beautiful puppy."

I had a little scowl on my face.

Sean looked at us and squatted down to our level.

"Becca, you once told me you dreamt of being the captain of your own ship."

I responded in a way to draw a distinction in how he said and how I said it.

"Well, yes. I had a dream where I was the captain of my own ship. I remember telling you about that earlier this summer."

"Exactly!" Sean looks at me with a smile.

I was very apparently scowling.

"Oh, don't put that beautiful face into such a scrunch, Becca. YOU and your vessel are the most beautiful things in all the neighborhood. Look around?"

Sean opens his arms wide while twisting his body and head to appear like he is looking far and wide across the neighborhood for anything more beautiful.

"Oh, Sean. You are so sweet. You make me blush."

Sean's face brightens into a laugh.

"You are funny, and cute."

Then a concerned look comes over his face.

"Becca. This is serious. Every Captain wants her vessel to perform to the best of her abilities. In order to get your vessel to perform to the best of her capabilities, a Captain and vessel must bond and become one."

"Once a vessel and Captain become one, the captain can know instinctively how the vessel will move or shudder in certain seas. AND", Sean continues very sternly and slowly,

"The vessel will learn to anticipate the captain's orders, so every tack and jibe are completely seamless and perfect."

Then Sean finishes,

"Every Captain that has ever bonded with a vessel has a name for her vessel. Every Captain the world has ever seen names her vessel directly, in a christening."

Sean looked at her wheels with a bit of concern. I watched him intently, while he pulled a cloth from his back pocket and gently cleaned off a bit of dirt from her chrome wheels, then polished the area for a second or two.

Then he looked up at me and said,

"Only once the captain has named her vessel, can the vessel and the captain truly become one."

Then Sean stands up erect and says,

"Your bike is your vessel, Captain. You must name her like you would name your own child. Make it mean something to you, Becca. Make it be a name your vessel will be proud to bear."

I was moved by his words. He truly got me thinking. 'Like my own child', he said.

Then I said to him excitedly,

What Little Girls Are Made Of- From the Diaries of Becka Skaggs, PhD

"Wow, Sean! That's a better pep talk than Grandma Fran!"

I had a big smile on my face as I began turning myself and my bike around.

"That Grandma Fran must be a very nice person?" Sean replies.

"She is. She's the best!" I respond with my mind more on a name for my vessel than thinking about Grandma Fran and all her great qualities.

I turned my bike back away from the bike shop door and into our parking lot. I was pointing right at the back door to our building and standing over the frame about to hop onto the seat and start peddling, when I tell Sean I am thinking about what he said.

"I'm going to sleep on it, Sean. I'll let you know tomorrow."

"Aye, Captain" was the first mate's response as I retired to my Captains Quarters.

One more quick foray into the alley and time to get back into the air-conditioned apartment. Yippee!!!

* * * PERIWINKLE PRINCESS – Day Two * * *

August 20, 2008

I am in heaven. I have a little bike from the bike shop next door. She's gorgeous! But we have yet to take our maiden voyage. There are evil spirits in the neighborhood, namely at "Iglesias de Maria". I don't like that church and I'm not sure why. It just has evil energy about it. I'm afraid to go very far in that direction down the block just because of that church.

This morning, as soon as I woke up, I threw my shorts and shirt on, from yesterday, and I ran outside to christen my vessel. I ran outside with a plastic bottle of drinking water in my hand to assist with the christening. I thought I would just pour the water over her when I am naming her.

Excited, I unlocked the back door and pushed the back door open. It's a commercial-sized door of a multiple-use building, so it opens outward, away from the room inside the building.

I took the three steps to my vessel, and I dropped to my knees. The bottle of water dropped helplessly to the ground. I covered my face with my hands and began to weep like a little girl. She had a flat tire. How could this happen?

Sean from the Desert Bike Shop was just unlocking the door opening the bike shop for the day. He saw me crying as he approached the door to the bike shop. As soon as he gets the door open and retrieves his keys he asks.

"You have some troubles, Captain?"

It's the first time I noticed he was there.

I looked over toward the voice and saw Sean standing there. He was a very gentle looking man, with droopy, puppy-dog eyes. He was in his mid-forties. His tone was always gentle and understanding toward me.

Sean, are you my friend?" I asked him sincerely. I began to walk my vessel toward the bike shop, and I looked at him forlornly.

Then, Sean said so kindly with a little humor,

"We can be friends when you let me fix your bike. What happened to our mighty vessel?"

He approached me and the bike with true concern as we got nearer to the door.

"She got a flat tire." I said while drooping my head.

"Ok. I'll be your friend," Sean said with a smile.

"And I'll be her friend, too. As soon as you introduce us properly, by using her name."

What Little Girls Are Made Of- From the Diaries of Becka Skaggs, PhD

Now THAT was funny. He got a laugh out of me, and I brightened right up. WE took the vessel into the shop and began our dry-dock repairs.

Sean placed her up on the bike rack and gave a twist to tighten the wooden jaws of the large vise-like tool. Then, he said what he was going to do to fix her up and he would have her patched in no time.

"Be careful of nails and glass in the alley. They can puncture her tires", as Sean pulled a small nail from the tire and showed it to me.

Live and learn, huh?

"Thank you, Sean. You are a good friend."

You are welcome, my good friend" Sean said to me. Then he added,

"She's still waiting for her name." Pointing at the vessel. Sean is now done patching her tire and removing her from the workbench-vise.

"What's it going to be, Captain?"

"I thought real hard last night, Sean. I have two names I really like, but I can't decide", I told him.

Then Sean gave me the breakthrough I needed.

"Why not use both names? People have two names. It's ok for a vessel to have two names."

He saw my eyes widen with exciting thoughts of all the possibilities I could now choose. Then, Sean added,

"You can even use a phrase as a name." Sean continued.

"Monkey Business is a very famous phrase people like to use for smaller vessels."

"Hahaha. Monkey Business? That's funny Sean." The name is funny. It gave me the mental image of monkeys running wild all over the boat playing pranks on each other.

"It's a true and infamous story", he added.

"Think about it, Captain. But don't think too long. Right now, Captain, this vessel doesn't know who she is supposed to be. Her name writes her destiny, just like the name Monkey Business wrote the destiny of that little vessel many years ago."

Sean walked us out of the shop, through the backdoor, and into the heat.

"You don't want her not knowing who she is for very long, Becca." He told me with experience in the matter showing on his face.

"A vessel could get lost without a name. She may never learn who she could become, if she's never given a name."

Right then, my life came into focus. At eight years old, I knew what was going to happen in my future. It all came in visions and images. Not all of it made sense. It was like someone had just opened the curtains covering a picture-window and I could see the entire world through that window. Not all detail in the view was going to be seen or understood until a few moments had gone by.

I had never seen the World before. Is this really it??

THIS little bike is the beginnings I need to make me who I will become.

I then told Sean, matter-of-factly what I decided.

"Sean, I would like to introduce you to"

Then I squealed a little before saying, "LOVE is ENERGY!"

Sean thinks for a moment and his face lightens up, and he asks a question.

"First, let me ask, how did this name come to mind?"

I explained she is purple and pink. I LOVE purple and pink. And she has a yellow lightning bolt, which means Energy. I was thinking about just calling her ENERGY, but that name never felt good. Not all the way."

What Little Girls Are Made Of- From the Diaries of Becka Skaggs, PhD

"This name feels right! LOVE is ENERGY!" I exclaimed loudly.

"Becca, that is a FANTASTIC name for your vessel! I love her! Well, done, Captain!"

Then completing the introduction,

"Nice to meet you, LOVE is ENERGY."

Then Sean says playfully,

"Look at her Captain." He's standing back looking straight at her handlebars and down her entire contour.

"I think she's smiling."

Then he looks at me with a serious look, "Are you keeping the exclamation point?"

I couldn't quite tell where her mouth would be. But I believed him. Sean was the bike expert.

And "Yes!" I said with huge, excited eyes over the sudden idea.

"I'm keeping the exclamation point! 'LOVE is ENERGY!' with Becka Skaggs, Captain."

"Bye, Sean" I pushed my peddles until me and LOVE is ENERGY! were back over to our side of the parking lot.

I jumped off my bike and ran inside to tell Uncle everything that just happened. Including the evil spirits at Iglesias de Maria. He needs to know there is evil energy over there.

* * *

SC MacAlpine

At another moment when Becca is outside riding 'LOVE is ENERGY!', perhaps coinciding with her King Pine Tar experiences, another conversation occurs by the bike shop.

Uncle Jack is talking with Sean of Desert Bikes N Trikes next door.

"You have little girls, right?"

Jack looked at Sean and extended his right hand. Sean reaches over and shakes Jack's hand.

"Yeah, 3 of them. Becca would be my number three if she was one of mine. I still have a six-year-old. Why, you looking for another?"

Jack gave him a chuckle.

"Not hardly. This one's plenty"

Then Jack got a serious look on his face.

"But I'd like to ask you a question, if you don't mind?"

Sean shook his head quickly. "No, I don't mind. Go ahead."

Jack wasted no time and gave Sean a direct Father-is-concerned question.

"What do you think of her speech? I noticed you were talking with her a bit."

Sean scrunches his face a little as he thinks. Then,

"What do you mean? How she pronounces her words?"

Yeah," Jack said. "That and the tone of her speech and voice." He finished.

"I noticed a little issue with her R's and L's, but it's not severe. Her voice is hoarse a lot. But she's still young. These things have a way of changing through maturity."

"Yeah, she's still eight." Jack volunteered.

What Little Girls Are Made Of- From the Diaries of Becka Skaggs, PhD

"I don't hear an issue" Sean continued.

"Lot of girls that age have small speech problems" Sean followed with a question.

"Do you think she has a big problem?"

"No, Sean. Not at all." Uncle Jack dismisses the idea of a 'big problem' with my speech and continues his thought.

"She was in an auto accident 4 years ago and suffered a lot of physical damage. She also has a Traumatic Brain Injury. I just wanted to know what you thought before you learned of her injury."

"Physical damage?" Sean asks himself more than he asked uncle. "I'm so sorry to hear all this, Jack."

"Thank you, Sean." Uncle responded to Sean's expression of male feelings, then let Sean continue.

"No. I see the small scar on her throat", Sean began.

"And only because you drew my attention to it, she seems to favor her left arm. She doesn't seem to grip with her left hand as well as with her right."

Sean shakes his head twice.

"But a lot of physical damage? I would never guess that, Jack."

Sean finished his complete and honest answer to Jack's complicated question. It sounded like an easy question, at first. But the more Sean threw these new facts around in his head, the more difficult it got to fully answer the question to his satisfaction.

"Like I said, I noticed a little something in her voice, but not anything that sounds different from my girls. Do you think it might be permanent, then? You think it might not transition away as she grows up?"

Then Sean added,

"I want to help with your concerns, but I'm not sure there's anything I can do."

Jack was looking nervously around the parking lot. He was thinking things over, in the way he does. Uncle Jack believes talking about bad things that have happened to you gives them energy and makes them harder to get over. That sounds a little too macho for me.

"Yes, we're thinking the damage is permanent. But whoever knows for sure with these things", Uncle Jack said.

"May I ask you one more thing, Sean."

Jack gets a little more comfortable in his stance in the parking lot. He pockets his left hand into his cargo shorts and puts a foot out ahead of the other, so they are loosely crossed.

"That little academy across the street from the end of the alley? I saw they have online classes. Think that school is any good?" Jack was gesturing with his hand in the direction of the school.

"Oh, yeah!" Sean was happy to respond.

"My oldest girl goes here because she loves science. They have the best science programs for kids of any school in the valley, as far as I'm concerned."

Sean gets a little frown.

"If you want Becca to have a rounded curriculum or if she was to favor the arts? Don't send here to this academy. They are a very good STEM Academy. Science, Technology, Engineering, Math only. There's not much else."

Sean gets a smile and says, "Hope that helps?"

Jack then turned toward his lab,

"Thanks Sean. You've been a wonderful help. I really needed to hear those words. ALL of them."

What Little Girls Are Made Of- From the Diaries of Becka Skaggs, PhD

Jack walked across the shared parking lot. When he looked back, Sean was still standing at the back door to the Bike Shop. Jack threw him a little wave. Sean responded. Uncle Jack entered the lab through the back door and immediately called Fran. There was even more to report than just his conversation with a neighbor. Uncle Jack just solved my school problem.

Is this what all adults do when the kids are out playing? Checking with the neighborhood adults and asking about us?

Hmmmmm....... **Note to Self**

* * * **PERIWINKLE PRINCESS – Day Three** * * *

September 10, 2008. Three weeks after my eighth birthday.

Uncle Jack has been asking me to go to the little Spanish church on the corner. He is aware I am avoiding the church on purpose. Jack has decided today is the day we gain complete understanding on the issue.

I've been arranging some index cards I made to plan my voyage, that I'm not sure I'm taking yet, on the floor in front of the television. The cards have locations of the places I might want to explore on my voyage. Should I approach the rising sun in the morning? Or should I approach the setting sun at night? Choices of a Captain can be hard to make.

Uncle approaches me and stands at the edge of the throw rug that defines the tv-viewing space.

"You've been riding LOVE is ENERGY! around here for almost a month and you have yet to go to the corner by the church. You ready to tell me what's going on, Becca?"

"I don't like that place, Uncle."

Uncle says, "Ok. But you can't figure out your feelings about them? So, you are suspicious?" I'm not sure those were questions from Uncle. But I'm giving him the benefit of the doubt.

"Do you just read that from my face?" I asked Uncle.

"How do you know I feel that way?" My left hand is on my hip that is tilted left for maximum effect, and my eyes are telling Uncle I want an answer.

"As a matter fact, you do. You display clear indications on your face of almost everything going on inside your pretty mind."

With a wink and a smile, he then walked over to me and added,

"I need to talk to the folks at the church, anyway. Why don't you come with me?"

Uncle Jack tells me,

"Once we get inside, use your love to feel the energy within the building. Try to feel everything present that can be felt. Notice it's energy, Becca, and understand each presence."

Then Uncle said,

"Use that energy and discover some real facts in life. Experience the energy and remember that experience. Weigh the experience against all the things you already know are true and factual. Then, when you make a discovery, you can compare this discovery against your accepted facts. This is how you know you are dealing in facts when something new arises while on your voyage through life."

I was sitting up and listening. Uncle is saying some interesting things. I like to talk to adults about my energy. Talking about my energy helps me understand what is happening to me. I have a deep need to understand what is happening to me. Father and Alisha are trying to learn things, but they aren't any closer to answers than me. This unexpected conversation from Uncle is sparking all kinds of understanding, like an enlightenment, I guess.

"Becca, when we get there, go inside the main hall and look at the people. Notice the ones who are praying. Reach into their souls with your love. You

What Little Girls Are Made Of- From the Diaries of Becka Skaggs, PhD

will likely discover their sincerity. Feel what they are feeling. Understand their experiences, sweetheart."

Uncle Jack bends down toward me,

"Feel the strength of their legend, Becca. Just because I'm not a believer doesn't mean I think it's not worth understanding. Rather, I believe understanding is the root of our human experience. Human's must gain understanding to fulfill our destiny among the stars."

Jack has a very serious look on his face. He has my complete attention. I am fully engaged in everything he's saying. He could easily be talking to one of his son's, the way he is speaking to me. But I'm understanding everything he is saying, it is making sense to me. I need to experience the universe and all its forms of energy. Uncle Jack is so smart.

Jack took a big breath, thought for a moment, and continued his thoughts and adult advice to me, a little girl.

"That's more in line with my beliefs", he finished his last thought.

"I would like you to create your own belief system, Becca. You have a unique ability to comprehend things at such a young age. By beginning on your belief system now, you will gain a big advantage in your future. You will use it against which to test all other suppositions in your life. The great thing about a belief system is that its dynamic. You will alter your beliefs, over time, as you gain further understanding of the universe. Most people don't begin the adventure into their belief system until they are in their teens. You, my beautiful Becca, are ready to begin that adventure."

I liked that confidence boost. I got a little smile, and my eyes became smaller. Uncle winked at me and continued.

"Go in there and feel the energy. Learn what is in there. Understand it, Becca. I'm not telling you to confront it and conquer it. I'm telling you to comprehend it. Touch that thing you fear and learn from it what it thinks of itself. I am right here with you, baby girl. I'm not letting anything happen to you."

I stood up and put my right arm around Uncle and gave him a kiss on his cheek.

"I'm right here with you, uncle. I love you." I stayed there, leaning my body against his while he was squatting, I feel comfortable keeping my arm draped over his shoulders.

"I love you, too, Becca." Uncle smiled and continued his very large point. We might be done circumnavigating the globe by the time he's finished.

"Sometimes, as an investigator, I have become uncertain of the path I have chosen for my research. One who is unsuccessfully searching for answers is always, ultimately, faced with one decision: whether to continue along the same line of thinking or go back and change your direction from a different point during the investigation."

"Humans have the ability to recognize that goals aren't being met. We can tell when successes aren't occurring through a set of actions. Once an investigator observes the lack of successes, unanswered questions enter his mind and cause uncertainty."

"You still with me, Becca?"

"Uh, yeah, Uncle." I guess I was looking like I was far off somewhere.

"Uncle, I hear your words and they give me images in my mind. I see all the things as you say them. It's like I watch what you say in pictures and movies."

Then I looked at him square in the eyes.

"I'm sorry, Uncle. But I'm enjoying the movie. I love you so much."

Then I asked him, though I really knew the answer already, "Is the movie over?"

Uncle chuckles at me. "No, Rebecca Dall, we're just at intermission", he says with a smile.

"If you want to hear more, I can come up with more."

What Little Girls Are Made Of- From the Diaries of Becka Skaggs, PhD

Then I got a big smile.

"I have to do a voyage and make discoveries, yet Uncle. I'd like to hear more about investigations or being an investigator."

I squinted my eyes, but didn't notice until after I had said,

"I can see the answers to the questions as they come up when you're talking, Uncle. Is that weird? Am I that strange?"

I realized I was thinking about how people – which includes kids and adults - think I'm strange and weird and unique. Okay. I decided to embrace my weirdness right then at that moment. It suddenly became very logical for me to be weird to my full amount of weirdness. Strange is good and mysterious and not normal. That is definitely me!

"You know, Uncle?" I asked him, and then paused and became lost in my mental images.

"You'll have to ask another question before I can say that I do, for sure." He winks at me.

He got me to smile when I was trying to be serious. That little stink bug!

"Funny, Uncle." You're a funny uncle." This time I winked big at him, in dramatic noticeable fashion.

"But do you think I'm weird, Uncle?"

Jack got a big, excited expression on his face.

"Becca, honey! I love you completely and absolutely. You know I love you, right, baby? But I cannot lie to you, Love Bug. You are the weirdest child I have ever been around in my life!"

THAT gave me a huge smile and I jumped into his arms.

"I just embraced my weirdness, too, Uncle! This is fantastic!!"

I let him go right after I was done kissing his cheek too many times to count. I climbed up onto the sofa and sat down by slowly sliding down the back until my tushy met the cushy.

Uncle stood up, shook out his arms and legs like I had cut off his circulation with my kisses, then sat beside me and put his right arm around me. I am warming up my left side against his father-like safety.

I'm glowing like LOVE, my Unicorn at grandma's. She does too glow, and I'm not discussing this any further!

"Okay, I'm ready now, Uncle. I'm ready for intermission to be over."

"Hahaha. Okay, my beautiful Love Bug." Uncle Jack has a big happy smile.

"Where was the movie? I forgot."

I must have pouted a little, because he got a loving expression on his face that just made me forget about all my worries.

"You were telling me about the uncertainty you would get sometimes as an investigator. I understand the doubts, Uncle."

"Well, thank you, Becca. Yes, it's true. I believe every investigator will have at least one investigation that will cause a lot of re-thinking, a lot of questioning of his methods and decisions he's made to that point."

Uncle squeezed me, and I managed to get closer to him. I didn't realize I had given him so much room on the sofa before that squeeze.

Uncle found a place to re-start the movie.

"Such uncertainty can create negative emotions that will cloud our judgement, as investigators. But it is up to that investigator to make that ultimate decision. There is no wrong way to come upon your decision when making ultimate choices in your life's path."

Uncle kissed the top of my head and continued.

What Little Girls Are Made Of- From the Diaries of Becka Skaggs, PhD

"You are at a juncture in your life, Love Bug. You must now make a left turn or a right turn. The road no longer extends straight into the horizon in front of you. You must change your direction. What will be the choice?"

Now Uncle Jack has bent his head to my level. His head is kind of looking sideways at me. I love this man.

"How do you, as the investigator, discover which is the best choice? You collect information along the way. You make mini decisions within your-self that shape your likes and dislikes along the way. Then, you get to the decision-point, and you weigh your options against all you have learned and already decided along the way."

His eyebrows are jumping up and down like crazy when he gets excited like this. Uncle doesn't miss a beat. He straightens his head and keeps looking at me.

"Once an investigator can get into the middle of the soul of that thing he is researching, he may find it's not as mysterious as he once thought. The investigator may find the fear he's been feeling is not fear, but apprehension of the unknown. He may find it's not worth fearing at all."

Then he looked at me most sincerely. Uncle has brought his lecture the full 360 degrees of the Globe.

"You may be correct about the spirit's evil nature. I'm not denying that, honey."

"Becca, my beautiful dove, you have a strong mind." He gives my forehead a peck.

"Learn your strengths and weaknesses by extending your powers and testing your limits. Reach out with your LOVE, baby. It will guide you through everything."

Uncle Jack raised himself from the slouching-sofa position he found him-self in over the time it took him to educate me. He hugged me with both arms, and said,

"LOVE is your energy. Trust your Love, Becca."

Then he released me, stood up, and shook the circulation back into his limbs. Uncle extended his refreshed hand to me.

I took his hand, climbed off the sofa, and he led us outside and toward the little church.

"Come on, Love Bug. Let's go meet this evil beast."

Uncle Jack looked down at me with the most beautiful loving smile and glint in his eyes. How could this man still be single?

We walked to the corner and up the twelve stairs to the wooden church door and made our way inside. There Uncle Jack stopped and leaned over to me and said,

"I'm going right in that door to their office. I'm not going anywhere else without getting you first. So, don't worry about the time or missing me. When I'm done, I will be in to find you."

"Now go use your mind and research something for reals." He finished me off with his gorgeous smile and twinkling eyes. Did I say I love this man?

When Uncle Jack talks to me in that very sincere way he just did, I have nothing else in mind but what he's saying. I don't have questions about what he says. I don't have misunderstandings or unclear moments. I just absorb it all as pictures and images, and my brain starts working in the ways he described it to me.

I've learned to search for understanding in Uncle Jacks words. They rarely mean only one thing. Words can be so tricky, you know?

I walked inside the main hall of the church. Wow! It's so big compared to what it looks like outside. The ceilings must be 20 feet tall. Stained-glass windows with pictures of people and artifacts. Wooden carvings. Rows of candles in one corner of the room, but only a few were lit. They were the little candles that can sit inside tiny glass. These were green-colored

What Little Girls Are Made Of- From the Diaries of Becka Skaggs, PhD

glass candleholders, that matched a lot of the blues and greens in the stained-glass.

There is a box of strike-anywhere matches, with its sandpaper strike-pad, in a metal box for the visitors to use to light the candles. This is very clever. I had to watch 3 people visit the table of candles to understand the ritual.

When they first approach, the visitor places a coin in a slot in the metal box. Then the visitor takes a wooden stick, or "strike anywhere match" according to the little box, and lights a random candle. At some points in time during the ritual, they make motions with their right hand. They touch their head then belly. Then right and left shoulders very rapidly. The three sample visitors in my study made this motion at different times in the ritual, so I couldn't gain complete understanding on any potential restrictions to their movement because of the ritual. They seemed to be moving and acting peacefully throughout the entire ritual.

The rows of benches are wooden and heavily stained with years of re-applied varnish built up. Some of the mars and pits in the wood from years past are covered by the newer varnish layers. Some marks look like they could have been writing from way back, but someone tried to sand it down. It looks like someone tried to match the previous stain and then applied new varnish over it. I can see a lot of these repairs the more I look. These benches could tell a lot of stories, I'll bet.

Not far from here, the Spanish conquistadors came through in the late 1500's, looking for the city of gold. Unfortunately for the Queen of Spain, Cortez stopped his men at the southern bank of the Arkansas River in present-day Colorado. Had they continued north, the Conquistadors would have found gold in less than another 100 miles, near present-day Pikes Peak. Instead, Captain Pike discovered the area for America and the railroad barons became wealthy. It's all timing.

Some of the native villages in our Phoenix-area of the Sonoran Desert are from before that time. The Yaqui people are descended from the very people that lived and hunted in this area more than 600 years ago. The town of

Guadalupe is an old Yaqui village that is now surrounded by Phoenix and Tempe. They are a very spiritual people.

I noticed the 5 people that were scattered about within this little church. The 3 people that lit candles kneeled for a few moments at the very center of the front of the church. Then they each made their way to different seats within the rows of benches.

The rows of benches were divided into two halves of the room with a central aisle going all the way to the front. At the very front is a little area with a lectern to its right side, and a big wooden cross hanging in the geographical center of that back wall of the church.

Or is that the front wall of the church? Did we enter at the front of the church or at the back of the church? And why does a church only have one door, anyway? Isn't that a fire hazard? Suddenly, these confusing thoughts entered my mind. It was like information was put in a blender and someone turned my brain onto "blend" and walked away. Ahhhhh! My brains are scrambled!!

Just as suddenly I am being mentally transported somewhere. The skies are a very beautiful bright green color and there are fluorescent blues and browns and reds and oranges.

A deep voice spoke slowly.

"Hello, Becka. How is our neighborhood Princess today?"

I am startled beyond belief and ask a million questions. It just happened that way.

"What? Who am I? I mean, where am I?" Who are you? How do you confuse me so?"

The deep voice spoke again.

"It's the fog of pitch. You wish to speak to the spirits? Then tell us of who you are and who you wish to be little human. Then, if the council deems

What Little Girls Are Made Of- From the Diaries of Becka Skaggs, PhD

you worthy, we will impart our secrets to you. I am Pine Tar. King of the local Pine Trees. Nice to finally meet you, Princess Becka."

"Huh? Uhhh, nice to meet you, King Pine Tar. But what is happening? I was sitting in the church, and now I'm sitting in a pine tree across the alley from our Laboratory? I don't understand what happened?"

A deep rumble of a laugh came from King Pine Tar.

"You summoned my spirit with your thoughts while stroking ancient wounds within the ancestor you now sit upon, young Princess."

While speaking to me, the image of the large pine tree seemed to be moving its branches like they were his arms.

"Princess? You have a special ability to use Pure LOVE. We trees have sensed this since you first entered the neighboring kingdom 2 years ago. But today you did something you have never done before. You felt the energy and the past of the piece of wood, our Ancestor. The wood you used to rest yourself on today was extremely touched by the empathy of your spirit. And do not worry. You are still resting on our ancestor in the church."

"So, you are just in my mind, King Pine Tar?" I'm just full of questions.

"Well, Yes and No, young human. This is a world where spirits of all kinds gather and can communicate without barriers. We have no language problems here. All is clear. But you are in a fog because you are not yet trusted by the others. So, they protect themselves by hiding from you."

A little breeze came through the tree and his needles bristled lightly. The King seemed to shudder just a little.

"Why do you fear the wind, King Pine Tar?" Am I up to ten yet?

"Ahhh, little human Princess. You are a very perceptive sort."

The King shook his dry needles off a bit and said something I will never forget.

297

"The rain is the friend of a tree, but the wind is not our friend. The wind can take away our destiny in an instant. So, though the rain is our friend, Rain and Wind usually travel together as companions. We trees are always leery when our friends travel with those that are not to be trusted."

The King rustles his needles a little, then continued.

"We Spirits of the Wooden Heart are passive spirits. We allow our friends to make their own choices, and we trust that LOVE will prevail in all things."

The King moved the limb I was sitting on just a bit to make sure he had my attention.

"You are strong in the LOVE. You will be given a special gift by the tribe of Pine Tar."

King Pine Tar gently touched a small branch to my hair.

"You shall be given a ball of Pine Tar stuck to your hair. The Periwinkle Princess must allow your uncle, King of the Periwinkle Tribe, to find the tar ball and remove it for you all out of love. You cannot tell him the purpose of the Tar Ball until he lovingly excises it from your hair. If he asks if it's okay to remove the tar ball, you must allow him. Only THEN will you have the trust of the wooden spirits."

Suddenly, there was only me and King Pine Tar. Nothing else seemed to exist for a moment. Then he said,

"Once you accomplish this task, you will have the cooperation of all wooden spirits throughout Earth. Should the Periwinkle Princess call us for assistance any time hence, we shall respond to her aid."

As soon as King Pine Tar was done, I was right back in the church in the back row of benches where I was sitting before. Nobody was staring at me. So, I must not have popped out of the church and popped back in. I was sitting here the whole time. WHOOAAAAAA! HUGE feelings of stuff!!

Okay, I am outta here!

What Little Girls Are Made Of- From the Diaries of Becka Skaggs, PhD

I scooted out of the pew and ran back out the door, where I ran smack into Uncle Jack.

"Hey, ENERGY!" Where're you going in such a hurry?" Jack holds me in a big hug as I surround him with my arms the best I could!

"I'm pretty sure I felt everything I need to feel in here. Can we go now?"

"Yes, darling. WE can go right now."

Uncle Jack extended his hand to me, and I took it. We went out the door, down the twelve stairs and back down the block toward our apartment in the Engineering Lab.

We were walking back to the apartment when he had reached up with his hand and stroked my hair. There he felt something sticky. He stopped us on the sidewalk to investigate the hidden treasure.

"How did you get pine tar stuck in your hair, young lady. Was that when you went in the alley? Wait. Has it been in there that long??""

Uncle inspects the nuisance further.

I'll need to cut that out with scissors when we get home. I have nothing else that can remove pine tar."

I got a big smile on my face and said,

"That's Okay, Uncle Jack. I kinda was expecting you would have to cut it out."

I was smiling big now.

"No, it just got there, Uncle. And that's okay, too. I don't mind if you need to cut a little hair."

I reached for Uncle's hand, and he held mine all the way home. I was SOOO Happy!!

Exactly what King Pine Tar said must happen is going to happen. YAYYY!!!

When Uncle Jack and I got home, he took me right into the bathroom. Surgery on my hair was about to begin.

"You can watch everything that is happening in the mirror. That's why I brought us in here. This way, you can see how much hair must go and you can approve beforehand. Okay?"

"That's okay, Uncle Jack. I don't mind, really."

"Alright."

Uncle Jack took the scissors to precisely excise the tar ball from my hair without taking any more hair than needed.

It was done.

"There, all better!"

"Wait." Nothing happened?"

Uncle, I was expecting something to happen."

"Well, that sounds confusing." He gives me a smile followed by a look of true interest.

"What was being expected, sweetheart?"

"I'm not sure, Uncle. A feeling, maybe?"

Uncle Jack gave me some of his fatherly advice.

"That is a problem with expectations. They are usually born on incomplete fact and finished off with a dose of fantasy." Then he added,

"Instead of expecting something to happen, wait for something to happen.... or not. Then have an opinion on it... or not."

Uncle Jack has many things he has said in the past about expectations. I'm finally starting to understand the depth of his words.

What Little Girls Are Made Of- From the Diaries of Becka Skaggs, PhD

Nothing happened the rest of the day. But that night in my dreams? A whole different story!

King Pine Tar came to me and told me the council had accepted me as their Periwinkle Princess. I shall now hold the secret to protecting the Spirits of the Wooden Hearts, the name of King Pine Tar's tribe.

Uncle Jack was right again! Wait for something to happen, THEN have an opinion on it…. Or not.

I LOVE IT!!! YES!!

* * * PERIWINKLE PRINCESS – Day Four * * *

March 30, 2009

I am back in Phoenix for the spring flu season in Washington. I am really excelling in my schoolwork. I go to the school once-a-week with my little paper hospital mask covering most my face.

I go to the academy every Thursday morning and talk to a counselor for about an hour, usually less. They ask me questions about the online work I did in the previous week. When they're satisfied that I'm the one who is doing the work, I walk back home.

No, I don't ride LOVE is ENERGY! to school. She's too pretty to be left alone by herself for so long, while I'm inside getting tested. Yawn! She's likely to get distracted and go find a fun social gathering to join. I don't want THAT to happen! Besides, the kids just make fun of us.

It's a beautiful spring day. The sun is shining – duh – but it will be a high of 78*. That is just perfect for bike riding. So, when I got home from school, it's time we went riding.

I decided I needed a REAL maiden voyage for LOVE is ENERGY! and her Captain….ME! So, I filed my maiden voyage plan with Uncle Jack, and he approved, if I don't cross any streets.

He said it's ok to use the alley, if I'm "careful and mindful of what you're doing". Then, I can stay on the sidewalks. That gives me a huge, big, beautiful ocean to sail across, or around, like a big city block cut in half by an alley. I also can use a half-a-block of vacated street. It's used by the apartments that King Pine Tar and his tribe protect on the other side of the alley from us and the bike shop.

I made my first command decision and sailed my vessel right over to the familiar territory of the Spirits of the Wooden Heart. I couldn't get directly to King Pine Tar because of the foul fence the landscapers laid in my way. It's not like I can't get in. I ride my bike 100 feet further and turn left into the driveway made for the cars of the people that live there. There is the car barrier thing, one arm that stays down and raises up when people key in the code or have a remote. But that isn't keeping anyone from getting in there if they wanted to walk.

Or if a kid was on a bike. Or aboard any small vessel.

I sailed over to King Pine Tar.

"King Pine Tar? I'm on a voyage. King Pine Tar?"

I waited for a branch to move or needles to bristle, but nothing happened.

"King Pine Tar? Are you here? Are you alive?"

Then an answer came.

"Hahaha. Yes, young Princess. I am here. I am alive. No need to be excited."

I wasn't so sure of that. I started getting a little scared something happened to my old friend. So, I had to give him a few questions to let him know I had concerns.

"Why didn't you answer me when I called you. I said I was on a voyage?"

"Hahaha, Yes, you did, Princess. And I was simply waiting for you to make another statement or form a question about your voyage, since you had not asked me any specific question. You did, however, say my name in the form of a question."

"As I think of your words, you are very correct King Pine Tar. I apologize to my friend. It was my mistake."

The King was very courteous and gentle, as usual.

"Mistakes can happen. Your apology is accepted, Periwinkle Princess."

Then I told the King of my Plan to investigate the evil church.

"Young Periwinkle Princess. The tribe has become concerned by the spirits at the little church you have spoken of before. During the darkness, when the light of day is at its shortest, the Spirits of the Wooden Heart see an eerie greenish glow coming from the church. The glow is not as visible when the lightness time is longer and darkness time is shorter, as is now. The Wooden Heart of King Pine Tar fears the evil that causes that glow in the church. All spirits of the Wooden Heart fear the evil within the church."

Then many of the King's branches shuddered at once. Thankfully, I wasn't sitting up there.

I told the King my suspicions.

"There is something happening in that church that shouldn't be happening, King. But I might have to do my real work at night, when the glow from the church is in full view.", I told the King quietly, so we weren't overheard.

"I must complete my maiden voyage, King Pine Tar."

I hopped onto my bike, ummm vessel, and started out of the parking lot.

"I'll report back when I find something." Then I peddled off onto my appointed grid coordinates.

The first destination was the corner where the twelve stairs to Iglesias de Maria lurked. I had to navigate that treacherous strait going full sail! There was no holding back. I had to get that beast's bad wind behind my wake, and directly at him was the best tack to make that happen!

LOVE is ENERGY! is flying toward our next move, the "Grand Tack" maneuver few have ever survived to talk about. I must make a complete ninety-degree right turn due west. I must shorten my sails before gaining velocity for the last leg of the maneuver.

The long-awaited foot-touch is coming, and we survived the jib touch to the surface and have skidded around the buoys to gain sails once again and off we goooooo to the penultimate flags in our voyage.

I am NOT going to miss this voyage. NOPE!

I'm now sailing so fast I am almost flying away from the twelve stairs and gaining momentum as I pass the old insurance store that's all boarded up. I keep my focus and am peddling, er, sailing, past the windows of the antique shop. There is some new clothing in the antique shop window. A steamer chest? I will make a mental note to investigate the antique shop further. I will need a separate voyage for the antique shop reconnoiter.

I almost missed my opportunity to observe the bike shop window, as I seemed to be hydroplaning by with the wind pushing at my stern. Nothing new. Focus? Yes, focus!!

I'm free sailing down the backstretch now, past our front driveway to our parking lot, then past our little building. Half-block to go before I must pull sails.

I peddled like crazy and gained every millisecond in time I could gain. Now, down the long back corner of my right-handed racetrack, in front of some more of the apartment buildings the tribe protects. These are at the far end of the alley from King Pine Tar, and on our side of the alley.

I turned right off the sidewalk and into the alley as if I would be completing a loop all the way back to King Pine Tar. But I will turn right into our parking lot first.

What Little Girls Are Made Of- From the Diaries of Becka Skaggs, PhD

"I will report back later, King Pine Tar."

I said it loud enough that trees can hear, but not the whole neighborhood. I'm not an obnoxious neighborhood kid.

I skidded my vessel to a stop right under the awning of the RV for Uncle's charity.

"Perfect Ten Point landing!"

I had to run inside to tell Uncle all about my maiden voyage. And King Pine Tar, and I was no longer afraid of the twelve stairs of Iglesias de Maria, or the evil spirits inside.

Uncle finally asked me a question.

"The evil spirits inside? Inside the little church?"

I shook my head in a BIG YES!

"Alright, let me get myself clear on some things. May I do that, please?"

Uncle always did that, like he was the stupid one around here. Hardly!

"Ya sure, Uncle."

"YOU are the Periwinkle Princess?" Uncle lets out a little chuckle. "THAT is precious, sweetheart!"

I crinkled my nose at Uncle.

"I love you so much, you know?" I threw that in quick, while I could still get bonus points.

"Yes, beautiful Becca. I know, and I love you so much too."

With a smile, he continues.

"Nice job, trying to distract me. But you aren't in any trouble, honey. I'm wanting to understand. Maybe, the Periwinkle King can do something to help you and your friends?"

That got a giant smile on my face.

"And King Pine Tar put the tar ball in your hair?" He asks with a sincere look on his face.

"Yes, Uncle. He made me swear I wouldn't touch it. I had to let you find it out of love and want to cut it out. And you did Uncle!"

I climbed into his unsuspecting arms. He accepted this little package.

"You did it right away!" I told him.

Now, my emotional floodgates opened and I couldn't hold back the tears. I was so happy that my great-Uncle loved me enough to find the tar ball and understand everything I have been telling him. That is so special, folks. I just kept crying and telling him "I love you I love you I love you!"

*** Our Princess LOVE BUG Breaks ***

Uncle is holding me tight, and I am just getting comfortable and calming down. I'm on the sofa with him. This huge room with 4 cubicles for computer workstations and a sofa at the far end where the tv hangs on a wall. There's also a leather recliner chair next to the sofa, for the times grandma is here, or when I take up too much room on the sofa. The recliner gives Jack a little refuge from the femaleness that gets all over the fluffy couch.

I'm very comfortable where I am right now, pretty much sitting on Uncle Jack, I mean. I've stopped crying. I know there are still more questions before this topic is put to rest. But I'm enjoying the closeness time we're getting, right now. This day with Uncle has been the greatest best day ever!!

I don't do a lot of touching with people. It's really great when I get to touch people with love. Then to have pure love in your heart, and the pure intent that you only want happiness for the other person? WOW! That is such an awesome feeling! Uncle is giving me all those feelings and more.

What Little Girls Are Made Of- From the Diaries of Becka Skaggs, PhD

We sat there in our quietness for a few moments. I was really feeling safe and calm. Then Uncle spoke.

"What did King Pine Tar say about the evil spirits in the church. Anything specific you remember, Becca?"

I thought for a moment just to get the words right.

"The King said all the trees feared the evil spirits in that church."

"The trees feared the evil...." I could see Uncle was thinking very hard on the problem. Then,

"I have an idea, Becca!" Uncle quickly got my hopes up. He began whispering his idea to me, like it was our little secret. Of course, we were the only ones in the lab and the apartment. But it was still our little secret.

The next day, Uncle went to the church and asked the Parish priest about exchanging the candles for LEDs – Light Emitting Diodes. Extremely energy efficient electric light bulbs – lights. Uncle would take care of the cost. It really was an experiment, and he would replace everything in a couple months if the church didn't notice an improvement in their expenses. "The energy cost would be less than what you spend on the matches in a year. That doesn't even include the cost of the candles you'd be saving", I overheard Uncle tell the priest.

The church agreed to allow uncle to exchange the candles for efficient little lights that can be turned on and off. No candles to be lit and replaced the next day. A person turns on the light when they want their loved one to be remembered by the Saints. Then, the light gets turned off by the angels later.

The next night, Uncle's plan was that I go see if there was any change with the Spirits of the Wooden Heart. I needed to see if they felt any safer. And I needed to gather my information when the light of the day was dim.

"Ask the King if he fears fire more than wind. I would guess he would answer you affirmatively, Becca. Then, you may ask the King how he would feel if he saw Wind and Fire together? He'd probably want to be covered by earth at that moment."

Uncle winked at me in a strange way. I think Uncle is weird like me.

"Okay, Uncle. Be right back." I called back to him as I ran to the back door.

I went out on my reconnaissance voyage to the grove of the Spirit of the Wooden Hearts. It was after dinner, so it was getting dark now. I stealthily rode my bike, ummm vessel, over to the grove of trees. I scooted around the pesky fence and went up to King Pine Tar.

"Hi, King Pine Tar. How are you doing? Nice evening, don't you agree?" I didn't want to say in the question how I wanted him to answer. So, I am practicing being coy. I read about this recently.

I can tell you guys more about being coy, if you wish. NO?? Ok, fine. Don't be grouchy.

"Hello, Princess." King Pine Tar answered my direct questions.

"I am doing fine. It is a fine night, is it not?"

"Yes, King. It is a fine night". Ok. I agreed. Now what?

Alright. I'll just ask another direct question.

"I was just wondering, King, have you noticed any differences in the spirits at the church?"

I hope that's direct enough.

"Let's see. Now that you mention it, Princess, we don't see the evil spirits there anymore at all. The evil spirits are gone."

Then I swear that big tree bent over and looked at me and said,

"Did the Periwinkle Princess vanquish the evil spirits from the church?" He shook his branches all about, like a gust of wind suddenly blew through in two seconds.

What Little Girls Are Made Of- From the Diaries of Becka Skaggs, PhD

"No, your King. I mean, No, your majesty, King Pine Tar." I finally stammered a response.

He caught me off guard, if a tree can do that at all, catch a human off guard, I mean. I took a step back, then answered further.

"It was my uncle, the Periwinkle King. He did some incantations that he hoped would work and I was supposed to find out from you tonight if they worked. Did they work?"

The big tree bristled all its branches again, and needles came down everywhere, including all over me, as he straightened up. He asked the whole tribe how they were feeling. I couldn't understand him because it was in TREE language – specifically, long-needle Pine. Soon the King responded.

"Yes, little Princess. The evil spirits are gone. Thank you eternally for your help, Princess"

I began reflecting on what Uncle Jack had told me about the trees and their fear of fire.

"It was the fire in the candles that are the evil spirits the trees fear", Uncle was explaining to me.

"And as long as the candles with their fire are in that church?" Uncle Jack continued,

"The trees are correct that the possibility exists fire could occur and spread to their little grove."

"Okay, King Pine Tar. I must go home now to my kingdom and rest." I began preparing LOVE is ENERGY! for the return sailing.

"Yes, little one", the King said as I began pedaling down the alley toward Uncle Jack's apartment.

"Travel with safety" The King finished his long goodbye, as I was turning into the parking lot and pedaling toward the back door, getting ready for my patented skid stop!

I still had Uncle's voice in my head.

"See, Becca?" Uncle asked.

"The trees are correct in having the fears they did. Sometimes it's okay to have fears, as long we understand them, and we don't let them control us."

Then he grabbed me up against himself and hugged me so much, it was great!

"Once we Periwinkles understood the entire problem", Uncle finished, *"we found a way to vanquish the evil from the kingdom."*

Then, he gave me his biggest kiss-on-the-cheek ever!

Thus, ends the story of Becca Skaggs and her LOVE is ENERGY! on their maiden voyage together! YAY!

I went running through the backdoor yelling,

"I'm home, Uncle! You were right! You were right about everything!"

**That's a keeper! I want this one for the archives, please? **

**Hehe. Good job guys! **

-FADE TO BLACK-

* * * **End of The PERWINKLE PRINCESS Meets King Pine Tar** * * *

CHAPTER – SUPERHERO LIFE:
The Early Years

August 27, 2013

"Not the entire spectrum of load calibre, Uncle. But maybe one subset of grain sizes would be more effective? I'm sorry, Uncle. My voice is bothering me. I'm starting to sound like a boy. And I've been having a hard time, lately, remembering most of 2004. Is that being blocked? Am I doing that to myself? Okay, sorry. Talk soon. I love you."

I'm leaving Uncle a recording on one of the lab computers. When he gets back with our groceries, he will be at this station before long. If I leave the poor guy alone long enough, that is.

I've become very obsessed on wave theory and started using sand from the beach at Grandma's to help me work out the mechanics of how waves move and transport things. So, I've been asking questions about observations Uncle remembers at beaches. I use the images he creates in my mind to help me solve the outstanding issue of building constructive waves for Father's ELF array.

Pardon me for a moment. I have one more thing to tell Uncle:

"If we make the refraction specific to a certain energy level, then we can selectively lift only a small range of grain sizes. This will result in a stable, shifting landform, much like a barrier island. I can then translate the success from that technology to create a device that will boost father's ELF array. I can create THE specific constructive wave-set to perform the exact task I desire to defeat Yuri. Uncle I love you so much! In case you couldn't recognize my voice, this is your little brother."

Before I turned 10, the CDC set up a hospital room at Stone Mountain just to deal with my pneumonia and immune problems. I had it twice more and Alisha helped me through both times. Alisha is the DHHS person in charge, after all! Alisha and I are doing great! I LOVE her! She is actually funny! That's not a slam!

Funding from Congress still helps Father, and they keep me and Rosalyn alive, but we are treated like tiny little kids. I am NO tiny little kid. Not anymore. I am Becka Skaggs, The COSMIC TWIN. Hehe.

Yuri has been using refraction waves to block Rosalyn and I. BUT, I have discovered a way to fractionate the constructive wave-sets from some of Uncles devices. And, EUREKA, Big Discovery!!

I can defeat his blocking device and rid the world of his evil! Buahahahaha.

* * * SUPERHERO JOURNALISM BREAK * * *

August 27, 2013 – Four hours later.

I am only thirteen, sheesh.

Feels like something much larger. Thirty, maybe. Not sure what that feels like, though. I feel a great weight with all the knowledge that continues to come to me. I am finding that I can suddenly feel overwhelmed by life. I mean, in an instant.

And I am only thirteen. Sheesh!

"Becca?" Uncle called me over to his worktable in the Lab portion of our building. I got a little sleepy, so I took a nap. My schedule allows for naps. I've been really good with my schedule over the years. I enjoy trying to see how close I can get to staying on time.

What Little Girls Are Made Of- From the Diaries of Becka Skaggs, PhD

Oh, "Lab" just means it has long tables that papers can be laid out on, or little pieces of equipment scattered out on, and then several computer stations along the wall. We do physics in our lab. No chemicals necessary, except water, and we can discuss that another time, if you wish.

Uncle sits me down and looks at me squarely.

"I listened to your recordings. Thank you, sweetie."

"Thank you, Uncle." I had to get that in fast. He's getting ready for a lecture. I can see it. I wonder what this one is gonna be about?

"I look at you and I can't believe my eyes. Look at how big you are? You have blossomed into a gorgeous young woman. More importantly, you are brilliant beyond belief!"

I was getting happy, then something changed.

"Why the fantasy worlds, Becca?" He shows me copies of my books I have written that Uncle Jack has placed on the table in front of us.

"Your particular Traumatic Brain Injury can easily capture you in a world that ignores your reality. I worry you could lose your Love, Sweetie."

He has discovered that I have self-published over twenty works of differing kinds. Technical manuals on proper care and handling of wire mesh sieves, to public health documents on residual oxidation needed to properly treat drinking water. A white paper to the City of Phoenix on how to extricate pharmaceuticals from water with only solar power. And many children's books of varying genre.

"This is actually my favorite, Love Bug." Uncle Jack is holding a textbook.

"No. Not just A textbook. MY textbook entitled "The Excitement of Quantum Mechanics", by yours truly, John Anderson Wilson II."

"I sold 2000 copies of that book, Uncle."

I couldn't help myself. It was like a bug got stuck in my mouth and I had to spit it out. Those words were accidently expelled with that bug. I didn't know the words were there until it was too late.

"When you were eight, I thought it was cute", Uncle continues.

"I thought you'd grow up and get past it, maybe get bored. But now, you are 13. You are still living with these imaginary worlds and now, along with your science books?"

"Uncle?" I couldn't speak.

I just started crying.

"Sweetheart. I don't doubt you. I know what you can do. I know your skills are off the charts in most things. And there are logical explanations for all of this. I love you so much, Becca."

Then he hands me a tissue and lets me wipe my tears with one hand while holding the other hand.

"The scientists at the health center aren't changing you into some super-hero cyborg, honey. They are helping you get better. And you have been getting better every year since you woke up. Alisha and you are so close together. You guys have worked miracles. I am truly proud of you and all your accomplishments, Becca."

"Uncle please. You're gonna me make cry again." I put the tissue to my eye and blotted a tear.

"I'm sorry Becca. I love you. I can't express fully how much I love you. But", then he paused most uncharacteristically and looked right at me. Ahh, the old great-grandma Wilson trait of gaining your attention carried on by her children to their children.

"I have some things on my mind, and you're the reason for them." Uncle finished his thought seeming to be somewhat distant himself.

314

What Little Girls Are Made Of- From the Diaries of Becka Skaggs, PhD

After gathering his thoughts, Uncle swiveled his chair all the way around, so he was now facing me. Uh-oh. This could be a while folks. He has this other look on his face.

"Indulge me for a moment, will you, Becca? Answer a couple questions for me? Then I may have a good story for you."

"Okay, Uncle. What do you want to know?" I'm looking right at him, waiting for what is to come next.

"What do you remember about your accident? It's been nine years today. What happened that day?"

It was a straight question. That's how I took it, anyway. I answered quickly,

"Not a lot, Uncle. I remember the moment when our car got hit and it felt like we were flying. I was stuck and I had more pain the longer I was there. I remember being awake for what seemed like a long time. I had to hold on for Carol. That's how I was feeling."

"Good. Thank you, sweetie. And you remember all those feelings. That is fantastic!"

"What's your next memory, Becca?" He looked at me with concern.

"What do you mean, Uncle?" Confused, I sort of answered.

"Waking up, of course. Why?"

"That's a great memory to have, for sure." Uncle smiles at me.

"Just generally give some highlights with time frame. Please humor me?"

He places an elbow on the table to rest his arm. He's sitting at a strange angle to the table. Or maybe holding up my book was too heavy for his little arm? I understand what he is asking me.

"Ok Uncle. I woke up and I was very sick, still. I had surgery so it was Friday when I woke up. Friday the twentieth."

"Uh, Ok, Becca." Uncle said it in a way that gave me confidence to continue.

"Then I had surgery again on Monday." I had a slight frown that disappeared quickly.

"Oh! Doctor Murdock came in and said I needed surgery in the morning. That would've been Sunday night. But I don't remember much after that. I was still asleep when the surgical staff came and got me."

"Yes, very good, Sweetheart! One more question, okay?"

"Sure Uncle?" I gave him a smile and a quick touch on his arm.

"When did you wake up after that Monday surgery? Do you remember anything at all?"

"Well, sure, Uncle. I remember, Father had sent testosterone into me, and I woke up on Wednesday. I have been getting better every day since."

"I am so proud of you, Honey." You are the light of my life. I am so blessed to have you in my life, Becca."

"Well, Thank you, Uncle. I love so much, too." And we hugged.

Then he said,

"I don't understand how you keep falling back to that story. You tell the story like you were awake the whole time after your accident until Sunday night. That's not true, Love Bug. If you were awake in there, you weren't responding to any of us. We all became very worried. Are you remembering any of this, Becca?"

I must've looked puzzled because he kept going.

"You awoke almost two days after your first surgery. Saturday you ate your pudding and went back to sleep. Hardly having dinner, and certainly not awake conversing. Okay? This stuff is in the nurses' notes."

Uncle was gaining momentum.

What Little Girls Are Made Of- From the Diaries of Becka Skaggs, PhD

"Then you were in a coma two days again after your second surgery, which was Monday morning. Those first two days, you were rarely conscious, but you did have moments of semi-consciousness, I'll give you that as moments of being awake. I was severely concerned about you. I remember the day of the accident like it was yesterday, honey."

Now he looks at me very closely. Tears bulging in his eyes.

"The second two days were a full coma. Somewhere, amongst all this coma and semi-consciousness, you gained incredible intuitive and deductive powers. You can now read English with no lessons. You love to research things. You ask questions and go find the answers. That's why you don't remember much after your accident, and even until you were 5. There wasn't a lot to remember. The days you were actually WITH IT? You were still pretty out-of-it, Love Bug. You were in your world of inside information; inside your own brain."

Uncle became serious…er.

"Becca. I know this is NOT what you want to hear from me. But you have been doing so well. I think it's time you had a hard look into your past. The world you have created for yourself, honey, it's killing you. You have to come to safety, sweetie."

Uncle seemed seriously concerned.

"This story with Yuri really worries me. You have been inside this for too many years."

Uncle holds both my hands, looks straight into my eyes and says,

"Please allow me to help you come home, Becca? You MUST get out of that world. It's all in your head. You live in there all day every day. It's not healthy. Even Rosalyn worries about you."

He saw my expression change.

"You hear from Rosalyn?" I asked Uncle quickly.

317

"Yes, through Malia. She wants to be sure you have what you need. "

Uncle shifted his chair.

"That's another thing. Sometimes you two sisters talk and sometimes you don't? What's with you and Rosalyn? I am too far out of that loop, too." He gives me a disgusted look.

"WE still communicate, Uncle. Rosalyn's a great sister."

And she never tells others when we make plans to defeat the evil Yuri Yurachenkov. Wink.

"That's right, honey. Ros is a great sister", he said with a glint in his eye. Then he turned serious, again.

"Is Ros part of all your books and manuals?"

Uncle asked this question as a slight change of topic. Interesting. Uncle is getting fatigued. This discussion is almost over folks.

"Only a few. I mean, she has helped me in almost all of them. But she didn't want her name in any of them. So, I had her as a co-author on those publications where no one cared about having co-author information."

"Ohhhh, I don't want to know all of this, Becca. Do I?"

Uncle is calling for the white flag on this conversation.

"Yes, Uncle. You do, and it's great! Grandma has a PayPal account with all the money, since I wasn't old enough to have my own account."

Uncle became a little flushed.

"You have a PayPal account in Fran's name??" Now he has genuine concern on his face. But his energy level picked up again. He may have made a countermove to his earlier request for the white flag.

"Yes, Uncle. I have all the passcodes and account numbers. You can have them anytime you wish."

What Little Girls Are Made Of- From the Diaries of Becka Skaggs, PhD

"I know that honey. I'm not worried about you making off with some money, sweetie." He looked more relaxed again.

"I'm concerned for your safety and your health, Becca. That's all." Then he looked down at all my publications on the table and looks up at me.

"How much money are we talking about? In your Grandma's PayPal account"

Then he quickly adds,

"Enough to go to Hawaii?"

Uncle gets a sly smile on his face.

"How much does 'going to Hawaii' cost?" I asked him, using my fingers as air quote marks in the middle of the question.

Let's say you, me, Fran and Carol all go. Let's say we want to spend Twenty thousand dollars. Could we, do it?"

"Sure Uncle" I said as a matter of fact.

Now Uncle is thinking of the costs of more luxury items included.

"Let's say we wanted to spend $30,000. Could we spend that much and still have money left over?"

"Sure, Uncle." Then I looked at him very seriously.

"We'd have enough money left over to go back 9 more times."

"WHAT??" Uncle jumped out of his seat and the chair flew backwards, still on its wheels, and fell over after it hit the wall.

"Yes, Uncle. There is $308,000 in grandma's account."

As I walked over to pick up his chair, I continued my explanation.

"We wouldn't have enough money to go back an eleventh time. In your hypothetical scenario you just gave me, that is." I wheeled his chair to him.

"Uhh, wow! What am I about to say? You didn't even finish sixth grade, honey. You think it's time we finally solved your school problem? I mean, once and for all?"

"Uncle, I know all this. It's Okay, Uncle. I have been planning. Please trust me, Uncle Jack."

I went over to him and hugged my surrogate father. "Please sit, Uncle-father."

He sat.

"Yes. We need to permanently solve my education challenge", I continued and stepped to the table, "and I have come upon a solution. I have an appointment next week to take the GED." I sat on the table edge next to him. Yes, I had a big smile! I knew what was coming.

"OH! I LIKE That idea. That's an awesome idea!" Uncle Jack has finally gotten rid of the sour looking frown he had most the evening.

"I have more plans for us, too, Uncle."

I can't hold it in, I MUST tell him. I jumped off the table and began,

"My book The Periwinkle Princess will give us all the support we need. With the money I make from that book, I can develop the equipment I need right here in this lab, Uncle. I almost have everything I need to defeat Yuri, once and for all."

"Equipment. Yuri??" There's that frown again.

"Becca? Have you been listening to me?"

"Yes, Uncle. I love you so much." I had already turned and immediately ran off to my room to make plans for my next bestseller.

"I love your voice!" uncle-father called out after my door had closed. I got a bigger smile on my face.

*** **A BREAK from MONEY WORRIES** ***

What Little Girls Are Made Of- From the Diaries of Becka Skaggs, PhD

While I was in my room making plans, Jack had to call his sister. Of course, adults!

"Yes, Fran, you heard that correctly, Three hundred eight thousand dollars and thirty-six cents."

A short hesitation, then he said, "Yes, it's in your name. It's all yours, as far as I'm concerned. I think Becca feels that way, too."

Another pause as Jack listens to Grandma Fran.

"My advice is to secure as much as you can. Leave Becca some operating funds and get the rest of that money somewhere safe."

I wish I could hear grandma. But I have pretty good idea what is going on between the two siblings, in all the un-said words they share. They don't really need to have these kinds of conversations. They are almost exactly alike the way they think and the way they provide guidance. All they are doing is giving each other high-fives for the great job they did parenting me.

Hahaha! They are so funny! I LOVE them both to pieces!! I am a very lucky girl to have parents like these two grandparents. They are awesome miracles of the universe.

"I know it's safe. That's not what I mean. Oh, you know what I'm trying to say." Uncle says to his younger sibling.

This is one of their shorter phone calls. Uncle has already told her to decide whatever she wants to decide. Did you guys hear that, too?

"Becca made an appointment for herself to take the GED test."

Yes, The General Education Diploma for completing the high school requirements.

"Oh! One more thing I keep forgetting to ask you. Have you been hearing the word 'scrumpdumptious' a lot lately?"

Pause.

"Yes, Becca. It's not from the Spirit Ancestors that are around here."

Pause.

"Yada Yada Yada. Or Dilly-icious?"

Pause

"Few years. Yeah, I guess it has been a few phoenix-visits ago that she started. Ok, you've heard that one, too."

Pause.

"No. She writes the words perfectly. She's meticulous in her books."

Uncle! I thought you were almost done. Geeez!

"Fran, you absolutely must read, "The Funniest Ferret". Becca's imagination is mindboggling. Where does she get this stuff? None of us have this sense of humor. We have a special talent in our midst, Fran."

Pause.

"No, not me! You are funny ha-ha, and a wacko cuckoo bird, Fran."

Pause

"Yes. I love you very much, too, sis! Okay, talk later. Bye"

I heard Uncle hang up the phone. I ran out of my room, and I ran over and hugged him the best hug I could give him.

"I love you so much, Uncle Jack!" I gave him my patented cheek-kiss.

Yeah, I just applied for the patent when I was in my room. So, its patent pending.

{Don't believe her folks. Becka is Miss Dizzy right now.}

Rosalyn! I love you, my sister, my light. I learned so much from this transformative experience. The Periwinkle Princess isn't an idea. I lived it. It was

What Little Girls Are Made Of- From the Diaries of Becka Skaggs, PhD

an experience I had the experience during my maturity toward the use of Universal Energy.

Rosalyn, you are incredible, my sister! Thank you for awakening me to all the wonders of the Universe!

{What? Huh?}

I would like us to be publishing our own works now, together. All our science and our information to help society run better and help people be happier.

{I will help you make people happier, Becka. I love that kind of work. But I do not need recognition, sister.}

My sweet sister, Rosalyn. I am not asking that we publish together so we can have more fame. We are The COSMIC TWINS. People know of us. We cannot hide because we don't want notoriety. We have gifts that must be shared with humanity. It is our destiny to share the gifts we've been given so that all humans may thrive and one day travel among the stars.

{Wow, Becka! That's the best pep talk I've ever heard. You are indeed my strength, sister. I will follow you anywhere, my love.]

Grandma and Uncle Jack are pretty good at pep talks. I'm sure it's rubbing off on me. Thank you, my beautiful sister, my love, my Light.

Uncle Jack is thrilled with my spontaneous surprise hug and kiss.

"Thank you, Love Bug! I really love your kisses and your hugs! They are very special to me."

He hugged me good, too. That put a smile on my face.

"I love you, too, Uncle Jack." ☺

*** **A LIBRARIAN SUPERHERO LOVE BUG BREAK** ***

Labor Day, 2016 – Getting you caught up

I had decided, right after talking with Uncle that day in the lab when he discovered my love for publishing the written word, to gather up all my science information and save it for our future. Which meant keeping it all in my mind, until further notice. Of course, I needed a better filing system so I could remember things when I wanted, and not just when my brain wanted to remember things.

I finally started getting good at my mental recall by practicing my filing system. I'm not telling you about my mental filing system any more than I just did. You can go create your own system for your own brain. It'll work better anyway.

I started doing more research and more outreach to universities. Also, that day in August of 2013, I decided to publish The Periwinkle Princess. It was a smash hit! The Periwinkle Princess became number 54 on the NY Times Bestsellers list and number 48 on the LA Times Bestsellers list for the Young Reader's Mystery genre! For one week in Chicago, it hit number 32 before dropping out of the top 50. Yes! I sold 132,000 copies in less than ten weeks on a website for publishing Baby Books! The Periwinkle Princess was noticed by someone important.

I was so excited for weeks!

This time I had the money go into our charity's PayPal account. That's what I told Uncle I was going to do. I was going to complete what I had planned. This is all about defeating evil in this world, you know. Let's not lose focus of our long-term goals.

*** **LONG-TERM GOALS BREAK** ***

January 23, 2018

I began planning online science courses in March 2016 for faculty at Western Oregon University. One teacher asked if I could make them an outline for lectures. So, I drafted an entire lecture for them. After that, many of the teachers started paying me for lectures. This part of my work, along

What Little Girls Are Made Of- From the Diaries of Becka Skaggs, PhD

with all that was shown to the University board, earned me a Bachelor of Science Degree in 16 months. This is a transcript from my first lecture used by one of the professor's:

Pay attention students. I'm going to tell you how to revolutionize our world so that we all may begin living sustainable lives in a sustainable way. This is BIG! It means NO more wars over lack of resources. It also means everyone saves money and energy.

Sustainable living means that what you do in your daily life uses just the number of resources you generate. USE = PRODUCTION. If a tree grows by your house, you get to use the tree. You benefit from its shade in the summer to help cool you off. If it's a fruit tree, you will nurture it and enjoy its fruit for years to come. Should you decide you need to use the wood in the tree, you may harvest your tree – that is, cut it down so it is no longer living. If you want to use another tree in the future, you must plant a tree to replace the fully grown tree you decided to harvest. Basically, if you use something, you replace that something. If you can replace double, do it.

Don't be getting yourself all hung up about ownership just yet. Listen up and see what you think, first. So, young man who is the late arriver? Login time is before class starts. Oh, Hi Jeffery! Glad to see you sneak in.

When a society lives in a sustainable way, our use of goods is in balance with our use of natural resources. Sustainable living, then, MEANS we never run out of water. Sustainable living also means we Never run out of food, land, trees, animals, fish, kelp, any natural resource you wish to picture inside your mind. There's NO reason to go to war over a resource if you will never run out of that resource, right?

Our laws that set up all our grids – Electrical, Water, Sewer, Cyber – were made to keep people healthy and safe. Convenience was a benefit, but not the primary goal. People were getting sick and dying from the collection of natural resources and the by-products that were generated. Rainwater was becoming tainted after it was collected, and microbes grew in the water.

People would drink the water and become sick and die. We have learned how these diseases occur.

Many illnesses and deaths are attributed to diseases caused by the pathogens within the sewage. It became a logical and easy solution for everyone to pitch in together and create a way to improve the health of all. So, we agreed as a society to improve the quality of life of everyone. No person left behind. Consequently, sewer lines were constructed to carry our poop away from our sight and give it to someone else.

Today, however, we have the technology to be self-sufficient in our own homes. We have solar panels that can be used to generate all the electricity needed by today's homes. We don't need electrical grids. We can also add windmills to supply some of our power on a very small scale.

The electrical grids waste our energy and resources. Our high-power transmission lines leak out kilowatts of energy daily. Someone is paying for that lost electrical energy and it isn't your utility company. It's all of us consumers of their goods. PROBLEM: we consumers already PAID for the entire grid with our tax dollars, and we continue to funnel tax dollars to those utilities for them to maintain our grid. They say the amount they receive from taxpayers is miniscule and pays for almost nothing. Then, if that complaint is true, we should stop all such subsidies immediately!

Something tells me that the utility companies would not be in favor of this idea.

Technology is also available for us to collect and store our own rainwater without it getting contaminated. We have the ability to keep our water supply safe for our entire family. We don't need to spend our rare resources to build and maintain grids to connect us all. Grid structures cost us more in rare resources than the benefits derived from them. The grid for drinking water has a unique transmission problem. The water lines will generate bacteria within them. So, we must use chlorine to kill the bacteria that reside along the entire water line route. Engineers call this "residual disinfection". Even though they treated the water at the source where they gathered the water or

What Little Girls Are Made Of- From the Diaries of Becka Skaggs, PhD

where the distribution lines begin, we still need residual disinfection to kill the bacteria that naturally grow within the water lines.

Finally, composting our sewage at home will allow us to stop dumping poorly treated sewage into our precious fresh water supplies. Our sewage treatment plants do 2 kinds of treatment, when 4 different kinds are necessary to make that water healthful to use again. Solids are settled out and dried to remove about 80% of the pathogen load. The remaining fluids are, then, aerated to kill the microbes and viruses by exposing them to the air. They only use the natural killing properties of the air to treat our sewage. There are many things that give us cancer and can otherwise kill us that are still in the fluids. But our sewage treatment plants simply discharge that contaminated fluid into a river or a lake, leaving our freshwater supplies unhealthy for us to consume. Consider the situation at Flint, Michigan with their high lead problems in their drinking water system in 2020. Not a sewage issue, but an issue over a freshwater supply for our drinking water that caused health problems and piping problems.

In addition, we have chemicals made from petroleum that don't break down in the sewage treatment plants. Pesticides and pharmaceuticals also don't break down within the sewage treatment plants. This contaminated water goes back into the waters we use for our drinking water sources. It is true!

In the 1980's, the United States Environmental Protection Agency (EPA) developed regulations requiring all cities over 50,000 population to install "Tertiary" treatment – the "third" kind we need - at the sewage treatment plants. This technology can rid our waters of some of the chemicals we find in our water today. But not all of them.

Unfortunately for the people, cities sued the federal government. They argued to the court that the federal government was putting undue burden on the citizens since the science wasn't settled on the health effects of the chemicals. EPA only had a list of a thousand or so chemicals they wanted to regulate. The industry brought a list of many thousands and asked, 'why aren't these also proposed to be regulated?' The courts decided the regulations were arbitrary and unfair, and voided them all. The cities won, but the citizens lost!

People don't realize this kind of contamination of our drinking water is planned and ongoing in communities all around the world. The authorities in control of the purse strings don't want to pay for the improvements because no one is screaming that they want the improvements to be constructed. Consequently, we continue to give ourselves cancers and chronic diseases by NOT adding these improvements to our sewage treatment plants.

Our cancers and chronic diseases, then, pass off the cost of improving our health through consumption of unhealthy water and food to our healthcare system. We still pay for the cost of acquiring healthy water. We are just paying many times more for our drinking water by waiting until it causes health issues and then, paying for a doctor or a hospital, instead.

It's time for the practice of governments ignoring the health of its citizens to stop. We are doing everything the wrong way!

Our technology for composting sewage in our homes is available today. But the private sector controls the technology and doesn't want just anybody having it without an obscene profit being collected.

There should be no profit for basic services that make a healthy community. A healthy community will return the resources spent many times over through trade and bartering and ensuing cooperation between citizens within the society.

Total costs of the society will go down as we become sustainable. So, why don't we? Because someone is collecting a profit and hoarding it for themselves. That drives up the cost of all our goods and services.

What if we decided to build our homes just 2 foot higher off the ground? This would give us room for composting our sewage and keeping the stuff out of our immediate view. 18 inches is all that is needed for proper breakdown to occur. One day, people will get over their disgust of poop. But until then, we need to keep it out of view. That's the only reason I am advocating to build it under the house. It could work perfectly well in the backyard.

What Little Girls Are Made Of- From the Diaries of Becka Skaggs, PhD

Apartment buildings can be set up to serve the dozens of families gathered under those roofs by simply tasking space for the technology to be installed. The space could be under the building or in an adjacent location.

Developing, installing, and using this technology is nothing like welding meteors together into a fireball and burying bad guys with it. It is MUCH simpler.

Many houses today are built with basements. Some of these basements are dark and dank, have standing water, may have dirt bottoms and could also be incubating molds that can make us sick or kill us. Our basements are already like that all over the world. We NEED to be better at building everything, and we can if we just take the extreme profiteering out of the equation.

Sustainable Living does exactly that. ALL the profits are transferred to each individual that is using her resources in a sustainable way. THESE PEOPLE no longer must pay the high prices of others when they have their own resources to use, and it is a virtual endless supply.

If your fruit tree is healthy, it will give you fruit for a hundred years or more. Such a fruit grower would never consider paying another person a profit for a product she produces herself. So, too, is the idea over all the sustainable ways we can change our lifestyles. We save money and we help all others by making the economy fair for everyone to enjoy EQUALLY!

Tell me, class, why shouldn't we be living sustainably? If we can become innovative without boundaries, maybe we can find a construction material that is stronger than a steel I-Beam with a specific gravity of less than one? And just maybe, we can innovate ways to transmit fluids, like water, within nothing but an energy field consisting of energy that already exists within and around the transmitted fluids? Perhaps, re-purposed universal energy is possible. Hey! It's just science.

For next time, I want you all to read about new innovative technologies for collecting and/or treating rainwater. I am expecting some discussion next time, too.

Class DISMISSED!

Wink wink

CHAPTER – LIFE with a LOVE BUG

April 10, 2018

Grandma said I could have accepted a commission in the National Oceanic and Atmospheric Administration (NOAA), as well. They have the same kind of DCO program as the PHS. But I decided to stay with my family. Besides, NOAA does a lot of research. I like to apply my skills to help people stay healthy, and alive. However, the Lieutenant JG that came to offer the commission was worth the visit.

Rosalyn will also receive a commission once she has received her PhD in communications from the Walter Cronkite School of Communication and Broadcasting at Arizona State University. She is on schedule to receive her diploma on June 2, 2021. Faster than ME in school time!

The COSMIC TWINS are officially part of the US Government in the Public Health Service. Rosalyn is their first and only cadet. All healthcare is taken care of, nothing to worry about in that department anymore. In fact, the US Congress decided it was in the National Interest to fund Father's future research into brain chemicals and neuroreceptors, and they are assisting him in further securing his ELF arrays by developing a dynamic system for switching between receptors in the array, in case of attack. This technical advancement allows the array to be kept intact while rotating the "virtual connection" between individual signal receptors placed around the Globe.

Father was required to build underground quarters for the Marine Light Infantry Detachment assigned to the COSMIC TWINS World Headquarters at Stone Mountain, Georgia. It's okay, though; they are very fun people, once they let you get to know them.

I wasn't thrilled about the way the government first tried to implement the COSMIC TWINS PROTECTION Act. Until sometime in 2008, I felt it was more like the COSMIC TWINS PROTECTION and ASSIMILATION Act. I was not very cooperative to the people wanting things from me all the time.

Alisha eventually got me to see the benefits. After I realized how people were being helped, I calmed down about that topic, and began to enjoy sharing my love with all the doctors and government research staff.

"I'm sorry, Lieutenant Abbott, Rebecca's been in her room all day. She has already made a promise to the PHS to accept their commission once she's done with her degree. I appreciate your offer, though, and so does Becca."

Frans pulls the Lieutenant by his lapel closer to her.

"Honestly, Lieutenant, my granddaughter is not physically built for the sea. Will you be candid with me? Why does NOAA want Becca as an officer?"

"Honestly, Fran? They want her brain. I'm the one who wants Becca. I know she will always have difficulty with her speech. I understand her physical problems. I can't help myself, Fran. I really have feelings for this girl of yours."

"Well," Frans says a little misty-eyed.

"That's fairly candid, Lieutenant. Thank you."

Fran releases Jeffery's lapel.

"Oh! She's on a new therapy regiment. So, she is practicing her R's and her L's. She especially likes words with double R and double L. She might be doing that right now."

Then, Fran looked back at the stairs,

"I thought Becca would be curious enough to be down by now."

and turned back toward the officer.

What Little Girls Are Made Of- From the Diaries of Becka Skaggs, PhD

"I'm sorry, Jeffery. Looks like she'll be in her room for a while longer."

As Fran was closing the door, I heard her say "You're very Welcome, Lieutenant."

"What Lieutenant? Who was that grandma?" I had just come downstairs from my room because I heard voices. I was busy studying upstairs when my podcast finished. Once I heard voices downstairs, I had to investigate.

I ran to the window to look outside as soon as I got into the front room.

"OMG! Grandma he's gorgeous!"

"Oh? Here, let me call him back in for you, Rebecca." Grandma Fran says easily. And approaches the front door again.

"No!" Then I covered my mouth in case I was too loud, and he may have heard. Of course, it was too late. If he heard my big mouth say "NO", covering my mouth now was doing nothing to take that away from his short-term memory.

I need one more peek out the window.

Then, Fran calls in the Cavalry.

"Lieutenant?"

Grandma calls after the NOAA officer, Lieutenant Junior Grade, Jeffery Abbott – "that's with two effs, two bees and two tees", he would say - just before he disappears into his car. He must have heard her because he bobbed right back up.

"Yes, Mrs. Skaggs?" The officer politely replies.

"My granddaughter just arrived from upstairs and would like to speak with you. If you have a moment?"

Fran sounded so courteous and concerned. Like she was concerned for my welfare and potential life-long loneliness.

Now I'm whispering and screaming at grandma at the same time.

"No! I don't want to talk to him, grandmother! Grandma, you are embarrassing me."

I looked out the window again quickly.

"Grandma, No! My hair's still a mess, No!"

In a very casual way, Fran says,

"Then tell him that, honey. He is just about to the door."

When the young officer arrives back at the front door, Fran invites him in, but I stop him using my instant close-proximity trick. I jumped between Grandma and the officer.

"No!" I said and grabbed the front door.

"I, uh, I..." I stammered my words to the young officer while twisting the doorknob to the already open door. Panicked thoughts suddenly struck me between the eyes.

"Oh crap! Get some words in that mouth of yours, Becka", I'm thinking to myself in a maddened state.

Finally, I put it together.

"I was wondering if you would, uh, if you might, um, like to walk to the Yogurt Shop down by the beach?"

I'm quickly trying to comb my fingers through my fine blonde hair. But it just sticks to my fingers. JEEEZ!

"It's just a few blocks. Then, you could, um, maybe you could, uh, tell me about your program you work in at NOAA."

And now my hair is a static frizzy attractant to nearby birds looking for a nesting site.

What Little Girls Are Made Of- From the Diaries of Becka Skaggs, PhD

"I would really like that, Ms. Skaggs. I think so highly of you, Becka", blushingly gushing, he adds like a star-struck cadet.

"Fine, Lieutenant. But don't start that Ms. Skaggs stuff and admire me and all that. Okay?"

Then I went through the door and down the 3 steps from our little concrete stoop at grandma's front door.

"You coming? Or am I going by myself?" I wise-cracked at the Adonis. I can't have him gaining his balance while I'm still reeling.

"Noooo…."

Gawd! That was out loud!!

"I mean", a slight pause for effect.

"Nooo?? Like a question?" Smooth Becka.

"Nooo! Like an answer." He gives me a sly smile.

Then like a gentleman and an officer, he volunteers,

"I am ready for some frozen yogurt, yes?"

Then with a smile Jeffery says, "let's go!"

I smiled at him and got in step with his military cadence. Off we go!

I asked him about his work and the program in which he works. He began telling me all kinds of exciting things about the deep seas below 2000 meters, like potential food supplies that could feed the world for centuries. He began about some engineering challenges they face and that when he gets his Captainship, he will be able to write some of his own grant proposals and do his own research.

Uh-oh.

What am I supposed to do with my hands?

Ok, so I can put my thumb on my pocket and kind of look cool. Then, I can walk really slow-like in my navy pumps kind of acting cool. Maybe I could kick a pebble along the sidewalk. No. That will look like I'm bored. I need to be coy. That's entirely different.

Can a five-foot eleven and three-eighths-inch woman walk slowly in navy pumps and look cool, while trying to be coy? I mean, is that even possible??

"And we have no idea what would even happen once we tried to bring them to the surface?" Jeffery is continuing his thesis on very-deep-ocean food supplies.

"We may need to do all our processing at depth, as well."

If I cross my arms across my chest, he might think I'm closing myself off to him. That's not the message I want to send out. I really think he's beautiful! I mean, I would do this again. Already! And we haven't done anything, yet!

There is a little chill. Oh, well. I'll tighten my arms to my body just a little and take it like a human woman. Damn! I didn't put on lip gloss. Do my lips look chapped?

"That sounds so exciting, Jeffery!" I launched that compliment as I noticed he had stopped talking.

That put a smile on his face, just as we turned the corner to the Frozen Yogurt Shoppe.

Jeffery opened the door for me. I managed to finally scoot my femaleness through the door with just a little physical combat training between the two of us. He wasn't quite used to larger women, was my first thought. I mean, he could've left a little more room for me to get through the door.

Once we were both fully inside the yogurt shoppe, I began in tour-guide mode.

"Well, Jeffery. The big menu on the wall is everything. Today's specials are listed on the lower left, as you can see."

What Little Girls Are Made Of- From the Diaries of Becka Skaggs, PhD

"Thank you very much. Rebecca. That's a large menu board, Rebecca."

"Oh, please. Call me Becka."

"Then please quit calling me Jeffery." He quickly followed.

"I have always been called Jeff. I really would like it if you called me Jeff."

"Oh, Jeff! I'm so sorry." I laugh a little.

I continued to buy him a little time to make his selection, so I blabbed out,

"I already know what I want. I hardly ever get something different."

I flashed him my best Viking-warrior-has-hair-like-a-birds-nest smile, and hoped it was sufficient for my cause. I really needed help here. I'm out of my romance league with this mister everything is nice.

"So, you go right ahead."

But Jeff insisted I go first.

I noticed the attendant on the other side of the counter was already smiling at the two of us. I'm having a hard time here. Why do I seem to think that this person has already been here before and knows everything that's already going to happen? I'm as nervous as I've ever felt.

"Hi, Lar-ry. What are you smiling about?"

Yeah, I know Larry. I just like his name in two syllables.

"Nothing, Becka. The usual?" Larry asks me. I ignore his question.

"Ahhh, I'll have a Strawber-ry Marshmal-low Twist cone, small-l-l please." I was saying each syllable the way I was training.

The attendant burst out laughing.

"What?" I shot at him.

Larry's known me since I was a little girl. But that's no reason for him to laugh at such an embarrassing time as this for me.

All I could think of was to scold him with his name.

"Lar-ry!"

"Oh, Becca." He straightened himself up a bit and started to calm down.

"That little cone won't last you 5 steps. Just get the Jumbo like you always do, Becca. You are a famous girl. Treat yourself." Larry gets a big grin.

Then, it's Jeff's turn.

"Jumbo?"

"Oh, I see it. Yes, there are 5 sizes. It's the largest, just above Giant. Which is above Large."

Now Jeff feels like he has leverage on me over something. I can't quite figure out these feelings I'm having, and Rosalyn is totally quiet. She's been running in stealth-observer mode ever since I squealed when I saw him pull up at the curb when I was still upstairs. Squealed the best I can, anyway.

Little sisters can be like that, you know.

Jeff has this odd smile on his face.

"No, Larry. But I'll take that Giant".

"There you go! You'll feel much better, Becca. I guarantee it." Larry says.

He spun the perfect twist cone and handed it to me with a smile and a tiny wink.

"I love you, Becca. You know that" finishing with a sincere puppy dog-look.

"Yes, Lar-ry. And I absolutely LOVE you, too."

Then, I got a serious look on my face and said,

What Little Girls Are Made Of- From the Diaries of Becka Skaggs, PhD

"But when a girl says small-l, you let it be. OK? You hand over the small next time, Lar-ry."

"Yes, Dear" Larry gets off his short wise-crack and feels much better for it.

Then I gave him an Air Kiss and a big smile and grabbed my Giant cone. I stepped back and let Jeff order his secret concoction that I haven't heard one peep about yet. The secret was finally released as I was grabbing enough napkins for a girl scout troop.

"Yes, Larry. Hi, I'm Jeff."

"Oh, Nice to meet to you, Jeff. Any friend of Famous Becca's is a friend of mine."

Then Larry got his ordering smile on,

"What can I get you, Jeff."

"I think I'll have the Large Chocolate Pralines cup, with the crunchies. Famous Becca?"

I had to have looked surprised, because I was.

"Oh, you go for the kibble. Grrrr....me eat things."

I couldn't help myself.

{Becka! Shut up! Your nervous mouth is gonna blow this for both of us.}

Oh, Hi, Rosalyn. Did I wake you up, sister?

Then I screamed to Ros in desperation.

HEEELLLP ME!!!

I'm DYING here! Rosalyn, I need major help! I can't talk about my books. I'm not ready. My cone's already dripping. Now, I have to lick the whole thing all the way around, quickly or there's gonna be a big mess. Right in front of this deep-sea Titan. What am I going to do?

Oh, the napkins. Okay, okay. Ohhh, I have too many. Wait! I can ask Jeff to carry some home for grandma. Yeah. That would seem logical.

{BECKA!!!! STOP YOUR MIND!}

Ros-a-lyn! I can't stop myself. I'm going crazy, sis."

{It's OKAY, Becka. Calm down and look at Jeff. Look at him, Becka. He is waiting for your next word. He'd be on the edge of his seat, if you'd let him sit down. He can't wait to see what that word is going to be from you.}

Yeah, I see that odd stupor on his face. Like, what, Rosalyn? Uhhh, I got nothing.

{Becka. I am asking you this question. Do you want your next word to be something stupendous like serendipity, or something stupid, like Duhhh?"}

Yes? I mean, yes! You're right, Ros.

I drew a breath

"Oh, I'm sorry, Jeff. I was teasing you. I can't ever resist those little punch-lines when they present themselves. Shall we sit down?" I led him over to a table for two near the door.

{B+ for Becka. Better than duh. I love you.}

"Oh, a joke? Hahahaa, that's funny! You got me good. Haha", Jeff says to me.

Now Jeff is looking like a gauntlet was just placed in front of him. I'm not sure I did that right, either. I wasn't intending to place a gauntlet in front of Jeff. Nor was I trying to challenge him in any way, other than romantically.

"You are funny lady. You like little jokes. OK. I like little joke sometimes, too. Maybe some time we joke together again, No?", in his worst fake Russian accent.

His lousy accent sure made me laugh!

Rosalyn isn't laughing.

What Little Girls Are Made Of- From the Diaries of Becka Skaggs, PhD

I got this, sis.

{I said nothing, Becka. Not one thing came from me. I am mum.}

Your silence is golden, my Light, my LOVE. I appreciate your wisdom little sister. Thank you.

I feel just knowing Rosalyn is there for me is enough to give me confidence.

{Oh, gag me, sis! Get going, Becka!}

"Come on, Jeff. Grab your cup of pralines."

I grabbed his hand and gave it a tug as I was leaving the table.

I was already done with my Giant Strawberry Twist cone. I get hungry when I'm nervous. What can I say?

"I have one more thing I want to ask you about," I told Jeff. Then I bend toward him and whisper. "Lar-ry is listening to everything. Let's go."

I start to stand up, still holding his free hand, and pull him toward the door. Maybe giving his hand a little extra squeeze. I don't know my own strength sometimes. I'm up, and Jeff is tugging at my hand while I'm trying to lead us out of this place.

Jeff says, like he's trying to sound defeated or something,

"May I have my hand to eat my Yogurt and Pralines, at some point in time before it melts?"

"As soon as we get outside." I rushed him out the door and we turned the corner toward grandma's house. Jeeez!

Once fully outside, I tell Jeff,

"And if you still have some yogurt left when we get back home, there's an old picnic table in the backyard."

But I got nothing from Jeff. He didn't look stunned or in shock.

Maybe I should have let Jeff lead in our dance inside the yogurt shop? It's so confusing.

Ros? I'm so bad at men!

{*No, sis. You are doing GREAT! So, kiss him already!*}

Rosalyn?? Quiet!!

I returned Jeff's hand so he could begin finally enjoying the circulation in his fingers.

Larry, inside the shop, has started laughing out loud again. Rolling-On-Floor-Laughing, pretty sure. Jeff and I can hear him from here.

"Do you mind if we walk back to your house?" Jeff asks me softly. "I mean, rather than standing here listening to that wild laughter?"

I am feeling like I could do anything this man asks me to do. I trust him completely! But walking home together was already on my growing list of things for us to do.

"Yeah, sure, Jeff. I just like talking with you. That makes you a special person right there, just the fact that you have no trouble getting me to blab."

He looked at me with a surprised smile. He was nervous too. I could hear it in his laugh at my little joke.

I'm trying to lighten the mood, Rosalyn. Is that good?

{*Becka, pay attention to Jeff. Not me! Silly sister neophyte in LOVE. Ha! Miss I AM THE LOVE is chicken! Yes, that's terrific, sister. Now, kiss him. He'll absolutely die in your arms!*}

I don't want him to die for 80 years, Rosalyn.

{*BECKA!! Jeff, with two effs. GO!*}

What Little Girls Are Made Of- From the Diaries of Becka Skaggs, PhD

We walked a moment in silence, while I dealt with secret demons in my head, and Jeff ate and ate. Then, Jeff continued revealing more thoughts that were swirling around inside HIS head.

"I really..."

I interrupted him when I saw he was done with his cup of yogurt.

"Jeff, let me hold that empty cup for you. I'll throw it away when we get home."

Oh, good! Now I have something to do with my hands, Ros.! Whew!

"I'm sorry. Go ahead", I urged Jeff to talk. Please!??

Once he is completely freed from the burdens of the yogurt shop, Jeff began again.

"Your humor is funny. You make me laugh, Becka. I really enjoy your company."

"Thank you, Jeff. I'm enjoying your company, too."

He's nervous and stammering, but he's doing okay, in my book.

I'll let him gather his thoughts without too much interruption. Something interesting is about to happen.

He looked up at me with these eyes that made my insides melt, even with all that frozen yogurt in there. Then he spoke,

"Becka, I really admire you. You are super smart. You are a famous lady. I know about you and your children's mysteries. You are the most drop-dead gorgeous Periwinkle Princess a guy could ever have the luck to set eyes upon."

Oh, My Gawwd!! He is SOOO precious! Grandma? Can I keep him?? He's so beautiful.

With that glorious icebreaker, we both laughed off some nervousness. WOW! Jeff has my complete attention. Our cherry-red complexions are matching. Our eyes are meeting.

We looked at each other with our embarrassed faces and big grins.

I wasn't totally unprepared for what came next. I'm not sure if Jeff intended to kiss me or not. But when we stopped on the sidewalk and he reached his recently freed arms around me, he WAS going to kiss me. I was determined to get that kiss!

Whether he intended it to be a hug or not, only Jeff knows for sure. My mind was not settling for a hug. Especially, the little demonic angel of a little sister inside my mind.

It may have begun a hug, but it was NOW a kiss!

Our heads tilted in unison and our lips touched and I exploded! I needed a little more pressure, so I grabbed onto him even harder. He is leaning into me, and we are in full embrace.

WOW!!!! What a kiss!!!! When do I stop???

Rosalyn? Is that you giving me visions of fireworks?

{No, sister. Those are your very own fireworks going off inside your brain. Isn't it WONDERFUL!?? And don't you dare stop!}

Jeff must've felt me melting in his arms. He held me just a squeeze tighter. I had no idea that was possible until it happened. He softly released our lips. My eyes were glued shut. Was I waiting for another? It's not coming, so, I should probably look at him, now.

I opened my eyes, and there was an angel looking at me with this beautiful little smile and the peace of heaven all over his face.

Jeff, leaned into me one more time, and kissed me. This time he intended to kiss me. He closed his eyes, and I couldn't help but watch. In a few seconds, he gently pulled his lips from mine. WOW!!

What Little Girls Are Made Of- From the Diaries of Becka Skaggs, PhD

I'm dead, Rosalyn. Cupid shot me right in the heart.

{Hehe. No, you're not dead. You're just numb, sister. I've been telling you that for years. I'm loving it! Hehe}

Neither of us spoke. We had the look we exchanged with each other. You know? That silent look romantic couples give each other that lets them know everything is with full loving intent and they both understand.

The newly romantic couple walked silently for a short period of time because we are scared to death about all the feelings and thoughts in our heads, and uncertainty whether the other person is feeling the same way. We humans are very strange beings, indeed.

We held hands all the way. I had already scrunched up the cup and was holding the future piece of trash to dispose of later.

Don't you ask me what I was doing with that cup while we were kissing. You girls KNOW what I was doing with that cup when we were kissing. I'll tell him later that I will pay to get his jacket cleaned. Why should I let such a little thing like dripped, melted, frozen yogurt on the back of a jacket spoil the mood?? It was delicious, after all.

As we were walking, I started thinking about this trash. We women will just hold things for other people while they fuss around with their lives in front of us. We will hold their bag, their baby, their trash, whatever might free them up so they can fuss about and move along with their day, and become happy, we hope.

People might even ask us to hold their keys, then start digging in their purse for their keys. We might stand there patiently because the person never told us they were looking for their keys.

Until they say, "What did I do with my keys?"

Then we can hold the keys high in the air for them. "Here they are."

As I came back to Earth, I realized I hadn't learned how Jeff got into NOAA, and I was suddenly interested.

"How did you get into the Administration, Jeff?" I mean, you could've been a civilian and work for NOAA. Why did you accept a commission?"

"I'm just a few years older than you, Becka", Jeff volunteered

"I am old enough to remember 9-11 and it touched me that someone could attack us and get away with it. At least, that is how the story was always told."

"All my life growing up, I wanted to serve our country and be sure we received justice for all those families. I would think of how many kids would grow up without a parent, or maybe grow up with no parents. I really didn't know how many children suffered through family loss. But I thought about that as a kid. It would make me sad to think about those children that lost parents. And as I grew up, that sadness just became more profound. My heart actually ached whenever I thought of those children, which was too often, truthfully."

Jeff changed the grip of our hands from fingers interlocked to palms clasped. It helps the hands breathe a little to change the grip from time-to-time.

"I know, Jeff. That makes me very sad, too. Your heart ached? My gawd, Jeff! Mine aches just hearing about it." I'm into this guy's story! I'm paying attention much better than when we first started this walk.

"Then, what happened with you?" I smiled to him with a sincere look on my face, I hoped.

"Please go on, Jeff." I gave him a gentle nudge in the ribs with my elbow.

Jeff continued, after a tiny smile and a look at me from the corner of his eye.

"I joined the ROTC program in High School", he said looking out into nothing but the past.

What Little Girls Are Made Of- From the Diaries of Becka Skaggs, PhD

"The Reserve Officer Training Corps can be used for any uniformed service", he said as he looked at me, and regained his presence from that far off place he was just visiting.

"So, I felt good that ROTC would be creating opportunities for me", he said, "even though I was choosing a path of service to the American people."

I looked down at the sidewalk and started envisioning what he had looked like in High School in that uniform. What an Adonis! Now a grown man in uniform, and he's telling me his inner thoughts of how he made his decision for his future. I don't know if I can resist this person. He could ask me to do anything, and I don't know if I would WANT to resist this man.

Jeff is still telling his story.

"Then in 2016, I changed my mind on a lot of things. I began to disagree with the wars the US had become embroiled within. I no longer had the desire to exact revenge upon our enemies. I could no longer be clear about the identity of our enemies. Everything was becoming so confused. Details were being revealed that the government lied to us about many things leading us into those wars. The wars became more about greed and power than ideals and protecting our way of life."

Jeff paused a moment and looked right at me. Jeff is about 6'1", so it's the perfect height advantage. Tell me, my love, everything on your mind.

Jeff turns toward me while we keep walking.

"Becka, I could no longer feel good about killing, or even trying to feel that our cause was superior to any other cause. There was no 'high morality' to fight for in this country. The cause didn't even matter anymore. We were no longer being a moral nation. Once I realized that, I couldn't support any cause."

Then he straightened us out as a walking unit on the sidewalk and we began strolling toward home.

"You decided to become a scientist instead?" I finished his thought with a question just to let him know I was paying attention. And I was interested, truly!

"Marine Sciences was always an interest to me. This discipline of life in the Very Deep Ocean just fell into my lap during my junior year of college. I'm really enjoying the research. I found a very profound way to help humans. Helping people is what fills my heart."

He stopped us quickly in the middle of the sidewalk a half-block from home. I'm getting good at following his lead in this dance. He turned and looked at me with the excitement of a dream in his eyes. Which dream is this going to be?

"Becka?" He says to me.

"Yes?" I instantly respond.

"I really like you, Becka. Even though the Administration sent me to recruit you, I need you to know that I accepted this assignment only because it was you, Becka Skaggs, the Periwinkle Princess that has had so much hardship in her life."

"Thank you, Jeff. You are very kind." Aren't his eyes dreamy?

Then my eyebrows went up and I leaned a little closer to him.

"Is that all you wanted to say, Jeff?"

"No, Becka. I do have one other thing."

My ears are wide open.

"Yes?" I give him a little prompt.

Jeff begins,

"We could have enough food at depth to feed the world for centuries in the deep ocean. We know almost nothing about it."

What Little Girls Are Made Of- From the Diaries of Becka Skaggs, PhD

"Oh."

I'm truly happy for Jeffery. I find myself still wanting to call him 'Jeffery'. Is that weird? But he likes Jeff, so…

I really was just teasing Jeff, by acting like I might be waiting for some big question. I wasn't necessarily waiting for any big question. No more than any girl my age might be waiting for some strange, obtuse, BIG question.

Jeff continues sharing his dream with his future dream girl.

"Now we can't just go down there and start harvesting, or we'd end up in the same mess we are in now. BUT, once we learn all about the ecosystem and how it functions, we can begin thinking sustainably about our future food supply. Of course, we need to know if the ecosystem is stable or not. One of the first questions to be answered should be whether the ecosystem is in decline, or is it thriving?"

Jeff stopped his presentation. He looks at me with the smiling eyes of a Greek god.

"I'm sorry, I…"

I think he was going to say something more, but that never got to happen. I reached over to Jeff, got on my toes and gave him a quick loving kiss on the lips. 1.0 seconds is all that was needed. Those lips are so soft, yummy.

"Always obey your mother, Jeff."

"Huh? What was that for, Becka?" Jeff asked with his giant precious sincere puppy eyes.

"I feel the Love in you. I am in Love with you. You will know the Love in me. I'm your Love Bug, Jeff!"

We both got big smiles on our faces. One more mutual scrumptious kiss to seal the deal.

We finished our stroll in blissful silence. Yes, the last 50 steps home seemed to take 50 minutes.

We arrived at grandma's house with sweaty palms joined together. Grandma opened the door as I began up the three little steps. I asked Jeff to come in.

"We could sit in the backyard a little bit", I said to Jeff in my best loving 'Come join me, I'm a woman who wants you' voice.

"No, I'm sorry, Becka. I must get back to the office," Jeff said.

Wrong choice, dude!!

Then his face brightened, and he said,

"I really enjoyed," he hesitated very briefly before finishing his sentence.

"The yogurt, the conversation, and the walk."

"Me too, Jeff."

{Ahhhh dummy!!! Is that all you can say, Becka???}

Hush, Ros! I didn't hear any suggestions from you, oh great communicator!

Jeff bids his final adieu.

"Ok, then, I better get the car back to the motor pool."

Jeff looks at grandma, "nice to see you again, Mrs. Skaggs", he gives a little salute to both of us as we are both waving goodbye to the Junior Grade Lieutenant. He climbs into his car and disappears into the afternoon.

Now grandma looks at me, as I continue into the house, and she just has to say something. She can't leave it alone.

"Hello, Rebecca, Dear. What happened to you?"

I hand grandma the cup-o-trash. She willingly accepts the little package and begins to hold it with both hands.

350

What Little Girls Are Made Of- From the Diaries of Becka Skaggs, PhD

I look up at grandma with my big blank blue eyes.

"My star went supernova." Then I looked up and stared at the ceiling while twirling in a circle about the North Star.

It wasn't the totally correct metaphor, but it was the only thing I could think of with lots of explosions and fireworks. I needed a LOT of explosions and fireworks to explain what happened.

There was only one person on my mind, and thoughts of him were generating a thousand feelings. A million, maybe!

"What happened, exactly?" Fran asked gently, even if a little confused.

"You wouldn't understand, grandma."

"Oh, I see", Fran lets out as I'm walking by her.

I just kept going right past her and up the stairs to my bedroom. I have a lot of feelings to figure out. I didn't even notice whether the stair squeaked on the way up the staircase. But I heard grandma throw the cup-o-trash in the garbage under the kitchen sink before I got to my room.

As soon as I opened the door, Rosalyn let out a squeal.

{THAT. WAS. AWESOME!!! I want one of those kisses!!}

Believe me, Ros. You'll want a LOT of those kisses. Definitely a million, at least.

{Why did you use Father's words on Jeffery. He can love no other, Becka. Not now. He has tasted the kiss of a Love Bug.}

I don't know, Rosalyn! I freaked out!! I feel so stupid!

I felt him tugging on my emotions. I felt like I needed to tug back. But just a little. They weren't totally correct words, Rosalyn. He's not under that kind of spell. He'll just miss me the rest of his life if he doesn't marry me. That's all.

{Becka!}

Well???

You saw him, Ros. I turned on my charm to have him sit with me in the backyard and he turned me down. What kind of spell is that? The backyard backfire spell?? I have no control over him, Ros.

He MAY just be a Love Bug, Rosalyn. He noticed when I told him to obey his mother. That shouldn't happen.

You want to occupy your nose with research on that topic for a while, my sister, my light?

{No reason to be snooty, My Love, my Strength. I accept your challenge. I will learn of our future lover, Jeffery. Hehe}

Not OUR future lover, sister! Let's be very clear on that fact.

{I love you so much, my sister, my strength, my love. Hehe}

* * * **Damned Pandemic Break** * * *

December 15, 2019

I'm sitting here in Stone Mountain getting frustrated by the latest turn in history. Events are out of my control, and they still drive me crazy! Okay, a little dramatic, maybe. I wasn't going to school anywhere, so it's not like I was waiting to graduate or anything. My only plan for a diploma is my PhD. And I'm going to finish next spring. I'm just finishing up the editing on my dissertation until then.

I had just returned from my quarter studying abroad on the Danube River Delta in the Black Sea. Now, there are rumblings in the science rumor mill of a coronavirus coming from China. It may already be here in the US. We have no confirmed cases yet. But we also don't have the genetics of the virus, yet.

What Little Girls Are Made Of- From the Diaries of Becka Skaggs, PhD

Epidemiology has advanced to the point where we now decode the genetics of an invading virus before we start to combat it. The CDC is stuck right now. They are officially under "Stand Down" orders. What will happen to my PhD work? I have no idea. We must press on. "Mush!", as the Alaskan dog-sled drivers would say when the snow became more difficult to traverse. Usually because it was all wet and mushy snow. Which made sense.

I discovered a way to distinguish the differences in universal energy between individual cells. I have been teaching this to Father, Alisha and Rosalyn. I believe this knowledge will lead me to a better understanding of the energy of cells, in general, and from an invading virus, more specifically.

Rosalyn feels like she will be able to communicate with the invading cells, once she gets the energy-signature things figured out. Each cell has a unique energy signature, just like each human finger has a different fingerprint.

I asked her to teach me how to talk to my cells. THAT would be cool!! SO, we are each helping the other. That includes Father and Alisha and Malia, too. We are all here enjoying each other's company and evolving our skills.

However, NOAA has Jeff working for these holidays. And we are discussing this on the phone right now.

"I'm not a happy about it, Love Bug."

Jeff went off to War College at Auburn University. That was almost a year-long secret hush hush training. I'm pleading with him to come to Georgia for the Holidays. Or Virginia, or Florida, I don't really care. I just want to be with him for the holidays this year. I'm here in Stone Mountain for the month, and maybe longer if this virus thing blows up, like they expect.

I have thought too many times about my Backyard Backfire spell. I am acting like I totally can't live without this guy. Pfffttt. What's his name again?? Ha! The big Love Bug can't live without ME! Listen to our recent exchange.

"Becka, my darling, I want to be with you so badly. But I have no control over the matter, little buggles." He sounded so forlorn.

"But, Jeffery, my buggles. I love you now, baby. Today. Who knows what will happen in 6 months?"

{Ok, Becka. You just lost your right to narrate this scene. You are SO bad with your understatements about your emotional anchor you have attached to Jeff. Time for some truths, sister.}

{You guys noticed that, right? The Love Bugs are buggles? Hehe. Oh! Listen up. I have some gushy gooey stuff on Becka and Jeff, first.}

{Jeff was tested for the Love Bug gene in 2014. He has known for a while now that he is special. Yes, he thought Becka would be a challenge to his newfound powers, at the time. These children are so funny!}

{So, Becka and Jeff both like each other but they are scared to death they won't be liked back. Yet they each knew they were Love Bugs. SO, they also each knew that, by definition, they must be loved by the one they kissed!}

{How crazy is Love?? It's paradoxical!}

{They are so wrapped up in the love for love, they are forgetting the spirits that are inside their bodies. These "Buggles" are ruining their love because they know too much about the topic.}

{Let it be!}

{Please, Guys? Get out of your heads, and into your beds!}

{THIS Love Bug has seen enough of their nonsense. No more throwing good love after bad love. I will intervene on behalf of all Love Bugs}.

{If we made Love just one-24th of the time we are given for our lives, can you imagine how happy this planet could be? Let this be a lesson to all of you Love Bugs: Don't over-think it. Just feel the Love, and let it be love.}

{I'm not sleeping in the same room with you tonight, Becka. You have bad energy, girl. Go clean yourself up! Work it out or shake it up. Something, my Strength. I'm not feeling the Love. Sheesh! *Eye roll*}

What Little Girls Are Made Of- From the Diaries of Becka Skaggs, PhD

{Rosalyn Valery, out!}

CHAPTER – ISLAND LIFE LOST

August 15, 2020 - GUAM

The couple was very happy together. They had just met yesterday, and they feel like their lives were just saved. They enjoyed lunch together at the hotel where they met. The couple then spent all day and all night together. They have not been away from each other since they met. They have become blessed with the love of their lives on the little island of Guam. They both have no doubts in their minds that they will spend eternity together.

Once they enjoyed the room service breakfast, and each other in a jacuzzi bath, the couple dressed for their day. They had planned only one activity for the day. They are to be the "Loving Couple" at Two Lover's Point.

Two Lover's Point is a famous little overlook on the Island of Guam. It has a story whose roots run deep into local legend. Two Lover's Point also has a snack bar and a gift shop, some observation areas, and the Leap Point itself, of course.

The couple got dressed for their day and drove off up the hill from the hotel zone to their destiny. Once they arrived at Two Lover's Point, they didn't go into the gift shop or any buildings. The loving couple went directly to the Point where the Legend of the Two Lover's is described on a sign for all visitors to read.

The Legend describes a Prince from one tribe and a Princess from another tribe desperately in love with each other. The tribal elders will not allow their marriage to each other as both have already been betrothed to

What Little Girls Are Made Of- From the Diaries of Becka Skaggs, PhD

another. The tribal elders decided these young lovers shall never be allowed to love each other.

In ultimate defiance, the young lovers ran away together to this geographical point. Here, they vowed to be in love together for eternity and that no elders shall ever separate them. The lovers then tied their hair together and leapt to their fate within the fringing reef just sixty feet below. They disappeared into the Pacific Ocean, never to be seen again.

When our modern-day lovers climbed the barrier to the Leap Point and began symbolically tying their hair together, they were very obvious to the tourists in the area. It certainly appeared to everyone that this couple was in love.

Witnesses said the elder lovers were wearing a hundred pounds of chains and irons each by the time they jumped off that cliff and into the ocean below.

The bodies were recovered by authorities later that day. The lovers were later identified as well-known, and wealthy, locals. One lover was the Chief Executive Officer of the Bank of Guam and personally worth over $100 million US. The other lover was similarly wealthy and was the CEO of the Bank of Saipan.

The United States Government has a large military presence on its territory of Guam. Saipan is a 90-minute flight away. They are next-door neighbors in the wide-open Pacific Ocean. Guam is the largest Island in the Northern Marianas Islands chain and is along the eastern edge of the Philippine Sea, roughly 1600 miles east of Manilla.

Guam is farther away from Honolulu than Boston is away from Los Angeles, by about one thousand miles. Los Angeles is closer to Boston than it is to Honolulu. That's the wide-open Pacific Ocean.

* * * ISLAND LIFE-TAKER BREAK * * *

In the Seychelles, Indian Ocean – August 29, 2020

Yuri is watching the monitor of the laptop computer sitting on the table of his private condominium. Vladimir Bostek is sitting in the chair at the table, occasionally hitting some keys to advance the screen, and thrill Yuri even further.

The numbers on the screen are getting larger by the second. Yuri is watching the value of his private bank account soar past 5Bn Euro and climbing fast.

"Oh, Vladimir, look at what time it is? We will be over 15 Bn Euro in 10 minutes, with Billions more to come!" Buahahaha

"I must go enjoy this moment in solitude."

Yuri begins to briskly leave the front room of his hotel suite and retire to his room for a bubbly jacuzzi bath.

"I will watch the world markets begin to fall while in complete relaxation in my bubble bath, Vladimir. Do not interrupt me."

Yuri closed the door to the bedroom and the Master Bath portion of his suite. Vladimir hears water running in the tub and continue running.

Sounds right.

Time to watch the money roll in for the Director.

Vladimir wasn't sure why he had that thought. It doesn't matter, he was going to watch the money anyway.

In less than two days, the Asian financial world was rocked to its knees.

* * * ISLAND LIFE in a PANIC BREAK * * *

August 31, 2020

What Little Girls Are Made Of- From the Diaries of Becka Skaggs, PhD

Rosalyn came to me in a panic. This is new. Rosalyn has never been like this before.

[Becka my sister, my strength. There has been an explosion at 38 Scotts Road, Singapore.

It's a high-rise apartment building. The top 5 floors have been lost in the explosion, my sister. Lives have been lost, Becka!]

Rosalyn? Calm down please, my love, my Light. Tell me what you know. Don't worry about the rest.

{There is a disturbance in the human spirit. It's not just this explosion that concerns me. The soul has been usurped from 1000 people. Becka? One thousand human beings have lost their souls. They have not died. Their souls have been stolen. The people are under the control of Yuri Yurachenkov.}

What is happening Rosalyn? You're not making sense. How can Yuri be doing this?

{The Bank of Kuala Lumpur has fallen to Yuri. Yuri is gathering up resources by using his control serum. The Bank of Singapore has fallen to Yuri, sister. The Royal Family of Thailand has become infected.}

Okay, Rosalyn. Stop the second-by-second running account, please. I get it. We are in big trouble if we don't stop that stinking aardvark, Yuri Yurachenkov.

{Sister, the finances of all southeast Asia are going to Yuri's accounts.}

Understood. Let's get going, Ros. We have many plans to prepare. I think I know exactly what we need to snake this long-snooted ferret from his underground lair.

*** ISLAND HOPPING LIFE BREAK ***

September 3, 2020

{Yuri has gone to ground, my sister my strength. He is still in the Indian Ocean but may not be in the Seychelles. It makes no sense, sister. Becka, my strength? The images I am receiving seem to be out of order. Did you know Jeffery is in the Indian Ocean?}

Jeffery is on "The Adventurer" supposedly acting like they are doing research, sister. Jeffery and the Adventurer are part of our task force. Is he in danger?

{Sister, my love, my knowledge. It seems that Jeffery is creating danger. It makes no sense, sister.}

CREATING danger? What does that mean, Rosalyn? Are you sensing this is NOT related to our capture of Yuri?

{That is correct, my Light. But I can't get a fix on what is happening. Images that make no sense keep flashing through my mind and melding together. That usually means something specific, usually bad, but I just can't get it. My mental powers are weak. I must power down and recharge. I will learn more and return to you, my sister, my love.}

ROSALYN!! Oh, jeez girl.

CHAPTER - CLIMAX for LIFE DOWN UNDER

September 15, 2020

Aboard the USS Eisenhower, somewhere in the Indian Ocean, west of Perth Australia.

Mom and I hadn't been getting along lately. I was getting so frustrated with her blind obsession with men. She is an addict in whatever she does. I expected something to be substituted for her giving up alcohol. I'm so proud of her. She is really trying hard with that addiction. But the substitutes?

"Men are people with feelings, too, Mom!" I have said too many times to remember. I would also follow up with,

"You can't just use them and throw them away."

And of course, her usual retort was an "Adults are Adults" kind of thing.

"Why not?" Sometimes she would throw that question out there, too.

Then the next is the rationale for doing everything. Because "They" do it, too.

"That's all they're doing. It's a mutual agreement." She would say.

I had to finally stop getting myself so emotional about what my mother is doing with her life. She has been damaged, and that's the way things are for her, until Father completes his cure.

Look at me! My big mouth went and opened a topic we decided we weren't going to mention until next adventure. I am so sorry everyone!

Let's go back now and get this louse, Yuri! He's just the kind of insect chickens are always trying to find.

Alisha brought Carol and Marjorie to give me inner strength. When they walked through the galley door, where we were all sitting, I felt the energy level skyrocket!

"Excellent idea, Ros! So full of surprises, today."

"That's not all", she came back excitedly. "Look out at the main deck" she commands with a sly grin.

When I saw it, I knew exactly what Ros had in mind. And now its in our mind. I'm not sure how I feel about her being able to keep secrets from me. I'll check back on that later. For now?

"I love it, Ros!"

Rosalyn presented me with a beautiful twenty-foot-diameter parabolic mirror. Once it was placed into position, we merely focused the intense beam of sunlight onto the Jupiter Well Bore. It was a little hard to control at first, but I quickly got the hang of it. Rosalyn was gathering energy from our guests and sending it to me. Soon, I learned how to capture that gift of energy and use it to steady a beam of light right into Yuri's lousy lair.

I had that beam centered on the bore and began to drill a hole on top of the old hole. I wasn't physically holding the mirror. It was my mental powers holding it. But I looked like I was holding something big. It may as well have been a giant parabolic mirror. I had to act like I was holding something to get my powers to work. Yes, that is something else I need to work on. *Note to Self*

As I began to increase the intensity of the beam, I suddenly felt something strange.

What Little Girls Are Made Of- From the Diaries of Becka Skaggs, PhD

What just happened, Ros?

{Why are you asking me, my strength? You did it.}

What did I do, Ros? Did I kill our ship? I wasn't trying to kill our ship!

{You killed our ship, Becka.}

The USS Eisenhower went completely dead. All systems were shut down. No engines were running. Not even a bilge pump could be heard, nothing stirred, for about 30 seconds, then everything started back up like it was a giant computer getting rebooted. Or maybe the backup systems came on.

"Oh, shoot! Sorry guys!" I hunched my shoulders to the admiral. What's a superhero to do?

I had to take all the energy I could find and re-purpose it for just a moment. I didn't realize I was also taking energy from the Eisenhower. I will need to ask for forgiveness. But later, okay?? My list is growing of personal things to work on.

I got the light beam going again by aiming the mirror to catch sunlight. I shifted my aim slightly so the beam would move to the east. Once I gained my balance with the instrument, I went after that mound like an aardvark going after its prey in an Australian Outback anthill.

"It's Dinner Time!"

I let out my big bellow blast of strength. A hot wind blew dust across the desert.

Rosalyn placed her left hand on my right shoulder. That was the steady hand I was needing.

In a slow steady movement of about 3 seconds, I had opened Mt Webb as if a COSMIC KNIFE had cut a slice of cake for the party. Would any-one else like a slice? It's layered cake. It's got crunchy bad guys in it. No? Your decision.

Australian Federal Police, FBI, Scotland Yard, Interpol, Deutsche Police were all represented as the Australian Military moved in swiftly. Apprehension was swift and complete. Yuri Yurachenkov is not going to enjoy the Island stay they have planned for him.

Yuri Yurachenkov learned that when The COSMIC TWINS say something will happen? It will happen. Right, Sis?

"Correct, big sister!" Ros has a wide grin. "And that is a marshmallow heart I placed in your mind. It's for your hot cocoa."

Rosalyn enjoys the set up to what she thinks is a perfect punchline.

"That nasty Rooster, Yuri, finally had his goose cooked! Bahahaha."

Ros is very proud of herself.

Grandma Fran Eye Roll, sis.

Soon the word came from the world's newest gaping fossil dig that Yuri was not among the captured. Unfortunately, Yuri got away. He was not in his evil lair. Most of his lieutenants and henchmen were apprehended, but Vladimir Bostek and Yuri were never seen, for quite some time.

Rosalyn was correct in that Yuri had left the northern part of the Seychelles Island chain, but we were wrong thinking that he had gone back to the Gibson Desert. Turns out he didn't move quite as far as we thought.

Coprolite Corner was the big winner of the "Mt Webb Dinosaur Lottery". Yes, The Australian government sold the merchandizing rights to all the dinosaur bones, and other fossils, found among the rubble of Yuri's Jupiter Well lair. Hats, Coffee Mugs, T-shirts, private-labelled "Rock Candy" and "Bone Taffy". Boom-Time came to the Gibson Desert.

* * * ISLAND LIFE LOST BREAK * * *

COSMIC TWINS Communication: September 25, 2020

What Little Girls Are Made Of- From the Diaries of Becka Skaggs, PhD

{Becka, my Love, my Strength. I have learned how to contact Jeff. I told him who I was. He thought I was part of your injury, you just made me up. Like the Pineapple Princess. Hahaha. You children are so funny!}

Periwinkle, Rosalyn! The Periwinkle Princess!

{Don't get all hurt, sis. That was the picture inside HIS head, not mine. He's not free to communicate like us. That's the impression, the feeling, I'm left with after reaching him. He was very happy to hear you are ok.}

{Becka, my Love, my Strength, Jeffery may need our help. He's part of our secret in the Indian Ocean, sister, and may already be discovered.}

Rosalyn, my sister, my love, my Light. Use your wisdom, sister. I shall wait for further word from you. I am your strength. I am ready to shine, Rosalyn. I have the energy. I have the Strength. I AM the LOVE!

* * * **WEE SWISS LIFE BREAK** * * *

September 25, 2020 - Geneva

At World Health Organization Headquarters in Geneva, Switzerland, Mary Aboagye is getting briefed on the destruction of the underground lair in Mt Issa and everything that was recovered. She's been going over the inventory of everything that was known to be in Yuri's possession. Mary has found something that is not making her very happy.

Mary checked and double checked the list. Again, and again.

She was frantically collecting up the papers. Something was terribly wrong. She called in her assistant and asked her to double check. The assistant was also unable to find the missing papers. Looking in the outer office, Mimi found nothing there either.

Mary asks her assistant to come into her private office.

"What happened Mimi? I thought we had recovered all the doses of Yuri's serum?"

"Yes, Director. We did, too. We have no idea where the samples could be. They aren't on any of our inventory sheets we've received from the Jupiter Well teams."

The Director asked her assistant, "Could this be some paperwork error, Mimi? Could those inventories have been sent to the wrong Agency, and someone else is sitting on our samples?"

"No one seems to be able to locate them, so far, Director. We have reached out to the Americans, Australians, British, French, Germans, and Japanese. Even the Chinese are saying they are helping. The Chinese are usually very direct when asked about their efforts on most things. We believe they are truly concerned about locating the missing serum, even if it might be purely for their own reasons. We don't believe the Chinese have the missing samples, Director."

The assistant finished and waited for a response from her director.

The director was thinking of bigger possible disasters looming ahead as she asked her next questions.

"What are we looking at, Mimi? How many samples of serum do we know are lost?"

The assistant hesitated for a moment, then answered in two parts.

"Well, Director", Mimi started.

"We know we lost 1200 samples," Mimi stopped to see if there was a reaction from her director that would require her to stop giving her answer to Ms. Aboagye.

"Yes?" is all that came from the Director. The assistant continued onto part 2.

What Little Girls Are Made Of- From the Diaries of Becka Skaggs, PhD

"We suspect a total of five thousand will ultimately be considered lost, Director."

Mary looked at her assistant and put up a silent hand, signifying no talking for now, but don't you dare move.

Mary dropped her hand to her desk, obviously deep in thought. Mary awakened from her deep thoughts enough to look up at her assistant while placing both hands on top of her head. She clasped her fingers together. Still trying to imagine some of Yuri's plans, she leaned back in her chair until it squeaked, and said one mis-courteous,

"SHIT!"

Quite loudly.

"Yes, Ma'am," came an immediate response from the assistant.

* * * BARBECUED SLIPPERY EEL BREAK * * *

{Becka, my Love, my Strength. Yuri has relocated his personal headquarters to the southern end of the island chain from the Seychelles. He's holed up in Reunion Island. He moved just where we had hoped he would, still in the Indian Ocean. Yuri doesn't realize that he just moved closer to Jeffery and his little ship "The Adventurer". Now, sister, Yuri Yurachenkov's goose really will be cooked. Bahahaha}

"Admiral, I would like you to take this ship to Reunion Island." I told the Admiral in charge of our special mission. WE have been steaming West from near Australia toward the Seychelles since Ros and I ripped open Yuri's underground lair. WE are still part of the International Task Force that has been amassed to finally filet this slippery eel.

Reunion Island will cause a slight southern course change to our steaming direction, but no need to slow down. This critter is NOT getting away again!

{Sister, my love my Strength. I have received a communique from Jeffery aboard "The Adventurer". You are in danger, sister. Heed the warnings found within the images. Transferring to you now:}

* * *

October 2, 2020, Reunion Island: Western Indian Ocean

"Bahahaha! The COSMIC TWINS cannot defeat the Great and Powerful Yuri Yurachenkov. I have my attack point shielded from their little counterattacks they learned from their father. I have only been working on my complexion in the Seychelles, while waiting for construction to be completed on my ultimate weapon against Commander Skaggs. She has foiled my plans for the last time, Vladimir!"

"Yes, Director", Vladimir responds with a kind tone to his voice.

"Now, Vladimir. I have perfected the ELF signal that will block Commander Skaggs's Kidney-Liver by-pass tool and she will simply fail on her own. It's so easy, Vladimir. I was really hoping, after all these years, they would finally prove to be a greater challenge."

Yuri turns to look out of the window of his secret hideout, situated along the eastern shores of the island. Yuri considers this location to be "Dom" …home. When he has gained all the money and the power he desires, this is where he will live out his days. Always being somewhat disappointed in the ability of others.

"Such is the life of a supervillain. Buahahaha."

"Yes, Director", comes a lonely response from Vladimir.

Sister, my Love my Light. I received the communique. I understand, my Light. Is Yuri aware we know he has not fled the Seychelles?

What Little Girls Are Made Of- From the Diaries of Becka Skaggs, PhD

{Yes, sister. He believes his plan will work because Yuri thinks too much of himself! MY plan is much better sister. My plan is the old 'fumblerooskie' mis-direction plan. I got this sister, my Love my Strength, my eternal happiness.}

Rosalyn, you are awesome! You are my Light, little sister. Okay. Tell me your plan.

{No.}

What? Maybe you didn't understand me.

{I understood. Not telling you}

Rosalyn, tell me your plan, please.

{No thank you, Miss Becka Love Bug. Jeffery and I have this all figured out.}

Jeffery? You are calling him Jeffery?? Rosalyn! You are planning things without me? How dare you! I will implant...uh, I will implant an image in your head...of what? What will I implant? Oh!!

I will implant an image of Jeffery that you don't really want to see! Jeffery...

{Hehe, silly sister. I already have all those images. SERIOUSLY, Becka!! YOU are in danger because Yuri knows the frequency of your artificial kidney-liver organ. It all makes sense now, sister!}

I guess my mental powers HAVE been slowed down. I'm not following you, my love my Light. And he's mine to call Jeffery, not yours.

{Ohhh, Becka. You are a mess, sister.}

I feel like a mess too. Ahhh, should I cry now, or later??

{Later! Besides, it's been 6 weeks since our birthday, so stop being silly.}

Rosalyn?? I promise not to tell. Please let me in on your plan??

{Okay! But don't you be thinking about this all the time. Yuri could steal it from your thought waves. I don't know for sure, but I don't want to take

chances. Hear my words and file them quickly away for rapid access. You will need to act fast during a part of my plan.}

Yes, my Light. I understand.

{Have your Navy men set up your parabolic mirror on a large dolly suspended on a single pole so you can redirect his signal when Yuri begins to attack your organ. You cannot simply reflect his signal back at him and think that will destroy him. The shielding he has installed will cause a perfect signal to rebound back at you. That will put you in a perpetual reflection loop with his laser beam. The one enemy who then blinks, gets obliterated.}

{My plan By-passes his reflective scheme.}

{More to come later, my love my Strength. But you need to know Jeffery and "The Adventurer" are essential components to my plan.}

You are working with my Lover boy? I mean lover buggles? Umm, Jeffery? I mean, Jeff??

{Ooooh, sister. You stink of too much fantasy on the brain. You can't remember 2 minutes ago. Go take a shower, sis. No, really. I love you my love, my Strength. But you need an adjustment in your mental balance. Go! Heal thyself!}

* * * BREAK for PINK NOISE * * *

I'm taking a shower in Father's ELF-shielded pink-noise shower they installed on the USS Eisenhower just for me and my beautiful skin, and it's waking me up. Yuri must also have a signal that is confusing my receptors. I don't like how cunning this little devil has gotten.

The warmth of the water with the roundness of the pink sounds makes me feel like I'm taking a tropical rain shower in a beautiful paradise lagoon. Just a slight bristle of the palm leaves is heard above the running water. My worries are melting away and I am feeling clear.

What Little Girls Are Made Of- From the Diaries of Becka Skaggs, PhD

Ros's images are coming into focus. Yes, she trusts me. She just doesn't trust Yuri.

In Rosalyn's images, I saw Nectar. Something about Nectar. A Bree Nectar has fallen. I saw that image. Yes, that's it. But what does that mean?

Nectar? I was thinking, while the tropical downpour of water and sound fell over my face and down my body. The mixture of sound and water rinsed away all the confusion with each drop that ran its length of the course, all 71 and 3/8 inches long.

Nectar? What is it about Nectar?

Wait? Hester wasn't spelled with 'ER on the end. It was spelled with 'AR. Hestar. The Russian H symbol has our 'N' sound. And the English 'S' sound is spelled with a 'C' in Russian.

HeStar = NeCtar

Bree Nectar means Bree Hester!

OH, MY GAWD!!

Bree Hester must've known Fred Hester had my organ. She saw Father dig him up and take it. It must've been Yuri's before Fred got it.

Oh, My Sweetness! I have Yuri's organ!!!

Yuri had Bree murdered because she saw Father and put 2+2+2+3 together to make fourteen. Her math is terrible, SO Yuri had her killed!

No wonder he wants my organ back!! That evil…. Oooooh… fowl!

Father! How dare you keep this from me for so long!!

When I get home, you will never hear the end of this, buster. I will tell you that! As soon as I get to Atlanta, your ear will be so sore from listening to my….

**Becka? **

Uh-oh. Daddy?

**Becka, Yuri's ELF Disruptor has been disabled."

Thank you, Father. (Whew!)

**Remember, a lot of people are depending on you tomorrow. You'll need all your energy. This day is why we have been training all your life, sweetie. No more ELFs interfering with your life. Do you need help getting to sleep? **

No, Father. I'm going right away sir. But tomorrow we need to....

Wait? Are you eavesdropping on me?

**It's called 'monitoring my child's activities'. Excuse me if I'm concerned for my daughter's safety. Even at age twenty. Now sleep! I can order you, if you prefer. **

No, Father. I got it. You don't have to be a Meany.

Heavy sigh.

Powering down now, Father.

Oh great. Am I gonna have daddy issues all my life?

* * * The JAVELIN BREAK * * *

October 6, 2020 – USS Eisenhower, Indian Ocean

We are idling 60 miles ENE of Reunion Island. I would've liked us to be closer to straight east from Yuri's hideout. But the Admiral assures me this attack position is one that the famous Chinese warrior, General Tzu himself would approve.

The Admiral assures me The USS Eisenhower will be coming at Yuri as if we were steaming right out of the sun at him. Yuri will not be able to tell exactly what we are until we are too close for him to stand down. He will be forced to execute his plan. THAT's when we get him!

What Little Girls Are Made Of- From the Diaries of Becka Skaggs, PhD

"Very Well, Admiral." I told him. Then I looked out ahead with my binoculars. Nothing out there.

"I'm waiting for final word to take action, Admiral. Begin steaming your ship so we are at that decision-point for Yuri as the sun is rising."

The Admiral is talking to me like we are just two parts of a much larger machine at work. We must work well together if all the parts are to work well together. This evil must be stopped at any cost. We are both professionals.

"Course is plotted and ready to execute, Commander." He is standing at the ready for the next command.

"Execute, Admiral."

I got the binoculars out again. Still nothing but ocean in the direction of my interest. I'm feeling some unease out there. It's a weird energy I'm not used to feeling. I still see nothing.

"Continue as you are, Admiral."

"Aye, Commander", the Admiral replied.

I stood in silence for a moment just watching. Now we trust in the energy.

Suddenly, on the far horizon, the energy signature I was searching for through the binoculars is barely in view. But it's a beautiful sight.

"The funny-shaped little football may have just showed for today's game, Admiral. Steady as she goes."

"Excuse me, Admiral." A female voice came from a doorway entering the bridge. "May I speak with the Commander, please?"

"Yes, Ma'am. I need a break anyway", the Admiral says to Carol.

"The bridge is yours, Commander", and the Admiral stepped off the bridge for a little break.

"Yes, Admiral. Thank you", I responded, still a bit confused by our guest's arrival here.

"Mother! What are you doing here? We must work well together if all the parts are to work well together. We could get attacked any minute!"

"I know Dear. That's why I needed to see you now. It's important", Carol said with a real look of concern on her face. "I want to use my energy."

"What? Mother what are you talking about? I don't have time for this."

I'm getting very nervous and perturbed that my mother is standing here trying to talk to me about something she has never paid attention to before.

"Mother, I could kill you."

The horror on my mother's face told me I said something wrong, again. Oops.

"Accidently, I mean. It's dangerous here. You don't know what you're asking."

She seems undeterred and is just staring at me waiting for me to finish.

"I don't know what you're asking me to do, Mother."

She is standing there with her arms crossed.

"Ok. Tell me what is important. I'm listening."

Now she has a happy face, and I have a...well, mine's not happy.

"I love you, Becky. I always have loved you so much."

"Mother, please. I am anxious and can't stop this feeling anymore."

"Becky, USE my energy. I love you. You will not harm me. You can use it to magnify your strength. I'm not stupid, Becky. I'm just injured. But I understand what you have told me about LOVE. And I believe you, Becky. I have all the faith in you that you will save all of us."

What Little Girls Are Made Of- From the Diaries of Becka Skaggs, PhD

Mom is really making sense, and she is winning my cold, damaged heart all over again. These are some sane words, mom.

"Becky? You must always obey your mother."

Did she just invoke Father's words?

"Use my energy to help you, Becky! Now!"

"No, Mother, that's not how you use the words. You forgot the audible breath for 1 point zero seconds."

Carol is looking totally confused.

"Now, I have no idea what you are talking about, little girl. But you will obey your mother."

This is indeed my mother. I have missed you for so long mother. My eyes begin to mist, but mom snaps me out of it. She clasps her hands onto my forearms. I clasp back in automatic response of a child needing her mother's touch. Welcome back, mother.

"LOVE is ENERGY! You taught me that. Now do it!"

She is staring straight into my still-moist eyes.

"Go save the world. Use my energy with yours. Bring us together, Baby."

She releases me and turns me on my path. I turn to object, and I suddenly see me scolding me.

Mom is standing there giving me MY hands-on-hip look. Is my child going to do that to me, too?? OH, nooo. She was telling me to obey her. Yep. It's genetic.

"Alright, Mother. Go to the galley and stay with Rosalyn. She will tell you what to do when its time."

AS Carol turned to leave, she heard a "I love you, Mother" come from behind her. Probably that brilliant child running the bridge of the USS Eisenhower, little what's-her-name, The Periwinkle Princess.

And it's almost time. When looking through the field glasses, I spied the energy signature of an underwater volcanic vent. Scientists have recently found some of these vents teeming with life that loves this odd mixture of heat, sea water, and molten rock. Our underwater vent is very excited and it's very hot. I can hardly wait for Rosalyn to introduce me to our new friends living within the vent.

Then the word came from Rosalyn.

{Jeffery and "The Adventurer" are in position, my Love, my Strength.}

"Alright, Admiral. Let's get these birds in the sky. It's time to empty our ship. Order them to safe distance while taking a defensive posture. Once he makes his first move, we'll counter him with everything we got. He'll be expecting that. But not what NOAA has in store for him."

At that same moment, the Adventurer contacted the Eisenhower through their secured line. The first mate relayed the message to the Admiral by speaking aloud to me in front of the Admiral. "The NOAA 'Adventurer' is standing by for orders Commander Skaggs."

"NOAA? Commander, there's a research ship out there?" Admiral has a real concern. That means civilians on board, usually.

"Yes, Admiral, on a covert mission for the Task Force. They're with us. The entire crew is uniformed personnel. Our surprise Yuri was not expecting."

The admiral gets a smile of interest and begins shaking his head in a bit of disbelief.

"Attack full force straight on, with the real javelins coming from the flank. Well-planned counter Commander. You truly put a smile on my face." The Admiral was smiling while nodding his head, now.

What Little Girls Are Made Of- From the Diaries of Becka Skaggs, PhD

"I'm glad you approve, Admiral. I do, honestly. But there is still another twist on top of that. I am not leaving anything to chance anymore. Not with Yuri. Today, his goose will finally be thoroughly cooked. Perhaps to a thousand degrees, Admiral."

{WE are ready for you to shine, my Love my Strength.}

Very well, sister. I am ready to shine. I AM the LOVE. I AM the strength!

I AM just waiting for Yuri to attack me.

{Yes, sister. We are ready.}

Pause

"I wish I liked coffee. I might have one about now." I must've sounded serious because the Admiral responded to me.

"There's a machine in the corner over by the comms center, if you desire", the Admiral points to the area.

"Thank you, Admiral."

Then a voice from somewhere yells "Incoming" and an explosion occurs next to the ship.

"What was that?" the Admiral barked out his question.

"That was no laser." I told the Admiral. "Yuri's firing metal projectiles."

He wants me to use my powers on those projectiles. Then Yuri will fire his laser.

"Very well, Yuri. I already had you fitted for a premium silk dunce cap, you nitwit."

Now it's my turn.

"I will see your projectiles, Yuri. And I will raise you one under-sea thermal vent. Right up your boxers, you little turd!" That was loud enough for the entire bridge to hear. Some chuckles could be heard. Enough that the admiral had to quiet down the bridge. We are on a dangerous mission, after all.

Rosalyn, it's time to shine.

Soon another projectile lands, and a third and a fourth. I'm making sure they aren't going to hit anything but water. By capturing them with our combined mental powers, I have the energy from these duds of Yuri's.

I couldn't help my glee. "I got you Yuri!"

Then just as suddenly, "Commander leaving the bridge", I shouted and ran down to the deck as fast as I could.

I had another idea for our new underwater friends.

*** MICROBIAL RESCUE BREAK ***

Rosalyn. Send Jeff an image of metal projectiles providing food and shelter for his new friends from the sea vent. Start using everyone in the galley.

{Very well, sis. Done!}

I grabbed Yuri's projectiles, squeezed them together into one lump and tossed them at Yuri's reflection defenses. Nothing happened to his defenses. I wasn't trying to harm his defenses.

When the projectile mass was in the air, I split the mass into pieces again. This time I was using the energy from each person with Rosalyn. When those masses of differing size fell to the sea floor, I was able to use their energy to force open a new fissure. I only achieved some of the length of fissure I needed. A few more projectiles would've been nice. It still needs help cracking more.

{That's why we have "The Adventurer", Sis. Hehe}

What Little Girls Are Made Of- From the Diaries of Becka Skaggs, PhD

Just then a flash of white light came from my left. The Adventurer's research mirror just caught the sun.

The red laser began from Yuri's fortress. One solid stream of light was unfolding like in slow motion. I saw this coming and yelled out,

"TIME TO SHINE!"

With my SHINE a ripple laid out across the water that rose to become a 30-foot tsunami by the time it reached Yuri six miles away. This caused Yuri to jump back. He was surprised by this young Commander. I was also surprised. But he was not deterred.

"Neither am I, you little weasel!" I whispered just under my breath. Yuri got my message.

"Fire at maximum voltage, Vladimir", the Director directed his servant.

"Yes, Director."

By the blank daze in his eyes, Vladimir is truly enjoying his work.

Rosalyn already had everyone in the galley concentrating, holding hands, while she re-focused their energy to me. That second-effort is all we needed.

The laser beam came at me, and I swiveled the giant mirror to reflect the laser over to The Adventurer, whose stationary mirror was already in position for this bounce of Yuri's weapon. The laser hit the mirror of the NOAA ship and bounced to Yuri's right flank where it appeared to land harmlessly into the water with a sizzle and some pop. Crackle.

But the reflected laser beam did exactly what the TWINS had planned. It added just enough energy to crack open that fissure a little more. Soon, a thermal volcanic vent had opened right in the middle of Yuri's hideout. And not only that, all the lava and spouting steam wasn't the only thing the new vent brought to Yuri's party. It brought party guests.

Real live microbes that have never tasted the succulent brain of an evil mastermind. A mastermind that wanted to destroy their world. And Yuri would have destroyed their home, if it wasn't for Jeff and NOAA, and The COSMIC TWINS.

Rosalyn got the microbes to agree to send some warriors to defend their homes. They did it gladly. It will fuel legends of the triumph of good over evil for generations and generations within their microbe world. Heroes were made today of all the microbe warriors that saved their home world when the Gods from above spoke to them and asked for the microbes' help.

Rosalyn and I summoned the energy from below and blew that little eel off that Island! YAYYY. Headline: COSMIC TWINS WIN Massive Victory over Yuri Yurichenkov! Yes! Now, we are free to explore the universe the way we humans were intended, as free individuals. Finally, I will never be blocked again by evil. I am free to be Pure Love. I am free to be a mother of my own children and show them how to love.

THE END

to

"What Little Girls are Made of -"

*** MY SISTER, ROSALYN ***

January 31, 2021

Special consideration to my sister, Rosalyn, MY COSMIC TWIN! I love you sis!

Rosalyn has received degrees in 7 languages, besides her PhD in communications from ASU, that is yet to be achieved. She runs a School for Girls in Ghana to help with the refugee problems and lack of educational opportunities for the young ladies. There are still so many missing girls from Mali, it's a difficult life she has chosen to follow. I admire her tremendously!

What Little Girls Are Made Of- From the Diaries of Becka Skaggs, PhD

Rosalyn has recently been able to reach out to the stars. She has located a possible home world for humans in the Alpha Centauri Galaxy. Now, the astronomers have a real target to study to see if it's viable.

My little sister says she senses life forms on this one planet in Alpha Centauri. She says they are benign life-forms, and there are not many of them. But Rosalyn said they would be accepting of our presence, if we are respectful to the planet. When Ros says she senses life forms, she's usually right.

Rosalyn and I are currently busy working on a new language for human artificial intelligence. We believe our artificial intelligence will need a more effective language to communicate with the Alien Race that is on their way here, to Earth. They will be here in less than 42 years. Their primary language appears to be binary. They don't seem to be in a hurry.

In the past 14 years, since we first announced their presence to the world, Rosalyn has learned a lot about the Alien Race that has chosen to visit Earth. They are a colonizing Race, like ANTS from earth. Ewwww!

And they are not friendly.

I do believe Congress reacted correctly to Rosalyn, when she first mentioned this possibility in the summer of 2006. Though it took me a couple years to fully be on board with The COSMIC TWINS PROTECTION Act, Rosalyn never lost confidence in me.

And in the year 2062, when those nasty putrid insects from outer space arrive here with their big Queen, the egg-layer??

The COSMIC TWINS will still be here, and we will still be strong. Because,

LOVE MATTERS!

LOVE is ENERGY.

LOVE is ETERNAL.

And we LOVE you all!!

THE END AGAIN

No, Really

*** **OKAY, NOT REALLY** ***

OFFICIAL ADDENDUM:

Letter from Surgeon General Yotes, dated February 15, 2021.

It is our solemn and sad responsibility to announce that Commander Rebecca Dall Skaggs passed away last night at our CDC facilities in Atlanta. Becka is just the latest of almost three-quarter million Americans that have lost their lives from the COVID-19 virus pandemic, so far. Because of her complete commitment to the health of all Americans, Commander Skaggs has been posthumously promoted to the Field Rank of Captain.

Captain Skaggs and her LOVE is ENERGY! have been commissioned to an eternal voyage of discovery for all humankind. We anticipate the Periwinkle Princess will speak with many beings and spirits along the way. The Service looks forward to receiving the captain's final Voyage Log aboard her LOVE is ENERGY! upon their return.

The following action is in memorial to Captain Rebecca Dall Skaggs, PhD, who succumbed to the ravages of the COVID-19 virus on February 14, 2021.

In commemoration to the steadfast duty and faithful execution of all laws pursuant to the Constitution of the United States of America, and in recognition of Captain Skaggs' persistent loving attitude in the face of all odds,

I, Surgeon General Devin David Yotes, do declare that February 14th shall forever be known as LOVE BUG Day throughout the Public Health Service.

To further commemorate the true nature of this fallen angel, forever our COSMIC TWIN,

What Little Girls Are Made Of- From the Diaries of Becka Skaggs, PhD

Three Bells for Captain Skaggs.

DING..................

DING..................

DING..................

*** **JUST a BIT MORE** ***

Author's Notes:

Muteness or mutism (from Latin mutus, meaning 'silent') is defined as an absence of speech while maintaining the ability to understand the speech of others.

Mutism is typically understood as an inability to speak on the part of a child or an adult due to an observed lack of speech from the point of view of others who know them. These people could be family members, caregivers, teachers, healthcare professionals to include speech therapists and language pathologists. Muteness may not be a permanent condition, depending on the etiology (cause). In general, someone who is mute may be mute for one of several different reasons: organic, psychological, developmental/neurological.

For Children, a lack of speech may be developmental/neurological, or psychological, or due to a physical disability or a communication disorder. For adults who previously had speech and then became unable to speak, loss of speech may be due to injury, termed aphasia, or surgery affecting areas of the brain needed for speech. Loss of speech in adults may occur rarely for psychological reasons.

Children are less likely to have a basic understanding of our world or our bodies than adults. Therefore, they are not as psychologically available as adults to comprehend the trauma and its effects.

Adults will be able to use some logic center to gain comprehension based on remembered experiences. Even if the adult experience results in reactions only because of muscle memory or rote memorization, it is more of a foundation to "normalcy" than a young child. Such a child, especially in their early developmental stages, has no experiences for context. They are trapped wholly within their own imaginations. They have no tether to our reality, so they create their own reality that soothes them.

As your author, I have chosen my Becka to have these experiences. I chose to let you decide what you thought about Carol and her injuries with my minimal development in this book. I invite you into all my worlds. Please join me, won't you? I love you all!"

Captain Becka Skaggs, PhD

Also discuss the kind of TBI that will cause enhanced brain activity or use

I tried to interweave this theme throughout our story. Becka's profound understanding of our reality could be genetic, or a physiological result of a change in brain structure from her injury. Becka has only slight damage. But slight damage to the brain can change the original packing of cells, alignment of energy grids – creating neuron clusters that didn't exist before – a thousand things we scientists have never thought to study or observe.

Please understand: DAMAGE does NOT mean something bad will be the result. It means a traumatic event occurred and things are no longer the way they were prior to the event. We humans only started looking at the issue of Traumatic Brain Injury because we scientists had observed effects we had labelled as "bad" in our minds. We scientists have prejudiced the language because we failed to fully understand the effects of the trauma on the organic human. The use of such judgmental words should be reserved for the Bible and not placed within the medical journals.

TBI to Broca's area of the brain CAN cause muteness. Science just doesn't know for sure if there is a finite trigger to muteness in this area of the brain.

Articulation of speech can be centered in this area, but, again, we don't know how much of our articulation comes from this area.

The Broca area also has a role in motor-memory functions, such as retracing your steps to find your house keys. Discovering this role has encouraged more investigation into this part of the brain. Our superhero may have enhanced effects in her motor-memory functions. Continue to watch for things that could be enhanced effects in our future stories.

BROCA's AREA = Left Inferior Frontal Cortex

TBI = Traumatic Brain Injury

*** **FINAL CODA** ***

In the morgue where the body of Captain Skaggs is interred for 24 hours before being removed for burial at Arlington National Cemetery.

I have been in the body bag chilling for just over 19 hours.

I was going for my hibernation record of 20 hours six minutes between heartbeats.

I was running my body on the universal energy of the invading virus. I simply spoke with the virus, and it agreed to allow me to re-purpose its energy to save my life. That means I have solved my own immune-system issues. If I get sick by an invading organism, I can now re-purpose their energy. My NEW Superpower! Father will be so pleased!

But it's more dramatic to say I sucked all the juices from the nasty virus until it was dust! It was the moth that flew into the spider's web. COVID-19 was exactly the trick I needed to finally outwit Yuri and his ELF blockers, and all his evil germs! I am FREE of his influences!

Since Vladimir Bostek is still on the loose, we thought it would be a good trick to make him believe I was killed by my own immune weaknesses. Rosalyn, Alisha, and I think he will let his guard down once he receives the news of my untimely demise. Then we will capture him, and the world will be safe once again.

I have recently noticed somebody turned down the temperature below my original estimates. So, I'm losing energy faster than in my calculations, now that the virus is gone. *NOTE TO SELF: Re-calculate hibernation formula for temperature variances*

I shall emerge the victor, however! I just will lose my personal record for hibernation.

Oh, well. It's the kind of sacrifices a superhero must make…. constantly.

For the chance to save humankind from evil alien insects just full of universal energy to be re-purposed!

Soon, the body bag began to open. There came from the bag a hand and an arm. The hand and arm appear to be clearing the way for …. the arrival of the captain from beyond the river Styx! Hallelujah!!

I jump out of the bag in excitement!

"TA DAH"!!

"I'm BA-a-a-a-ack" Hehehe. You glad to see me?

YEEESSSSSS? You are????

I LOVE YOU SO MUCH!!!!

I WIN, AGAIN!!! YAYY!

You guys didn't think I was I dead, did you? Heck know! Wink!

PSYCH!! Hahaha

Who says I have no command over my words? Bahahaha!

What Little Girls Are Made Of- From the Diaries of Becka Skaggs, PhD

***Stay Tuned for our next episode of From the Diaries of Becka Skaggs, PhD.

Tomorrows Adventure: The COSMIC TWINS and The Science of Love.

Don't miss it. ***

***ALRIGHT, YOU GUYS!! This is the BEST one yet! I want this one published. Archive this and publish it, okay? Is someone calling the cemetery?

***That means, YOU, Becka! Don't forget to publish this book AND call the cemetery. Wink

FINAL FINAL END

I promise.

You trust me, don't you?

Kiss Kiss Hearts N Marshmallows.

EPILOGUE – WHAT LIFE??

Alisha received a promotion after we cockled that lousy chicken, Yuri Yurichenkov. Even though Yuri met with his due justice and became food for microbes from a boiling cauldron, his lab rat Vladimir got away. We know he can't get far enough away to elude The COSMIC TWINS. Authorities say they are confident Vladimir will be rounded up before more terror and disasters are beset against the people of the World.

I am now a Commander in the PHS. They took away my field promotion to Captain when they learned I wasn't dead. Well, field promotions are temporary anyway. So, I'm okay with it.

You guys remember those marines that were assigned to Alisha before I died? Well, they are MY detachment now. They have been assigned to me. Isn't that great!?? Now, there are people who must listen to me. It's all good! I LOVE all you guys so much!

It's true that Alisha is my commanding Officer. She is now the captain of this ship. Our ship is the underground bunker known as The COSMIC TWINS World Headquarters. So, Alisha is the boss of us all, but the marines all report to me. Therefore, those marines are all mine. If Rosalyn is nice, she may get an introduction to my marines.

Bye all! Have fun and stay safe!!

{What do you mean if I'm nice!?? What are you going to do with a dozen marines? You are loved by a love bug! You can't do anything with a dozen marines!}

What Little Girls Are Made Of- From the Diaries of Becka Skaggs, PhD

{Why would you waste a good marine like that, Becka?? Sister? Are you hearing me? My love, my Strength, are you listening??}

{Becka????}

{Hey!! This isn't funny! I'm always nice, Becka. I'm your LOVE.}

{Becka???? Where are you going?}

{I'm your COSMIC TWIN sister. Pleeeeze!?? Becka?? Come back here! We need to talk about this.}

{Becka-a-a-a-a??!??}

Then I heard a *"BECKA STOP!"* that was felt to my toes.

I looked down the long hallway ahead of me and said, "Roslyn enough, please."

When I turned to look back down the hall toward her and give her grandma's eye roll, there she was just one step away with a look of terror on her face.

I saw her eyes watering. Something serious happened. Yes, we were just being sisters teasing each other. But things can change instantly when Ros receives information.

"What is it my light?"

Then the words struck me from somewhere down the hall, as if they were an echo from my hurtful, damaged past. I realized they were my future. And when they fully penetrated my feeble brain, my body dropped me to my knees and then to the ground. I had no mind at all.

Now, all I could do was lay there and cry like the little baby I wish I was again.

{"Jeffery is missing at sea."}

Then I felt the big hug and the gentle rocking.

Rosalyn's real voice was soothing. She was whispering very nice things to me.

"I love you, my light, my strength. I promise you this is not over. Not even close, my sister. We will find Jeffery and we will make Vladimir pay for his transgressions!"

Yes, Ros, I agree. Now, where's Jeffery?

I remember hearing her whisper something about clicks and clacks and alien voices, but I couldn't focus on anything but Jeffery now. This moment was like no other moment I had experienced in my young life. Breathing was getting more difficult. My chest was pounding.

Then I found I couldn't even focus on Jeffery. I couldn't call up his image. He was no longer in my memory. Am I having a panic attack? Or worse, a stroke? I couldn't think of anything to do. Is this how it ends? All I could do now was look at Rosalyn with my soggy eyes, and fade to black.

THE END

Kiss Kiss